THE ART OF HUSBANDRY

A MACKENZIE COUNTRY STORY
BOOK 1

JAY HOGAN

SOUTHERN LIGHTS PUBLISHING

Published by Southern Lights Publishing

Copyright © 2023 by Jay Hogan

This is a work of fiction. Names, characters, places, and incidents are either the product of the author's imagination or are used fictitiously, and any resemblance to actual persons, living or dead, business establishments, events, or locales is entirely coincidental.

All rights reserved.

This book is licensed to the original purchaser only. Duplication or distribution by any means is illegal and a violation of international copyright law, subject to criminal prosecution and upon conviction, fines and/or imprisonment. No part of this book may be reproduced in any form or by any electronic or mechanical means, including photocopying, recording, or by any information storage and retrieval systems, without written permission from the author, except for the use of brief quotations in a book review. Any ebook format cannot be legally loaned or given to others.

To request permission and all other enquiries contact the author through the website.

https://www.jayhoganauthor.com

Trade Paperback ISBN:978-1-99-110411-3

Digital ISBN: 978-1-99-110410-6

Digital Edition Published June 2023

Trade Paperback Published June 2023

First Edition

Editing by Boho Edits

Cover Art Copyright © 2023 Reese Dante

Cover content is for illustrative purposes only and any person depicted on the cover is a model.

Proofread by Lissa Given Proofing and L. Parks

Printed in the United States of America and Australia

For my family who read everything I write and keep on saying they love it all, blushes included.

THE REAL MACKENZIE COUNTRY AND ACKNOWLEDGEMENTS

The Mackenzie Basin in the South Island of New Zealand is one of the most stunningly beautiful and scenic places in the world. Home to the Southern Alps that form the backbone of our small country, it is also the site of New Zealand's highest mountain, Aoraki Mount Cook. The region is riddled with glaciers, majestic lakes, braided rivers, and towering peaks. A dark sky reserve blankets the area making it one of the best places in the world to stargaze and maybe even catch a glimpse of the Southern Lights.

The high country sheep stations that call this spectacular land home are a farming legacy unique to New Zealand, and they take their role as custodians and guardians of the environment very seriously. The stations mostly farm the sturdy merino breed of sheep who spend their summers traversing back and forth over some of the highest ranges in this area, many only accessible by foot. Tourists from all over the world book to be part of an annual muster—a down under term similar in meaning to roundup—where the mobs of sheep are brought down from their high altitude summer grazing to lamb and to overwinter. It's a once in a lifetime experience.

In my research for this series I spent time at two South Island high country stations and I am grateful to the owners and shepherds who let me tag along as they worked, and who put up with an endless barrage of questions from this clueless townie not to mention all the follow up emails. I am also grateful to my expert beta reader Jill

McCaw who made sure I got my high country farming terms right and everything in its place.

Any mistakes are completely my own.

In this series I have tried to stay true to the dominant landmarks, towns, and the general feel of the Mackenzie Basin, but for the purpose of the storyline itself I 'added' the fictional Glendale River and its glacial valley—home to Miller Station. On a map this fictional valley would sit somewhere east of the Macauley River. I also created the fictional supply town of Oakwood, so please don't add it to your sightseeing list.

As always, I thank my husband for his patience and for keeping the dog walked and out of my hair when I needed to work, and my daughter for her incredible support.

Getting a book finessed for release is a huge challenge that includes the help of beta readers, editing, proofing, cover artists and a tireless PA. It's a team effort, and includes all those author support networks and reader fans who rally around when you're ready to pull your hair out and throw away every first draft. Thanks to all of you.

THE ART OF HUSBANDRY

When life drowns you in lemons, to hell with making lemonade. I wanted to burn the whole world. But eighteen months from the day my life was torn apart, I'm tired of the anger. Tired of the nightmares. Tired of putting one foot in front of the other just trying to survive. Three months on a high country sheep station in the middle of nowhere is precisely the reboot I need. A chance to break free. To breathe again. To find a way forward.

I put my entire life on hold and head south to Mackenzie Country. But falling for the captivating young station boss was never part of the plan. Holden Miller might be smart and sexy and push all my dusty buttons, but we come from two different worlds. I'm not looking for a relationship. I'm not interested in love. I'm done with all that.

But Holden doesn't care about my rules. Nestled safely in the arms of the spectacular Southern Alps, on an isolated sheep farm at the top of the world, Holden begins knitting my battered heart together one careful stitch at a time. And with every pass of the thread, every braid of the river on our doorstep, I catch a tantalising glimpse of something I'd almost given up on.

Happiness, and maybe even love.

If I have the courage to reach out and grab them.

Note: This book contains references to the past death of a child and PTSD.

READER NOTE

This book contains references to the past death of a child and PTSD.

PROLOGUE

Gil

"I'm sorry I forgot Hannah's present." I pulled away from the kerb and merged like a zip into the stream of school pickup traffic. It was Callie's best friend's birthday party and I'd dropped the ball. "I had my mind on other things, okay?" Like a phone fight with my husband about his flight schedule—a continuation of the fight we'd started the night before.

Callie stared doggedly out her side window, her shoulders tense, her expression the practiced pout of a ten-year-old girl who felt let down by her father. "She's my best friend, Daddy, and I'll be the last one there," she snapped, as if it was the end of the world. And maybe it was. To be honest, I had little clue when it came to best-girlfriend etiquette and birthday parties.

"It's only going to take ten minutes to whip home and pick it up on the way. No one will even notice." Thirty, max, depending on traffic, but I wasn't about to mention that.

Callie fired me an impressive 'do you think I was born yesterday' look, and I winced.

"Okay, so maybe twenty," I amended.

She rolled her eyes and returned to staring out the window.

"Come on, baby girl. Cut me a break here," I pleaded. "Yes, I should've put it in my bag last night, but to be fair, last night was kind of busy." As in spousal-domestic busy. "And don't forget I was the one who came up with the awesome idea for the present to start with."

It had been one of my finer moments. A signed T-shirt from one of Hannah's favourite New Zealand bands. I'd called in a favour from their drummer who I'd happened to attend university with.

Callie's shoulders loosened and she finally turned in her seat, her scowl slipping just enough to let me know we were almost there. "Hannah *will* love it. Maybe enough to forgive me for being late to her party, although I doubt it." The kid had a great return serve. "And I'm still mad at you."

"I totally get that." I briefly raised my hands from the wheel in a gesture of surrender. "And I deserve it. Would it help if I bake lemon meringue cake on the weekend?"

Callie's mouth twitched. "*And* your bacon-and-egg pie?"

I flinched. It wasn't Luke's or my favourite, but I was on a mission to garner some brownie points, so what the hell. "Sure."

She chuckled. "Boy, you must *really* feel bad."

I snorted and nudged her with my elbow. "Am I forgiven?"

She side-eyed me. "I'm getting there."

I'd take that.

I manoeuvred in and out of three lanes of traffic, determined to get home and pick up the damn present as quickly as possible and get Callie to the party. But traffic was barely crawling. A misty rain slicked the windscreen, playing chicken with my wiper blades, and it seemed every man and his dog had suddenly decided they needed to go somewhere.

"What is it with the traffic today?" I grumbled, changing lanes again as our off-ramp came into view and sticking my indicator on. "Nearly there, honey."

Callie was fiddling with the hem of her school uniform and when she finally spoke, her voice was so soft, I almost missed her question altogether. "Are you happy, Daddy?"

I blinked, my heart leaping in my chest. *Fuck.* I kept my tone neutral and my eyes straight ahead. "What do you mean, honey? Being with you always makes me happy."

She sighed and faced me, tucking a leg underneath her. "Not with me." She hesitated, then added, "I heard you and Poppa arguing last night."

Fuck. Fuck. Fuck. Luke and I had both thought the other had closed the hallway door after Callie had gone to bed. By the time we realised, it was too late, and I'd just prayed she'd fallen asleep quickly. It wasn't a bad argument. No name-calling or anything like that. We didn't go in for dramatics. We kept it all very civilised, very . . . sensible. Mostly we just sounded disappointed with each other.

"All parents argue sometimes, sweetheart," I explained in my best everything-is-fine voice. "That's all part of living with someone for a long time. Sometimes we annoy each other just like you get annoyed with us. That doesn't mean you don't love us, right? Or that you aren't happy?" I really needed the conversation to end, but her eyes were hot on my face and I wasn't at all sure I was selling the line convincingly.

"But you and Poppa don't kiss in front of me anymore. Hannah's parents kiss all the time."

Oh Jesus. "Don't we?" I tried to sound surprised, sliding my foot onto the brake as we approached the last set of traffic lights before the turnoff to our street. "I'm sure we do. Maybe you just missed it." Me too. Since I couldn't remember the last time Luke had kissed me outside of the bedroom, and even there . . . yeah, well, it wasn't like I'd been that great at that stuff for a while either.

"Yeah, maybe." Callie turned back to her side window. I knew Luke and I needed to have a talk and then one with Callie as well. This couldn't go on.

The lights turned from red to green before we had to stop, and the three cars ahead began to move. I followed, a couple of car lengths between us, happy the journey home hadn't taken as long as I'd feared and I was on course for getting Callie to the party at the lower end of the late scale.

I'd barely gotten halfway through the intersection when a blue Mazda going the opposite direction ran its red light and careened toward us, its tyres sliding on the slick tarmac.

I never even heard the crunch as the Mazda slammed into our car. Never felt the jolt that broke three of my ribs, my tib and fib, and put me in a neck brace for weeks. Never saw the other driver as they pulled him from the wreckage, high on meth and alcohol.

But until the day I die, I will hear every microsecond of Callie's terrified scream just before her door was hit.

"Daddeeeeee!"

CHAPTER ONE

Eighteen months later

Holden

I blinked the sleep from my eyes and stared up at the shade hanging above my bed, noting the dense criss-cross of cobwebs that filled its interior. Adding cleaning to my mental should-do-but-will-never-get-the-time list, I wriggled my arse and smiled at the familiar ache.

An excellent start to the day.

The grey pink of dawn striped the ceiling behind the shade and I tracked its path to a thin break in the curtains, the soft grey fabric shifting gently in the tiniest of breezes.

In and out.

The familiar pulse of the Southern Alps breathing life over the land, and the hearts of those mad enough to try and farm them.

Like me.

Like my grandfather.

And his father before him.

I filled my sleep-sour lungs and took a minute to simply lie there, quiet and peaceful, welcoming the silence of the still-dark mountains that loomed just outside the walls of my cottage, letting them settle in my heart and work their magic as they did most every day. Then I drank in another deep breath, slid my legs off the side of the bed, and wrangled my protesting body into a reasonable sit.

Damn. When had I gotten so fucking old?

Nobody warned you that by thirty, the youth-fuelled superpower you once wielded, capable of acing endless late nights followed by arse-crack-of-dawn starts, was about to be wiped away in the passage of a single year. A long, back-breaking afternoon of fencing rolled out before me, and my thirty-year-old body protested the very thought.

What the hell had I been thinking?

A welcome lick of cool air pebbled my nipples but I wasn't fooled for a minute. By afternoon I'd be sweating bricks in the late February summer heat while the lower alpine valleys, with their pockets of bush and rocky shelter, would fill with sensible stock seeking a shady place to while away another scorcher.

Welcome to Mackenzie Country—hot and dry as the devil's throat in summer and cold as a witch's tit in winter.

Home sweet home.

A series of soft rumbling snores had me turning to appreciate the long run of a pale naked back parked smack-bang in the middle of my bed, the top sheet puddled over a pair of lean thighs and exposing the tasty swell of a bare arse I knew only too well.

My best mate and sometimes bed companion, Zach Lane.

Zach stirred in his sleep and the smattering of summer-darkened freckles that dusted his shoulder slid over the lithe muscle beneath. Messy auburn waves framed a strong but pretty face that carried a light blush tan in contrast to its usual winter pale. Together with a pair of bright green troublemaker eyes, they paid tribute to the Irish heritage that ran thick in Zach's veins. The remainder of the man consisted of almost two metres of mouth-watering high-country male deliciousness, right there for the taking.

All of which reminded me exactly what I'd been thinking last night.

The sight still stirred my cock.

Then I remembered the fencing and sighed.

Still, a little tiredness was a small price to pay for what had been an epic night of fucking made better by the fact I hadn't been laid in almost a month. Bonus points for a ten-second booty call that pretty much guaranteed this particularly lush body at my door in under thirty minutes. It sure beat a forty-five-minute drive into Tekapo and a potentially wasted night if tourist pickings were slim.

I usually avoided local *entanglements* like the plague—the Mackenzie Country community was just too damn small. But Zach was different. We'd grown up together on neighbouring stations, attended the same primary school, and although we'd boarded at different high schools in Christchurch, we'd always kept in touch. But whereas I'd been out since I was sixteen when Mum caught me sneaking out of the implement shed with one of the teenage shearing gang sweepers, both of us laughing and zipping up our trousers, I hadn't known Zach was gay until we were in our twenties.

His parents still didn't, for very good reason.

After university, we'd fallen into a casual friends-with-benefits arrangement that suited us both. It wasn't like there were a whole lot of opportunities for hookups in the high country, but we'd been clear from the start. I wasn't looking for a boyfriend and Zach wasn't out. But he was always down for a bit of fun.

I slapped his bare arse, his skin still toasty warm. "Get up, sunshine. Time to go."

He groaned and pulled the sheet over his head. "Go away. You fucking wrecked me. I might never ride again."

I chuckled and whipped the sheet off his legs. "Your dad's gonna ask some very tricky questions if you don't get that motorbike back in time for the morning conflab."

Another groan. "Damn, I hate it when you're right." Zach swung his legs over the side of the bed and sat for a second to get his balance, squinting into the weak light. "Jesus, what time did we get to sleep?"

"Fucked if I know." I snorted. "Literally, as it happens." I threw his jeans on the bed for him.

He laughed but made no move to pick them up. "What, no blowjobs in the shower before I go?" He sounded almost wistful.

My brow creased. We'd only ever done that a couple of times over the years. Most mornings it was just a slice of toast on the fly as Zach ran out the door.

"Nope." I zipped up my jeans. "You and me in that tiny shower has only one possible ending and I don't have time for that today. I've got to get to mat time with the team and then head into Tekapo to pick up our new domestic manager on the nine o'clock bus from Christchurch."

Zach frowned. "He's not driving in? And also, that's the most ridiculous term for the morning meeting I've ever heard."

I chuckled. "You don't work here. And the guy was a psychologist in Wellington. Guess he's leaving his car up there since he's only here for three months. Mum promised him the use of the old Ford Ranger while he's here."

Zack looked surprised. "A psychologist?"

I shrugged. "The cousin of a friend of a friend, or something like that. Anyway, he was in a car accident about eighteen months ago that messed him up a bit. Mum's a sucker for a sob story, right? But if we hate him, it's only a short-term hiccup."

"Right." Zach was still sitting on the edge of the bed, staring at his feet, his jeans untouched at his side.

"So, how many dogs do you have in at the moment?" I tried to lighten the odd mood that had settled in the room. Zach had made a name for himself as one of the best dog trainers in the high country, which was no small thing.

"Three." He still didn't look up.

What was I missing? I moved to stand in front of him. "Hey. Are you okay?"

He looked almost nervous. "I'm fine. I've just been doing a bit of thinking . . . lately."

I chuckled. "You wanna be careful about that." I grabbed my T-shirt from the back of the chair and gave it a shake.

"Yeah." He shot me a smile that didn't quite reach his eyes. "How long have we been doing this, Holden?"

"Doing what?" I tugged the T-shirt over my head.

"Hooking up."

I blinked, wondering what the hell he was banging on about. "Jesus, I don't know." I did a quick calculation in my head. "Around six years, I guess, on and off."

He nodded. "And it's been fun, right?"

I grinned and waggled my brows. "Damn right. You're a sexy beast, Zacharia."

The comment earned me a more genuine smile. "Yeah, well, you're not so bad yourself." He hesitated long enough for me to look up from where I was gathering the duvet from the floor. "So, I've been thinking about coming out." His words came out in a rush and I'm pretty sure I gaped, because holy shit, Zach and I had both just turned thirty and I'd almost given up on him ever coming out.

"Wow." I patted him on the shoulder. "Good for you. You know I'll be there if . . . *when* . . . shit goes down with your dad, right? I've got your back."

He stared at me like he was maybe waiting for something more.

I added, "There's always a bed for you here, and I can always do with an extra pair of hands. Mum would be absolutely fine with it." Which was true, since she was one of the few people who officially knew about what Zach and I were up to, although I suspected it was a poorly kept secret with the rest of the team as well.

Zach leaving my cottage at dawn a couple of times a month was never going to fly under the radar with my mother whose own cottage stood barely fifty metres away. Not to mention, the roar of Zach's

Kawasaki Ninja was loud enough to rattle the scree loose from the mountain and wake everyone else along with it. The only positive was that none of the team had actually said anything, which I guessed was down to respect for the fact Zach was in no way out about his sexuality.

Zach studied me with an odd expression. "I thought you were moving into the homestead?"

I hesitated. "Not yet, if I can avoid it. But there's a spare guest cottage out back you can have. It's an older one we haven't renovated yet. It just needs a bit of cleaning."

Zach gave a slow nod and then looked back down at his feet. "Right. The spare cottage." He huffed almost dispiritedly. "I'll keep that in mind." He got to his feet to pull on his jeans, and I wondered what I was missing. "I just wanted you to know. I, um, well I guess I thought . . . maybe hoped . . ." He hesitated, then buttoned his fly and reached for his T-shirt. "Forget about it."

I frowned as he tugged the shirt over his lean-muscled frame. Something wasn't right. "Would you like me to be there when you tell them? I'm happy to do that."

He stared at me for a few seconds, clearly thinking about it, then shook his head. "No, thanks."

And I was struck again by the way he wouldn't meet my eyes. "Zach, what's going on?"

He shuffled his weight from foot to foot and then sighed. "If I did come to work here, what would you see happening . . . with us?"

Us? The question threw me, and after a few long seconds when I didn't answer, Zach sighed and dropped onto the mattress, snatching his socks from the floor. "Yeah, I thought as much. It doesn't matter."

What the hell was going on? "No, it clearly does," I argued, taking a seat beside him. "If you lived on the station, then I guess we'd need to talk about whether it was a good idea to carry on doing what we're doing. I mean, it would be different, right? With me in charge now, things could get . . . complicated."

Zach tugged on his boots, not looking up. "Yeah, complicated."

He sounded resigned, maybe even upset, but when I reached for his arm, he jerked it away and got to his feet. But he made no move to leave, and as he continued to stand there, an awkward silence filled the space between us.

What the hell? I racked my brain. Zach and I didn't do this. We didn't have these types of conversations. We didn't feel awkward around each other. We had fun together. We laughed, and we fucked, and then we said *Catch you later*. We didn't do *this,* because *this* felt a whole lot like something else, like he was—

Oh fuck.

I blinked hard as the answer hit like a freight train and I cursed my stupidity. *Dammit.* Somewhere along the way I'd missed the signs. I'd missed a shift in Zach's feelings. I looked back to find him watching me with sad eyes and knew I was right. I shook my head, slow and apologetic. "Zach, I—"

"No. Don't say anything," he interrupted with the tiniest quiver to his voice. "It's me who should say sorry. I know this wasn't what we agreed to. I get that. But I figured it was worth a shot to see if things had changed . . . for you too. I got my answer."

Oh shit. Shit. Shit. Shit. I stood and put my hands on his shoulders. "I'm sorry too, Zach. We're good mates. The best. And I'll always be here for you, you know that."

He snorted with an edge of disappointment he couldn't hide. "Yeah, I know. It's one of the things that made it so easy to fall for you." His gaze slid to the window and he shrugged free of my hands. "I'll just take a piss and then be out of your hair." He turned away before I could think of anything to say that might make it easier, if that was even possible.

I waited until the bathroom door closed and then headed to make coffee, more as a distraction than anything else, my hamster brain spinning in free fall. *Fucking hell.* I'd never wanted a serious relationship with Zach, or anyone else for that matter, and I'd thought he felt the same. But I sure as hell didn't want to lose him as a friend, either. Friends like Zach were gold in the high country.

Way to be an oblivious arsehole.

I poured two coffees and took them outside. A minute or so later Zach found me leaning on a veranda post staring at the growing wash of lemon and pink staining the horizon. It was my favourite time of day. The rich night with its crisp starlit sky dancing toe to toe with a slowly spreading sunrise.

Zach slid in behind me, his arms snaking around my waist as he pressed a kiss to the back of my neck. I stiffened without thinking.

He gave a sad chuckle. "For fuck's sake, Holden. Don't make me regret checking in with you. I'm not about to take to my bed with the vapours. You're not *that* irresistible."

"Says you." I gave a snort and spun in his arms, my body relaxing. "I'm sorry." I held his gaze, willing him to believe me. "I mean it. I'm sorry I can't be that guy for you."

Zach shrugged and glanced over my shoulder to where the sun was beginning to peek over the sawtooth range, his green eyes turning almost gold in the light. "Yeah, me too." He turned back. "Still mates?"

I nodded and kissed him softly on the lips, once, and for what I suspected would be the last time. "The best. And I meant what I said. I'm here for you. Nothing's changed."

His eyes held mine for a long minute. "I think maybe they have, just for a bit. So, no more booty calls, yeah?" His smile was soft and a little sad.

I slid free of his hold and took his hands instead. "Agreed. But don't make me come and nail your sorry arse for ghosting me."

He snorted. "Like you could ever track me on my own land."

I waggled my brows. "Spider would do it for me."

Zach groaned in acknowledgement. "Fuck me. You're right. That dog has always had a thing for me."

"And he won't be the last," I pointed out. "There's someone better than me out there for you, Zach. I know it."

Zach shrugged. "Gotta come out first, right?"

"Only when you're ready." And I didn't envy him that. "I made you a coffee." I nodded to the cup sitting on the railing.

Zach stared at it like it might bite him and shook his head. "Not today." He stepped back and jammed his helmet on his head. "Catch you later, Holden."

"Make sure that you do." I let him pass, then watched as he straddled his bike and started it up, spitting dirt loud enough to wake the rams in the shed pen before taking off down the gravel drive without once looking back. I kept my eyes locked on his silhouette until all trace was gone and the ache in my heart eased enough for me to swallow.

Dammit to hell. I could've thought of a million better ways to start a Friday than stomping on the heart of my best friend. We'd been so damn clear at the start that it was just sex between mates that it never occurred to me things had changed for him. Then again Zach had always been the more romantic of the two of us, talking about some distant future for himself that included things I barely even thought about. A husband. A family.

"Fucking, fuck, fuck." I threw the remains of my coffee out onto the dusty drive, then looked up to find my mother standing on her own porch, watching. I had no doubt she'd caught at least part of the exchange. Emily Miller had a finely tuned nose for drama. I gave her a jaunty wave and headed inside. Her curiosity was going to have to wait.

CHAPTER TWO

Holden

Two hours later, with the mercury rising and the station crew briefed and headed upriver, I threw my supply list on the passenger seat of the Hilux and pulled out my phone. I ignored the missed calls from my grandfather and texted Zach instead.

__Just checking in. Are you okay? Are we okay? I'm sorry__.

His reply came almost immediately. *__I'm fine. We're fine. Take your worry hat off. I'll get over it. You're not that special__.*

I snorted. Fucker. I wasn't particularly happy with *fine* as an answer, but it could've been worse.

__Okay, hat removed. Don't be a stranger. And I am so that special__.

Dots came and went for a long time before my phone finally buzzed with a reply.

__You aren't and I won't. Now piss off and let me work__.

I supposed it could've been a lot worse, and I wondered again how the hell I'd missed the warning signs. I threw my phone on the passenger seat and snapped my seat belt in place.

"Holden, wait up." My mother jogged down the path, her blonde bob bouncing loose under her wide-brimmed hat. One look at those shrewd grey eyes and her determined expression and a groan escaped my lips.

I lowered the driver's window and summoned a bright smile. "How may I be of help?"

She rolled her eyes and pinched me on the bicep. "You're not cute. Thought you could sneak away, didn't you?"

"I *am* cute, and I have no idea what you're talking about."

"Yes you do." She eyeballed me. "You and Zach. What happened?"

My fingers drummed on the steering wheel. "Really? You don't see me asking about you and Harry. I take it that was his Merc parked around the back of your cottage again last night?"

She never even blinked. "No, it was another of my fancy men. I can't remember all their names."

I laughed. "Lucky you. He must've been late getting in."

Her cheeks pinked. "A little after midnight. He was on his way back from Christchurch and just decided to stop by."

I chuckled. "Because an hour's detour is exactly what everyone needs at that time of night, right?"

Her pretty eyes sparkled. "Which is why I asked him to stay. I was concerned about his safety on the road."

I rolled my eyes. "I just bet you were."

She batted her eyelashes. "Contrary to what you young guys think, sex doesn't stop at forty, you know?"

I gave a dramatic shudder. "As long as *you're* happy, *I'm* happy. You deserve some sunshine in your life."

Her smile was radiant. "I *am* happy. He's a good man, Holden."

I sighed. "I know he is. We could've had breakfast at the house together if you'd wanted. I won't bite."

"Really?" She nibbled her lower lip in a manner so unlike my mother that it suddenly registered what a total dick I'd been . . . again.

It was obviously a day for it.

My mother and Harry had been seeing each other for six months and all I'd done was ignore the elephant in the room, seeing it as yet another adjustment in my life. Losing Gran and Grandad from the station into town had been bad enough, but I wasn't sure what I'd do if Mum decided to marry and move away too. God, I couldn't even think about it.

"So, you'd be okay with seeing more of him around here?" She looked so hopeful I wanted to slap myself.

"Absolutely. And make sure he knows that, will you?"

She visibly relaxed. "I'll tell him."

I hesitated. "You two are really serious, then?"

She blushed prettily and my heart did another anxious flip. "Yeah, I think maybe we are. Now what's up with you and Zach?"

I groaned. "Do we have to do this?"

"Yes. Trouble in paradise?"

I counted to five. "There *isn't* any paradise. It's never been like that with Zach, not for *me*. And I thought it wasn't on Zach's side either, but apparently I was wrong." I left it at that.

My mother took a second to work that through and then patted my arm. "I'm sorry. Will you two be okay?"

I pressed a kiss to the back of her knuckles. "I hope so." I really did. "And in case things go tits up for him when I'm not around, I think you should know he's debating coming out to his parents."

"Well, shit." My mother cast an eye toward the line of mountains that marked the boundary between Zach's station and ours. "Paddy's not gonna like that."

"Tell me about it." I followed her gaze and thought of Patrick Lane's sour expression every time he laid eyes on me. "Anything you need from town?"

She shook her head. "Just those twenty-kilo bags of flour May set aside for me. Gil says he can bake." She waggled her brows. "I aim to see just how good he is."

I grinned. "Poor guy won't know what's hit him."

She smiled and shot a glance toward my cottage. "Have you packed up?"

"There's no rush."

"Holden, sweetheart." She cupped my face and I felt twelve all over again. "I know it feels strange moving into your grandparents' house—"

"*And* their bedroom," I reminded her with a visible shudder.

"*And* their bedroom. But you're running this place now, and part of that entails moving into the homestead."

"But Gran—"

"Is where she wants to be, close to Grandad's care unit. It's the right move. She wants to be close while he still recognises her."

"But what if you and Harry—" I couldn't finish. "I mean, you guys might want it."

"Nope," she said crisply like they'd already talked about it. "If Harry and I make it long-term, who knows where we'll end up?"

For the sake of my mental health, I decided to ignore that disturbing remark. Just the thought of her leaving the station spiked dread in my heart.

"It's yours now, and it needs to be lived in." She eyed me affectionately. "It has history. *Your* history. One day you might even have a family of your own to fill it up."

I snorted derisively, which only turned her smile a little sad. "I guess I never imagined living in this valley without Gran and Grandad and you here," I admitted. "It feels . . . weird."

"I know." My mother blew a shaky sigh and I was reminded she had to be missing them as well. "We're all gonna need some time to adjust. But if your gran was still here when I left for the UK, even at eighty, she'd have felt duty-bound to help. Employing Gil was the best decision for everyone."

"And you're sure he's up to the job? He's a psychologist with

PTSD and no farming background, for Pete's sake. I won't have the time to hold his hand, Mum."

A flash of uncertainty flickered behind her eyes, then disappeared just as quickly. "He'll be fine," she insisted. "The farming part is your job. Gil has worked in a professional kitchen before, and the PTSD is mostly nightmares and related panic attacks to those. He even let me speak to his therapist. Plus, it's only a three-month contract and we were hardly drowning in applications, AKA none. And it was exactly what Gil was looking for—a short change in lifestyle."

"I know. I know," I huffed. "It's just one of our busiest times of the year."

She stroked my cheek with the backs of her fingers. "I'm sure you'll cope. I've got a few weeks to get him up to speed, and he'll have all my recipes and a ton of spreadsheets and instructions. There's seven of you to get through a week and a half of muster, and then the shearing gang is just belly crutching, so they'll be done in a few days. It's not rocket science, Holden."

I raised a brow.

"Okay." She flushed. "I'll admit it's a little trickier than that. But what's the worst that can happen?"

"We all come down with food poisoning, the muster doesn't happen, the first snow comes early, we lose a ton of stock and set my breeding program back a whole year, and the shearing gang spit the dummy because Gil's food's not up to scratch or he doesn't understand what they need." I was only half-joking.

My mother rolled her eyes. "Such a drama queen."

I sighed, sensing the battle had been lost before it even started. My mother had an answer for everything. She was also right. I wasn't sure which pissed me off more.

I grumbled, "Well, he better be able to follow through on the cooking thing, that's all I'm gonna say. If not, there'll be a mutiny and it won't be pretty. Are you sure you have to go?"

My mother snorted and ruffled my hair. "I want to see my best friend before she dies, sweetheart, *and* attend her living memorial. But I'll make sure to let her know what an inconvenience it's been for you."

I flushed hot. "I'm an arsehole, I know. You know I want you to go."

"I do." Her eyes softened. "And you're more than capable of running the muster on your own."

"I'm not sure Grandad would agree." I studied the mountains through the windscreen, avoiding my mother's shrewd gaze.

"Your grandad loves you. I know he didn't really acknowledge you being gay, but he always recognised the born farmer in you, which we all know was far more important to him than who you took to bed. The fact he was planning for you to take over this place says it all."

I was tempted to point out that there wasn't really a Plan B. Only grandchild, after all. I glanced at my phone sitting on the dash with all his missed calls and hoped she was right. I lifted her hand and pressed a kiss to the back. "Thanks, Mum."

Her mouth tipped into a wide smile. "You're welcome. Now go, or you'll be late for Gil's bus. And promise you'll be nice. I'd really like him to consider staying longer than the three months. I could do with easing back myself."

"He's a psychologist," I scoffed. "Why the hell would he choose to stay and cook for us lot instead?" I plugged L.A.B. into the sound system, gave my mother a jaunty wave, and headed out.

I checked fences as I drove, estimated feed volumes, and evaluated the muscle mass of the Angus cattle moving lazily over the lower slopes. Worries about Zach, my grandfather's calls, and the endless to-do list in my head faded into the background as the land worked its magic.

The station road tracked alongside the Glendale River, its braided waterways sparkling in the sun, and everything, as far as the eye could see was Miller land, *my* land. I still couldn't believe it. Thirty-five thousand acres made up of golden-brown tussock river flats, occasional runs of green pasture, wide shingle fans, thickets of thorny native matagouri, rugged hill country, impossible bluffs, steep runs of scree, and at the very top, the jagged walls and sawtooth ridges of the Southern Alps piercing the sky.

    I sprawled in my seat, dialled the volume up to drown the bump and rumble of the road, and rested my elbow through the open window. And with the soft reggae beat smoothing the rough edges of my mood, I started to sing.

CHAPTER THREE

Gil

I fisted my hands and then shook them out in a vain attempt to stop the trembling.

Not a chance in hell.

I sat on them instead.

It was already nine forty and I'd been told someone would be there to collect me at nine fifteen. I scouted the road left and right for the millionth time, my patience as thin as the slice of shade I'd found on the bench outside the crowded café. The stunning view of Lake Tekapo was some recompense, I supposed. If I was going to be kept waiting, I could do worse than having one of the most stunning lakes in the world as a distraction.

Not everyone was as anal about punctuality as me, I reminded myself. Didn't mean they were bad people, right? Yeah, I wasn't going to be drawn on that. Then again, it could've been the fact my eyeballs were hanging out of my head from lack of sleep. Not to mention, the growing pit of bile churning in my stomach was a hiccup away from making itself known at my feet.

Mostly that last one.

I ferreted in my satchel and downed one of my pills with a swig from my water bottle. I considered what lay ahead for the rest of the day and popped a second. My therapist would undoubtedly disapprove, but my therapist wasn't there. I made a mental note to come clean in our next session.

Or maybe not.

It didn't take my eye-wateringly expensive PhD in Psychology to work out that little avoidance gem. Then again, maybe he really didn't need to know. I stopped that particular thought in its track and rolled my eyes at myself. There was no *then again*.

I was taking too many pills.

Period.

Eighteen months, and it was time to take stock. That's what I was here for, right? Get out of my head, and my staid routine, and my crippling indecision, and shake things up a bit.

I scowled at my hands. Just not *that* kind of shaking.

The large car park opposite the café was jammed with tourist buses, their occupants busily making their way across the McClaren footbridge toward the teeny tiny stone Church of The Good Shepherd set on the lakeshore itself, just metres from the crystalline waters. Couples came from all over the world to marry in a place that burst at the seams if you got above fifty-five guests, including the wedding party. All set in a pretty town with a permanent population that weighed in at well under a thousand.

Still, the location was pretty unbeatable. Picture postcard sapphire glacial lake, with New Zealand's tallest mountain at its back, and a Dark Sky Reserve above. Ka-ching.

I'd discovered in my research that the Mackenzie Basin covered an area of about one hundred kilometres north to south, forty east to west. It was mostly known for two things: tourism and sheep farming, the latter evidenced by the statue of a sheepdog on the foreshore not far from the famous little church.

And the small town of Tekapo might be stunning but it was also late summer, blistering hot, and about to get hotter. Pushing into the high thirties by afternoon, according to the forecast.

I glanced at my bags, briefly considered swapping my trainers for jandals, then decided I was too damned hot to put in the effort. I checked the road . . . again, grumbled at the heat, and pulled out my phone, intending to reread the text Emily had sent the night before.

But before I could, the screen flashed with a text from Tucker. I missed him already. I pretended my hand wasn't still shaking as I swiped it open.

Are you there yet?

I smiled. ***Waiting to be picked up. They're late.***

A laughing emoji appeared followed by, ***I don't even have to see your face to know how pissed you are.***

I'm trying to be chill. What's up?

Why does something have to be up?

Because I know you. You're babying me.

If you don't want to be babied, then don't sneak away a few days early and not tell anyone, or even say goodbye.

I didn't sneak. I did.

You did.

I ignored him.

Because if another person looked at me like I'd lost my freaking mind or regaled me with all the very sensible reasons I was making the wrong decision, I was going to lose my shit completely. Maybe I *was* making a mistake. But it was a whole lot better than sitting on my couch and flicking through photos in my way-too-empty apartment with all its bland rental furniture, or chugging back pills to stop the nightmares, or drinking too much tequila. Although right about then, all of those options sounded perfectly reasonable alternatives.

But the decision didn't *feel* wrong.

That said, I hadn't felt much of anything *at all* for a long, long time, which was the very reason I'd said yes to the offer to start with.

I had zero to lose.

I continued to wait while Tucker composed his answer in whatever way he thought would upset me the least and tried to ignore the stab of guilt I felt at his words. I *should've* said goodbye. Tuck was my best friend and the man with whom I'd built a successful Clinical Psychology practice. A tall, squarely built, generally jovial guy, with sparkling grey eyes, a gauge in one ear, and an epic dark brown beard that hung almost to his chest, Tuck looked more like a monster truck driver than a psychologist, something that usually worked in his favour with his clients who adored the ground he walked on. As did I. I was frankly amazed he'd put up with my shit for as long as he had over the last year, but that was Tuck, and I owed him more than I could say.

Dots came and went until eventually they dried up completely and my heart sank. I wouldn't have blamed him for calling it a day. There's only so much a person can take, and my free rides on self-pity drama had to be running low.

Then my phone chimed loudly in my hand and I almost jumped high enough to land in the lake.

"Jesus Christ, Tuck. You scared the shit out of me."

"Good."

Oh yeah, he was angry. "I'm sorry. I know I should've at least called you. Emily asked me to come a few days early and . . . well . . . there was nothing holding me in Wellington . . ." I trailed off, flinching in anticipation.

"Except good manners," he pointed out. "And the tiny issue of not bailing on your best friend three days early without a single fucking word!"

Ouch. Apparently jovial had taken a back seat to thoroughly pissed off for a bit. "Fair point."

When I didn't offer anything more, Tuck sighed. "Not enough, Gil."

Dammit. "You're supposed to wait until your clients are ready to talk."

He grunted. "Newsflash. You're not my client. You're my arsehole friend who's had a hell of a time, and who I feel extremely sad about, but who is rapidly making a home for himself on my shitlist."

I'd have been mad if it weren't for the fact Tuck was right. No one had been there for me more than him. "All right," I conceded. "I admit I didn't call because I didn't want to fight you anymore on this. I know you think I'm a sandwich short of a picnic—"

"I never said—"

"Let me finish."

He paused. "I'm listening."

I blew out a weary sigh. "Tucker, I love you, you know that. But you thought stepping away from my patients and our business partnership for a while was . . . premature. You thought renting the house and leasing an apartment was a knee-jerk reaction. You thought I should hang around and work through things, do the hard yards. Which I have, by the way. You thought I had as much to do with Luke leaving as he did, which, okay, fair call. But I know you think taking this job is a bad idea as well. You think I'm running away. You think I should start dating again. Have I missed anything?"

"I never said *any* of that." He sounded pained.

I softened my voice. "No, you haven't, and I love you for that. But that doesn't mean it isn't true. I know because it's what I'd think as well if we traded places. I can see it in the way you're so careful with what you *do* say. I'd like your support, Tuck, but I don't need your permission."

The line fell silent for a while before he finally broke it, his words cut with emotion. "God, I hate that this happened to you. I hate all of it. Every fucking day."

I swallowed around the lump in my throat that never seemed to go away. "Me too, Tuck. Me too."

I listened as his breathing hitched.

"And you really think this will help?" he croaked. "Jesus, Gil, I looked it up. The place is in the middle of nowhere. You're practically sitting on top of Mt Cook and you don't even like sheep."

I snorted. "I don't *dislike* them; I just know nothing about them, well, other than how to cook them, and I do that part really well. Besides, it's only a half hour from Tekapo. It's hardly Scott Base. I hear they have internet and everything."

He barked out a laugh. "Arsehole. It doesn't change the fact that you're supposed to be there to help during autumn muster. But unless you've had a brain transplant, I figure you know absolutely nothing about mustering sheep, right?"

I huffed out a sigh. "My job is to cook and look after the guys doing the actual mustering, not traipse all over the Southern Alps bringing the sheep down myself?"

He snorted. "Riiight."

The silence bled out as I watched a line of tourists heading single file back across the bridge like a line of ants. "I know you're worried, but I have to try *something*, Tuck. I'm a few tablets a day short of a real problem. I know grief runs its own race, but I'm doing all the right things and nothing's working. When I got the call about this opportunity, Jesus, Tuck, it was like the first fucking ray of sunshine in a shitty year and a half."

He mumbled something about shoving a personal ray of sunshine somewhere I least expected it, but I ignored him.

"Okay, so maybe it *is* a mistake," I rambled on. "Then again, maybe it's not. Either way, at least I'm fucking *doing* something. Three months isn't forever, and maybe I'll learn something important. I need to at least try. I might not know where this is leading, but I know it's not back to who I was. I barely know that person anymore." I finished on a gasp and a pair of trembling hands, but I'd said what I needed to. I blinked hard, tears welling. The last thing I wanted was to lose my best friend.

My outburst was greeted by silence for far too long to be reassuring, but eventually I caught a sharp intake of breath followed by a drawn-out sigh.

"First off, I hate that you're right," Tuck grumbled, and I very nearly smiled. "I just want to get that out there, you know, for posterity. That way you can never say I don't give you credit." He took a breath. "And secondly, I hate that you're right."

This time I did laugh.

"And I'm sorry that you didn't think you could say all that to my face, before you ran out on me that is, but that's on me."

He really was the best. "It's not on you. I'm not even sure I understand it myself. I just want to take some control back, Tuck. I have to start moving forward again."

"And I think you're being too hard on yourself. Eighteen months isn't a long time, Gil, not considering what happened."

"I know. But I think at some level, I'm ready. Luke clearly is." It was hard to keep the bitterness from my voice. "I need a kick-start. And maybe this is it."

Tucker sighed. "The accident wasn't your fault."

"I know that." *Mostly.* Because nothing could take the hamster wheel of guilt-ridden *what-ifs* from my brain. The ones that woke me at night with whispers of accusation and held my lungs captive to their lies.

What if I'd just remembered to take the goddammed gift that morning? What if I'd been travelling slower? What if I'd just turned my head and fucking looked? If I'd spun the wheel a second quicker? Would she have lived?

"And you're sure you're not just running away?"

And there it was. "No, I'm not sure. But I've got nothing to lose."

After a long minute in which my heart rose in my throat because I needed him as a friend more than I could say, Tucker finally spoke. "Promise me you'll keep talking to Leonard. He's good at what he does, Gil."

Relief coursed through me. "We've already agreed to sessions online and extras, if I need them, and—oh, hang on, I think my ride just arrived." I lowered the phone from my ear and squinted at the dusty blue Hilux pulling in at the kerb. It had *Miller Station* stamped on its door, windows rolled down, and music blaring.

The driver killed the volume, pushed his sunglasses up his nose, and leaned across the passenger seat to speak through the window. "Are you Gil Everton?"

"Yep." I raised a tentative hand in greeting.

"Cool. I'm Holden Miller. Let's get you on board." His full mouth curved up in a high-wattage smile that made my stomach do a weird-arse, vaguely familiar flip.

Oh boy. Attraction. Just freaking dandy. Eighteen months with my libido on military-grade lockdown, and it chose that moment to wake up and get with the program. Not only that, but I already knew Holden was gay from my conversations with Emily. Go fucking figure. It was a wrinkle I sure as hell didn't need in my reboot plan. I hadn't been laid since Callie's death and I wasn't looking to change that state of affairs anytime soon even if I had been able to summon any interest, which I hadn't . . . for a while. So, yeah, there was that. Which was why my reaction to *any* man was . . . surprising.

"Gil, you there?" Tuck's voice broke into my thoughts just as Holden disappeared back into the cab and the driver's door opened.

I raised the phone again. "Yeah, but I'm gonna have to—" I stopped abruptly as a ruggedly handsome dark-haired beauty with a mass of lazy brown waves bouncing around his ears emerged from the Hilux. And since I was a hot mess but not dead, I drew in a sharp breath and whispered, "Wow."

"What?" Tucker interrupted my gawping. "What wow? Gil?"

I cleared my throat and mumbled. "Nothing. I'll call you in a day or two. Say hi to Gail and the kids for me."

"They don't like you either."

I laughed. "They love me."

"Fuck it. You're right."

"Bye, Tuck."

"Wait, Gil. Gil!"

I hung up on Tuck's protest and shot to my feet, by which time Holden had circled to the back of the Hilux and was busy opening the hatch. It gave me a few seconds to appreciate the way his dusty jeans hugged a pretty spectacular arse, and an equally dusty black T-shirt showed off lean muscular arms sporting a golden tan.

Holden caught my eye and that broad smile widened, no doubt because I was standing there staring at him like a total idiot. "First off, let's exchange numbers," he said. "I think you only have Mum's. I tried to call to say I was running late, but whatever I had in my phone didn't work."

"Oh." *Shit.* Great way to start. "Yeah, I ah, changed my number, sorry. I updated your mum, but maybe you've got my old one."

"No problem. Here." He gave me his phone and I corrected the number he had stored and then he sent me a text.

I called him back to make sure we were right, and Billy Joel's "Uptown Girl" rang out through the car park.

I bit back a smile and raised a brow. "Really? I think I should be offended."

He chuckled. "Don't be. Besides, it was before I met you and it kind of fits, right? You're from the big smoke. You've even got your Roberto Cavallis on." He pointed to the label on my jeans and heat rose in my cheeks. "Pretty fancy for the station."

I narrowed my gaze and fired back, "But you recognised the brand which says you have an eye for those things."

He grinned. "Of course. They're a great jean. Just don't wear them in the woolshed."

I laughed. "Kind of goes without saying."

"Are those it?" He nodded to four bags of varying sizes siting in a tidy line at my feet.

I gave a mute nod, because I was well-educated like that, and wiped my hot palms down the front of my jeans.

"Great." He sauntered over in that loose-gaited way perfected by many farmers like they had all the time in the world. About a metre away, he stopped, lifted his glasses onto his head, and a pair of coffee-brown almost black eyes locked with mine.

And just, damn. I was in trouble.

"Welcome to Mackenzie Country, Gil." Holden offered his hand

and I appreciated the firm warm grip and rough scrape of his calloused palm against my own.

"Thanks. I appreciate the lift."

He smirked. "We're a little far out for public transport, but maybe you've got talents I know nothing about." He winked and heat instantly fanned across my pale cheeks.

I was blushing? What the fuck? I cleared my throat and took a bag in each hand. "I just hope I didn't drag you away from something important."

Holden chuckled. "You might be the new domestic manager, but you're also the new cook. And *nothing* is more important than that."

I snorted and relaxed, my attention caught by a singular dark beauty spot sitting high on the man's left cheek. "So, no pressure then?"

"You wish." A smile tugged at Holden's lips as he grabbed the other two bags. "We're all about our stomachs, Gil. But fair warning, the guys will be hella disappointed if all you dish up on muster are hockey sticks."

I gawped. "What the hell are hockey sticks?"

He shot me a smile. "Lamb chops, mutton chops, name your death sentence. Also known as 365s due to the fact that hardly a day passes without eating them in some form. There's never a shortage of lamb on a sheep station."

I laughed. "Noted. Steer clear of lamb chops or versions thereof."

Holden laughed. "That'll earn you some brownie points. But just don't mess too much with breakfast. Shepherds are creatures of habit when it comes to how they like to start the day. And you got me out of fencing this morning, so it should really be me thanking you. I hope you've got some warm gear packed in these. Don't be fooled by this heat. In three weeks, it'll be a fond but distant memory."

I nodded. "I brought everything on Emily's list, although she mentioned the station had some spare winter jackets that I might be able to borrow for the short time I'm here."

Holden nodded like he'd expected that. "Yeah, Mum's a packrat when it comes to clothes." He stood back and ran his gaze over me from top to bottom, and it was all I could do not to squirm. "You're not far off Grandad's size, which means you're in luck. There's a store's worth of jackets in every weight imaginable still hanging in the mudroom. Boots as well if you want. Check before you fork out any money in Oakwood. It might be bigger than Tekapo by a few thousand residents, but it's still a small town and you'll pay for the pleasure."

I blinked. "I couldn't possibly wear your grandad's clothes."

Holden huffed. "Of course you can. He's got no use for them anymore. Besides, when you're on the hill, your clothes are survival tools, not personal fashion statements. The right gear in winter can mean the difference between life and death."

I frowned. "On the hill?"

Holden chuckled. "Up the mountains. We talk about stock being on and off the hill. Currently, over summer, they're on, roaming far and wide in the high altitudes while the lower pastures get a chance to grow. We get about four months' grass-growth time max at our altitude and we have to make the most of it. At autumn muster we bring the stock off the hill to overwinter and lamb."

I smiled. "There's clearly a whole new language to learn."

He snorted. "You'll catch on quick. And in case you're wondering—" He indicated the two huge bags of flour sitting alongside my bags. "—those are for you. Mum said you can bake." He arched a brow as if looking for confirmation. "I sure hope you can follow through. She runs a tight ship and you've got big shoes to fill. An angry shepherd is a dangerous man. Get in." He closed the hatch and headed for the driver's door.

"Oh, I can bake all right." I grabbed the door handle and caught Holden's eye over the roof of the cab. "Just never said I was any good. And just so you know, I'd back an angry baker over an angry shepherd any day of the week. I don't have to go anywhere near those damn sheep of yours, but you lot still have to eat."

He stared at me for a moment, then barked out a laugh. "Damn, I think you're gonna fit in just fine. Climb aboard and we'll go get some fuel."

I slid into the cab and buckled up. "Oakwood is your main service town, right?"

Holden nodded. "Yeah. It's about fifteen minutes southwest. But today we'll fuel up here since I don't need anything else. After that, we'll get you home."

Home. I rolled the word around in my head. I hadn't felt *home* since the accident. Hadn't felt I belonged *anywhere*. Hadn't known what to do about it. I took a deep breath and debated the chances of that changing in this strange new environment. I figured slim to none, but I'd take slim.

The Hilux burst into life and Holden turned in his seat, his eyes hidden behind those dark glasses. "But before we go anywhere, there's one very important question I have to ask."

My stomach knotted. "Sure."

His gaze narrowed. "How do you feel about reggae?"

I huffed out a laugh, mostly from relief. "Will my answer make any difference?"

His eyes danced. "I'd like to say yes, but the truth is, not a chance."

I snorted. "Then why ask?"

His smile turned wicked. "Because my mother said I wasn't allowed to scare you off."

I laughed and spun to face him. "Well, just so you know, it takes more than a little reggae to scare me off. I was raised on a relentless diet of eighties punk music, courtesy of my mother. Very loud and very . . . angry."

He winced. "Ouch."

"Exactly. Eighteen years of that and I can pretty much survive anything."

He chuckled and that damn beauty spot winked at me from his cheek. "Well, don't get too cocky. My shearing contractor gets off on old school country and western. Like *really* old school. By the end of the first day, you'll discover homicidal tendencies you never dreamed you had. Be thankful they're just belly crutching this muster. It'll be done in a matter of days. A full shear and you're looking at weeks of torture."

I blinked. "Something to look forward to, then. And also, belly crutching?"

He grinned. "Arse, bits, and bellies. Cleaning them up for lambing and winter."

"Oh."

Holden's brown eyes locked on mine, his mouth tipping up in a smile. "Don't say I didn't warn you." He switched the music on low, and pulled away from the kerb.

I slid down in my seat, my hands still and relaxed and resting on my thighs. The pills, or the magic of this place, or the man I was sitting next to?

I'd take it, regardless.

I focused my gaze forward, away from any glimpse of those lean denim-clad thighs, and silently grumbled to the universe. *You couldn't have gone with old, cranky, and smelling of sheep manure, could you?*

CHAPTER FOUR

Gil

WHEN WE PULLED IN FOR FUEL, THE SERVICE GUY HOSING DOWN the forecourt immediately drew Holden into conversation about some Oakwood café being sold to a city guy that no one had a clue about, and wasn't it a shame to see the business leaving local hands? Oh, and did Holden know that Brent and Maria from the drycleaners had split up and people were worried what was going to happen to that business as well.

I smiled at the small-town feel of it all and used the time to grab a suitable ringtone for my new boss. When he climbed back into the cab, I asked him to give me a call.

He shot me a look, then did as I asked, laughing out loud when "Long Haired Country Boy" by Charlie Daniels filled the cab. "I can see you're gonna be trouble, Gil Everton."

I was hoping he was wrong.

We drove out of tiny Tekapo in silence, travelled five minutes down the highway, and then turned left onto a gravel road that followed the eastern lakeshore. Flanked by tussock and browned-off pasture, it was barely wide enough for two cars to pass and my head continuously cranked from side to side to take in the views. The clear blue water of Lake Tekapo shimmered on our left, steeply rising hill country sat on our right, and the Southern Alps lay stacked in the distance like rows of shark's teeth, some still tipped in white. It was like watching a tennis match, my gaze darting from side to side so I didn't miss anything.

"Did they ever catch James Mackenzie, the infamous sheep rustler the area is named after? He was a bit of a Robin Hood or Ned Kelly figure, right?"

A smile stole over Holden's face. "A fan of the man, are you?"

"I confess to liking a good hero-villain tale as much as the next person, sure."

He laughed. "As a matter of fact, they did, although he always claimed his innocence, so it's hard to say who the villain was. Some say he had a thousand sheep with him when he was captured, but his story was that he was hired to drive them to Otago or duped into it. Anyway, they'd no sooner caught him than he escaped, only to be captured again and convicted before escaping another couple of times. Eventually his trial was found to be flawed and he was pardoned. I think they were pleased to get rid of him. His escapades had become an embarrassment to the authorities."

"Do you think he was innocent?"

Holden shrugged. "Who knows? But he kind of personifies that self-starter, tough, resilient, and irrepressible spirit of high-country people both then and now, and so I'm not sure it matters."

I thought about that. "You know, I think you're right."

After a moment's silence, Holden continued. "I assume Mum gave you a rundown on the station and why you're here?"

"Some." I angled my back to the door so I could see Holden better—it wasn't exactly a hardship. "I know your grandad's been moved into a care facility, that the station has been in your family three . . . no, four generations, and that Emily is heading to the UK to see a friend who's dying from cancer. But I'm keen to hear more."

Holden smiled. "Be careful what you ask for." He briefly explained his family history in the area—how his great-grandfather had taken over the land lease on a failing station and made it profitable through careful husbandry; how his grandfather had hoped Emily's marriage to a farmer would see the property left in safe hands; his disappointment when the marriage failed and how he'd planned for Holden to slowly take over under his watchful eye. But everything had fallen apart when he developed dementia, and Holden had the whole shebang thrust upon him three years earlier, at the ripe old age of twenty-seven.

"Wow." I shook my head, trying and failing to imagine all that responsibility at such a young age. "Sink or swim, then."

He gave a grim chuckle. "Pretty much. Grandad's an ornery old bastard. He never suffered fools gladly, and he never took kindly to *any* interference in the running of the station, family or otherwise. It made the last few years a freaking nightmare, both before and after I took over. The station was in bad shape by the time I picked up the reins, and we're still recovering."

I took a few seconds to study him, noting the first glimpse of frustration I'd seen since we'd met—the tight set to his jaw and the worry lines that flickered in the corners of his eyes. "That must've been gut-wrenching for you," I observed. "Watching things slide and having your hands tied."

He shot me a grateful look. "It was. And Grandad wasn't exactly a fan of planners or filing systems, let alone computers. Nothing was written down. All I had was my experience growing up on the station, his old diary, and stacks of invoices and accounts on his desk. I knew my way around the broad seasonal planning, but I had to wing a lot of the other shit. We were damn lucky we survived."

I wasn't sure luck had much to do with it. Holden Miller might have had a laid-back manner, but my sharply honed sense for people recognised the palpable air of competence and leadership running just below that calm surface. It was a potent mix.

"How many stations are up this way?" I asked over the noise of the tyres humming on the metal road.

"Four." Holden pointed out general directions. "Upper McKay, McEldowney, Calendar Peak, and Miller Station. Most stations are on crown-owned land—leased in perpetuity to the farming families who work them, and who often go back three or four generations. There are about one hundred and fifty high-country families left, so we're a tight group. There are tight restrictions on what we can do, and more and more consent is required to change anything at all, like increasing stock numbers or running tourism operations. It's getting harder and harder to make these places profitable. Who knows what the future holds for families like ours? One day these iconic stations may no longer exist. Hopefully not in my generation."

I frowned at the worried edge to his voice. "I had no idea."

He shrugged. "The average person doesn't. Anyway, Miller Station sits right at the top of this valley, where the Glendale River feeds into the Havelock. But we share boundaries with stations on the other side of the mountain ranges as well." He indicated further up the valley. "We're actually closer to Lane Station the next valley over, than we are to McEldowney's, our neighbours on this road. I can get to Lane's homestead in about fifteen minutes in summer via a track we had cut between the two. In winter, not so much."

I shook my head. "That's crazy."

"There's also a small local ski field over that range." He indicated a run of peaks on our right. "It brings a bit of winter traffic, and most of the stations, including Miller, have tourist accommodation of some kind." He gave a half shrug. "Diversify or die, right?"

"Are they part of my responsibilities?" I didn't remember Emily mentioning anything about that.

"Normally, yes," he answered. "Muster is a really popular time for international tourists who want the full enchilada experience of a high-country station. But with this year being my first muster without Mum, and with you stepping in as a newbie, we figured we wouldn't invite trouble. Mum managed to transfer the existing bookings across to other stations with tourist accommodation. That means you only have us to worry about."

Thank God.

I cast another look over the landscape and shook my head. "The scale blows me away. I don't suppose you get many casual drop-ins looking for a cuppa."

Holden snorted. "You'd be surprised. There's always a few randoms, mostly tourists, who come to see what's up here. They're not a problem unless they leave gates open or get themselves lost. But we do get a bit of poaching, and then there are the idiots who decide releasing deer or pigs to illegally stock the valleys for hunting is a good idea."

I stared at him. "You're kidding. On *your* land."

He shrugged. "Fucking entitled, right? I guess they figure because it's a crown lease that they have some kind of claim. But a single pig can do a shitload of damage in just a few weeks, and I have to send one of my guys to track and kill the thing. It's a pain in my arse."

"Do you have a lot of pests to manage?"

He shrugged. "Rabbits, of course. They're the scourge of the earth around these parts and we spend a fortune trying to control them. And there are stoats which seem to love our alpine conditions and all its fragile fauna. Plus, the infestation of wilding pines. They grow like wildfire from self-seeding and can choke good pastureland in a matter of years. Managing all that has to be factored into the seasonal work every year." Holden tapped my arm and pointed. "That's Mount Cook." He indicated a peak way off in the distance across the other side of the lake. "I'll see if I can fly you over it sometime, if the weather behaves."

My eyes widened. "You fly?" I couldn't believe it. *Another* damn pilot.

He grinned. "Just a fixed-wing. I'd like to get my helicopter licence one day. The station has an airstrip. Most do. It's a huge bonus in our line of work. We don't use a chopper to muster like some do, but it's a whole lot easier if you can scout the territory beforehand.

Saves a ton of time, not to mention blisters. But we had to sell our plane a few years back." He went quiet, and I wondered if his grandfather had something to do with that as well.

"So, what do you do now, without the plane?"

He dodged one of a never-ending succession of potholes and glanced my way. "I used to do some piloting for Wild Run, a heli-ski company operating out of Oakwood. I'd fly their overseas clients from Christchurch to wherever they were staying, sometimes here at the station. I don't do it anymore, obviously, but the company still gives me a good rate on a piloted chopper when I need one."

The Hilux hit another series of ruts, and I steadied myself with one hand on the dash and the other through the strap above the door.

Holden shot me a grin. "You'll get used to it. I probably know every damn hole on this road. Same with the station. The riverbed tracks can be a bit gnarly when the water starts to rise, but once you get to know them, it's a blast as long as you keep your wits about you."

Oh, dear God.

When I didn't reply, Holden glanced my way. "You *have* driven off-road before, right? There's a fair bit of back country commuting to get your head around, especially during muster."

I swallowed hard. "A paddock or two back in my youth, but that's about it. Your mother said she'd show me the ropes."

Holden took what looked like a calming breath. "Of course she did. Well, buckle up, buttercup, cos driving lessons with my mother are not for the faint-hearted."

I sucked in a breath. "Thanks for the heads-up." It wasn't that I didn't like driving because I did. In fact, I used to love it. But it had taken me a long time to replace my car after the accident.

Holden threw me an apologetic look. "I'm sorry. That was kind of a stupid thing to say to a guy who's been in an accident. To be perfectly honest, the tracks you'll be using to and from the muster huts are pretty good. There are a few riverbed crossings, but they're a piece of cake this time of year, and *no one* tackles them when the river is up unless they know what they're doing—*my* rule. We've got a young graduate working with us who I won't let drive the steeper climbs even as dry as they are now. You won't be expected to do anything you're not comfortable with, Gil. You have my word."

Which helped, a lot, enough for me to qualify, "It's not so much the accident. Being behind the wheel doesn't trigger me like you might expect. It's more my lack of recent driving experience. I took a while to replace my car, and when Emily talked about *tracks*, I guess I was imagining dirt roads like this. Riverbeds hadn't even crossed my mind." I scouted the landscape and sighed. "I guess they should have."

Holden gave me a calculating once-over. "I'm not worried. My mother has a knack for choosing the right people. That's why I leave all the hiring to her, including the shepherds. And I was joking about the lessons." He gave a sly grin. "Kind of."

I groaned. "Oh great."

"Nah" He cuffed my shoulder. "Trust me, she won't let you loose on the station if she's not happy. She's a better driver than me—just don't tell her I said that."

I gave him a hard stare. "That's not as comforting as you think it is."

Holden chuckled. "You'll be fine. Although I have to say, I've been wondering what brain explosion made you think leaving your city comforts for the back of beyond was a good idea?"

"Shows what you know," I said drily. "I've only just shaved my beard, and my flannel shirt is packed in my bag along with my subscription to *Woodsman* and my favourite axe."

Holden barked out a laugh. "Cute, but all lies." He turned and scrutinised my face. "I admit you've got an *almost* decent blond scruff going on, but as for growing a beard worthy of these mountains on that carefully groomed peaches-and-cream complexion of yours?" He pulled a less-than-impressed face. "I'm just not seeing it."

I laughed because he wasn't wrong. Not that I was telling him that. "Hey." I gave an indignant huff. "I can grow a beard."

Holden arched a brow but said nothing.

I bit back a smile. "Given a few weeks."

He cupped his ear. "What was that?"

"All right, months. Are you happy now?" I gave him a friendly shove. "Just drive."

Which only set him off again. "I think I'll wait on the outcome of the driving lessons before I bow to your inner Bear Grylls."

I groaned. "Oh god, I'm gonna make such an idiot of myself, aren't I?"

"We can only hope." He shot me a smug smile that elicited another groan.

We drove in silence for another few minutes, the breeze rushing through the open windows into the cab, a welcome change from air conditioning. It felt so . . . country, just like the man sitting next to me.

"You haven't asked about the PTSD." I exposed the elephant in the vehicle while keeping my gaze on the road ahead. "I expect you have questions."

Holden's eyes burned two holes in the side of my head before he faced the front again. "My mother has good instincts. I trust she checked things out. She told us that you were in a bad car crash and had a tough recovery. That you were taking time out from your psychology practice to do a little thinking and that you were a great cook. She said the PTSD was mostly nightmares and associated panic attacks. Was she wrong?"

"No," I answered truthfully. "Although if I'm stressed, like today, I can get a bit shaky." I held out my trembling hands and Holden glanced over, his mouth a thin, tight line, his expression unreadable. I slid them back under my thighs. "But I have a therapist that I'll be talking to while I'm here, I have a routine I go through if I have a bad night, and I haven't had a panic attack during the day for over six months."

"That's good then," he said with a quick and clearly relieved smile. "Like I told you, Mum knows Miller Station almost better than I do. She knows what it takes to work *and* live up here. If you passed *her* critical eye, then it's a done deal as far as I'm concerned. You're sure about the driving not being a problem?"

I blinked. "If you're asking, am I slightly terrified at the idea of manoeuvring sideways up gravel banks and riverbeds? Hell yeah, I am. But I think that's a point in *favour* of my mental stability, *not* against it, don't you agree?"

He laughed, those gorgeous brown eyes crinkling at the corners. "Fair point."

I slid my hands free and clasped them firmly in my lap. "I appreciate you not asking about the accident, but it's okay, really."

Holden's gaze flickered sideways. "It's not my place to pry, but sure, I'll admit I'm curious."

I took a deep breath. "I'd left work to pick up our ten-year-old daughter from school and drop her at a friend's birthday party."

Holden shot me a surprised look.

I shrugged and answered his unspoken question. "My marriage was another victim of the accident."

He grimaced in sympathy. "I'm sorry."

"It is what it is. Anyway, I'd forgotten to take the birthday present with me that morning, and so we were swinging by our house to pick it up when the accident happened. I was on a green light and halfway across an intersection when a car going the opposite direction ran his red light and smashed straight into us."

Holden's gaze jerked sideways. "Jesus Christ."

I pushed on, not sure I could finish if I stopped. Eighteen months and I still avoided the topic if I could. To be fair, most people, most *friends* had stopped asking. Nobody knew what to do with it. Hell, I didn't know what to do with it.

"It happened so fast. One second, we were slowly moving through the intersection, the next, we were sandwiched between this vehicle and a power pole on the other side of the road."

Holden shot me a lengthy look before turning back to the road, like he knew there was worse to come. "Mum said you were in hospital for a while. She, ah, she didn't mention your daughter."

I'd guessed as much. "Yeah, well, I had a couple of broken ribs, whiplash, concussion, bruising from the seat belt, and a fractured tib and fib that still ache like hell. But Callie . . ." I swallowed hard and turned away. "The passenger door took the brunt of the impact. She, um . . . she . . . was killed instantly."

Daddeeeeee!

I wasn't sure how long I'd been sitting there, but the next thing I knew a hand landed on my shoulder and I realised Holden had pulled over. "Oh, Gil, I'm so fucking sorry."

I scrubbed a hand down my face, my stuttering breaths the only thing to break the silence. I stared out the windscreen and huffed apologetically. "I bet you're really glad you hired me, right?"

His silence made me turn around.

"First off, I'm not that kind of arsehole," he said flatly.

"I didn't mean—"

"Second—" He arched a brow, which snapped my mouth shut. "—life fucking sucks sometimes. That much I do know. And although I don't pretend to imagine what you've been through, I get how it would fuck with your head."

I nodded wordlessly, struggling to hold his intense stare.

"I once rolled a quad bike twenty metres down a scree slope ending arse-up in a hole in the river with the quad weighting me down. To this day I can still taste the water in my mouth and gushing down my throat and the panic as I tried to get myself free. It took almost a minute, the longest damn minute of my life." He snorted. "Mum still doesn't know. I had nightmares for months, so I get it . . . at least a little."

I met his soft gaze and wondered how a man I barely knew had seen me so clearly in a way few others had in the past year. My lips curved up in an unexpected smile. "Yeah, maybe you do."

He returned the smile, the reassurance enough to smooth the rough edges of my embarrassment. "Sounds like you're lucky to be alive," he observed, those brown eyes quiet on my face.

He wasn't wrong. "So they say, although there's been more than a few times I haven't been so grateful for that fact since it happened."

A thick silence filled the cab, broken only by the *zonk-zonk* of a pair of paradise ducks making a fly-by on their descent to the river.

"I can imagine" was all he said. No questions. No pressing for more. No platitudes.

"It doesn't matter that I know it wasn't my fault—"

"You second-guess everything you did?" he speculated.

I huffed a joyless laugh. "The mind knows, but the heart can't deal with it. Still, I'm a lot better than I was."

Holden studied me for a moment. "Well, that's something, right?" He put the Hilux into gear and eased back onto the road. "And thanks for telling me. I can totally understand why you might need a bit of thinking space after all that, in which case, you came to the right place." He swept his hand over the landscape. "Welcome to space, Gil. Lots and lots of space."

I laughed, and the sound of it almost startled me.

Holden glanced sideways. "Just keep me in the loop if anything changes that I need to know about, okay? When we're on muster, you're our hub, Gil, our touchstone, our backup. You're it."

I rolled my eyes. "No pressure then?"

He snorted. "No more than on the rest of us. One thing you'll learn pretty quick on the station is that we're a team. Lose any one of us and the wheels fall off. I have to trust that you'll be there if we need you or that you'll get help if you can't. God knows it wouldn't be the first time shit happened during muster. It's life. But if things go tits up for any of us, for any reason, the rest can pick up the slack and get things done. That's how we work. It's how the whole Mackenzie Country works. We support each other. Just don't keep us in the dark."

I was smiling before I knew it, and for the first time in a long while, I felt the welcome pull of being part of something bigger than myself. "I won't keep you in the dark."

He shot me a broad grin. "Good, because the guys are betting on you being some kind of super chef and I'd like to keep you around long enough to find out."

I huffed and shook my head. "In that case, they're gonna be hugely disappointed. I love to cook and I know my way around a kitchen, but a chef? No way. Working in back of an Auckland restaurant to put myself through university doesn't make me a chef, just a masochist."

He laughed. "Since we appear to be having a show-and-tell moment, and on the back of the whole *team*-speech thing, I imagine my mother has already made you aware that I'm gay. She's pretty good at discreetly ferreting out the homophobes before they make it onto the station's payroll, but I always like to check."

I schooled my expression and reached out a hand. "She did. Hi, Gay. I'm Gil. Nice to meet you."

Holden's face lit up. "Funny guy. But on that note, you should know I have a zero-arsehole policy when it comes to bigotry of *any* kind on the station, contractors included. I don't tolerate it in my shepherds, my shearers, anyone who sets foot on the property."

"That's good news as far as I'm concerned." I was tempted to come out to Holden right there and then, but common sense kicked in. Because really, tell the gorgeous man sitting next to me who I was already attracted to and who I was about to share a house with for the next three months that I was also gay? Not the smartest move if I was here to get my head back in the game. The last thing I needed was any awkwardness between us. I wouldn't lie about it if he asked, and I had no idea if Emily knew, but right then I just wanted to keep things simple.

Holden seemed satisfied enough with my answer. "As long as we're all on the same page."

"Understood."

He shot me another sideways look. "Well, if anywhere can scrape the city and all that crap off your soul and get you raw enough to find some of those answers you're looking for, then I reckon it's the high country." His gaze swept the landscape flashing past. "This place wields its own kind of miracles. Welcome to the twilight zone, Gil Everton."

I stared out my side window, blinking back tears that had appeared from nowhere. Holden might be almost a decade younger, but in that moment, he felt a whole universe wiser. "I hope you're right," I said in an almost whisper. "I wouldn't turn my nose up at a miracle or two right about now." I stuck my arm through the open window to surf the air currents, feeling the thrill of the draught through my fingers, and added, "I guess we'll find out soon enough."

The intensity of Holden's stare drilled into the back of my head, but he didn't press, his fingers drumming in time with some catchy Bob Marley song that I couldn't remember the name of. When I started to hum along, he chuckled. "See, it's working already."

I turned and rolled my eyes and he laughed, lightening the sombre mood. And after that, we drove in silence, the mountains growing closer by the minute, the sun glinting off steep scars of scree, a few wispy cottonwool clouds catching on the sharp razorbacks to soften their tips. The wind cooled my arm, and my gaze wandered over the sea of tawny tussock rippling in the heat-faded breeze blowing down the valley.

A few kilometres later, we passed a boulder the size of a truck with the name Miller Station chiselled into it.

I sat a little straighter. "So, we're on *your* land now?"

Holden favoured me with one of those dazzling smiles. "We are indeed. Stocking rates sit around a few sheep per hectare, more or less. Usually less."

"A few sheep per . . . ?" My mouth dropped open.

He laughed. "Yeah, rush hour traffic in the paddocks isn't a thing. Look." He pointed to my right. "There's the homestead now."

CHAPTER FIVE

Gil

I spun in my seat and drew in a sharp breath because . . . wow. At this distance, it was like something out of a magazine. A sprawling homestead with a long sweep of lawn that ended at a small blue-green lake, a rowboat pulled up on the grass like a prop on a landscape painting. It was everything I'd hoped for at three in the morning when I was lying awake and trying to feel positive about my crazy decision.

"It's beautiful." My attention focused on a solitary hawk sweeping lazy circles high above the lake. Riding the currents. Ready to dive and risk everything for what it needed.

I gave a soft huff. Better than waiting for what you need to somehow just magically appear, right? The jarring thrum of the tyres hitting the cattlestop jolted me awake to the fact that Holden was still talking, pointing out the woolshed and other buildings and points of interest along the final stretch of drive.

I'd missed half of it.

"That's Dunwoody's beat you can see snaking up directly behind the house. You'll hear that name a lot as it's one of the most frequently used tracks on the station. It branches in three directions over the back of the hill. But the most frequently used access way is the river track. It follows the Glendale River along its shingle course and eventually crosses over to where the mustering huts are situated. That part of the station leads to the summer altitude pastures which we muster in two stages because of the sheer acreage involved."

I raised a brow. "You used the word beat?"

Holden nodded. "It's high-country lingo for a particular mustering route or track. A shepherd might be given a top, middle, or bottom beat. On the top beats you're likely to be on what we call marrowbone country, land too steep for horses." He shot me a grin. "Newsflash: ninety percent of the muster on Miller Station is done on foot for that very reason. Unlike some stations we don't have much horse accessible country at all, and almost zero in the high altitude summer grazing. The man on the top beat sets the pace as they have the most difficult terrain to work, and then the middle and bottom beat shepherds work in sequence to sweep their areas and bring the growing mob down."

"So, it's really steep?"

He snorted. "Like a razor back in places, with rocky climbs and dangerous scree slopes that can skin you in seconds if you take a tumble."

My brows peaked. "Okay, so not the leisurely romantic muster on horseback version that I'd been imagining?"

Holden chuckled. "Hardly."

"You called that beat Dunwoody's?"

Holden nodded. "Yeah. Apart from being labelled top and middle and bottom, beats often get nicknamed. Sometimes it's after the shepherd who favoured that route or an infamous incident that occurred on it. Dunwoody was a towering, grumpy shepherd from my great-grandfather's era who refused to muster on any other beat. And we have funny names for places that hark back to the history of the station. Like George's Mistake, a large boulder formation in a ravine halfway up Craggy Peak where my great-grandfather and a hundred merinos had to hole up, waiting for a two-day storm to blow over. He chanced ignoring the hogsbacks—" He shot me an apologetic look. "They're nor'wester arch clouds that form over the mountains and indicate a storm's coming. He gambled on having time to make another sweep before it arrived. He was wrong. He survived but landed himself with frostbite and lost three toes."

I gaped. "Holy shit."

"And here we are." Holden flicked his head to the right and I turned just as we rounded the drive at the bottom of a long sloping lawn. The homestead sat at the top, like an elegant if slightly shabby-chic duchess. Holden parked the Hilux alongside the path to the front door and cut the engine. "Home sweet home."

Home. I rolled the word around in my head once again, then drew a deep breath and followed Holden out of the ute for a closer look.

A dense windbreak of trees cradled the house on three sides, while a second layer protected the station buildings that lay in the distance behind, and a third stood beyond that.

All righty then. Three-tiered protection. Couldn't get much clearer than that.

A quiver of anticipation skipped over my skin at the thought of the wicked winter storms that I knew from my research could blast down these valleys, channelled by the towering alps that were almost close enough to reach up a hand and brush their jagged peaks.

"So, what do you think?" Holden appeared at my side.

"It's pretty amazing," I answered honestly, taking in the single-storey home decked out in cream weatherboard and grey stone. It nestled comfortably at the foot of a rugged mountain that climbed steeply at its back, and even the house itself seemed to rise from the landscape like it was a part of the earth rather than simply set upon it.

A covered veranda ran along two sides, wisteria twining around the uprights to steal over the grey iron roof. Wicker furniture dotted the shady deck, and pretty double sash windows fronted the rooms on either side of a wide front door thrown open in welcome.

In contrast to the dramatic but stark landscape, colourful gardens tumbled down the more sheltered sloping lawn, the planting admittedly a little the worse for wear after the long summer's heat, but still charming. And on the other side of the lawn about a hundred metres away, two stone cottages enjoyed equally stunning views of the lake.

The biggest domestic vegetable garden I'd ever seen lay to the right of the house, and opposite Holden's Hilux, a patchwork of machinery buildings, carports, and pens followed the driveway back behind the homestead toward yet more cottages and what appeared to be the woolshed and one or two other large structures in the distance.

A deep-chested bark spun me in place just in time to clock a huge brown blur of excitement barrelling down the path in a beeline for Holden. I took a reflexive leap back to avoid imminent collision with what had to be thirty or forty kilos of canine muscle, while Holden merely sank to his knees, his arms open.

"Hey, boy." He scruffed the big dog's neck and endured a good licking that made me wince. "Gil, this crazy boy here is Spider."

"Hey, Spider." I stroked the dog's head, and he gave me a curious once-over before deciding I could wait. The large sturdy dog with its mostly black body, tan legs and muzzle, and a splash of tan at the end of its tail was solely intent on Holden. "Interesting name," I observed.

Holden chuckled and got to his feet. "Yeah, the station's had a superhero theme going on for a while now. This bad boy is Spider-man, but we also have Thor, Batman, Elektra, Hellboy, and Wolfie."

I snorted. "That's pretty cute. He's a huntaway, right?"

Holden scruffed the dog's neck. "The bark gave it away, huh?"

I nodded. "Pretty distinctive, even for this city boy."

He chuckled. "Yeah, they can sure make a racket." His smile told me Spider wasn't just a useful farm tool, though. Holden loved the dog.

"Are they all station dogs?"

He shook his head. "The shepherds usually bring their own. They come as a team. Spider here is one of two huntaways we have right now. The rest are a mix of border collies and one bitsa. But Spider is the only dog allowed in the house. The others have their kennels out back." Holden grinned and patted the dog's head. "To be honest, he's a bit of a powder puff."

"A what?"

"All noise and about as much use as tits on a bull. Aren't you, boy?" Holden kissed the end of the dog's nose and Spider stared up at him with sappy eyes.

I made my way around to the back of the Hilux to get my bags. "Your mother sent photos of this place, but they don't do it justice. And these mountains." I spun to take in the valley once again. "You're a lucky man to live with this on your doorstep."

Holden gave a wry smile. "Talk to me again when it's minus ten and blowing sleet hard enough to slice your cheeks."

My eyes widened. "Does that happen often?"

He laughed. "*Once* is too often for my liking, but I might let you find that out for yourself."

"Welcome, welcome!" Emily Miller strode down the path, wearing a huge smile and an even bigger apron tied around her waist.

I grinned and went to meet her. "Emily, this place is ama—oof." I was cut off by a lung-crushing hug and the familiar vanilla-coffee fragrance of Opium. It propelled me right back to my childhood, sending a pang through my heart. My mother had worn the same scent.

Holden grinned at my helpless expression. "I'd just run with it. The woman has no boundaries."

I took his advice, not that I had any issue with the rare joy of being tucked up in a mother's arms. Hell, I could count on the fingers of one hand the number of times I'd even been touched in the last year, not counting Tucker, of course.

When she was done almost re-breaking my ribs, Emily stood back with her hands on her hips and ran a shrewd gaze over me, head to foot. "Yes. You'll do nicely."

I gave an amused snort. "You wanna check my teeth as well?"

She stared at me for a moment, then slapped me on the arm and broke into a huge laugh that was way too big for her tiny frame. "You're gonna fit in just fine."

"That's what I said." Holden shot me an amused grin.

"Now, let's get inside." Emily clapped her hands. "I have a chocolate cake and a bowl of icing that needs tasting. I figure you're just the man for the job. Let's test that palate of yours."

Holden groaned. "Give the poor man a chance to settle in, will you?"

"Fiddlesticks." She waved Holden ahead. "I've got the west wing ready for Gil, and I've moved all your stuff into the front bedroom."

Holden blinked, paling slightly at her words. "But . . . I wasn't . . . not . . ." He closed his eyes and sighed. "Dammit, Mum."

Emily raised a brow that dared him to argue, which I noticed he didn't. "I only moved your clothes and toiletries. And I asked Tom to help swap the mattresses. The rest can wait."

Holden gave a resigned sigh and a curt "Fine."

Emily's mouth turned up in a wicked grin. "I also cleared your bedside drawer. Come on, Gil. Grab your bags and follow me."

"You did what?" Holden's sun-kissed cheeks flashed scarlet, but his mother was already halfway up the path, leaving lingering notes of Opium and a trail of cheeky smiles tumbling in her wake.

I grabbed two of my bags and leaned close to Holden. "Your mother sure is something."

He winced, his gaze tracking Emily's departure. "Yeah, but don't ask me exactly what that something is, because I have a few choice answers on the tip of my tongue that probably shouldn't see the light of day."

I bit back a smile. "I'm going out on a limb and guessing there wasn't a Gideon Bible in that top drawer, huh?"

He looked mortified. "Oh. My. God. She's the worst. And no.

Not unless Gideon International has undergone a serious change of direction."

I laughed. "Yeah, I'm not seeing it."

Holden grabbed the remaining two bags and headed up the path. And if my gaze lingered for just a second too long on all that firm flesh moving under faded denim, it was nobody's business but my own.

I followed them up the stairs, past a higgledy-piggledy row of boots by the front door, and into a wide entrance foyer decorated in warm creams, greys, and a soft pastel yellow. While Holden disappeared up the hallway with my bags, I kicked off my shoes, and Emily began the two-cent tour.

"The original homestead started life as a two-bedroom weatherboard-and-stone cottage in the mid-1930s," she explained, coming to a stop as Holden reappeared from wherever he'd dropped my bags and kissed her on the cheek.

"I'm gonna leave you two to do your thing." He stuck his head into the bedroom alongside the front door and grimaced. "That wallpaper has to go." He took another look. "And most of the rest of it as well." He shot his mother a blistering look. "You're lucky I love you."

She patted his cheek. "I tell myself that every day. Don't forget to grab the chilly bin from the kitchen. You won't be forgiven if you forget everyone's lunch."

I watched him go and then followed Emily down the hall.

"The basic footprint was added to over the generations," she explained, giving me a snapshot of its history while my bare feet padded over exposed wooden floors worn smooth with age and past walls covered in family photos.

Spider dawdled behind us, his damp nose occasionally nudging the back of my legs like he was still gathering data on my relative worth. I let him do his thing and kept walking. The inside of the house proved to be just as welcoming as the outside with all the loved-up ambience of a family home. A year or two shy of needing some fresh paint and maybe a little updating, it wrapped around me like a warm hug, and my battered soul breathed a soft sigh of relief. Living here for three months was going to be a pleasure.

"There are eight bedrooms in two wings," Emily continued. "A spacious office, three living rooms, four bathrooms, and this." She flung open the door at the end of the hall and gestured for me to go ahead.

I narrowed my gaze at the smile threatening to burst over her face as I walked past and then immediately gasped at the sight of a spacious country kitchen that any catering business would be proud to call their own. "Wow."

"You like?" She appeared beside me as excited as a teenager on their first date.

"I love it."

The spotless prep and work area took up the back half of the huge room, a large central island separating it from the dining space in front that housed a long wooden dining table with a dozen or so chairs. To the left, a floor-to-ceiling bookcase packed with recipe books stood beside a pretty sash window, a small study desk and computer at its side, and two armchairs and a side table that faced the window, making the most of the view. On the right, an open door led to what looked like a mudroom or laundry, and at the back of the kitchen, another open door offered tempting glimpses into what looked like a large scullery or pantry.

Dark grey flagstone floors contrasted with bright white kitchen panelling, the crisp impression softened by accents of pale green and cream furnishings and similarly coloured gingham curtains. A wooden countertop the colour of warm honey ran along the back wall, while the one facing the lake sported an expansive stainless-steel worktop, a huge double sink, and a door leading directly out onto the covered deck. Copper pots and baking dishes of all shapes and sizes hung from a massive black metal frame in the centre of the space, and a variety of large potted plants added a homey, lush feel.

"Oh, my goodness." I ran a greedy hand over the marbled grey-and-cream slab of granite that topped the massive island, looking like it had been sliced straight from the mountains outside. "Emily, I may just have to kiss you."

She flushed bright pink. "If you weren't far too young for me, I might just let you." She watched as I wandered the space, opening cupboards and checking out the appliances.

"My mum and I renovated it about ten years ago."

I flashed her a huge smile. "It's fabulous. You don't mind me being nosey, do you?"

She swept an arm around the room. "Help yourself. This is your office now and I want you to feel like you own it. That's what you're here for."

Mine. The idea sparked a warm rush of gratitude in my chest, and I crossed to the twin oven and the six burner cooktop and tried not to drool as I stroked them covetously. "Just so you know, I spoke to Holden about Callie." I glanced Emily's way.

"Oh?" Her attempt at innocence failed miserably.

"Yes." I shot her a pointed look. "Something he apparently wasn't aware of."

Emily raised a brow. "Losing your daughter is *your* business, Gil. He didn't need to know unless you wanted him to."

I gave a soft sigh. "Thank you, but I'm happy for people to be aware. It avoids some of those awkward getting-to-know-you questions."

"Good thinking." She headed for the electric jug, and I made my way into the enormous scullery, my excitement building. Before I'd ever thought of becoming a psychologist, I'd wanted to be a chef. A kitchen like this was a dream come true. "You could feed an army from here," I called out.

Emily appeared in the open door with a huge grin on her face. "It's pretty great, right? In earlier days when the station didn't have shearers' quarters or enough cottages to house all the shepherds, they stayed with the family in the homestead, hence all the extensions and remodelling over the years, *and* the large kitchen. Those days are long gone, but we still have a small street's worth of two-bedroom cottages out back. Tom and Charlie get one each to themselves, while Alek and Sam share. The other cottages and the old shearers' quarters are for paying guests, extra muster help, and any of the shearing gang who don't bring their own camper vans."

"It must keep you busy." I wandered back out to the dining table and Emily followed.

"It does. The team look after their own breakfasts and evening meals, and that mostly goes for me as well, but I make sure to slip some garden produce and goodies into their cottages whenever I can. When my parents were here, I used to eat with them, but now that you're here, I'll mostly eat in my cottage. Holden needs his own space, and you two need to get to know each other without me propping conversation up."

I eyed her appreciatively. "You're a shrewd woman, Emily. Holden's lucky."

She looked pleased. "Coming from a psychologist, I'll take that as a compliment."

"It is. Is your cottage one of the ones out front?"

"Yes, the far one. The other was Holden's until this morning." She bit back a smile. "Everyone gathers for lunch in the kitchen if they're close enough to get here—that's four shepherds plus you and me and Holden. That ensures this space still gets a regular workout. Plus, when you're cooking for muster or shearing, it's worth its weight in gold. For a while, Mum and I ran a bed-and-breakfast farmstay out of the bedroom wing you'll be staying in, but that stopped when Dad got sick. All we do now is rent the cottages for heli-skiing accommodation, muster experiences, and general tourism,"

"Holden mentioned that."

She cocked her head. "Did he now?" She eyed me speculatively.

"You must have made an impression on my boy. He doesn't generally like to talk about his grandfather."

I cast her a sideways look. "Don't get too excited. It was the same time I was talking about the accident. It was this weird sharing-circle moment. Makes me shudder to even think about it."

She laughed. "I can imagine."

I took another look around the room I'd be spending most of my time in over the next three months, and my gaze landed on the mudroom door. I walked across and ran my fingers over height marks notched into the doorjamb. "Holden's?" I couldn't help but smile.

"The one and only. My mother wouldn't have dreamed of marking up the wood like that when my sister and I were growing up. Viv and her husband are lawyers in Sydney now. But Holden was always different. I lost a fair number of babies before he came along, and my parents spoiled him like you wouldn't believe." She was smiling, but I recognised the grief still lying just under the surface.

"I'm sorry," I offered quietly.

She looked up and held my gaze. "It was a lifetime ago. My body simply didn't like being pregnant. Five miscarriages in a row. We almost gave up." She hesitated, then brightened. "But then Holden came along, and I did my best to forget about the rest. Come on, I'll show you your room."

I followed her out of the kitchen and around to the left.

"Consider this whole west wing as yours," she said with a sweep of her hand. "Holden's office is next to his bedroom out front, and if he wants to watch television, he'll use the main lounge in the east family wing."

"It's a big house." I calculated the cleaning in my head and winced.

What the hell was I doing chucking in a profitable psychology practice to cook and clean on a sheep station?

Learning how to live again.

"There's a small lounge with a television and books and a comfy couch in here." Emily pushed open the door to a pretty room with grey-and-white striped wallpaper, blonde wood floors, and cream and pale blue furnishings. "And there's a bathroom and toilet over here." She crossed the hall to a sparkling white-tiled bathroom with a large shower. "Linen is kept in the end cupboard behind the double doors." She indicated further down the hall. "But your room is here."

She ushered me into an airy bedroom decorated in a sandy colour with splashes of dark grey. Two fluffy towels sat on a king-size bed that bore a grey-and-white geometric quilt, referencing the stunning view of the Southern Alps through the large window alongside. An armchair parked in front of the window made the most of the view, the door to the ensuite open at its back.

Spider made a beeline for the large sheepskin rug at the foot of the bed and collapsed, stretching his big body out with a protracted doggy moan.

Emily gave an exasperated huff. "It's one of his favourite places. You'll have to shut the door if you don't want him in here."

"He's fine." I looked around and couldn't keep the smile from my face. "The room is beautiful. Thank you, Emily. I love it."

Her mouth quirked up in pleasure. "Good, it was our most popular room when we ran the farmstay. I'll leave you to get unpacked. If you need anything, come find me. Once you're settled in, you can take the afternoon to look around, as Holden suggested." Just a hint of a screwed-up nose went along with that option. "Or you can jump in the deep end and join me in the kitchen for taste-testing."

Like there was any choice. "Door number two, please. I'm all yours."

"Excellent. I'll warm the espresso machine so it's ready when you're done. We take our caffeine very seriously here."

"Music to my ears." I met her smile with another of my own, and it occurred to me that I'd flown past my usual daily smile quota by a fuckton already and it was still morning. Maybe this would work out after all.

The soft patter of Emily's slippers disappeared back up the hall and I collapsed on the bed to revel in the silence and catch my breath. It had been a day already, but I'd arrived in one piece. My hands might have been a little shaky, but I was okay. I laid them at my sides, closed my eyes, and took a few deep breaths to calm the fuck down.

A minute or so later, I opened them again and looked around. The accommodation was far better than I'd expected. My own wing, my own space. I lifted my hands and was surprised to find them still. I rolled to my side and took in the view of the mountains through the windows. Spider wandered from his mat to rest his chin on the mattress, and I stroked the soft folds on his brow as he frowned up at me.

"You wanna meet someone?" I pushed to my feet and rummaged inside the smaller of two duffels, pulling out a framed photo of Callie sitting on my shoulders at the Auckland Zoo. I held it in my hands for a moment, one finger tracing her beautiful face, my heart catching at her wide-eyed delight, my throat thickening as it always did whenever I remembered. It had been taken on a family holiday a year before the accident. A time when things were . . . better. Luke was hamming it up behind the camera, making Callie and me laugh. It had been good between us then, before . . . well, before everything.

"This is Callie." I held the photo for Spider to see and then placed it on the bedside table before crossing to the window. Spider followed.

"So, this is home for the next three months, fella." I scratched his head and thought of my central Wellington apartment, the busy streets, the cafés, and the shows. All wonderful places to get lost in, to forget, or at least try to.

"There'll be no hiding in this place," I mused, my hand moving over his smooth coat. "Running away? I have a feeling this is going to be the exact opposite of running away." I stared into Spider's soft, brown eyes. "But it's what I asked for, right?"

An image of Holden popped into my brain and I groaned. "Well, some of it was. We're gonna have to see about the rest."

CHAPTER SIX

Holden

I slept like a log the first night in my grandparents' bedroom, waking to the alarm at five thirty and rolling to my side to drink in the last of the full moon's golden reflection on the lake. I might've hated the room's cutesy theme but there was no faulting the outlook.

Maybe my mother had been right. Maybe I *had* needed a shove. I couldn't play the grandson anymore. I was running this place. No shifting the blame. No hiding. For better or worse, from now on the buck stopped with me, and maybe moving into the main house drew some kind of line under that reality.

A line I needed.

Not that I'd tell my mother that.

I rolled out of bed, paused, and groaned at the soft hum of music coming from the kitchen. Another distraction I was going to have to deal with, sooner rather than later—my body's response to our new resident hottie.

Gil had consumed a fair amount of headspace since I'd picked him up the previous day. All of which made zero sense since I'd only just been laid the night before and had said no to a relationship with Zach.

Still, the man intrigued me. And the fact we were living under the same roof meant there was going to be no ignoring him. The occasional noises coming from his wing, along with the rattle in the pipes when he'd used his shower the night before were testament to that. They'd felt strangely comforting more than intrusive, but those knocking pipes had raised a few other images in my brain that were definitely less than PG and needed quashing.

Hard to do when the guy was quite simply gorgeous.

I shook my head and put the temporary madness down to stress. I needed to pull up my big-boy pants and leave the man to do his job. I had a station to run, a muster coming up fast, and a contract to nail down. Shit was getting real.

The shower pep talk worked a treat until I walked into the kitchen and found a sleep-rumpled Gil standing over a cooktop, shaking his hips and singing along to some band I'd never heard of while looking ridiculously . . . adorable.

Jesus fucking Christ. Since when had I found the idea of a guy cooking me breakfast adorable? Domestically inclined had never featured high in my Rolodex of traits I looked for in a man. Although to be fair, those usually didn't venture too far from hot, available, and preferably able to form complete sentences that didn't contain the word *dude*.

Or have hands that held a pair of shears. Those liaisons were relegated to past me. The past me who didn't employ said shearer, or have to face them twice a year, every year, to infinity and beyond.

Nope, I'd never done domestic. Never encouraged sleepovers if I could avoid it. No smiles over a shared breakfast in the morning—Zach was proof of that. And yet there I was, all but drooling over a man wielding a spatula and in need of a shower. It was all I could do not to sidle on over on some pretext and satisfy my urge to know exactly how he smelled straight out of bed.

Which would have been all kinds of creepy.

And yet the thought persisted.

Gil turned and caught me studying him and his cheeks pinked a little. "Oh, good morning. I didn't see you there."

Busted. "Good morning. And sorry, it's all still a little strange, I guess."

"I can imagine." He shot me an almost-shy smile, waved me to a chair, asked how I liked my eggs and how many slices of bacon I wanted and whether I liked the rinds soft or crispy. Then he got on with his job.

I, on the other hand, sat and pretended to scroll through my iPad while surreptitiously watching him work. Because I could. And because he was, as aforementioned, gorgeous. Although we were of similar heights, around two metres, Gil had the lean, rangy body of a runner, an interesting bump halfway down his nose, and a small scar bisecting one eyebrow. Choppy dirty-blond locks bleached white at the tips fell in casual disarray around his ears, and those hazel eyes carried large splotches of gold and green that looked like a paintbrush had been flicked their way. They'd made me smile the first time I'd seen them, along with the smattering of light hair peeking from the loose neck of his faded Nirvana T-shirt, and those damn Cavalli jeans.

Gil was a city boy for sure and well outside his comfort zone, but I kind of liked that about him. To survive what he'd been through, he clearly possessed courage and grit and seemed more than happy to throw down as good as he got. Both were character traits needed to earn any kind of respect in the high country. The land and the people who worked it didn't suffer fools gladly, and a bit of chutzpah—as Gran loved to call it—went a long way.

Breakfast arrived on a plate in front of me and I looked up to find Gil watching almost nervously. "Let me know if you'd like anything done differently."

"I can't imagine any improvement on this," I said honestly, taking in the creamy scrambled eggs and crisp bacon—almost charred at the edges, just as I preferred. "This beats the hell out of anything I'd whip up for myself."

"Good." His pale cheeks flushed and he gave a pleased nod. Then he slid a notepad and pen across the table, along with a freshly brewed latte, courtesy of our too-fucking-complicated Italian espresso machine that I'd watched him handle like a pro. "I'll need a list of your food likes, dislikes, favourites, and anything guaranteed to get me canned."

I almost rolled my eyes. As if I'd fire the best eye candy I'd had to look at over breakfast in a long time. "Honestly, I'm easy." I focused on my plate to hide the awkward look that no doubt accompanied my words. "I have to say I'm surprised Mum let you loose in the kitchen on your own so quickly. You could've taken the weekend to settle in."

"She did give me the option." He pushed the salt and pepper my way. "But I wanted to jump right in. It's what I'm here for, right? And I'm quite capable of cooking breakfast without a minder."

I winced. "Sorry."

"I'm joking." He gave me a quick smile. "But you *can* help by writing that list. Everyone has likes and dislikes."

I pushed the notepad aside and squeezed a little hot sauce on my eggs. "I swear, I'll eat anything. To be honest, it feels kind of weird to have someone wait on me."

Gil tabled his knife and fork in deliberate fashion, and I looked up to find him eyeballing me. "It's my *job*, Holden. I haven't had a chance to focus on cooking in far too long, so believe me when I say it's going to be a pleasure. But if you really want to help me out—" He slid the notepad back my way. "—then tell me what you like and what you don't."

He turned to grab his own plate from the island, and I absolutely did not watch the way his criminally thin grey sweats hugged his arse, or the line of smooth, pale skin that appeared between them and the hem of his crumpled white T-shirt, or the glimpse of blond hair that gathered thickly under his navel.

Nope, I saw none of that.

He settled into the chair opposite, and for a while we ate in comfortable silence. I stole a look from time to time, feeling like a newly minted gay teenager—checking out boys for the first time after discovering Hamish Carmichael did things for me his pretty sister never had.

Get a grip, Miller. I glued my eyes to my plate and focused on the day ahead.

"Are you back fencing today?"

I looked up at the question and lost myself for just a few seconds in those haunting splashes of green and gold. "Yes. The guys get Sunday off and another day of their choosing that fits with the work schedule. This breakfast is amazing, by the way. The eggs are perfect."

It made me smile to see him fluster just a little before he answered, "Glad you like it."

"Who's this?" I stabbed my fork in the direction of the Bluetooth speaker since we were clearly doing the small talk thing.

He hesitated. "Sorry, I probably should've asked. It's Soundgarden. I can turn it off if you like?" Then the corners of his mouth quirked up. "It's a far cry from your beloved reggae."

I rolled my eyes. "Are you taking the piss?"

He kept his eyes on his eggs. "Never."

I narrowed my gaze. "Mmmm. I take it this is *your* kind of music, then?"

He looked up and nodded.

"Fits with the Nirvana T-shirt vibe from yesterday." I talked around a mouthful of bacon. "Very . . . nineties of you."

He arched a brow. "Now *you're* taking the piss."

"Absolutely. But it's actually pretty cool. It can stay."

He snorted and sat back in his chair. "It wouldn't offend me if you hated it." He spun his cup slowly in small circles on the honey-coloured oak. "My parents could blare their punk full volume, but I was made to use headphones for what I listened to."

"Ouch. My mum wasn't too impressed with mine either." I

smiled at the memory. "I'm pretty sure she turned my room over on a regular basis, looking for a stash of weed, figuring the two went together."

Gil gave a sly grin. "Did she find any?"

I waggled my eyebrows. "I refuse to say anything other than old houses have the best hiding places."

He gave a loud laugh and the clear sound of it brightened the kitchen.

I qualified, "To be honest, I was never *that* kid. I wasn't interested in much beyond the occasional toke up Dunwoody's beat with a mate or a few too many beers in Oakwood on a Saturday night. How about you?"

He studied me with those bright eyes and my idiotic pulse ticked up. "I had a false bottom inside the Cluedo box on the top shelf of my wardrobe."

My eyes widened. "Wow, that's impressive . . . and kind of devious. A step up from under the mattress, for sure."

His grin broadened. "I know, right? I was into John le Carré in a big way at the time. One night, Mum got it down for a family games evening, and I had to endure the whole night knowing what was hidden inside not a metre away."

I laughed. "Did they ever find out?"

His expression sobered. "Yeah. Mum decided to replace the set with a new one and I got busted in the process. I was grounded for three months."

I chuckled. "Ouch. Do your folks live in Wellington?"

He didn't look up. "They used to. My dad died of a massive heart attack when I was sixteen, a year after said confession incident, and my mother died of leukaemia five years later. She'd been in remission for fifteen years."

Jesus Christ.

He looked up and caught me gaping. "It was a long time ago."

My brow creased. "How long? I haven't actually looked at your employment contract to find your age."

"Really?" He seemed surprised. "I'm thirty-nine."

Older than he looked, then. "But still, losing both your parents by twenty-one is pretty huge. Then you lost your daughter as well. Jesus, Gil."

A storm brewed in his eyes. "Yep. Figure I must've pissed someone off, right? But there's nothing much left to say that hasn't already been said. Time and a fair bit of therapy helped."

I broke off a piece of bacon and popped it in my mouth. "No offence, but I'm not sure people know what they mean when they say time heals."

He sniffed and pushed his plate aside. "I'm not sure either."

"Any brothers or sisters?"

"Nope. Only child."

I fell back in my chair. "Well, that sucks. Going through all that on your own."

"I had friends—" His voice carried a note of defensiveness. "*Have* friends. And this is pretty heavy for breakfast conversation."

"Sorry." I held up my hands and checked the clock. "And I should get going or I'm gonna get shit for missing mat time."

Amusement flashed in his eyes. "Mat time? As in kindergarten mat time?"

I walked my dishes to the sink. "It's what we've always called our regular morning planning meeting, and I don't even know where it came from, but yeah, kindergarten isn't too far off some days."

He grinned. "Well, we can't have you missing that, seeing as how you're the teacher."

"I wish." I began stacking the dishwasher. "Tom's the real boss out here."

Gil nudged me out of the way and I finally caught a whiff of that scent I'd been craving—coffee, a slight sourness from sleep, the sweet remnants of the cologne he'd worn the day before, and something that reminded me of fresh sheets or the smell of a new book.

"I thought *you* ran the station?" He sounded confused. "Your mother said you have big plans for the place."

I met his gaze, expecting to find a smile to prove the joke, but there was only a curious intensity that left my heart banging in my chest. "I do. I'm just . . . still getting used to it, I guess."

Gil frowned and we stood there a moment, gazes locked, a peculiar stillness hovering between us that felt like—

"Anyway—" He broke eye contact and headed for the pantry. "—as per Emily's instructions, I packed lunch for five." He reappeared, carrying a large chilly bin which he put on the table. "Here you go."

When I walked over to take it, Gil immediately returned to the sink, saying over his shoulder, "Have a good day, Holden."

I blinked, feeling almost dismissed, the turnaround in mood jarring enough to have me second-guessing what I thought I'd felt just seconds before.

"Yeah, you too," I returned. "Don't let my mother boss you around too much."

That earned me a welcome chuckle. "Yeah, I'll get right on that."

I was about to leave when I saw him hesitate. Then he turned and made his way back over. He tucked the notepad and pen into my shirt pocket and gave it a gentle pat. "Do the damn list, Holden."

I drove to the woolshed and cursed when I found it empty and all the station utes gone. Since I was going to get shit from the others for missing the meeting as it was, I took another half hour to clean out and restock my ute, which hadn't been done in weeks. Then I headed up the valley with the windows down in an effort to clear the Gil Everton fog effect from my brain.

The track forded several watercourses and the Hilux clambered up and down a number of bone-jarring banks, which thankfully forced me to focus. I'd travelled the watercourses all my life, but I took nothing for granted. I'd been caught out in the breeziest of shallows at the cost of a carton of beer, and each and every time, I'd needed to be pulled out.

It was all part of the high-country experience, rubbing shoulders with others along the rugged spine of the Southern Alps—massive ventures thrust high into the throats of glacial valleys. The peak of our foraging land tickled the snow-tipped summits, while the lower pastures wet their feet in the wide braided rivers at their base. It was farming the impossible on the knife-edge of failure.

And I fucking loved it.

With the Hilux back on track after a particularly gnarly traverse, my mind drifted again to Gil, because of course it did. Whichever way you looked at it, Gil Everton was fine with a capital F. Not that I needed to be lusting after the hired help. Gil as eye candy was one thing, but an inconvenient crush on our new domestic manager was another thing entirely.

A flash of red behind a stand of tall matagouri caught my eye and I spun the wheel toward Tom's battered Ford Ranger. The ute slid and bucked through the shifting gravel of yet another chugging stream before accelerating up the bank on the far side, the engine revving hard before I dropped down and slid sideways into a park. Nine heads turned my way—four human and five dogs, the latter stretched out under the shade of a scrubby thicket next to the water.

I jumped from the cab and a cloud of dust rose from the parched ground where I landed. "Howdy, kids."

"Hey," Alek and Sam replied almost simultaneously. Charlie gave a wave, her mouth otherwise occupied with a few staples shoved between her teeth, and Tom grunted something that sounded like, "Good evening."

I took a few seconds to appreciate their efforts. "Jesus, who lit a fire under your butts?"

Tom looked over from where he was working the strainer, sweat running down his face from under the brim of his hat. "It's about time you got your sorry arse here. Sleep in, did you?"

"As if," I fired back and Tom smirked. He knew damn well I was always first on and last off. "I had a few things to discuss with our new domestic manager, and then I cleaned the ute," I fudged.

"A likely story," Tom muttered. A forty-eight-year-old loveable grump, he'd worked our station since he'd hitchhiked into Oakwood as a wide-eyed teenager, ran into my grandad in the supply store, and been offered a job. He was a no-nonsense shepherd with merino blood in his veins, kind grey eyes, and spiky dark brown hair. Without his experience and advice, the station might not have survived that first long winter with me in charge.

I owed him more than I could ever repay.

"You'll never know." I sprayed sunscreen on my arms before rubbing some on my face and neck. It was as good a way as any to avoid his astute gaze.

"Besides, it looks like you've done just fine without me." I jammed my hat on my head and grabbed my leather gloves from the back seat.

"That's because we're the A team," he responded drily, ratcheting the winch.

"You're the *only* team," I reminded him. "And does that include the dogs?" I indicated the mismatched pack of canines who were watching like hawks in case I happened to have a biscuit or two about my person. Which, of course, I did.

As I reached into the cab, every one of them sat bolt upright in anticipation. "I gather they're here to help us *fence*." I shot Tom an amused look and those freckles disappeared in a wash of pink.

"Obviously," he huffed. "They need a break from the homestead just like everyone else, and we all know every one of them is worth two of us." He flashed me a grin. "And three of you. Quit spoiling them with those treats. They're working animals for Chrissake."

"Says the man who brought the entire pack along for an outing," I said drily, before turning back to the dogs. "Attention!"

There was an immediate flurry of tails and paws and barking as the pack scrambled into a well-rehearsed line from tallest to shortest like soldiers on parade. I walked a line in front, dropping a biscuit in front of each one's paws. Their eyes locked on the treats, but not one of them moved a muscle, and everyone stopped what they were doing to watch.

I circled back around and stopped in front, pausing for a long second before saying, "At ease."

The treats disappeared in two seconds flat, after which the dogs raced across for a quick hello and investigative sniff to find out where I'd been and who I'd been with and whether I had any more treats. When they were satisfied with their interrogation, they headed back to the shade to sleep.

Tom went back to work with the strainer. "So, what's the verdict on this new guy that you ditched us for?"

"I did *not* ditch you. And it's not like you can talk, traitor." I made my way to the back of the ute. "Just as well you were on your day off yesterday. You just had to help her move me, didn't you?"

Tom wiped his brow. "You have met your mother, right? There's only one way that conversation was ever gonna end. Besides, she's right." His look dared me to disagree.

"Says you," I grumbled, reaching for a roll of fencing wire. "It just feels . . . wrong. And it's not like I need the space."

His expression softened. "It's *your* place now, Holden."

"Oh my god, it's like an echo chamber," I griped. "I don't need—" A familiar ringtone split the thick humid air like a knife. *Shit.* Just what I needed. I considered not answering, then decided I may as well get it over with. He'd only keep trying until I did. With a bit of luck, the connection would cut out as it often did this far upriver.

"Hey, Grandad."

Tom rolled his eyes, and I turned my back and walked off a way to answer.

"Did you get them all?" my grandfather's gruff voice bellowed down the line.

I closed my eyes and counted to five. "The muster's still a few weeks away."

"Don't give me that," he said waspishly. "They're always off the hill by the end of March."

"You're right." I did my best to soothe him. "But it's still February."

"Lies," his voice rose in anger.

I glanced over at Tom who shot me a sympathetic look. "I'm not lying, I promise." I kept my eyes on Tom. "I promise I'll have them off by the end of March, just like we always do."

"Hmph. See that you do. And I hope you're not using that shearing gang you contracted last time. You had no right to change behind my back. There's nothing wrong with the lot we've always used."

Except you cancelled them without telling anyone.

"I didn't like their boss. Too full of himself. Didn't listen to a word I said."

Because I told him not to. Because you took a swing at him and told him to fuck off. Because he almost took his gang and left us completely stranded and in a shitload of trouble.

But I said none of that. I simply closed my eyes and let him rail at me like he'd done for almost a year whenever he could get me alone. Nice as pie when Gran and Mum were around, but like a pissy rattlesnake if it was just him and me. It was the dementia, for sure. But why *I'd* become public enemy number one, who fucking knew? Probably because he'd been forcibly stepped down two years before and he hated that. Hated that I was running the place without him. He still had his lucid moments, enough that he was able to talk on the cell phone Gran had given the care unit so they could help him call when he wanted. Mum and Gran loved hearing from him, of course. Me? Not so much.

"I'll look after the station exactly like you taught me." I tried to stem the welling tears.

"Pffft. You're not ready," he continued belligerently. "It needs a steady hand."

And a new fucking contract so we don't go under. And a better breeding program. And a solid plan for the future. And sustainable practices. Everything I'm trying to do, Grandad.

And everything I couldn't say.

"Don't think I don't know what you're up to," he muttered angrily.

Oh god. Here we go again.

"Turning my own shepherds against me."

"I'm not turning them against—"

"Do they know about you?" His words fell like a dead weight on my heart.

"What do you mean?"

"Do they know you're . . . *queer?*" He said it like the word tasted of shit in his mouth, and I reeled, tears pricking my eyes. He'd said a lot of ugly things when the dementia took over, but never anything like that. "And as for that worthless girl—"

"Enough." I raised my voice to him for the first time ever. He could say what he wanted about me, but I wasn't having Charlie or any of the team spoken about in that way, even if it wasn't really my grandfather talking. "The station is doing fine and Charlie is one of the best shepherds in the Mackenzie basin. And yes, they know about me. And they still work for me. For the station. For *us*. Just like they did before you got sick."

He growled. "I'm not sick—"

"Sorry, Grandad, but I have to go." I hung up and watched the phone blur in my hand before shoving it into my pocket. *Fuck. Fuck. Fuck.* I gave the front tyre a solid boot and was about to give it another when a hand landed on my shoulder.

"Quit that. You'll break your toes, and then how will you muster?" Tom dropped his hand. "You need to tell them, son. Your mum and your gran. They should know what's going on."

I scrubbed at my eyes, then turned and leaned back against the driver's door. "I can't. They'd be devastated. He still calls Gran most days. Mum too. They see it as some kind of miraculous sign that he's still in there somewhere." I sighed and squinted up at the bluebird sky. "I can handle it. He doesn't mean it."

Tom studied me closely. "Are you sure about that?"

No, I wasn't sure at all. "I'll be fine," I lied. "It was just the first time he's ever—" When I couldn't finish, Tom pulled me into a tight hug, which likely astonished him as much as it did me. It certainly had the other three gaping.

"Your grandad would never speak to you like that if he was in his right mind." He let go but kept both hands on my shoulders. "This is your place now, not his, and you're doing a great job."

My place? Fuck me. I huffed out a slightly hysterical laugh. I'd barely mastered stacking my Weet-Bix into a Jenga-worthy pile, and yet somehow, I'd become responsible for a handful of staff, over thirty-five thousand acres, ten thousand merinos, and a side order of three hundred cattle just to keep things interesting.

How the fuck is this my life?

"A. *Great*. Job," Tom repeated with emphasis, and the words rang like hammer blows against Grandad's bitter comments. "You're doing stuff your grandfather would never have thought possible. That breeding program to reduce foot rot, no-spray zones to improve biodiversity, carbon monitoring . . . the list goes on, son. You're taking this station into the future and we're all proud of you. Your grandad would be too if he wasn't lost in the muddle in his head. Hell, even I thought you were crazy selling off eight hundred head of the wethers so we could spell that hard-grazed land for a bit. But look at it now."

I swallowed hard and met his steady gaze. "Thank you."

Charlie looked up from the post hole she was digging, her short brown bob wet with perspiration. At five foot three and fifty kilos soaking wet, you crossed her at your peril. "Jesus, Tom." She pushed her damp hair off her face. "Keep that up and next thing he'll be wanting us to call him Boss. And I have to tell you, *Golden*"—I winced at the nickname bestowed on me in primary school and which had unfortunately stuck—"no amount of bleach can erase the image of you and your tiny wiener in those godawful budgie smugglers you used to wear to the school swim meets. It left an indelible impression on my young mind and means the whole *boss* thing is kind of a big ask— Hey!" She ducked as I lobbed a clod of dry mud, and it sailed past her head to land in the river.

"Nice one." Sam, our graduate student watched on with amusement, his shaggy blond waves catching in the longest lashes I'd ever seen.

"Watch it, kiddo," Charlie teased, and Sam scowled.

"I'm twenty-one, for fuck's sake."

Tom clasped a hand to his chest. "Just a baby."

"You're just jealous cos when I'm as old as you, I'm still gonna look thirty, whereas you need a fuckton of Botox and a hefty crane," Sam fired back.

I laughed because he wasn't wrong. Fresh-faced and with skin as soft as a baby's bum, and a five o'clock shadow that needed a microscope for proof of life, Sam got carded everywhere he went, teenage girls swooned, and mothers wanted to hug him. It royally pissed him off, especially since he'd had the biggest crush on Charlie from his first day on the station, and she'd done nothing but remind him of their age difference ever since.

"What are . . . budgie smugglers?" Alek leaned on his pile driver, his broody Russian features darker than usual. After being granted asylum in New Zealand, Alek had been looking to work on a sheep farm when a friend of mine in immigration had tapped me on the shoulder. The land and farming practices were hardly comparable to where he'd come from in the Rostov region of Russia, but I figured a sheep was a sheep and at least Alek knew his way around one. I could teach him the rest.

Charlie pushed her hair off her face and regarded Alek with a widening smirk. "They're Speedos, gorgeous. Those tight nylon swimming togs guys wear in competition. The ones that hug every nook and cranny of a man's—" She cleared her throat. "—wet appendages."

"Oh." Alek flushed to the roots of his black hair and the furrows on his brow deepened. "Why . . . budgie smuggler?"

"Well." Charlie clapped her hands together far too gleefully. "A budgie is a small soft bird about this big, right?" She made a budgie-sized shape with both her hands. "And if you shove that sucker down the front of a nylon swimsuit . . . and maybe even imagine it moving—"

"Ooooooh!" Alek's blue eyes flew wide and his mortified expression caused everyone to crack up. He scowled, muttered a string of Russian expletives, and lugged his post driver on to the next upright. "But—" He looked directly at Charlie with his finger pointing downward. "Al-ba-tross, not budgie."

Which left us all gaping in stunned silence.

"Oh. My. God." Charlie spun around. "Did you hear that? Alek made a joke! Our boy is growing up." She turned back to Alek, her eyes dancing. "But I'll need proof of that claim, mister. Just saying."

Alek turned an even deeper shade of crimson and Tom finally called an end to the ribbing before turning to me. "You still haven't told us what you think of the new guy. Is he going to fit in?"

That caught everyone's attention and I filed away an image of Gil *fitting in* just nicely, thank you very much.

But I opted for a more PG response. "He'll be fine." I kept my eyes on the wire in my hand, because *fine* was something the man undoubtedly was. "But I have a heads-up for you all." My gaze swept the group. "Gil lost his kid in that car accident. So, no prying, understand? As for whether he'll fit in, I'll let you make your own minds up when you meet him."

Charlie blinked. "His kid? Damn, that's rough."

"But he can cook, right?" Sam's brows scrunched in obvious concern. "Emily said he could cook."

The one-track minds of youth. "Apparently so. But we'll find out soon enough."

And with that, I shoved all thoughts of Gil Everton aside and got down to work.

CHAPTER SEVEN

Holden

By four thirty, the relentless heat had taken its toll. All teasing and bantering had evaporated into the ether, and there was barely enough of a breeze to raise a relieved smile let alone a laugh. Drenched in sweat and gasping for any air that didn't feel like it had come straight from a furnace, I was quite suddenly done.

I leaned on the post driver, wiped my face with my T-shirt, and considered my weary team. Nobody talked, everyone's eyes glued fast to their work, the ripple of water, the jangle of wire, the slamming of metal on wood, the only sounds to break the thick heat.

"Okay, that's it everyone. Tools down," I called out, and four pairs of shoulders drooped in relief.

"Thank Christ for that." Charlie fell to her butt on the ground. "Goddamn, it's hot. I vote we hit the lake for a swim."

"Oh, hell yeah." I was all over that idea. "Last one in gets pre-muster woolshed cleaning duty."

Charlie snorted. "God loves a trier, Holden, but you're a sucker for punishment." She referred to the fact I'd lost a similar bet the previous year.

Everyone laughed, of course, but none of them knew how much I loved that day to myself in the shed—my music cranked up and not a single soul to bother me. Bring it on.

"I'm calling the start, and no one sets off until we're *all* ready." Charlie, ever the stickler for rules, shucked her sweaty T-shirt, leaving her standing in an equally sweaty crop top and jeans that left Sam's tongue hanging out his mouth.

He caught me smiling and quickly looked away.

"*And* we leave how we arrived," she continued. "Alek's with me, and Sam's with Tom. No breaking the station speed limit on the gravel sections, which means it's gonna come down to whoever negotiates the fastest water crossings." She winked at Tom. "Good luck getting off of a shingle bank relying on *those* scrawny muscles." She nodded Sam's direction and Tom snorted.

"What about me?" I protested. "I'm on my own. How the hell is that fair?"

Charlie returned an innocent look. "But you're the boss man, remember? If you can't get *yourself* out of trouble, we're all in the shit."

I scanned the sea of grins and nodding heads, and grumbled, "Pack of arseholes. I suppose you want me to take the dogs as well?" More nodding heads, and I sighed. "This whole thing is rigged."

When we were done packing up, I turned to the dogs. "Come on, you lot. I only hope one of you can push." I slapped the roof of the Hilux and whistled through my teeth, and three dogs leapt into the back seat, leaving the other two to claim the dog cage on the bed.

Then, under Charlie's onerous directions, we set the utes in a line for a standing start and the race was on—AKA creeping along at the station speed limit which we hadn't a hope in hell of meeting on the rough riverbed tracks, anyway.

Tom had the most experienced eye for the river shortcuts and took an early lead. I stuck to the tried-and-true routes, happy to maintain a strategic position at the rear of the field while trying not to look like I was faking it. Charlie almost got herself wedged on a shingle bar, trying to outsmart Tom, and only made it out of a large hole by the skin of her teeth and a lot of swearing.

Jockeying for position was confined to the straight runs on dry land, the station cattle raising their heads to see what all the fuss was about. The wide, dry berms on either edge allowed three vehicles to run side by side for short periods. My grandfather would've been horrified, but after a hellish day of labouring in blistering heat, it felt good to cut loose, and the beaming smiles of my team made it worth every bone-jarring second.

Fifteen minutes later, amid blaring horns, dogs barking, and much whooping and hollering, the three vehicles whipped past the homestead and headed for the lake. Charlie hit the baked-brown grass at the end of the front lawn first, kicking up dust as she spun her Ford Ranger toward the lake with Alek leaning out the window yelling, "Faster. Faster!"

Tom's red ute followed a close second with Sam's arm out the open window, his hand slapping the door as if to make it go faster.

Happily bringing up the rear, I was almost at the lawn when movement caught my eye and I turned to see Gil and my mother race down the front steps to see what the hell was going on. I gave them a quick wave, slid the Hilux to a stop, loosed the dogs, and headed for the crystalline blue lake.

But Charlie and Alek were already up to their necks, with Tom and Sam not far behind. I hopped/stumbled toward them, barely getting my boots off before launching sideways into the welcoming icy water, clothes and all. The bone-chilling shock sucked the air from my lungs, and for a few seconds, silence reigned as everyone's brains checked out and took a second to reboot.

When we could all breathe again, the shouting, splashing, and water-bombing began, and all bets were off. In seconds the sparkling mirrored surface turned into a churning turbid cauldron of glacial flour, excited dogs, and ridiculous adults.

Charlie surfaced, spluttering from a particularly spectacular dunking by Alek and then flipped him off with a laugh. "Arsehole." Then she set off in an elegant breaststroke with two dogs at her side. "Oh my god, this feels amazing."

Alek floated on his back, arms wide, and staring up at the sky, while Tom bobbed like a large buoy, treading water, and keeping an eye on Sam who was the weakest swimmer of the group.

I made my way to the shallows, stripped off my shirt, and took a seat on the silty lakebed. The chilly water lapped around the waist of my sodden jeans as I cupped handfuls of frigid water and splashed the perspiration from my face.

"Bunch of idiots," my mother scolded from somewhere close behind.

I turned to find a fresh bunch of towels waiting on the shore and my mother hoisting up her dress for a paddle. "I should brain the lot of you," she grumbled. "But trying to track down any in those thick skulls of yours would be a futile waste of time."

"Pfft. We barely got out of second gear." I flicked a little water her way and she squealed and jumped back.

"Looked like fun." Gil stood on the silty shore behind my mother. His eyes were hidden by the shade of his cap, and yet there was something about the intensity of his stare . . .

Oh, for fuck's sake. The fact I was half-naked and wet like everyone else shouldn't have mattered and yet somehow it did. Heat raced into my cheeks. "Yeah, it was," I said, hearing the gravel in my voice. I returned his gaze for a second or two and then looked away. *What the hell?*

My mother put her fingers in her mouth and blew a shrill whistle. "Listen up, everyone. This is our new domestic manager, Gil Everton."

"*Temporary* domestic manager," Gil corrected, bestowing a winning smile on my mother. "I doubt you're replaceable, Emily."

Oh, he was good.

My mother smiled at the flattery and then introduced everyone, one at a time.

That over with, Charlie waved Gil into the water. "Are you just gonna stand there, new guy, or are you going to join us?"

I knew that interested gleam in Charlie's eyes only too well, and a slither of something unexpected ran through my belly.

"Sure, I won't say no to a dip." Gil stripped off his shirt, revealing altogether too much smooth, creamy skin for the thin hold I had on my libido. A better look at the chest hair I'd glimpsed the day before confirmed my suspicions that it was indeed sexy as all fuck, as was the golden-haired treasure trail that wound down his soft, flat belly to dip under the waistband of a pair of shorts that hugged the man's arse like I'd been thinking about doing all day.

He threw his shirt onto the grassy bank, lifted his hands above his head, and stretched those long back muscles from side to side. My mouth ran dry in a lake full of water, and I was still staring when his eyes landed on mine, his gaze lingering long enough to send my cheeks blazing . . . again. I turned away before my dick had a chance to get in on the act as well, but not fast enough to avoid Charlie's knowing smirk.

She mouthed, "You're welcome."

"Fuck you," I mouthed back, which only made her laugh.

I ignored her and turned to watch as Gil approached the lapping edge. There was a palpable anticipation, and everyone held their breath.

Three . . . two . . . one—

As he stepped into the water, his eyes flew open and he blurted, "Holy Jesus, fuck!" Then his horrified gaze jerked to my mother, but she was hooting with laughter along with everyone else. He rolled his eyes and snorted in amusement. "Okay. Yeah, yeah. I get it," he grumbled. "Screw with the new guy, right?"

Then he was gone under the water in a fast and furious dive before shooting back to the surface like a rocket just seconds later, his arms wrapped around his chest. "Jeeeeesus!" He jumped up and down in a vain attempt to warm up—numbness really was the only relief—and his narrowed gaze swept his still laughing audience. "Having fun? Enjoy the show?"

"Hell yeah." Tom slapped the surface of the lake, sending a spray of water toward Gil.

He lunged sideways, tripped, and disappeared back under the water, which only set everyone off again. When he resurfaced, spluttering, my mother was standing on the shore holding a towel at the ready for him. "It's a rite of passage, Gil. Be thankful you didn't arrive in winter."

His mouth dropped open. "You're kidding, right?"

My mother grinned. "As I said, be thankful."

Gil eyed the towel longingly, then shook his head. "In for a penny, right? If I stay in long enough, my balls might actually defrost and drop back where they belong, right?" He dove under the water and began slicing through it with a smooth freestyle stroke that barely chopped the surface.

"You did well with that one, Emily." Tom waded out of the water and accepted the towel my mother offered. The others quickly joined him, followed by the dogs who bounded up the lawn with more energy than I'd seen from them in days.

I stayed where I was, my dick slowly turning into a popsicle as I watched Gil make a turn and head back.

"He knows his way around a kitchen as well," my mother told Tom. "You'll be able to taste-test his skills soon enough."

And nope, I wasn't going near that one.

With goosebumps appearing like popcorn over my body, I dragged myself from the freezing water while continuing to steal sideways glances at Gil as he drew close to the shore—occupational health and safety and all that.

But as he waded from the lake up onto the narrow stony beach, water dripping from the ends of his dirty-blond locks to run in rivulets down all that lean muscle, my tongue landed somewhere south of my chest and planted a white flag. Because damn—with those full lips, shiny wet, and almost blue from the cold, taut pebbled nipples, and fine golden chest hair fanning wet across his pecs—there was no pretending I wasn't in full lust-mode for the man.

I really needed to get off the station more.

I slapped my horny self into submission and threw Gil a towel. "Here."

He grabbed it with a smile then turned to my mother. "Sorry about the language earlier, Emily."

She waved it aside. "Wait till you catch an earful of *me* when things don't go right in the kitchen."

"Still, I should make an effort."

"We all should," Tom piped up, looking smug. "But especially Holden."

I flipped him off. "And why is that?"

He grinned. "Because Emily's *your* mother, and you have a mouth like a sewer rat."

I snorted. "Charming."

"Holden not swear?" Charlie gave a booming laugh. "Holy crap. I give it twenty minutes max."

Sam stuck his hand in the air. "I'd take that bet."

"Fuck off," I snapped, which of course set *everyone* laughing again, including my mother.

Gil bit back a smile. "It's not a bad idea," he mused. "Are you up for a little competition?" He directed the question my way and I looked behind me, then back, much to everyone's amusement.

"Who me?" I acted surprised.

"Yeah, you. Swear off swearing. We can keep a running total. First past thirty loses."

I'm pretty sure I gaped. "Thirty? Are you serious? You mean a day, right?"

He shrugged. "Nope. I think I can make it a couple of weeks easy. Don't think you can do it?"

I narrowed my gaze. "Sure, why not?" It would be good for morale if nothing else. "As long as it only applies between you and me. I can't be held accountable for my language on the hill with a few thousand merinos, and I won't have these bozos dobbing me in if you're not around."

Gil considered that and gave a sharp nod. "Fair enough. What are we playing for?"

"Bragging rights," my mother interjected. "Anything else has to be kept simple. That's *my* rule."

She had a point. "Simple, huh?" I waggled my eyebrows and licked my lips. "Well, you're the cook, and I'm partial to an excellent cheese scone or six, *with* cayenne *and* spring onions."

Gil quickly agreed. "But what do *I* get?"

I smiled. "I cook a mean pancake."

He raised a brow. "Seriously?"

"I'm not completely hopeless in the kitchen, you know." I caught my mother's look of surprise and repeated, "I'm *not*."

"All right," he finally agreed. "But they better be as good as you're saying."

I held those vibrant hazel eyes and smirked. "Doesn't really matter if they are or aren't. I'm pretty sure you're gonna crack the limit before I do."

Gil raised my smirk with a mocking, "We'll see about that."

And we grinned at each other like a couple of loons, his smile lighting something warm in my chest.

"We'll need rules of engagement, of course."

"Yes, rules!" Charlie fist-pumped the air, which startled me since I'd almost forgotten the others were still there, and a sideways glance confirmed that we were indeed the centre of everyone's attention.

I tapped my lip thoughtfully. "I think we should permit a few low-level contenders, like hell and damn."

"Agreed." A smile tugged at those pinking lips and I couldn't look away. "And let's round it out with crap, so to speak. I mean, technically, is it really even swearing?" His grin was contagious.

"This is true." I eyed him up and down. "Be afraid, Everton. Be very afraid."

He regarded me with mock disdain. "Bring it on, Miller." Then he offered his hand and I took it, his fingers closing slow and warm around mine in a firm clasp that I absolutely did not imagine happening around something else, and in other circumstances which would remain forever unspoken. Neither did I keep hold of his hand for one or two seconds past simply polite.

I didn't.

At least I didn't think I had until Charlie cleared her throat. "Well, you two seem to be getting on like a house on fire." She looked between us with a teasing smile and a waggle of those saucy eyebrows.

Gil looked suddenly uncomfortable, and I wanted to wipe that smug smile off Charlie's pretty elfin face. And also; *Fuck. My. Life.* Because silent swearing didn't count.

I immediately dropped his hand and shot her a warning glare. "Okay, you lot." If in doubt, change the subject. "Let's get these utes unloaded. Then I suggest you make the most of your day off tomorrow, cos it's back to fencing Monday along with a whole list of jobs that need doing. I want this place spotless for the SX Merino buyer's visit, and we're gonna be busy as f—" I glanced at Gil to find him smirking. "—as *hell* with muster coming up. And just so you know, the buyer is gonna want to talk to all of you as well."

Sam's eyes bugged. "Us?"

I shrugged. "The sustainability component encompasses conditions of employment and best practices. They'll be checking I'm treating you right."

Charlie snorted. "And just how much are you gonna pay us to lie about that?"

I rolled my eyes. "For f—" I glanced again at Gil who was clearly struggling not to laugh. "—Pete's sake, go finish up before I'm tempted to drop a salary or two just to save on the irritation factor alone."

Charlie grabbed her boots and started padding up the brown

crispy lawn in her bare feet. "Aw, you love us. And you are so gonna lose that bet."

"Am not," I fired back petulantly.

Tom waved for Sam to follow the others. "I'll meet you there." Then he wandered down to the lake to wash the dust off his boots.

"That's our cue, Gil." My mother scooped up the pile of wet towels. "That lamb needs basting and you're on gravy duty. Why the heck I thought a roast was a good idea on a stinking hot day is beyond me."

Gil caught my eye and nodded to my mother heading up the path. "She's pretty great. You're lucky."

I couldn't stop from smiling. "Remember that next time the power goes out and there's baking in the oven. My advice? Run for cover. Catch you later, Gil." I gathered my boots and started walking to the Hilux, feeling his eyes on me all the way.

When I reached the driver's door, I risked a glance back to find him heading up the lawn with his towel and T-shirt slung over his bare shoulders, and that arse looking all kinds of scrumptious in soaking wet shorts.

Fuck me.

I blew out a long, frustrated sigh and turned to find Tom standing not a metre away, his warm grey eyes studying me with something that looked too close to sympathy to be comfortable.

"Come on, son." He ruffled my damp hair. "Get yourself in that Hilux before you blow a gasket."

I rolled my eyes. "I keep reminding you, you're not even twenty years older than me, so the son thing is just a little bit creepy. Besides, I've no idea what you're talking about."

He slapped me on the back, almost sending me to the ground. "Of course you don't. You probably look at everyone the way you look at him, like they're your favourite lollipop."

I choked out a laugh and gave him a friendly shove. "Wow. That was actually pretty good."

"Fuck you." He shoved me back, then slung an arm around my

shoulders and steered me toward the Hilux. "It was hardly rocket science. There was a puddle of drool to rival the damn lake at your feet."

He wasn't wrong. "God, it's so embarrassing." I glanced up at the house. "I have a crap poker face, don't I?"

"The worst." Tom smiled a little sadly.

"Still, you can't deny he's hot."

Tom blinked. "Ah, he's a good-looking man, I suppose."

I stared at him. "You suppose? He's way more than . . ." I groaned and didn't finish. "What is wrong with me? He's straight, for fuck's sake."

This time Tom didn't laugh. "It's natural. He's a nice guy and you're clearly attracted to him. It gets lonely up here. We all feel it. And it's not like there's a whole bunch of nice available gay men tripping over each other in Oakwood, right?"

I held my thumb and forefinger barely apart and he chuckled.

I glanced again toward the still open front door. "Lusting after straight hotties is a pointless waste of time and energy."

"It is," Tom agreed.

"Plus, the guy's been through a lot. He's trying to get his shit together after losing his daughter, and here I am, checking him out. I'm such a jerk."

Tom's eyes burned into mine. "You know, I always thought that you and Zach might—"

I spun to face him. "Jesus, are there really no secrets on this station?"

He shrugged. "Are you really telling me you think there are?"

I slumped against the door of the ute. "It's beginning to feel like *Love Island*. But no, Zach and I were . . . casual. Besides, it's finished." I remembered something and grimaced. "Does everyone know?"

"Yes," Tom answered flatly.

"Shit. Well, I hope they've kept their mouths shut, because Zach's father—"

"No one would say a word, you know that."

I did. "Yeah, thanks. But can you please tell them that there's nothing happening between us anymore? I don't want Zach exposed to any throwaway comments during muster, not even in joking."

Tom held my gaze. "I'll make sure they get the message." He pulled me around to face him. "And maybe it's for the best. The station needs all your attention right now, Holden. We're at a turning point and you can do without the distraction, *any* distraction."

I sighed because he was right. "Are you telling me to step up?"

He looked uncertain for a moment, then gave a sharp nod. "I am. But also . . ." He glanced down to where the fly on my jeans lay unzipped with just the waist button holding the fuckers up. An eyeful of bright red lightning-bolt briefs poked through the gap.

"Not. A. Word." I zipped up and pushed him toward his vehicle. "It's washing day. That's all I'm gonna say."

He laughed and threw his shirt onto the passenger seat of his Ranger before climbing in and leaning out the open window, that serious expression back in place.

I sighed and steeled myself. I owed everything to Tom for getting me through the previous few years, but it wasn't easy to step up when the shadow of another man's experience dogged your path.

"There's no room for half-hearted commitment in the high country, Holden, we both know that." He sounded so much like my grandfather I almost looked around to watch for him coming down the path. "It'll eat you alive and spit out your bones sooner than look at you. The rest of the team, including me, might work on the station, but only *you* have to live with the long-term consequences of what you do the next year or so. This is *your* family's station, and *you* are running it. Period. The rest of us can walk away, and that makes all the difference."

I said nothing for a few long seconds, shocked silent by the edge of frustration in Tom's tone.

At my lack of response, his expression softened. "You need to start believing in yourself, Holden. The rest of us already do."

I swallowed hard, my answer little more than a whisper. "I'm trying."

We locked eyes—the experienced shepherd, and the young, so out-of-his-fucking-depth owner. I felt like I'd received a warning, one I couldn't afford to ignore.

Because Tom was right. It was the same as the epiphany I'd had in bed that morning. I was *it* from then on. And the team needed me to step up and secure the future of this place. Nothing mattered more than that.

I gave a sharp nod to let Tom know I'd got the message, then I slapped the roof of his cab and watched him head up the drive toward the woolshed.

"Come on kids." I whistled to the dogs. "Let's get you fed."

They leapt in and onto the Hilux while I took a moment to stare at the homestead. Whether I liked it or not, the success or failure of this station rested on my shoulders. It was time to get serious, to grow the fuck up, and stop lusting over unattainable sexy men.

And it started by establishing some professional distance with the station's newest employee. Limiting the amount of time I spent with Gil was the first thing on the list, at least until I got this stupid crush under control.

Piece of cake, right?

CHAPTER EIGHT

Gil

D<small>ADDEEEEEE</small>!

"Callie!" I shot bolt upright in bed, my heart banging against my ribs, my foot slamming down on some non-existent pedal like my life depended on it. Gasping for breath, stomach clenched, acid welling up the back of my throat as my gaze jerked left, then right.

Nothing but darkness.

Thick, choking, merciless darkness.

I managed to suck a thin breath of air through the tight fist of fear around my throat and a reedy wail escaped my lips.

She was dead.

Oh god. Oh god.

She was dead.

Falling back on the sweat-drenched sheets I focused on slowing my breathing, trying to bring my racing heart down from the stratosphere.

Missed by a galaxy or two.

In and out.

In and out.

Lapping waves and warm sun. My therapist's voice dripped like honey in my ear.

I didn't even like the tropics. Liked therapists even less. Go figure.

In and out.

In and out.

Falling snow.

Didn't much like snow either.

In and out.

In and out.

Mountains and glacial valleys.

Down a notch or two.

In and out.

Clear rivers and icy lakes.

Slower now.

In and out.

Eyes the colour of coffee.

In . . . and . . . out.

In . . . . . . and . . . . . . out.

In . . . . and . . . .

Out.

I pushed the sheet aside and blew a long, slow breath, stretching it out, the night air licking at my sweat-soaked skin.

The clunk of my mind slotting back into reality.

Even if my body still trembled.

Even if my heart was broken all over again.

Daddeeeeee!

I curled sideways into a ball and drew my knees up to my chin.

Are you sure you weren't going too fast?

No.

You always push the limit.

I wasn't.

Are you sure you couldn't have slowed down, or sped up, or done something?

There was no time.

Why didn't you see him? The driver in front said he saw him. Why didn't you?

I don't know. I don't know. I don't know. I was focused on the car ahead. He was going slow. Do you think I haven't asked myself all those same questions?

My skin pebbled, not from the cold but from the unrelenting punishment of guilt. I scrambled for the ever-present bottle of pills on my bedside table, dry swallowed two, rolled onto my back, and waited for the soothing calm to kick in.

"It wasn't my fault," I whispered into the dark room. "It wasn't my fault."

Because, so help me, I was sick of the tears.

Sick of my prayers soaring into nothingness.

Sick of the panic attacks and the guilt and the raging anger at my daughter's life taken from us, from all of us.

Sick of myself.

Sick of the constant questions and empty answers.

Sick of the bleak loneliness that seemed to have become my life.

I missed my family.

I missed waffles on Sunday mornings, the three of us crowded into bed, Luke moaning about syrup on the sheets.

I missed my life, my work.

I missed my *home*. My *old* home, not the sterile apartment I'd been renting with its child-friendly nothing.

"For fuck's sake." I groaned and swung my feet to the floor, swallowing my tears. More fucking tears. A glimmer of light breached the gap in the curtain and I threw it open to find a blanket of stars hanging over the valley like a glittering ocean.

"And what've you got to say that's any different?" I fired the question out into the night. "Where are all these miracles I've heard about?"

Figuring I wouldn't get any more sleep, I pulled on some clothes, gathered my phone, and the brightly coloured throw from the chair, and crept from my room. Picking my way carefully through the kitchen to the covered deck, I ignored the temptation of the deep-cushioned chairs out front and instead sank onto the wooden stairs farther from Holden's open bedroom window. The relative coolness of the night fanned across my overheated skin and my body began to relax.

Seconds later, a familiar warm body stretched out at my side.

"Hey, Spider." I scratched the huntaway's ears and my heart ticked down another notch or two. "You having a restless night too, huh?"

Spider groaned and pushed his nose onto my lap, seemingly asleep again in seconds.

I gave a soft chuckle. "I guess that answers that."

I kept lightly tugging at his ears until breath by breath my body and squirreling mind calmed—the dark peace of the mountain night and the animal at my side working their magic. Five nights in a new bed and my first nightmare in the high country. I supposed it could've been worse.

Starlight sparkled on the black skin of water at the bottom of the lawn, and as I stared out across its surface, images from Saturday's hijinks rose unbidden in my mind, along with a bundle of other thoughts and feelings I could well do without.

Thoughts and feelings about . . . Holden.

I still didn't get it. I'd felt pretty much nothing, let alone desire for over a year since Luke had packed his bags. And if I were being honest, for a long time before that as well.

Until a few days ago.

Until Holden Miller.

I wasn't sure if what I felt *was* even desire. Maybe it was simply deep gratitude for a man who saw me in a way I hadn't been seen for a long while—without pity or sympathy or concern. Just me. And I'd laughed more over those first couple of days than I had in eighteen months. But that didn't mean I should do anything about it. Jesus, I could barely tie my shoelaces again. What the hell would I do with another man in my bed? It would be a disaster waiting to happen.

Not that Tuck would see it that way. He'd spent the previous six months trying to get me laid, thinking it might get me out of myself, but not even my starving cock had been on board with the idea.

Except when it came to Holden, apparently. Go figure.

With my mind on Tuck, I pulled out my phone and stared at the string of unanswered texts that wanted to know how I was doing. And yes, I was a shit mate.

I wrote a reply for him to read when he woke.

Sorry for the radio silence. Just settling in. Things are fine. The local wildlife is friendly. I'll call when I can.

I pressed Send and set the phone on the step, only to jump a few seconds later when it buzzed with an incoming call. I blinked at Tucker's name on the screen. He and the term early riser were not a match made in heaven.

I put the phone to my ear and whispered, "What the hell are you doing awake at this hour?"

"I'm due at the airport by six," he answered sourly. "The conference, remember? And why are you whispering?"

"Because I'm outside on the deck and Holden's bedroom is just around the corner. He's my boss, remember?" And a lot of other things I wasn't about to mention.

Tuck took a few seconds to process, then asked, "And why exactly are you on the deck in the middle of the night? Oh—" He put the pieces together. "You had another thing, right?"

I snorted. "A thing?"

Tucker huffed. "A nightmare. A PTSD *thing*."

I snorted. "Yes, Tucker, I had a PTSD *thing*. No one would guess you were a psychologist. But I'm fine now." I drew the blanket around my shoulders and wrapped my feet in its warmth—the mournful bellow from one of Holden's cattle the only sound to break the silence coming down the line.

"Are you sure?" Tucker asked guardedly. "We've never bull-shitted each other, so don't shut me out. And switch to video. I need to see you."

"Oh, for fuck's sake," I grumbled but did as he said, a surge of warmth tugging at my heart as his concerned expression, huge beard, and sleepy ash-grey eyes came into view. I'd missed him. More than I cared to admit. "Happy now?"

His mouth turned up in an affectionate smile. "Very. Even if I can hardly see you."

I turned a little to catch the glow from the kitchen.

"Much better." He studied me closely. "Okay, you look passable."

I rolled my eyes. "I'm fine. And I'm not shutting you out. I just need a little space. It's good here, Tuck. PTSD aside, I feel like I can breathe for the first time in months. You really don't have to worry."

Tuck's shrewd gaze travelled over my face and he let loose a heavy sigh. "Okay, fine. I'll try not to worry . . . until I do."

I snorted, and from somewhere in the dark another deep-chested bellow split the night.

"What the hell is that?" Tuck squinted into the camera.

"Just one of Holden's steers."

"A steer?" Tuck chuckled, his grey eyes dancing. "Look at you getting all countryfied and shit. So, how is this boss of yours, then? You getting on okay?"

Oh boy. I smiled to myself. "He's nice enough." *In a hot as fuck kind of way.* "We're still getting used to each other, I guess."

"Nice enough, eh? This is the guy who warranted a holy shit when he collected you from Tekapo?" Tucker narrowed his eyes. The man knew me far too well.

"That *holy shit* was entirely unrelated to Holden," I whisper-lied. "And keep your voice down."

"Hmmm." Tuck clearly didn't believe me for a second. "Seems kind of young to be running a station."

"He is, but like I already told you when we first talked about it, he didn't have much choice. What's really going on here, Tuck? You're cagey as shit about something."

Tuck paused long enough for me to know I was right and his gaze skittered sideways. Then he answered on an outrush of air, "I got a call from Luke."

My stomach dropped and a groan escaped my lips.

"He wants to know where you are. He says he needs to talk to you. And what the hell, Gil? You didn't give him your new number?" Tucker's confused expression made me wince.

"No. Did you?" *Please say no.*

"Of course not. Although he could tell I was totally gobsmacked that he didn't already know. I mean, Jesus, Gil. What were you thinking? What if something had happ—" He stopped and shook his head. "Forget about it. But I did promise I'd ask you. Did you tell *anyone*?"

I grimaced. "Just you and Leonard."

He blinked, and silence screamed down the line.

Shit. I'd been an arse . . . again. "Look, here's the thing, Tuck," I raced to explain. "I wanted these three months to be a clean slate. I wanted to keep this time separate from everything else, at least for a bit. Apart from you and Leonard, there really isn't anyone else I want to talk to. Not while I'm here. And I suppose I figured you'd tell me anything I need to know."

And because I need to not have Luke's voice in my ear, his words in my head, his . . . anything, just for a little while. And I'm tired of the friendly check-ins from my friends, the awkward silences, the well-meaning pep talks. I'm tired of it all.

His sigh reeked of frustration. "So, you landed it on me to act as go-between without even asking?"

Fuck. "You're right and I'm sorry. It was unfair."

"Damn right it was. You're cutting people out of your life who care for you, Gil."

"Luke doesn't—"

"Yes, he does, and you know it. You two—" Tuck paused and drew a frustrated breath. An awkward silence spun out between us, a silence I couldn't fill. Tuck shook his head, looking like the picture of exasperation. "What happened to Callie, to both of you, was fucked up and the saddest fucking thing I've ever seen. But just because you couldn't find a way through it together doesn't mean Luke doesn't care about you."

I gritted my teeth. "He walked away, Tuck. He couldn't deal with it and so he fucking walked away and left me to drown. And six months later he's cosying up to someone else? Who the fuck does that?"

Tuck said nothing for a minute, one hand pulling at his beard, his grey eyes sad. "You were *both* drowning, Gil. *Both* of you. And you know as well as I do that other guy was just a fling. You'd been separated for six months, and from what I hear, it finished as quickly as it started. And haven't I been encouraging you to maybe try and get out there as well?"

"Nope. No, thank you. I'm not even close to ready for that," I huffed before an image of Holden popped into my brain and I rolled my eyes at my blatant hypocrisy.

But Tuck was right about one thing. Luke probably did deserve to at least have a contact number since we hadn't finalised anything between us.

"All right." I blew out a long sigh. "You can give him my new number and tell him what I'm doing, but I want you to make it clear he's not to call unless it's an emergency. I'll call him when I'm ready."

"Thank you," Tuck said, his frown smoothing. "It will get him off my case for a bit. But you're going to have to talk to him sometime. You two have things to work out."

"We're done, Tuck."

"Doesn't mean there aren't things to talk about."

"I . . . know." I sighed because he was right. "But don't analyse me, Tuck."

He laughed. "Jesus, I don't have to. You do more than enough of that for both of us. Too bloody much, if you ask me. Sometimes the answers aren't going to be found in your logical brain, Gil. And maybe that's a good topic to raise with Leonard?"

The high country works its own kind of miracles.

"I realise that, Tuck. But can you please stop pushing?"

He studied me for a minute, then a soft smile spread over his face. "I can do that. But on the understanding that you do a better job of keeping in touch, or I swear I'll hunt you down and it won't be pretty."

I couldn't stop a wide smile at his words. "I promise."

We said our goodbyes and I pocketed my phone—thoughts of Luke and the painful unravelling of our marriage scratching at my raw heart. Tuck had been right. We had *both* been drowning. And what could you do when the person who'd been your life raft for fifteen years was suddenly too busy sinking in their own grief to save you from yours? Luke undoubtedly felt the same, but I wasn't far enough along my own angry path to be bothered to listen, at least not yet.

The psychologist in me knew we had to talk. The angry abandoned husband and grieving parent wanted to tell him to go fuck himself.

I couldn't even blame Luke for having a . . . fling. Tucker was right about that too.

Hell, just the memory of Holden watching me from the water, his gaze hot on my body set sparks sizzling under my skin. It was the most alive I'd felt in over a year. There'd been no mistaking *that* look or the way my body had instantly lit up. Oh yes, I could understand Luke only too well.

But there were a billion ways that scenario could and likely would go wrong. Then again, as a psychologist, I liked to believe in things having meaning beyond the obvious. So, if coming to the station was the right decision for me, then meeting Holden might not be just a random wrinkle either. Maybe he was in my life for a reason. Maybe it was just a reminder of a life beyond grief. Maybe it was something more. But I needed to figure that out before I did something stupid.

I thought back to what Holden had said that first day. *If anywhere can scrape the city from you and get you raw enough to find some answers, I reckon it's the high country.*

Perhaps there was some truth in that, after all.

The minutes crawled by until I stumbled back into bed around four, accompanied by Spider who seemed to have taken it upon himself to keep an eye on me. The alarm startled me awake an hour later, and I peeled open my eyelids against a headache that felt like a small army had marched through my brain with steel-toed combat boots.

Tired, grumpy, and frustrated, I headed for the bathroom, tripping over an unconscious Spider who groaned in protest but then fell back asleep in seconds. Standing at the basin, I threw a cold wet flannel around my face—for all the good it did me—and then stumbled out to start breakfast.

Emily had given me the day to *play* alone in the kitchen for the first time while she caught up on paperwork. I was tasked with covering the morning and afternoon teas for the rest of the week and anything else I took a fancy to.

She'd schooled me on her recipes, equipment, and stores. I had a printout of all her suppliers, and I'd made a list of all her preserved, canned, and frozen goods, including those she hid from Holden and the shepherds. It had been years since I'd worked in a commercial kitchen, and although this didn't compare in scale, it somehow felt equally important.

And that didn't even include the preparations for the upcoming muster in three weeks. Seven hungry shepherds for seven days meant a mountain of food for human and canine consumption, not to mention the shearing gang following. Plus, the logistics of stocking two remote huts for occupation, all the driving back and forth over terrain I was barely getting my head around, and a million other things that all had the potential to go south. But I was determined Emily wasn't heading to the UK with any concerns about my ability to do the job. I'd be carrying more than enough worry for the two of us.

I made a beeline for the coffee machine only to be brought up short by yet *another* note left on the island from the elusive Holden Miller, who not unlike the black robin, was a creature I'd seen so little of that I was tempted to question if he existed at all.

Gil
    I made an early start and packed my own lunch. I have a lot of work to get through today so I might be late. Don't bother with dinner. I'll grab a sandwich.
    Holden

I crumpled the note, three-pointed it toward the bin, missed, tried again, missed again, and left the damn note on the floor.

"And the crowd went wild." I glared at the bin.

Dammit, Holden. What the hell are you playing at?

My sixth day on the station and the fourth in a row where he seemed intent on avoiding me. I didn't know his work routine or the man himself well enough to be certain, but it was sure looking that way.

Way to make the new guy feel bad, arsehole.

So much for our friendly cursing wager. Holden had barely spoken a word to me *at all* in three days, let alone swear. To be honest, I was flummoxed.

I wandered to the window and stared out at the blush of dawn reflecting off the lake, its surface as yet unruffled by the warm nor'wester that seemed to rise each day around mid-morning. But in the weak light of morning, the air still lay cool and calm inside the mountain walls.

I sighed and tried not to take Holden's ongoing absence too seriously. But it was hard when Emily herself had been surprised, commenting that he rarely missed meals. And looking after Holden, the house, the cottages, and the shepherds who gathered for lunch most days was what I'd been employed for, after all.

Those first couple of days had been fine. We'd chatted easily over breakfast and had fun at the lake. And then Saturday night Holden had suddenly become quiet, disappearing into his office as soon as dinner was done. Then on Sunday he'd grabbed two pieces of toast with nothing but butter and disappeared back into his office with a parting comment to not worry about him for lunch or dinner.

On Monday he was gone once again before I got up, leaving a note to say he was heading up Dunwoody's beat for the day and would grab something for himself later. I'd ignored the latter instruction and left him a plate of food, which subsequently went untouched. Tuesday saw a variation on the same theme. Colour me a little pissed off. Because Emily had been *crystal* clear; looking after Holden and the team was my number one priority. It was my job to make sure they were healthy, supported, and well-fed to enable them to handle both the social isolation and the hard physical labour of station life.

That's how you hold on to your best shepherds, she'd said.

According to Emily, left to their own devices, most of the team would work all hours of the day and night, not get enough sleep, and live off noodles, toasted sandwiches, and microwaved meals. It was my job to make sure that didn't happen, a role that was apparently just as important to the success of the station as any of the others.

No pressure then.

Which had been fine with me. Caring for people was kind of my jam. But doing it successfully so that caring didn't become smothering, or even worse failing to reach the mark, relied on partnership. I could only do my job if people *let* me *and* worked with me. Kind of like psychology. And doing my job meant *nobody* skipped meals on a regular basis without me following them up, not on my watch. Holden not turning up for meals was kind of a slap in the face, and I was pretty much done with it.

Something had changed.

Holden had been fine until . . . it suddenly hit me. He'd been fine until that damn swim. Until Charlie had piped up and said something about how well we were getting on. She'd been calling Holden out for flirting, and he'd been . . . shit . . . he'd been red-faced embarrassed.

The boss caught flirting with a supposedly straight guy in front of his whole team.

And I'd totally missed it . . . because I'd been enjoying it . . . because I wasn't even remotely straight.

Dammit.

I was already fucking things up.

Which left me the morning to come up with a solution.

I brewed myself a fresh coffee and stood at the sink to drink it while staring through the window at the lightening horizon. The shepherds' windows blazed bright with everyone getting ready for the day, but my attention was drawn further up the track to a faint glow on the shelter trees at the top end of the track . . . opposite the woolshed.

Huh. But there was something else as well. I froze and listened. And as I listened, my gaze narrowed. I opened the sash window and a low thrum of music floated inside. Bob Marley.

"So that's where you sneaked off to." My words came out closer to a growl than I would've liked, but fuck me, the frustrating man wasn't exactly so far away that he couldn't damn well make it back for breakfast.

He was definitely avoiding me.

"Well, buckle up, buttercup." I poured myself another coffee and raised it to the woolshed in a kind of toast. "You don't scare me,

Holden Miller. If this job is going to work out, I guess it's gonna need a little more honesty than I'd hoped for."

Crap or get off the pot, Everton.

And if Holden Miller thought he could just ignore me and I'd settle for his scraps, he was about to find out how wrong he was.

CHAPTER NINE

Gil

Four hours later, with Spider at my side, a cool bag slung over my shoulder, and my heart jumping in my chest, I made my way up the track toward the woolshed. I'd donned a wide-brimmed hat I'd found hanging in the mudroom and was busy focusing on the ground to shield my eyes against a mini dust storm created by the nor'wester, which had rolled in once again like clockwork.

All the cottages were quiet—the team having left for the top of the valley to finish the last run of fencing. And with Emily still holed up in the office, that left just Holden and me. Perfect for that little chat I'd planned.

Still staring at my feet, my gaze jerked up just in time to step off the track and out of the path of a Ford Explorer so dusty I could barely tell its colour. It slowed to a stop alongside, a good-looking, dark-haired, fortyish man sitting at the wheel. The logo on the door said Oakwood Veterinary Clinic, which answered my first question.

"Hey there." The driver offered his hand through the open window, but Spider got to it first, giving it a sniff before adding a lick of approval. The man chuckled, wiped his hand on his shirt, and offered it again. "You must be Gil. Holden mentioned the station's new domestic manager had arrived. I'm Spencer Thompson, one of the local vets, for my sins."

"Nice to meet you, Spencer. And *temporary* manager." I shook his hand, then absently wiped my palm down my shorts, having quickly learned that most people in the high country seemed to come with a side order of lanolin, especially if they'd been in the woolshed.

Spencer laughed. "Damn stuff gets everywhere, right? Occupational hazard. I can't tell you the number of the woolly beasts I handle on a weekly basis. The locals call my vet partner and me the Teflon twins. Get us on a rugby field and we can't land a ball to save ourselves." He gave a booming laugh. "Mind you—" He held his hands out and turned them over. "—they're soft as a baby's bum, so there's that."

I was smiling before I knew it, immediately warming to the man's affable nature. "Are we keeping you busy?" I nodded toward the shed.

"Nothing serious." He reached a hand down to scruff Spider around the ears. "Holden's been closely monitoring a few of the station's top performing ewes for his breeding program to try and improve the stock and fleece value, and today was ultrasound day. We've been measuring foetal development. After lambing, we'll track weight gain and wool growth. So far, it's looking promising. Holden has an excellent nose for bloodlines. He's a clever lad."

That didn't surprise me. "I'll have to ask him about it."

"You do that. Then grab a comfy chair for the long haul."

I chuckled, and Spencer gave me an all-too-familiar once-over.

"So, how are you enjoying station life?" he asked. "Holden said this was all new for you."

I cast a look around the mountains and opened my hands. "What's there not to love? It's beautiful up here."

He followed my gaze, nodding. "That it is. But I'll check back with you after the first winter storm." He gave another of those booming laughs.

"I take it I'm in for a shock?"

He laughed. "Far be it from me to spoil the surprise. Nice to meet you, Gil. Don't take any shit from these bozos. And come find me if you feel like a change of . . . scenery." He looked me up and down for the second time so there was no way I'd miss the innuendo.

Caught off guard, I tried to think of a snappy reply, couldn't, and settled for a half-smile and what I hoped came across as polite but non-committal. "Oh, ah, thanks."

Spencer gave another chuckle and was gone with a wave and a cloud of dust. I watched until he made the turn at the bottom of the homestead lawn and idly wondered if I had the words *Hello, my name is Gil and I'm gay* tattooed on my damn forehead. Or maybe it was just this place.

I shook my head and kept walking, Spider slotting alongside as if we did it every day. The woolshed sat at the top of the track, about half a kilometre from the homestead. It was an old but well-maintained, sprawling wooden structure, whose corrugated iron roof extended well past the building itself to cover a large number of pens. One of those was currently housing a half-dozen head of sheep who were no doubt grateful for the shade.

The pungent aroma of lanolin and dried animal manure hung ripe in the air, and by the time I reached the door at the side, the tang lay thick on the back of my throat. I placed my palm on the wood worn smooth with age and use and immediately thought of all those shepherds who'd gone before and fought to make a home in this inhospitable country.

There was an odd romance to the moment, a palpable history, and the thought made me smile, along with the sound of a soft rock band I didn't recognise but could get used to—something that couldn't be said of Holden's singing, which lacked anything resembling a key, let alone the correct one.

I shot a look at Spider who'd dropped into a shady spot next to the door and was watching me with soulful brown eyes. "Staying out here, huh?" I glanced at the door and winced at another of Holden's attempts to reach a high note. "Yeah, I don't blame you. Wish me luck."

I gave the door a good shove and . . . nothing. I made a mental note to get the damn thing fixed and put my shoulder into the second attempt. It scraped open along the floorboards and a hundred years of lanolin, sheep manure, wool, dust, feed, oil, sweat, and wood assaulted my nostrils. Every beam and plank of the old building was steeped in it. Farm animals, wool, and dozens of hardworking bodies. The sound of electric shears and the chatter of men and women working the *board* was just a flick of the imagination away.

But all those thoughts were forgotten the second I laid eyes on a lean, half-naked Holden, broom in hand, the muscles of his bare back bunching and stretching with every to-and-fro sweep over the wide-plank floors. With his back to me, he never even looked up, his filthy jeans hugging his spectacular arse, his lean hips swaying slowly to the beat of the music, and I couldn't take my eyes off him. And when he dipped the broom to the side and shimmied up and down putting that tight hard body on full display, the sight made me smile for all the right reasons, and blood pulsed low in my belly.

Fuck me, he was pretty to watch.

Shields up, red alert. I shook my common sense free of my dick and rapped on the door. "Hello?"

Holden spun, his palm slamming against his chest. "Jesus Christ, Gil, you scared me."

I waggled my eyebrows and mimed giving myself a point.

He threw his broom to the floor and stabbed a finger my way. "Dammit. You did that on purpose." He reached for his phone and dialled the volume right down.

"What? Came in the door and said hello?" I scoffed, raising my palms. "Guilty as charged."

He grumbled something that sounded suspiciously like *cheeky fucker*, but I let that one go. "Is this your first time inside the shed?" He picked up the broom and leaned it against the wall, seemingly avoiding my gaze.

"It is." I set the cool bag on a long wooden bench and wandered over, watching how his gaze immediately skittered away. "I like what you've done with the place."

He shrugged. "Inflicting some semblance of order before chaos descends in a couple of weeks." He swept his arm around the space. "Welcome to the woolshed—shrine to the hallowed merino, den of iniquity, and leveller of egos. Where the sheep get their own back."

I laughed, mostly to be polite because it was clear he wasn't comfortable with me being there, something borne out by the ensuing silence that fell thick and awkward between us.

With only the shuffling of the ewes and the low bass beat of the music for accompaniment, I wandered to the nearest shearing stand and pretended to look around. Holden watched, his gaze intent, like he was trying to work me out.

Well, good luck with that.

"I ran into the vet outside." I made my way over to the penned sheep who took one look at me and headed for the opposite railings. "He's a very . . . *friendly* guy." I glanced back in time to see Holden's frown deepen.

"Oh god," he groaned, following me over. "He came on to you, didn't he?" He sounded more than a little cross. "I can have a word with him if you like. The man has zero boundaries."

"Nah, he was just fishing." I leaned over the top rail and studied the ewes, their fleeces grey with dust. They'd formed a small circle, nose to bum, and were eyeing Holden speculatively.

"So, I gather he's not straight?" Doing a little fishing of my own.

Holden joined me at the rail, our elbows almost touching, and shrugged. "Spencer is bi and not in the least bit shy about it."

There was something about his amused tone that pricked my

ears, and I wondered if the two men had crossed paths . . . and beds . . . somewhere along the way. It would make perfect sense, but still, I pushed the uncomfortable thought to the back of my mind.

"He mentioned you've got some new breeding program you're trialling?" I hoped Holden's favourite subject might open him up. "He's impressed with your work, by the way."

A note of surprise crossed Holden's face. "Oh. Well, yes, I'm doing a bit of tweaking. Adding a few new bloodlines to see if we can improve the overall health and yield of the stock. It all helps future-proof the station." He wiped his hands on his thighs and waved for me to follow him over the railing and into the pen.

I stalled, and Holden's pretty brown eyes grew merry. "Come on. They don't bite."

"Says you," I grumbled, eyeing the sheep who stared back like they knew the lineage of every item of merino hanging in my wardrobe and weren't impressed. I swallowed my nerves and climbed the railings while protesting, "Your mother was very clear I wouldn't have to get up close and personal with the stock." I landed on the packed earth and the sheep stomped their feet in obvious disapproval. *Oh god.*

Holden leaned sideways, his breath fanning hot over my ear. "Stay close. They hunt in packs."

I shot him a wild look and he laughed.

"Just kidding." He patted my arm. "Wait here while I grab one for you."

My eyes popped. "What?" I squeaked. "No. No, no, no. *Not* for me. That was never in the contract."

Holden snorted and then approached the ewes, who eyed him warily but calmly stood their ground. "Grandad did a good job with his early breeding program." Holden's tone was relaxed and steady. "I'm just fine-tuning those lines for better disease resistance, winter resilience, better lambing percentages, and a finer wool yield." He made a grab for the closest ewe who gave a bleat of disapproval before quickly settling in his competent hands. And yes, my mind totally went there. "But even with the best genes, if you don't look after them right, you may as well not even bother."

He flipped the ewe onto her back, and to my surprise, she barely even protested. Holden inspected her face, took a look at her teeth, and cleared the dust from her eyes. "Poor feed, weather stress, inadequate shelter, and a whole list of other things will screw with your perfect little breeding plan. There's a saying; breed well, feed well, and keep them well. Animal husbandry is about the whole package."

Like all husbandry, I mused drily.

"And this little beauty is my favourite girl." Holden graced me with one of those high-wattage smiles I'd missed. "What do you think?"

I blinked. "About what?"

"About my girl, here." He nodded to the ewe.

I stared at him incredulously. "Who me?" I ran my gaze over the animal who looked . . . all right . . . I supposed. What the hell did I know?

Holden was obviously struggling to keep a straight face. "Sure. Why not you?"

I narrowed my gaze. "I have a feeling I'm being had, but whatever." I took a minute to study the ewe. "Okay, well, she's very . . . pretty?" I raised a brow and Holden's eyes sparkled with humour. "Cos I gotta tell you, Holden, that's a lot more believable than me saying she smells good because . . . whoa." I raised my hands and took a step back.

He laughed. "Yeah, you get used to it. They've been on the hill all summer, although I've grazed these ones a little closer to home to keep an eye on them."

"So, the others just wander around the mountains for months on their own?" It seemed so strange.

He shrugged. "Pretty much. I fly over the whole area at least once during the season to get a general feel for the spread of the mob, sometimes more if the weather's been dodgy. Then we do another scout pre-muster to help us plan. Some of the stock prefer to hang around the lower slopes and we catch sight of them fairly regularly. But otherwise, yeah, we turn them loose and they do their thing. Isn't that right Aunty?" He continued to coo to the ewe in some kind of secret sheep language that I wasn't privy to.

"Aunty?" I raised a brow.

"Yeah, she's the matriarch of this little group. Keeps the girls in line."

"Aw, you talk to them," I said delightedly. "That's pretty damn cute, just so you know."

"Of course I talk to them." He gently dragged the ewe closer, and I reflexively backed away. "We all respond to a little conversation and flattery, don't we, beautiful girl?"

I eyed him dubiously. "Not that I doubt your knowledge of women, but . . ." I left the comment unfinished.

He looked up with surprise and then barked out a laugh. "True, but then I've never met a woman with such a lovely crop of wool. If I had, who knows? I might've been tempted to change my . . . preferences."

I waved a hand in front of my face. "Thank you for an image I could've well done without and which I now can't unsee."

He chuckled. "You're welcome. Now, get over here. I want to show you something."

I stared at him for a moment, then flatly said, "I am *not* holding her."

"Understood." He swallowed another smile.

I warily closed the distance between us and was almost at his side when Holden's head whipped around and he hissed, "Look out, she's gonna charge!"

I reached the railing in a single bound before I caught Holden's strangled snort and spun to find him pissing himself with laughter.

"Arsehole," I muttered. "I'm out of here."

"No, wait, please." He laid a hand on my arm. "I'm sorry."

I arched a brow.

"Okay, I'm not. But you have to admit it was pretty funny." He gave me a shining look.

"No I don't." I straightened with mock indignation. "I have PTSD for f—eaven's sake."

He gave another snort, which I tried to ignore before eventually caving and laughing with him. "You're an arsehole. And it's not swearing if it's fact."

"I know. I know. And I'm sorry. I genuinely forgot about the PTSD thing." He tried and failed to look suitably contrite.

"Hmm, then it's just as well rogue sheep aren't on my list of triggers then, isn't it? And not a single word of this will pass your lips to the others, got it?"

Holden alternated between shaking his head and nodding. "Yes. Absolutely not. Affirmative."

I glared at him. "Shut up and just show me whatever you were going to."

Another ewe arrived to investigate Holden's leg and he glanced down. "Well, hello there, Dolly."

I frowned and shook my head. "They're so calm. I had the impression sheep were pretty scatty animals."

"They can be," Holden agreed, still cooing. "But these girls know me pretty well. I've been handling this group a lot over the last year. You'll notice the others will be much less amenable when we bring them down. Now look." He refocused on the ewe between his legs, parting her dusty dark grey wool to expose a deep rich layer of brilliant cream fading to almost white next to the skin, the long fibres formed in tiny, corrugated crimps.

"Oh wow," I marvelled, taken aback. "It's beautiful and . . . unexpected given how filthy they are on the outside."

"That's only dust." Holden rubbed his hand up and down the ewe's back, sending a grey cloud into the air. "The land's so dry at this time of year, the rabbits have to take a cut lunch." He again parted the wool. "But the fibres are dense enough that the dust doesn't penetrate far. Have a feel."

I shot him a horrified look.

"Come on. You can trust me."

"Yeah right." I regarded the ewe for far too long, aware of Holden biting back a smile at my obvious discomfort. Then I finally got my shit together, shoved down the niggling uncertainty, and joined him. "What I do for the sake of work relations," I grumbled, and reached a tentative hand toward the open fleece.

Without warning, Holden wrapped his hand around my wrist and buried my fingers in the thick spongy softness, my pulse beating in my throat under the electric sensation of his touch.

"It feels amazing, right?" He looked up from the fleece and our gazes locked, his bare shoulder hovering within licking distance, our faces close enough for me to make out the deep pools of black in his brown eyes and register the slight flare of his nostrils and the sharp intake of breath that matched my own.

"Y-yes. Amazing." I cursed my foolish brain and broke free of his hold, steering the conversation to safer ground. "What's the market for merino like?"

Holden released the ewe and wiped his hands down the front of those filthy jeans that had suddenly become the sexiest damn things I'd ever seen. "Up and down—"

I almost groaned.

"But there's been a solid resurgence with the sustainability angle. Wool's biodegradable, it requires less energy than polyester to produce and a lot less water than other natural fibres. It can even replace some plastics." He motioned for me to follow him out of the pen, which I gladly did. We crossed to a large wooden table where Holden grabbed a plastic bag hanging off a nail and tipped the bundle of wool it contained onto the slatted tabletop.

"This is called a classing table." He ran a hand over the smooth slats. "A classer sorts through the fleeces as they come from the shearers, cleaning, identifying, and documenting them ready for sale. This wool is from last year's shear. I keep it to show visitors. Take a look." He stepped aside, but not by much.

And just like that, the hot skin of his bare upper body was once again just a turn of the head and a lick away; the sweet-sour tang of his sweat mixed with the smoky spice of whatever cologne he wore playing havoc with my senses. I stared unseeing at the fleece, every cell in my body attuned to the man at my side.

CHAPTER TEN

Gil

"This is called a staple." Holden separated out a small section of the crinkly wool fibres and pressed them flat, and with considerable effort, I dragged my attention from his body to where it belonged. "These crimps are kind of like tree rings. We can tell a lot about wool growth and the animal's health from these alone. How long and strong the staple is, any weak points, and the diameter of the individual fibres, which are measured in microns. All are crucial for the sale price. The lower the micron, the softer the wool. But too low and it can lose its strength."

His passion shone through every word, reflected in the gleam in his eye and the way his hands moved excitedly, as he talked about warmth and wicking and breathability and a whole host of things that sailed right by me because . . . he was just so fucking there, taking up all the oxygen in the room.

Every maddening centimetre of him.

His bare shoulder tip formed a circle of fire against my own. His hand brushing scorch marks over mine as he moved the fleece and pointed out this and that. The soft brown hairs on his forearm, so close I could count each one. The wash of his breath across my cheek, sending goosebumps crawling down my spine as he talked and talked and talked—the words rattling in my head like scattered pinballs, their meaning eclipsed by waves of sensation, of vibrant, tingling living colour on a greyed-out life.

Second by second, Holden was forcing my body to remember, forcing it to break that dusty seal of grief. To bring me back to life without even trying, without even knowing what he was doing, and in a woolshed for fuck's sake. I was coming alive in a smelly, dusty, cobweb-strewn woolshed. I was feeling something more than grief and anger for the first time in forever.

And all I could do, all I *wanted* to do, was absolutely nothing. Nothing but let it happen. Nothing but let *him* happen . . . to me.

Holden suddenly stepped away, breaking the spell. "Buyers can stipulate the micron size range they want—"

I blinked and gulped a shaky breath.

"—which means we have to be consistent in what we deliver, or risk losing the contract. And contracts are a game changer. They give a guaranteed buy price for a number of years, which means stability for us and the confidence to invest money into the station. Without a contract, we're at the whim of the market from one year to the next. High-country farmers play the long game, not the short one."

"And that's why this buyer's visit is so important." I finally understood. "Your mum said you'd lost a contract before you took over."

Holden sobered, his face a mask. "Yeah. Grandad wasn't exactly thinking very clearly those last couple of years. Gran had her head in the sand and Mum was caught in the middle. Which meant Grandad was allowed to keep making decisions way longer than he should have, and we had problem after problem. Feed, the weather, a delayed muster, and a whole lot of other issues that stressed the animals and affected the quality of the wool. Those two years produced the worst fleeces we've put up in decades. The truth was, we deserved to lose that contract." He stared blankly at the fleece on the table, and I suppressed the urge to lay a hand on his arm.

"Knowing how much you love this place, it must've been unimaginably hard to watch that happen," I sympathised.

"We were *all* devastated." He looked up and I swallowed at the heartache swimming in his eyes. "I was lucky I had Tom. We kind of tag-teamed Grandad after that. Tom flat-out refused to do what Grandad asked most of the time, although he was careful not to argue face to face, and I acted like a buffer between them, taking the blame if Grandad started ranting about anything we did. The crazy thing was most of it slipped right past him. He hardly remembered what he said from morning to afternoon. But there were some big decisions he'd made on his own that we couldn't salvage, like cancelling orders that ran us low on winter feed."

"Oh no."

Holden opened his hands in a what-can-you-do manner. "And he'd switched around mustering dates so often that the stock was left on the hill almost a month too long, and it was pure luck we weren't hit by an early storm. We also lost our slot with the usual shearing gang and had to settle for a ring-in crowd who weren't up to scratch. The fleeces suffered. *Everything* suffered."

I drew a slow breath and tried to imagine Holden coping with such an impossible situation. "But your grandad eventually stood down?"

He gave a heavy sigh. "Was forced to, more like it. It was the one good thing that came from losing the contract. Gran had her blinkers ripped off and got Grandad properly assessed. That changed everything. She was told he shouldn't be making any important decisions and that was that. I was thrown the keys and told to get on with it."

"How'd that go down with your grandfather?"

He sighed and leaned his back against the table. "About as well as you can imagine. Something he made a point of letting me know every . . . single . . . day." There was a soft hitch to Holden's voice that made me want to hug him.

"I wouldn't have made it without Tom. I was . . . *am* still pretty green. It's pretty humbling to try and run a station this size when most of your staff know a hell of a lot more than you do."

It was the first obvious chink in Holden's confidence, and for a second I was thrown. Something else I'd been wrong about. "Seems like you've done a good job so far," I tried to point out.

He huffed. "Don't take offence, but I'm not sure you'd know the difference."

"Ouch." I chuckled. "The practical side of that might be true, but reading people is very definitely in my wheelhouse. And I've seen how your team are around you, Holden. They're open and warm, but they also listen. They respect you. You're a natural leader. And that's why I think the station is in good hands. Your mother certainly thinks so."

His brows scrunched, but a pleased smile rode his lips. "She *has* to say that."

"Maybe," I conceded. "But Spencer doesn't, and he was talking you up big time outside. Batting on about your keen eye and good instincts."

Holden stared at me, clearly lost for words.

"So maybe you should try trusting those instincts of yours a little more and see what happens."

Holden blinked. Then his mouth drew up in a rueful smile and his shoulders relaxed. "Thanks. It's entirely possible I needed to hear that to—"

John Denver's "Country Road" filled the woolshed and Holden winced. He took out his phone and stared at the screen. "My grandfather," he explained. "I should probably take this."

I nodded. "Go ahead."

"Hey, Grandad." Holden walked off a few metres to talk and I headed back to where I'd left my bag, glad for the chance to calm the fuck down.

I didn't know whether to feel horrified or grateful for the flood of hormones reintroducing themselves to my body at an alarming rate. I settled for cautiously optimistic and chose to see it as nothing more than a sign of moving forward. Which was exactly what I was there for, right?

Right.

Didn't mean I was going to act on it. Not at all. That would be a bad move. A very bad move.

I started unpacking the bag onto the bench while continuing to steal the occasional look Holden's way. His tone grew louder and more frustrated by the second, the tension returning to his shoulders, his fingers dragging through his hair, the toe of his boot kicking lightly at the bottom railing of the pen.

The call ended abruptly, and when Holden rejoined me, his distress was palpable.

"That sounded... tricky," I offered in sympathy.

He pocketed his phone with a nod. "Yeah, he gets pretty confused sometimes. It can be hard to take."

I wondered how far to push. "Dementia is a godawful thing."

Holden said nothing, just stared at the woolshed floor, and my heart squeezed for him.

"Well, I'm here if you ever need to talk," I offered. "I'm a pretty good listener. Kind of goes with the territory. Not that I can sort my own shit out, of course."

Holden looked up with that playful glint back in his eye, and it suddenly clicked I'd just sworn.

"Damn," I grumbled. "I guess that makes us even. I've started a running total on the fridge."

"Yeah." His gaze slipped sideways. "I . . . saw."

It was as good a segue as any. "Oh really? That's good to know. I'd begun to think you'd developed a sudden allergy to the kitchen, or maybe just to me."

He grunted something that sounded like, "Don't be ridiculous."

I bristled. "You wanna try that again?"

He finally met my eye, his expression guarded. "Sorry, I've been a bit—"

"Busy, I know." I fired him a long level look which said I wasn't buying his bullshit, and a red stain crept up his neck. *Excellent.* I ferreted in my bag for the tea towel I'd packed, spread it over the bench, and began opening the containers.

Holden watched with obvious confusion as I poured a tumbler of ice-cold lemonade and sat it alongside two tan slices oozing with still-warm caramel and two cheese scones with their accompanying wrapped slice of butter. "What's all this?"

"Morning tea. Thought that might be obvious even to a man who seems to be surviving on fresh air." I let the pointed observation hang and watched with satisfaction as the colour in Holden's cheeks deepened.

He stared blindly at the array of food. "But . . . why? I left you a note. I'm fine. I don't need food delivered for f—Pete's sake."

"Why? Because this is my *job,* Holden. The one you and your mother employed me to do." I eyeballed him. "I have detailed instructions from Emily like you wouldn't believe. And included in those was morning tea, along with every other meal of the day, at least as far as you're concerned. Not that you're making it easy for me."

Holden still hadn't met my eyes, his teeth too busy worrying his bottom lip.

I took it as permission to continue. "You've blown off every meal I've prepared since Saturday, and although I'm trying not to take it personally, it's hardly the vote of confidence in my ability that I was aiming for."

A pair of horrified eyes finally met mine. "No, that's not it at all. I just . . . I wasn't sure how to . . . ugh." He groaned, and his shoulders slumped. "Okay. I screwed up. I'm sorry."

I shrugged. "I don't want or need an apology, Holden. I need you to talk to me. You told me on that first day that I'm part of this team, so how about you treat me like that. We seemed to be getting on well until you did a one-eighty on Sunday. If my being here makes you uncomfortable for any reason, then it's not too late to get someone else. You can't head into a muster if you don't gel with the person who's manning home base—something else Emily drummed into me. And just so you know, your mother wears the same perfume my own mother did, which means I'm obliged to do everything she says." I tried for a smile. "It's a law or something. But she also told me that you rarely miss meals, so . . ." I raised a brow and left the unspoken question hanging.

Holden blinked, looking suddenly miserable. "You don't make me feel uncomfortable." He shook his head and sighed. "At least not in the way you think."

You wanna bet?

"So, enlighten me." I pulled one of the scones apart and began slathering it with butter—the aroma of warm cheese, onion, and melted butter rising between us.

Holden licked his lips like he couldn't stop himself. "Oh god. Are they—"

"Yes. Cheese and onion and cayenne pepper. That's what you said, right?"

He looked confused. "But that was for the bet."

I shrugged. "I'm not above a little bribery. The bet still stands. I just want you to see that I'm actually a pretty good cook."

His smile faltered and a warm hand landed on my forearm. "I was never worried about that. Sorry if I've been a jerk."

I tried to ignore the buzz riding my skin from the pressure of his hand. "Just a little bit." I reached for our drinks and out of his grasp, handing him one of the tumblers before taking the other for myself. "Nothing we can't get past."

He stared at the lemonade for a long second before taking a sip. Then he swallowed and looked up. "Full disclosure?"

I put my back to the wall and gave him my full attention. "Sounds interesting."

He smiled thinly. "This is going to be embarrassing."

"I can't wait." I felt a little bad for putting him through the long version, but I needed to know if I was right.

He rolled his eyes. "So, you're kind of hot."

I blinked. It wasn't exactly what I'd been expecting.

"And . . . well . . . I'm *gay*." He stared like he was willing me to understand. "Do I really have to spell it out?" He fell back against the dusty wall and stabbed at the floor with his boot. "See, embarrassing."

I hid my smile behind my lemonade and waited him out.

"It's not an excuse for ghosting you, I know," he continued earnestly. "But let's face it, I don't get out much." His mouth curved up in some semblance of a cheeky smile and I laughed.

"So maybe I'm not *that* hot," I teased. "Just . . . here . . . and alive, right?"

He rolled his eyes. "Oh no, you are definitely *that* hot."

I ignored the flutter in my chest as he continued.

"Anyway, Charlie called me out for making my . . . *appreciation* obvious that day of the swim, and let's just say, I was made aware it wasn't a good look . . . as their boss, as *your* boss." He shrugged. "It's something I'm still adjusting to."

It was just as I'd thought, which was a relief of sorts.

"And it was disrespectful to you," he clarified. "If I made you uncomfortable, I apologise. I was embarrassed, and I suppose I thought it might be wise to create a little distance."

"Yeah, thanks for that," I said drily, then hesitated just a second before adding, "But what makes you think I'm straight?"

Holden froze, like he was unsure if he'd heard correctly. "Ah . . . maybe the fact you didn't say anything on the drive in when I told you *I* was gay?"

I screwed my eyes tight for a second, then opened them again. "Yeah, sorry about that."

He stared at me, slowly shaking his head, but he wasn't smiling. "I've been beating myself up for three days thinking I'd made you uncomfortable, and all along you were—" He hesitated. "What, gay?"

I nodded.

His lips pursed. "Right."

I gave a tentative half-smile, which wasn't returned.

"Can I ask why you didn't say anything? And why you made me go through all . . . this?"

And there it was. My heart thumped wildly against my ribs as I answered. "Call it self-preservation."

"Self-preserv—" He gaped, then squinted at me again. "And what exactly does that mean?"

I threw his own words back at him. "Do I have to spell it out?"

His eyes widened. "You mean you—" He wiggled a finger between us but didn't finish.

I held his gaze, sinking into those beautiful brown eyes that admittedly looked less than impressed with me in that moment. "Yes. I'm attracted to you as well."

He looked positively thunderstruck, and it was far, far too charming. He huffed out a laugh. "Well, at least I wasn't crazy. When we drove back from Tekapo, there were times it felt like maybe you . . . like we—" He stopped mid-sentence.

"Yeah." I shrugged. "We have chemistry, I guess."

"Chemistry." Holden said the word flatly, continuing to stare like I was a bug on a slide.

I shrugged. "I hoped that if you thought I was straight, then *I* wouldn't have to deal with *my* inconvenient and unexpected attraction."

"*Were* you going to tell me?"

I winced. "Possibly." I waggled my hand. "Maybe?"

Holden gave a disgusted shake of his head. "Don't get me wrong, you don't owe anyone any explanations. It's your life and I get that you're here for a very specific purpose. I'm just pissed for entirely selfish reasons."

"It wasn't just that." I slumped on the bench and set my beaker of lemonade aside. "I haven't been with a man since my ex-husband left six months after Callie died."

"Oh . . . fuck." Holden sank at my side, reaching out as if to take my hand before sliding his safely under his thigh.

"It's a long story." I leaned back against the dusty wall. "And one that started well before the accident. In the end, we couldn't be there for each other when it really counted, and things . . . fell apart."

Holden stopped fighting himself and took my hand. It felt . . . nice, and I covered it with my own. "I'm so sorry." He squeezed gently. "That must've been really hard for you on top of everything else."

I snorted derisively. "Yeah, the timing could definitely have been better." But then I hesitated, adding, "But if Luke *had* stayed, who knows? Things between us might've been even worse at the end. Because I have no doubt we were heading there, regardless." I thought of Tucker's comments, and for the first time, the idea didn't sound like a lie anymore.

"It still had to hurt."

I couldn't find the words to tell him just how much, and so I let it go. "After that, I pretty much went into complete lockdown, emotionally at least. I haven't so much as hooked up or even been attracted to a man since he left, and if I'm being honest, things weren't that great between us even before Callie died."

Holden winced. "Ouch."

I shrugged. "Marriages have their moments. The sex part is no different from the rest. I hadn't quite given up hope, even if Luke had."

A frown creased Holden's brow. "I guess I can understand that."

"Said in the tone of a what I'm guessing is a perpetually single guy who can't imagine sex never featuring at the top of the list."

Holden blushed furiously. "Guilty as charged."

"Nothing to feel guilty about. I remember it only too well." I lifted my hand and he quickly slid his back to the bench. "Anyway, next thing I know, I meet you and find myself inexplicably thinking about stuff I haven't considered in a long time. It took me by complete surprise. I didn't know what to think other than it was terrible, terrible timing. And so, I said nothing, figuring the alternative had the potential to majorly complicate my time here."

Holden huffed somewhat indignantly. "I hate to burst your

bubble, but just because you're gay and, okay, *hot* doesn't necessarily mean I'm going to jump into bed with you. I could've had a boyfriend. You're not *that* irresistible."

I snorted. "Yes, I do realise that, Holden, but thank you so much for reminding me."

The corner of his mouth quirked up. "Any time."

I met his soft gaze and found myself saying, "I think I was more scared than anything else."

And there was his hand again. "About being hurt?"

My eyes remained steady on his. "About feeling *anything*. Anything at all." I blinked furiously and looked up at the huge cobwebbed beams above our heads.

Holden stood and pulled me up into a hug. I went without thought, without any fight at all, my hands sliding around his waist as easily as they'd done in my fantasies, the first time in another man's arms, other than Luke, for over seventeen years. A man who wanted me in ways I wasn't at all sure I could give.

And it wasn't terrible.

Not terrible at all.

It was the exact opposite.

And Holden didn't push, he kept his hands high and safe. In fact, he barely moved at all. He simply held me, and I clung to him in return, his burning skin flush against my cheek, my lips, the palms of my hands, my entire body alert to every nuance of his—the quickening of his muscles, his breath against my hair, the soft rumble in his throat. I felt safe and seen and appreciated, and it was so fucking good I never wanted to let go. But then I felt the warm press of his lips against my hair and froze.

Holden immediately loosened his hold and leaned back, keeping his hands steady on my shoulders. "Are you okay?"

I lifted my hands to wipe my eyes, but Holden pulled them away and ran his thumb under each one instead, his pupils darkening. The salty tang of his skin sat fresh on my lips, teasing, tempting, impossible to ignore. And I realised with a jolt that I wasn't even going to try.

I lifted up and pressed a gentle kiss to the corner of his mouth.

Once.

Twice.

He gave a soft gasp but didn't move.

I went back for more, smoothing my lips over his, one side to the other, my tongue sliding over the plush surface while he stood still but not frozen, his mouth moving ever so slightly against mine, his needy groan filling my mouth.

It would've been so easy to just crawl into his lap and take what I wanted, what I craved, and what I was pretty sure Holden wanted as well. But instead, I found myself pulling away.

He chased my lips for just a second before giving a soft grunt of understanding, the huge black of his eyes slowly receding to brown.

We shared a shy smile, and I tucked one of those long, dark waves behind his ear before running my fingertip down his throat. He shuddered, his nipples pebbling under my touch.

He took my hand and turned it over, studying the slight shake I'd been trying to hide. "I'm sorry if I did this," he said, looking into my eyes.

And those walls just kept crumbling. "*You* didn't. It's just a big change for me, feeling all these things again. Like walking out into a storm. I'm not sure if I'm exhilarated or terrified."

He lifted my palm to his lips and planted the softest of kisses there. "I wish I knew what was going through that pretty head of yours."

I huffed. "Maybe then you could tell me and we'd both know."

He smiled. "I'm not such a bad listener myself, just so you know. Any time."

I swallowed around the sudden lump in my throat. "Thank you."

"And also—" He leaned in again, stopping just a breath away. "—that was the saddest first kiss of my entire life." He brushed his nose against mine. "Like hello and goodbye all wrapped up in one."

I had no answer for him because he was right. And because I was having trouble even breathing.

And so, I reached behind me, nabbed what I was looking for, and offered it between us. "Scone?"

He stared at it for a second then blurted out a laugh and took it, saying, "I take it we're done talking?"

I ran the back of my knuckles along the scruff of his jaw, feeling the jolt of want going right to my balls. "Please. This has been a lot for me."

He frowned and his eyes searched mine. "Gil, I know I'm not a good bet for much of anything, but if you ever—"

"Shhh." I put a finger to his lips. "I'm not a good bet *at all*, Holden. Not right now. And to be honest, I never was much of a casual sex kind of guy." I rolled my eyes. "Married at twenty-three, right? Kind of says it all. But I'm pretty sure that part of my personality hasn't changed, which could be a big problem with how fragile I am right now. I'm not sure I have it in me to handle another loss of *any* kind."

I watched as he fought some internal battle before finally giving a nod. "Got it."

"Thank you. So . . . friends?" I ventured.

"Definitely friends." His mouth tipped into a huge fucking smile and all I wanted was it back on mine.

I cleared my throat. "Well, that's good then."

Holden smirked at the rough cut to my voice, and I found myself blushing.

I gave him a playful shove. "Shut up and eat."

He chuckled and took a huge bite of his scone, sending melted butter running through his scruff.

I swallowed hard, absolutely *not* wondering how it would feel to brush that oily smear clean with my thumb, and certainly not my tongue. And by the unapologetic grin spreading over Holden's face, he'd known exactly where my mind had gone.

"You're so not funny." I scowled, which only made him laugh and make an even bigger performance out of wiping the crumbs from the dark curls on his chest.

Give me strength.

"The guys are gonna go nuts for these." He moved on to one of the tan slices, downing it in two bites before finishing his drink.

"So, we're good now?" I flicked a finger between us. "No more skipping meals or leaving notes that piss me off?"

His brown eyes softened. "We're good." He hesitated like he had something to add, then closed his eyes and sighed.

"Holden?" I put a hand on his arm.

Another sigh. This one heavier. "I brushed you off before, when you asked about my grandad." He opened his eyes. "Gran gave the staff a cell phone for him to use. The nurses dial the number, then leave him to talk. Mum and Gran love it and he's fine with them."

"But not with you?"

He shook his head. "Ever since he was made to step down, he's been nothing but angry with me. I know it's the dementia, but it doesn't make it easier. He berates me, the other shepherds, everything we do. And lately he's started in on me being gay."

"Oh, Holden. I'm so sorry."

His glassy eyes met mine. "He wasn't like that before. He was always tough but kind. He never once mentioned me being gay after I came out, but he never said a word against me either. He loved . . . *loves* me. I know that. It's just that sometimes it's hard. I want to do him proud with the station, with his legacy, but it kills me that he'll never know. That all his brain will let him do is resent me for it."

"Does Emily know?"

"No," he said emphatically.

Oh, Holden.

"She and Gran would be horrified. Besides, I can handle it, and I do . . . most of the time . . ." He trailed off, his gaze sliding away.

I turned his face back to mine. "You've got a lot going on, Holden. The muster. Crutching. Your mum heading to the UK. Me arriving. The contract. That's a lot of stress for one man. Maybe it's time to think about telling them what's going on. It's hard work absorbing the punches. It wears you down."

The look in his eyes sharpened. "Is that your professional opinion?"

I stepped back and studied him. "As a matter of fact, it is."

His annoyance dissolved. "I'm sorry."

"No, I get it," I reassured. "I've done the same thing for over a year, rejecting any and all suggestions and offers of help. We're ready when we're ready, right? Maybe it's time I took some of my own advice."

He cocked a brow.

"I've yet to make my next appointment with my therapist, like I promised I would."

"Ah." Holden finally smiled. "Then here's the deal. You do that this afternoon, and I'll promise to think about telling Mum before she leaves."

"Psychologists don't make deals," I said loftily.

Holden shot me a patient look. "Then it's just as well I'm not asking you as a psychologist, isn't it?"

I huffed. "Okay. It's a deal. Now will I see you for lunch?"

He nodded. "You'll see me."

"Good." I gathered my bag. "Better make it one o'clock. I'm delivering lunch out to the others at Folly Hut first."

"River Hut," Holden corrected with a smile.

"Right. River Hut." I cursed my memory. "Your mother drew me a map."

"You want company? I can ride shotgun if you're not sure of the track."

"Nope." I dusted off my hands. "The rivers are low, I've officially graduated from the Emily Miller off-road driving school, and I've got a radio if I get into trouble outside of cell reception. How hard can it be?"

Holden's expression was curiously neutral. "I'll keep the radio close."

"Oh, ye of little faith." I finished packing the bag and then paused at the open door. "Besides, your mother said I was way easier to teach than you. A natural, according to her."

Holden scooped something from the floor and my eyes flew wide.

"You wouldn't dare!" I lunged for daylight but not quick enough to avoid the balled-up wad of dried, smelly dags that hit me on the back.

CHAPTER ELEVEN

Gil

I tiptoed my way across the front deck, sidestepping the two creaky planks so I didn't wake Holden, whose bedroom sat just metres away on the other side of the front door. Since our tête-à-tête in the woolshed, I'd given up hiding around the corner, opting instead for the comfort of the outdoor couch and chairs piled high with bright cushions. I sank into the pillowy softness, put my glass of water on the deck, and pulled the handknitted throw over my legs.

Two weeks into my time at the station and the temperature had quickly shifted from dusty, scorched earth, into the pleasantries of autumn—cooler nights and mornings, with warm dry days bridging the gap between. The first frosts were already on the horizon, and I felt a palpable excitement for a change from the endless heat and dry winds.

A cool breeze nipped at my face, and I gathered the edge of the throw under my chin. The half-moon painted the surface of the lake like a skin of shimmering silver against the shadowy mountains, the soft chatter of the braided river softening the stillness.

Stealing these few moments alone at the beginning of the day had become a precious routine. Up at four thirty—a half hour before Holden—I put the espresso machine on along with the oven, then took myself onto the deck for thirty minutes of silence . . . peace . . . magic . . . solitude . . . all of the above.

Whatever you wanted to call it, my battered heart soaked it up, and piece by piece my tangled world was beginning to smooth out. It was slow but it *was* happening. Almost like the mountains were pressing me flat to the edges—exposing parts of me that had been hidden in the folds of grief and anger for eighteen months.

I'd told my clients time and time again, *'You have to see it, you have to feel it, before you can work on healing it.'*

And I'd avoided precisely that for eighteen months. I hadn't been ready. It hurt too much to shine a light on a lot of it. To remember. To feel. And I still felt raw and exposed. Most days I wanted to crawl back into those folds and disappear once again, but day by day it was slowly getting easier not to. The genie was out of the bottle.

I'd kept my promise to Holden, called my therapist, and we'd had an honest discussion about my medication, talked more about Callie's death and Luke's leaving, and I'd even told Leonard about the unexpected awakening of my libido. Rather than be cautionary, he'd been encouraged, saying it was progress. I'd almost laughed. It was high praise from the buttoned-up man.

Holden had checked I'd followed through on my side of the agreement and assured me he was still considering speaking up about his grandfather as well. He had a couple of weeks to go before Emily left, and I wasn't sure which way he would go.

In addition to my morning time, I'd fallen into a satisfying rhythm in the kitchen. Somewhere along the way, I'd forgotten how creative and soothing it was for my soul. I was contributing again. I was appreciated. A sense of purpose was slowly creeping back into my daily life, and my heart was lighter for it.

But it wasn't a miracle cure. The nightmares hadn't stopped. I still woke some nights with my hands shaking and a suffocating panic gripping my chest, guilt sour in my throat. I still needed my pills, although I was doing my best to cut down where I could with Leonard's guidance.

Even Tuck had felt the difference, saying he could hear it in my voice, that I was laughing more, and was definitely more relaxed. I made no mention of Holden, but then again, there was nothing to say.

Which was the lie I kept telling myself.

In two weeks, Holden, Emily, and I, and sometimes Harry, had become this odd little domestic unit. And along with the often-raucous station lunches held around the kitchen table, they'd gone some way toward filling the family-shaped hole in my life.

I drew a long, slow breath and let it fall from my lips into the cool morning air.

In and out.

In and out.

The last of the stars danced in my head, and I watched them drift and tumble into the lake.

In and out.

Until a rumbling snore dispelled my carefully woven peace and made me smile.

Holden.

How very apt.

Breaking into my stillness just as he broke into my thoughts on an all too regular basis, his quick humour and warm smile always at the ready.

Less clear was whether that was a good thing or not.

Even less was whether I cared a damn about the answer to that anymore.

I glanced over my shoulder toward Holden's open window—images of him all sleep-rumpled in his bed loosening feelings I'd given up trying to ignore.

I wanted Holden. I wanted him badly. I wanted him in my bed, and it was getting harder and harder to keep a lid on that.

Every day we did this polite dance around each other, chatting and organising and planning, but the space between us sparked and crackled. I knew the minute Holden walked into a room. I knew his scent and the weight of his footfall. I knew his irritated voice from his tired one, his genuine smile from his patient one. I knew when his grandfather had called. I saw it on his face and felt it in the way he looked to me as if seeking comfort.

I found myself tracking his every move, stealing looks, and finding reasons to drive out to wherever they were working that day to make him laugh, getting close in any way I could. Every night we cleaned the kitchen up together, elbows jostling, hips brushing, a touch, a laugh, electricity flickering over my skin like a play of lightning. We both knew I didn't need the help, but Holden never missed, and we both knew why. And if our feet met by chance under the dining table when everyone was gathered for lunch, neither pulled away, but neither was willing to catch the other's eye and acknowledge this unnamed *thing* between us, either.

I hadn't packed lube and I was running out of lotion. I couldn't decide whether Holden was just this delicious distraction keeping my mind occupied and off the work I needed to do, or whether the fire he lit inside me was one of the threads helping to piece me together. But without an answer, all I could do was watch him and want him, too paralysed by uncertainty to do anything more.

My phone flashed to signal my thirty minutes were up. I picked my way back to the kitchen, stepping through the open door and—

"Shit!" My hand flew to my chest, the dregs in my water glass sloshing to the floor. "Alek?" I took a moment to calm my racing heart. "What the heck are you doing here?"

Alek stepped back with his hands raised. "I'm sorry. I saw the light and wanted to ask Holden something."

"He's still in bed." I counted slowly in my head, the warnings of a panic attack starting to recede.

Alek's cheeks coloured. "Yes, of course. I'm sorry. It was—" He hesitated, clearly struggling for the word. "—stupid of me." He spun on his heels, but I grabbed his arm.

"Stop. Please." I glanced at the clock. "Take a seat. He won't be long. I'll get you a coffee while you wait."

Alek glanced longingly at the espresso machine and nodded. "Thank you."

"You like it strong, right?"

Another nod and I smiled to myself. The big Russian wasn't known for his small talk.

I carried our coffees to the table—Alek's being strong enough to strip the enamel off your teeth—and sank into the chair opposite.

He took a tentative taste and beamed. "This is good."

"Don't sound so surprised. I know how everyone takes it."

His gaze swept the kitchen before landing back on me. "So, you like it . . . at the station?"

"Yeah, I do."

He seemed perplexed. "But this . . . very different for you, no?"

"It is." I tapped my chest. "But right now, it fills my heart."

Alek's normally stoic expression grew soft. "That was a terrible thing that happened. I am sorry."

"Thank you." I rubbed the back of my neck. "How about you? Do you like it here?"

Alek nodded. "Farming—" He tapped his chest just as I had. "—fills *my* heart. Helps me . . . breathe."

My throat thickened because I knew exactly what he meant, but I was not going to fucking cry. Instead, I said, "It is who you are."

He processed that for a minute, his brow furrowed, then he smiled almost shyly. "Yes. Yes." He glanced nervously in the direction of the hallway where the thump of pipes announced Holden was in the shower. "Maybe I wait. Another time."

I ducked my head to catch his eye. "Alek, is there something *I* can help with?"

"No," he said quickly, then shrugged. "I don't know." His gaze slowly lifted to mine, and the misery I saw there made my heart hurt.

My hand covered his without a second thought and he stared at me with dark, penetrating eyes that sometimes reminded me of Holden's.

"My brother, he is in . . . trouble . . . back home," he said haltingly. "My cousin says I must stop writing."

Shit. "I'm so sorry, Alek."

He broke into a stream of Russian that needed no translation. "I'm sorry," he apologised. "I . . . worry."

I waited him out.

"My brother . . . he is . . . different." Alek freed his hand and dropped his eyes to the table. "I think maybe he is . . . like Holden?" He stole a quick look at me through those long, dark lashes.

Oh. I schooled my expression. "Do you mean gay?"

Another quick look, then a curt nod.

I guessed it was as good a time as any. "Well, I'm also gay, if that helps?"

Alek's expression was almost comical. "You?"

I shrugged. "Last time I looked. It's not a secret, Alek." *Well, not anymore.*

"But . . ." He sighed and fell back in his chair. "This country . . . crazy."

I chuckled at that.

Things fell quiet for a moment before Alek said, almost under his breath, "I miss my family."

"I can imagine," I sympathised. "My parents both died separately before I was twenty-one, and I have no brothers or sisters. There's no filling that hole, right?" I put a fist over my heart.

Alek's bleak expression said he knew exactly what that felt like.

"But it is possible to create a new type of family for yourself *here*, if you wanted. It would be different, but maybe just as important."

He looked sceptical.

"You have friends here already. The team. They might not replace your family, but they could help fill that hole inside if you let them. None of us thrive in a bubble." *Including me.*

"And I'd be honoured to be one of those people." Holden's steady voice came over my shoulder and I spun to find him standing in the open doorway.

"Well, good morning." I smiled and got to my feet. "We have an early visitor."

Alek leapt to his feet. "I am sorry. It was rude of me."

Holden and I traded glances, then he waved Alek back into his chair. "That's what Gil and I are here for, right, Gil?"

I warmed at being included and at the way Holden's bright eyes caught mine in obvious approval.

"You heard?" Alek eyed Holden nervously.

Holden took a seat. "A little. How about you tell me the rest?"

Without thinking, I reached out and squeezed Holden's shoulder. "I'll get more coffee."

"Thanks." Holden laid his hand over mine and our eyes locked for a beat too long.

The exchange wasn't missed by Alek judging by the curious look he sent our way. I wasn't sure if Holden had considered how that easy touch would look to Alek now that Alek knew I was also gay, but since I'd already said it wasn't a secret, I was betting news would travel fast.

So be it. Leonard's recent counsel rang loud in my ears. *Maybe try not to control every tiny little thing in your life. You took a huge step moving out of your comfort zone and the world didn't end. Just a thought.*

I headed into the kitchen and left them to talk, stealing glances from time to time and appreciating Holden's warm inviting manner with his staff. When they were done and Holden reached across and squeezed his hand, Alek almost startled at the touch.

"You've earned your place here, Alek, and we'll support you in any way we can if you want to try and get your brother into the country. We can guarantee him work, whatever. You only have to ask. I'll give you my friend's contact, and if you need me to talk to him as well, I can. Like Gil said, you don't have to do everything on your own. Maybe give us a chance."

Alek looked warily between us before a sigh broke on his lips. "Thank you."

Holden smiled warmly. "Good. Now drink your coffee. You're staying for breakfast."

He was?

"I am?"

He was. I smiled and readjusted my quantities of huevos rancheros while Holden engaged in a slightly mind-numbing conversation with Alek about stock numbers, drenching schedules, merino prices, and finally, which dog they'd choose if they could only have one.

I didn't have to think too hard about that last one. Spider was lying atop Holden's feet, totally oblivious and secure in the knowledge he was best loved of all, at least in his own mind . . . and mine. I cast him a fond glance, and as if on cue, he rolled onto his side and farted.

Holden grimaced and gave the dog a soft boot with his foot. "Dammit, Spy. You have to be dead inside to smell that bad."

Emily arrived halfway through and did a good job at hiding her surprise when her eyes landed on Alek chatting at the table with Holden. Twenty minutes later, with a full stomach, a box of Emily's homemade caramel crunch in his hand, and the biggest smile I'd yet seen on his face, Alek excused himself and left the kitchen.

Holden lingered to help me clean up, again, and we skirted around each other in a comfortable domestic dance like we'd been doing it for years. Emily cast us an amused glance from time to time but said nothing.

When we were done, Holden grabbed his keys and paused at the mudroom door. "What've you two got planned this morning?"

Emily looked to me. "A trip to restock the firewood at River Hut, wasn't that right?"

I nodded.

Holden shot me a look. "I was thinking about heading into Oakwood later on. I need to replace one of the electric drills, and I thought maybe Gil might be interested in coming along?"

My heart kicked up, because of course it did. An opportunity to spend more time with Holden? Hell yeah, I was interested.

"Oh." Emily looked between us, her gaze narrowing. "Actually, that's not a bad idea. So far, he's only been to the supermarket and a few of the supply stores. You could show him the rest of what our fair town has to offer. Gil?"

I caught Holden's determined stare like he was willing me to say yes, and nodded. "Sure. That'd be great."

He grinned. "Cool. We can take the Ranger. How about you pick me up from the woolshed at ten?"

I nodded and a smile broke over my face. The day was looking up.

I followed Holden into the mudroom with the weight of Emily's stare heavy on my back. We chatted as I watched him pull on his boots—another of those odd little rituals we'd developed that neither of us acknowledged.

I was losing the battle in spectacular fashion against whatever this was between us, and I knew Holden felt it too. It was in the way he tracked me across a room, and how his eyes lit up when he saw me at lunch, and the lightness I felt in my chest in return. The way we'd gravitate to *my* lounge in the evenings to watch a show or talk about nothing in particular. Or how he'd ask me to stay and have a seat when I dropped a coffee into his office, telling me his plans and what he hoped for the station. I'd started taking two mugs.

We both felt it. We both ignored it. Or at least we tried to.

But we were getting clumsy.

Getting overly familiar with each other.

The slip with Alek was a classic example.

"You do realise that everyone will know I'm gay by the end of the day," I warned, as Holden laced his boots.

His fingers fumbled for a moment but that was all. "I figured as much." He looked up. "Are you okay about that?"

Am I? "Yes. It's just . . ."

He waited, searching my face, for I didn't know what.

I gave him the only answer I had. "People are going to think—"

"What they want to think," he finished for me. He glanced into the kitchen and nudged the door closed. "Look, I don't know what's happening between us either. Do you think I planned this?" He hesitated, dragging a hand down his face. "Can we maybe not over-analyse things? You're not interested in starting anything, and so, whatever they think, *nothing* is happening, right?" He tipped my chin up. "Besides, I kind of like what we're doing. It's . . . nice . . . wholesome, even. Unless you don't like it?"

But I did, far too much, and that was the problem. "Holden, I—" But I didn't even know what I wanted to say, except, "Yeah, I like it too. But wholesome?" I snorted disbelievingly. "You clearly haven't seen inside my brain lately. And that doesn't mean it's okay."

"It is if we say it is." He smiled and reached for his hat. "Or am I wrong about that, *Doctor* Everton?"

I sighed. "You're not funny."

"Are you sure about that?" He smirked.

And I found myself smiling. He seemed to have that effect on me. "But that won't stop people wondering and likely talking."

He arched a brow. "Wouldn't have thought you'd be the kind of guy to care much about that?"

"I'm not. But I'm also not the one running this station," I reminded him. "I'm not the 'boss.'" I made air quotes.

He closed his eyes for a second and sighed before opening them again. "I know. I haven't forgotten. But the truth is, there's nothing to hide. We're not *doing* anything, are we?"

I handed him his windbreaker and eyed him pointedly. "Aren't we?" Because it sure as hell felt like we'd crossed a million lines somewhere along the way, emotionally if nothing else.

Holden peered up at the sky, deftly sidestepping my question. "We better not get an early storm. Grandad will have my hide."

"Is that likely?" I could ostrich with the best of them.

Holden shrugged. "I've seen snow in December *and* February, so yeah, anything is possible." He faced me again and I caught the hint of apology in those brown eyes.

"That was a nice thing you did for Alek," I said quietly. "You've got a good touch with your staff, Holden. You should be proud of that."

He blinked, looking surprised. Then he clasped a warm hand around my bicep, which caused my stomach to flip-flop in an alarming fashion. "That's the most Alek has said in one go, ever, and Lord knows we've *all* tried to open him up. This morning was down to *you,* Gil, *not* me. You're the one who should be proud of yourself. I know I am." He licked his lips, and for an explosive second, I thought he might kiss me.

My entire body screamed *yes,* but instead his mouth slid past to whisper in my ear, "Thank *you* for coming out and for telling him about your parents. Thank you for taking the chance." He leaned back and we locked eyes. "I think we could make a good team, Gil Everton."

There was so much unspoken in those innocent words. That current between us, that irresistible magnetic pull, like we both knew exactly what would happen if we gave in and let it.

But we didn't.

Holden let go of my arm and leaned back against the wall. "So, what do you want me to say if the others ask . . . *when* they ask? Because they sure as hell will."

I sucked in a breath and blew it out slowly. "Yeah, five bucks says three hours max till the ribbing starts. And just tell them what you feel comfortable with. I trust you."

"Okay then." He brushed a tangled nest of bed hair off my forehead, the soft look in his eyes making my toes curl in my thick woollen socks. "And I'll take that bet."

I watched until he disappeared around the back of the chicken sheds, my lungs tight, a lump in my throat the size of a softball, the touch of him fresh and hot on my skin.

"Gil?"

I spun to find Emily standing in the doorway, watching me with a curious look in place. I wasn't sure how much she'd heard or seen as she looked from me to the chicken sheds, then back again, a frown creasing her pretty brow. But whatever she might have wanted to ask, she didn't. Instead, she took her hat off the peg and banged it on her thigh, sending a cloud of dust flying. "Are you ready to drop the firewood at River Hut before the heat gets up? I'll have you back by ten."

I nodded enthusiastically. "Good idea. If you can stand me unshowered, that is?"

"I'll survive." She watched as I tugged on my boots, the heat of her gaze and all those unspoken questions burning a hole in the top of my head.

I sighed and shot her a look. "Just ask, Emily."

Her cheeks brightened and she drew a sharp breath. "This is a tough life, Gil, maybe even harder than it used to be, with all the conservation pressures. It wears on a person, and the high-country scenery provides zero immunity from mental health issues. We're no different from the rest of rural New Zealand. Only last year we lost a station owner up Hopkins River. Depression is a bitch and no one saw it coming. Isolation is a huge factor on these stations, and there's something about the 'just shut up and get on with it' attitude that we all wear like armour out in these parts that makes it even harder to talk."

I waited as she formulated what she wanted to say.

"Holden's a good man, Gil, not that I'm biased. But I worry about his heart, and being gay in these parts still has its challenges. It can add to the isolation."

I finished tying my laces, then looked up. "I'm not quite sure what you think—" I stopped at the don't-bullshit-me expression on her face and groaned. "Okay. So, how did you know?"

Emily's mouth curved up in a warm smile. "Because I know my son. And I've never seen him look at someone the way he does you. If you're in the same room, he can hardly keep his eyes off you."

Oh god.

"And the same goes for you."

"We're not *together*." I rushed to set her right, heat racing into my cheeks. "And also, is there a sign on my forehead or something? Because your vet picked me for not being straight as well."

"Spencer?" Emily looked amused. "No surprise there. That man is like a homing pigeon for dick. Just please don't hurt Holden if you can avoid it."

"And as *I* said, nothing's happening between us. Sure, we like each other, but we figured it wouldn't be a good move, for a lot of reasons."

She gave me a calculating look. "It's a tricky complication for a man who's looking to find himself."

I shook my head and stared out into the grey wash of morning brightening the backyard. "You'd be right about that."

"Mmm." She grabbed her jacket and ran her hand over my shoulder. "Doesn't mean it's wrong, Gil."

My gaze jerked up to find her regarding me with an indulgent smile.

"I thought you psychologist types would be experts on the whole 'you get what you need, not necessarily what you want' scenario. Now get a move on, it's a lovely morning for a drive."

And with that she turned and left, like she hadn't just dropped an emotional grenade into my backpedalling brain.

CHAPTER TWELVE

Holden

"But I can save you a trip and grab a drill when I head into town tomorrow," Sam insisted, and I considered shoving the container of drench I was carrying right down his throat just to shut him up. "Ow!" He jumped at the elbow Charlie landed in his ribs. "What was that for?"

"Oh my god." She gave in to the laugh that she'd been fighting for the past few minutes. "Sometimes, I really worry about you."

Sam flushed red, looking totally baffled. "I don't get it."

Charlie took him by the shoulders. "Okay, read my lips." Then she spoke in exaggerated slowness. "Holden is going into town *with Gil.*" She paused. "To pick up something that we don't really need."

"I know," Sam protested. "That's why I said I could—"

"*And—*" She talked over him. "—we just learned that Gil is *also* gay." She tossed me a meaningful look and I rolled my eyes. It had been like this ever since I'd arrived that morning.

Sam looked from Charlie to me, and I saw the moment it hit. "Oh. Oooooooh. Do you mean . . . are Holden and Gil—"

"No." I gave Charlie a playful shove out of the way and freed Sam from her grasp. "We're not *anything*," I corrected, glaring at an unrepentant Charlie. "We're just friends."

"But you'd like to be more." She waggled her eyebrows. "You forget I know you, Holden."

"Charlie, stop," I warned.

But all she did was roll her eyes. "Oh, come on, Holden. You've been mooning after the man since the first day he arrived. And I don't blame you. He's hot as fuck. Who wouldn't want him?"

Tom shot Charlie a warning glance, but all she did was smirk.

"Well, it's true," she said airily. "And why not? Holden deserves a bit of romance in his life."

"Oh, dear God." I dropped my chin to my chest and groaned. "I repeat. There is *nothing* romantic going on between Gil and me."

"Riiiight." Charlie stared at me, along with everyone else, and my cheeks did their thing, which was becoming a bit of a habit since Gil had arrived.

"You do realise that I'm technically Gil's boss." I spoke to everyone but kept my eyes on Tom, hoping to reassure him that I'd been listening to his advice. "It would be wrong to cross those lines."

Nobody said a word.

"Well, it would," I insisted.

"Say it loud enough and maybe you'll even convince yourself," Charlie deadpanned. "Jesus, Holden, do you really think any of us would give a damn? You're grown men. It's nobody's business but your own."

I shot her a pointed look.

"Well, and ours, of course," she added sweetly. "But only because we love you. Right, guys?"

Alek and Sam immediately nodded, while Tom said nothing.

Unexpected irritation sparked in my chest, along with something that felt shockingly like a protective urge. "That's enough." The order came out sharper than I'd intended, and everyone's heads snapped up. I took a breath and counted to five. "You all know that one of the reasons Gil came here was to work through losing his daughter. So how about we show him a little respect? He's been through a lot. The last thing he needs is us gossiping about him like he's cheap news. Me too, for that matter. Whatever you think about it, I'm supposed to be your boss."

Silence descended like a final curtain, swift and heavy. I'd never spoken to the team like that and I immediately regretted it. "I'm sorry guys, I—"

"No, you're absolutely right." Charlie moved closer and put a hand on my arm. "I *was* being a jerk. It's me who should be sorry. What you two have or haven't got going on is none of our business."

I caught Tom's nod of approval, whether at Charlie's apology or my unexpected outburst, it wasn't clear.

"Thank you." I pulled her in for a quick hug. "And yes, I like him, okay. But let's cut him *and* me a break."

Tom appeared alongside Charlie. "I should've shut it down before you got here, sorry."

Everyone gaped, including me. Tom rarely apologised. Admittedly, he rarely had anything to apologise about, but hey.

"I'm sorry too," Sam piped up. "To be fair, I didn't even get what it was about, but fucked if I'm going to be the only one who doesn't apologise."

"And of course, Gil's gay," Charlie stated. "I should've guessed. It's the only explanation for why he hasn't succumbed to my charms."

Sam rolled his eyes. "Oh, I could think of one or two others."

The sound of Gil's SUV approaching put an end to the banter.

"Behave." I glared at them, one by one, hoping for the impossible and groaning at Charlie's exaggerated zipping of her lips.

Gil parked alongside the cattle pens and jumped out. "Hey, guys."

"Well, good morning, Gilbert," Charlie returned ever so politely, and everyone turned to stare at her.

Oh, for Pete's sake. I'd kill her later.

Gil's narrowed gaze swept over the too-quiet group before focusing on me. "They know, don't they?"

I nodded.

He gave them another once-over before snorting and flipping them off. "Pack of arseholes."

"Already established," I deadpanned. "And you get a pass on that. They deserve it."

"Much appreciated." He flicked his fingers at me. "Pay up, loser. That was well under three hours."

Charlie gaped. "You took a bet on us? I think I'm offended."

"Damn right we did." I smirked. "You lot think you're funny, but you're really just way too predictable."

Gil held his hand up for a high five and I obliged.

"Right." I got everyone's attention. "Tom, can you check on that beefy we saw carrying a limp? Pen him here and I'll get Spencer to take a look. Charlie, work with Alek in the drafting race, will you? He needs the experience. And will *everyone* stop putting the half-empty drench containers back with the others?"

There was a sea of nodding and Charlie slapped Alek on the back. "I guess you're with me, handsome."

I took a final look around. "Right, then. I'll see the rest of you later. Alek, can I have a word?"

Alek frowned then made his way over. "Everything all right, Boss?"

"It's fine. I just wanted you to know that I gave my friend a call about your brother, and he'd like to talk to you. No promises, just the first step in a long process, he said. I'll email you his contact details and maybe you can set up a call or video link as a first step. But if you need to fly to Wellington, the station will cover all the costs and your time."

Alek's eyes widened. "But—"

"No buts. Like Gil and I said, we're a team here at the station, and that's what a team does."

Alek's eyes brimmed and he blinked furiously. "Thank you."

I patted his shoulder. "You're most welcome. But as you know, the process can take months or even years, and there's still no guarantee of success. This is just a start."

Alek nodded soberly. "I know."

"Good." I looked back to find everyone still standing and watching us. I opened my hands. "Do you all need a kiss goodbye or something?"

"Fuck, no." Charlie laughed along with everyone else.

"Then maybe you could get to work." I turned and held my hand out to Gil who stared at it blankly, so I added, "Keys?"

He snort-laughed and headed for the driver's side, giving my empty hand a slap as he passed. "Like hell. This is my vehicle, sunshine. Help yourself to the passenger seat."

He climbed in and fired up the engine, leaving me standing there looking like a jackass. I spun to find the others doubled over in not so silent laughter, because I always drove. *Always.*

I shot them a dirty look. "Not. A. Word." Then I climbed in the passenger seat and Gil turned to me, wearing a smug as fuck smile.

"You all right there, *Boss?*"

I shook my head but couldn't stop from smiling. "Just shut up and drive."

He murmured something that sounded like, "Yes sir," but I couldn't be sure. I was too busy staring in the side mirror and smiling at the reflection of my team howling with laughter.

Gil

We breezed into Oakwood with Peter Tosh jamming in my ears and the music wasn't . . . terrible. I knew zip about reggae beyond Bob Marley, but I hadn't been kidding when I told Holden I could pretty much listen to anything. Holden had taken that as permission to 'educate' me. And since I'd insisted on driving—I'd have paid good money to see that particular expression again—I figured I'd let Holden choose the music.

We chatted about nothing in particular all the way in, carefully avoiding the subject of whatever conversation I'd interrupted when I'd gone to pick him up. The team seemed pretty cool about me being gay, other than Tom, who'd been hard to read. Then again, he was always hard to read, and I figured it was more concern for Holden than about me. Tom was a shrewd man.

"I could be twenty minutes or longer," Holden warned as I passed the town's supermarket and pulled up in front of the hardware store. "Why don't you take a walk down Main Street and I'll meet you at Meg's Place, the café opposite the church? They have great coffee." He extended his hand for the keys and I laughed.

"I wasn't born yesterday, mister." I slapped them in his palm. "I'm still driving home."

His eyes danced with mischief. "Of course you are."

Oakwood was a pretty town with a pretty name and an eclectic mix of modern and old stone pioneer buildings. Large trees—presumably oaks—lined both sides of the street. In the early throes of autumn colour, they provided welcome shade, and along with colourful baskets of petunias hanging from the verandas, they created a welcoming ambience. But for all its appeal, the street was quiet, *too* quiet for eleven thirty on a weekday when tourists and locals alike should have been scouting for their daily hit of caffeine and sugar or even lunch.

The signs of lean times were hard to ignore. Pretty and historic buildings, the likes of which should've had tourists detouring and retailers clamouring, instead had lease signs hanging in their windows. There was a lazy, sleepy feel to the place, and although that wasn't without its charm, I didn't imagine it filled many wallets. Oakwood might've only been a sharp left off the main road, but judging by the quiet streets, it clearly didn't feature on many must-stop tourist agendas, which was a shame.

I passed a sizeable veterinary clinic with Spencer's name on the door, along with Matt Nicholson, presumably his business partner. Next to that was a modern concrete and glass building that housed a lawyer's office and an accounting firm—essential services for any rural district. A double-fronted shop had been converted into a small library, and there was the usual line-up of clothing shops, a bakery, pharmacy, a medical centre/emergency clinic, a dairy, and a few tired-looking restaurants.

On a corner at the end of the road sat the Oakwood Pub, an historic building with a wide second-storey veranda. The beautiful place was begging for a renovation that would likely cost a fortune. There was a metal shoe scrape outside the main entrance with a sign above that reminded patrons to please not walk sheep shit into the public bar. A second sign on the door itself informed patrons that food was available in The Fleece Bar at the back. I smiled at the cutesy name.

Opposite the pub stood an old stone bank with a plaque dating it to 1890 and a battered sign that read Blue Bird Café. A haulage van was parked out front, its team of men emptying furniture and assorted catering sundries into the old premises under the eagle-eyed direction of a blond, sharp-tongued young man clutching an iPad and barking instructions in a voice far too big for his slim frame. He was dressed in denim shorts, a white tank, and jandals and offered me a tight smile as I passed.

I returned a big grin, hoping to win him over, and he narrowed his gaze. So much for the friendly locals.

Next to the pub sat a tiny historic church clad in white weatherboard and with a cutesy bell tower and well-tended gardens. The busy noticeboard spoke of an active community, announcing the usual hodgepodge of activities from yoga to antenatal classes, coffee mornings, social media for the retired, the summer cricket tournament ladder, and so on.

"If you need your sins forgiven, the priest comes every other Sunday, or so I'm told."

I turned to find the young blond man eyeing me up, his iPad

clasped to his chest. He was older than I'd first thought, maybe mid-thirties, and his eyes were an arresting shade of light grey. Creamy pale skin clung to model-sharp cheekbones and an equally sharp mouth. A twisted silver feather hung from one ear and his tank offered a teasing glimpse of a tattoo stretching over one shoulder.

"Personally, I gave up on forgiveness years ago." His gaze narrowed on the church door. "But on the other hand, if you're looking for a good coffee—" He smiled and flicked his head toward the café opposite. "—Meg does one of the best in town." A sly look crossed his face. "And tell her I sent you. That'll put the cat among the pigeons. She thinks I'm gonna steal her squillion customers." He gave the empty street an exaggerated once-over. "The hordes have obviously got more important things to do today."

I couldn't help but laugh. "I'll keep that in mind. I'm Gil Everton, by the way." I offered my hand and he took it with a firm grip.

"I'm Roz Chandler. Nice to meet you. I'd like to stay and chat, but I better get back before one of these bozos drops another box. See you around, Gil Everton." And with that, the intriguing man was gone in a cloud of spicy cologne.

Still smiling and with no sign of Holden, I wandered around the back of the church and perused the tiny but immaculately kept historic graveyard. Every headstone told a story, and as I read one of a young girl taken in eighteen ninety-four at the age of nine, just a year younger than Callie, I thought of our daughter's ashes sitting on the bookshelf in my Wellington apartment and felt a stab of guilt.

I picked the worst of the lichen off the engraving and read it again. *Loving parents . . . angel in heaven . . . always be missed . . .* As I imagined her parents standing where I stood, I sucked in a shaky breath and reread the words over and over until they blurred. More than a century between us, but there was a kinship there that disregarded time.

"Long Haired Country Boy" rang softly in my pocket, and although I knew it meant Holden was looking for me, I wasn't quite ready to break away. Just a little longer.

A minute or so later, a hand slid into mine and stopped it shaking.

"There you are," Holden breathed the words close to my ear. "Are you okay?" Then he must've read the gravestone because he quietly added. "Yeah, I'm thinking not so much."

I couldn't find the words to answer, and so I just stood there. At some point Holden let go of my hand and circled my waist instead. I didn't move away, didn't want to. I let myself be held, let Holden take some of the weight for a while, leaning into him, drawing from his strength, staring at the grave, remembering.

How long we stood there, I had no idea, but eventually I found myself talking.

"Things fell apart really fast for Luke and me after the memorial service." I kept my eyes on the headstone. "Like she had been the only glue left holding us together. I like to blame Luke for leaving me when I needed him most, but the truth is, I didn't exactly make it easy for him to stay."

Holden squeezed my waist, pulling me closer, and I sighed and settled against him.

"We'd been having problems for a couple of years before the accident, but we were working on it, and I stupidly believed we'd come through it. But then Callie died, and Luke and I were like two planets orbiting the remnants of the dying star that had been our daughter. Without the force of her presence, we simply drifted away from each other."

My breath hitched and Holden cradled my head against his shoulder.

"We stopped talking." I fisted his T-shirt. "Stopped living in most of the ways that count. We were consumed with our grief and too angry with each other to talk. I thought he blamed me for forgetting the present that day. I was always doing that kind of stuff. Or for driving too fast, something I was also guilty of, although not that day. He never said it directly, but I knew he was thinking it. Not that it mattered. I blamed myself enough for both of us."

"Oh, Gil," Holden whispered into my hair.

"But the person I was really angry at was me," I pushed on. "Not that it stopped me tearing *him* down every chance I could, or just not talking at all. There was a lot of that. A lot of silence between us. And then there were the nightmares and the panic attacks, and neither of us was getting any sleep. Eventually Luke had enough and decided to leave. Honestly, I don't blame him. The way we were carrying on, neither of us had any chance of healing. If he hadn't left, maybe I would've gone myself? Who knows?"

Holden turned and brushed his lips over my temple. "I'm so sorry."

I slipped from his side and squatted beside the headstone. "We never buried or scattered Callie's ashes before Luke left. We didn't even decide which we wanted to do. She's just sitting on my bookshelf. What kind of father does that, Holden?" I stood and Holden pulled me back into his arms, my face pressed against his neck. "What kind of father leaves his daughter's ashes sitting on a shelf and just fucking walks away?"

"Shhh." Holden cradled the back of my neck with his hand. "The kind that loved his daughter so much, his heart crumbled, and he didn't know what else to do. You weren't ready, Gil. But one day you will be. You both will be. Luke must be feeling it too."

I pulled back, surprised to find his eyes glassy with tears. "Luke doesn't know where I am."

Holden frowned.

"I know, I know." I swallowed hard. "Tuck says he wants to talk to me. Maybe he wants to do something with her ashes, but I haven't felt . . . ready. Not yet."

Holden picked a sprig of lichen from my hair and flicked it aside. "That's a decision only you can make."

I groaned and for some reason stopped lying to myself. "It's not just that. I think I wanted to punish him a little. Keep him in the dark about me. God, I'm such a prick."

He gave me a quick, sad smile. "No, you're just grieving."

I buried myself in his arms once again, continuing to talk as he stroked my hair. "Luke had a fling with some young guy a while back, and it . . . hurt. I felt . . . forgotten, I guess, and it seemed like he was moving on from Callie, leaving me behind. I was so fucking angry with him. I still am if I let myself feel it. But I know it's not fair. I know he was just trying to have a life again, and it's not like we were together. Tucker told me it didn't last long, but I just couldn't understand how Luke could do that."

I stepped back and let my gaze drift over Holden's face. "And then I kissed *you* that day in the woolshed." I ran my thumb over his full lips. "And I felt more alive than I'd done in years. And suddenly —" I looked him in the eye. "—I understood."

He took hold of my hands. "What did you understand?"

I took a few seconds to think, wanting to get the words right. "I understood that grief and attraction and like and love don't compete in some kind of linear race where only one can be in the lead at any one time. It's more like a washing machine—everything present at the same time in a tangled, messy jumble. Sometimes one thing is on top, sometimes another. But paying attention to one doesn't mean all the other stuff disappears."

Holden smiled and kissed my forehead. "And that's why they pay you the big bucks."

I snorted and clutched him against me, enjoying the warmth of his arms around my waist, the fresh scent of his cologne in my nose, the heat of his skin on my cheek. It would've been so easy just to tip my head up and kiss him, but I felt too raw in the moment, like my skin had peeled away from my flesh and I was still bleeding.

Holden seemed to understand because he didn't push. Instead, he loosened his hold and let a little space come between us. "That's a lot of big thoughts for one afternoon." He ran the back of his knuckles down my cheek. "How about a coffee to digest them with?"

I nodded wordlessly but didn't move, and we stood there a moment, a million things left unsaid between us.

Holden ran his thumb under my damp eyes. "There, much prettier."

I snorted and swatted his hand aside. "You're still not driving home."

"We'll see." He took my hand and we strolled back to the front of the church where I expected him to let go. He didn't.

I waited for a rush of anxiety that never came.

Roz was still standing outside the old bank clutching his iPad. I gave him a wave as we crossed the street, and when he saw our joined hands, he gave a thumbs-up in return.

"Who's that?" Holden cast a long glance over his shoulder at Roz. "I didn't know someone had bought the old Blue Bird. Place needs a hell of a lot of work."

I chuckled. "And I've absolutely no doubt Roz is just the man for it." I filled Holden in as we entered the quaint café filled to the brim with large leafy plants and about a dozen smart dark-stained tables with matching cushioned chairs. The greenery gave the place an almost tropical feel—not exactly in keeping with the landscape but charming, nonetheless.

Meg turned out to be in her mid-twenties with a wide smile, happy blue eyes, and a bunch of dark curls bouncing lazily on her shoulders. When I mentioned that Roz had recommended her coffee, her mouth dropped open and her gaze immediately darted to the window but the man in question was nowhere to be seen.

We ordered lattés and two apple crumble slices to go, and then chatted about nothing in particular as we waited. Five minutes later, with our orders in hand, we left Meg still frowning at the window, and I speedily made my way to the driver's side of the SUV where I paused and snapped my fingers at Holden. He laughed and threw me the keys, which I snatched out of the air.

"Someone has to keep you in line," I said drily as I buckled my seat belt. "Can't have you thinking you can just click your fingers and the whole world stands to attention, even if you are the boss."

Holden huffed. "Like there's even a remote possibility of that while you're around."

I smiled and pulled away from the kerb. "Then I'll count that as a win. Now where are we going to eat? I vote that river we passed on the way into town. After that, you can give me a tiki tour of Oakwood's highlights."

Holden chuckled. "It'll be a short tour. And if you want the river, then the river it is."

I shot him a wink. "You catch on fast."

I followed Holden's directions to the river and chatted as I drove. "I'm surprised how quiet the town is, considering it's quite pretty with all those trees."

Holden nodded. "It used to be a lot busier, but these days, most of the tourists stop in Tekapo, so only being fifteen minutes down the road doesn't really work in Oakwood's favour. If it wasn't for the farming community, it would've died a slow death years ago. There's talk of trying to reinvigorate the main street and maybe push the bed and breakfast and foodie destination angle since we have a lot of local artisan producers. So far, it's just been talk, but there is potential. In summer there aren't enough beds for all the tourists who want to stay, especially if you don't want to fork out a premium. Time will tell, I guess."

He directed me into a car park next to the river and we wandered down to the water's edge where we spent the next hour finishing our coffees with our feet dangling over the icy water and talking about anything except what was happening between us.

Holden asked about my coming out—a non-event since there really wasn't one, at least not with my parents who were liberal flag wavers and who'd known about my interest in boys from my first major teenage crush on our pool maintenance guy.

"A cliché maybe," I admitted. "But that guy had an arse to die for. The only people taken by surprise about me being gay were my strict church-going grandparents. They looked a little faint for a few weeks before my parents rounded them up for a heart-to-heart chat. I have no idea what was said, but the next time I saw them, they were changed people. How about you?"

"Much the same," Holden said, dipping his toes into the water.

"Mum was great, of course. She'd pretty much guessed by the time I was ten. Dad wasn't in the picture at that stage, but when he found out, he was okay about it. Nothing particularly supportive, but he didn't feature much in my life anyway."

He fell quiet for a moment, and although I wanted to ask more since he rarely mentioned his father, I figured he'd tell me when he was ready, or not, considering I wasn't going to be in his life for long.

"My gran was a little leery," Holden admitted. "Mostly because it wasn't something that was really talked about in rural communities, especially in the small niche of high-country farming." He deepened his voice to add, "*Real* men's territory, if you know what I mean."

We both laughed.

"And so, if you were gay in my gran's day, you certainly didn't broadcast it. And although things have progressed a hell of a lot since then, being anything but straight still has a stigma attached that has a particular rural flavour. I still get side-eyed far more than you'd expect."

It didn't surprise me, which was a sad statement in itself.

"And you know about Grandad." Holden picked a few pieces of straggly grass from the bank and wound them around his fingers. "He never said anything against me. He just never said anything at all. Not that I made it easy for him. I wasn't exactly a wallflower as a teenager, and I imagine he took some shit from a few of his contemporaries, like Paddy Lane." He wrinkled his nose and gave a half shrug. "Maybe that's why I struggle with what's happening now. We never really had those conversations for me to be sure about *what* he thought."

I slipped my hand into his and squeezed. "Can I offer a suggestion?"

His gaze turned to mine. "More pearls of wisdom?" But there was a hint of a smile with his words.

"Maybe?"

He snorted. "Maybe, my arse." Then he swivelled to face me. "Go on then."

I reached for his hand, well past giving a fuck who saw us. I liked this man. And it appeared we were having an afternoon of taking chances, so the world could go to hell.

"You can't control what your grandad says," I offered simply. "You can't change how he is or turn the clock back. But you *can* control if and when you take his calls. You can control when you've reached your limit and when you finish the call and when you tell your mum and gran. In my understanding of dementia, he likely won't even know *why* he feels like he does or even remember one call to you from the next. And so, if his calls upset you but you're not ready to tell the others yet, then just don't accept them until you're in the headspace to deal with the repercussions. You're entitled to protect yourself, Holden. That doesn't mean you don't love him or that he doesn't love you."

Holden frowned, his gaze sliding sideways and down to the water gurgling around his feet. After a minute or so, his knee nudged mine. "Not too shabby, Mister Psychologist. I think I can maybe work with that."

I grinned and held my hand out. "That'll be two hundred and fifty dollars."

He gaped. "Is that what you charge an hour?"

I gave him a shining look. "No, that's mate's rates, sunshine."

He blanched. "Oh my god. We barely pay you that a week."

"Now, that's an exaggeration."

He took my hand and kissed the palm. "There you go. Can I get a receipt?"

I stared at my hand, surprised there wasn't a ball of fire where his lips had been. I swallowed hard and arched a brow. "Are you saying your kisses are worth two hundred and fifty dollars?"

Holden licked his lips and winked. "No, that's mate's rates, sunshine."

And okay, so that particularly saucy look went straight to my dick. Do not pass go, do not collect two hundred dollars, do not come anywhere near me or I will strip you where you stand and take you over that boulder in the river.

And damn, where the hell did that come from?

And then, like he knew exactly what I was thinking, Holden shot me the filthiest wink that practically melted my balls. While I was still recovering, he stood and held out his hand. "Coming?"

I rolled my eyes and deadpanned, "Not even close. It takes a lot more than that, just so you know."

He grinned. "I'll bear that in mind." He helped me up and then kept hold of my hand until we arrived back at the Ranger.

I handed him the car keys and he looked surprised. "Don't get too excited," I cautioned. "I want a tour, and the simplest way is for you to drive. But if you're a good boy, I might let you take the wheel on the drive home."

Holden barked out a laugh and swatted me on the butt before heading for the driver's side. "Get in the car, Bossy," he said over his shoulder. "And just so you know, I'm always excited when I'm with you."

It wasn't until I was seated with my seat belt buckled that I realised I was still smiling.

CHAPTER THIRTEEN

Holden

I woke to muffled scrapes and the murmurings of someone outside on the deck, the slide of a chair, a quiet cough, a familiar lilt to the whispered words—

"Spider, get over here." Gil was awake.

I smiled at the tick-tick answer of Spider's nails on the wood.

It wasn't an unusual happening in itself. I woke most days to the comforting sound of Gil working in the kitchen, along with the aroma of pancakes or pastries or bacon. I'd lie there smiling and imagining him busy at the oven, or packing lunches, or jotting endless notes on that growing stack of spreadsheets on the island. The cringing domesticity of it all had somehow become shockingly reassuring.

Not that Gil stuck to the tried and true. We'd all had our palates extended. I'd found myself eating smashed pumpkin and ricotta on toast with poached eggs, and kimchi mayo, which had blown my socks off. I hadn't even known what kimchi was. And the previous day, our team lunch had been crispy bacon-and-egg tacos with pico de gallo. While the day before that had seen Tom staring suspiciously at spinach and potato gnocchi in a creamy tomato sauce, only to end up scoffing two plates of it. Not bad for a man who hadn't met a pasta he didn't hate.

I rolled over and checked my phone. Just after midnight. *Shit.* I tried to block out Gil's presence and give him the privacy he needed. I pulled the sheet up over my shoulders and closed my eyes. With the oppressive summer nights having finally blown through, there was a welcome chill in the night air and a chance to get cosy. I took a deep breath and willed sleep to come.

I already knew Gil liked to grab some quiet time on the deck before the day started. But I'd also heard him out there in the middle of the night and knew they had to be his bad nights, the ones broken by nightmares. That had to be the reason he was out there then, right?

But Gil had a practiced routine that worked for him. He'd been clear about that. There was nothing more *I* had to offer, right?

Yeah, right. Like that rationale had a snowball's chance in hell of working. I groaned and fell onto my back, wide awake and staring at the ceiling. There was absolutely zero chance I was going back to sleep knowing Gil was out there. Not after what happened at the cemetery. Not now I knew how he felt in my arms.

Something had changed between us.

He'd let me in.

Jesus, had it only been twelve hours?

Fuck it. I threw back the sheet, grabbed my sweats and a T-shirt, and padded to the window for a peek outside. A sliver of moonlight fell across the bed as I parted the curtains to find Gil, as expected, curled up on one end of the outdoor sofa with Spider lying across his legs. With his back to me, he seemed unaware of my presence, and I took a minute to run my eyes over his lean frame.

There was just enough light to catch his shattered expression as he stared out across the lake, his chest heaving, his shoulders hunched in exhaustion, his hair slick with sweat on an otherwise cool night.

But one look at the glass of water trembling in his hands and my decision was made.

I made my way to the ensuite for a piss, grabbed the blanket from my bed, and took a five-minute detour to the kitchen. After that, I headed for the front door.

Gil turned at the first squeak of the hinges, his tired gaze landing on mine in obvious apology. "Damn, did I wake you? I'm so sor—"

"Unless you want me to throw this cup of cocoa at you, you better be quiet."

He glanced at the cup in my hand and a small smile broke over his lips. "You made me cocoa?"

"Shut up and shift over. I'm freezing."

Gil lifted the blanket and made room while I ejected a protesting Spider from the sofa and snuggled in close—so sue me. I swapped Gil's water for the mug of cocoa and spread the extra blanket over the two of us.

He wrapped both hands tightly around the warm mug, and I was gratified to see his breathing settling. "Thank you for this."

"You're welcome."

"I see Harry's here." He nodded to the vehicle parked alongside Mum's cottage.

I smiled, remembering my mother's last-minute panic about the duck breasts she was cooking for dinner. "I'm happy for her. I think Harry might become a permanent fixture around here . . . or wherever they decide." A hollow pit opened in my stomach.

Gil shot me a look. "How would you feel if they didn't choose to live here?"

He was too fucking smart. "How do you think I'd feel?"

He nudged his shoulder into mine. "I think you'd both miss each other like crazy, but I think you'd be okay."

I wasn't convinced and I was pretty sure Gil knew that already, so I just shrugged.

Gil took a sip of his cocoa, froze, and his gaze immediately jerked to mine. "Oh . . . mmm . . . nice." He managed a smile, but the swallow had been forced, the words kind of strangled, and there was a wince in there somewhere.

I groaned. "Okay, so what did I get wrong?"

He was clearly biting back a smile. "Nothing, it's just . . . very . . . sweet?" He took another sip and shuddered. "Like a dozen-instant-cavities sweet."

"Crap." I took the mug from his hands and tried a sip, the sugar exploding in my brain like a small nuclear detonation. "Jesus." I almost retched. "I thought about stopping at two teaspoons, but you looked like you could do with the energy burst."

"Well, I got it." Gil reached for my hand, and I felt a faint lingering tremble. I squeezed and he smiled. "It was a very kind thought, but I think I like my teeth just where they are."

I snorted and set the mug on the table. "I'm better at pancakes, just so you know."

His mouth quirked up. "Based on your current total on the fridge, chances are I'll find out pretty soon." Then his smile slid away. "I didn't mean to wake you."

"'S fine." I pulled his legs onto my lap and he leaned back as I began to massage his cold feet through his socks. "Was it a panic attack?"

He nodded; his gaze fixed on where I was kneading under his toes. "No surprise after yesterday."

I worked my fingers into his sole and his eyelids fluttered closed. "Yeah, I figured as much. And your feet are blocks of ice by the way."

He shrugged. "Spider stole most of the blanket."

"Such a bad boy." I shot the huntaway a glare, which he duly ignored. "You realise you've stolen my best working dog, don't you? He doesn't even bother pretending to be pissed when I leave him behind anymore."

Gil huffed. "According to you and everyone else, he's a crap working dog. Even Spencer laughed when I asked whether I should be buying a high energy dog biscuit like the others get instead of the regular stuff you keep in the house for him. I believe Spencer's actual words were and I quote, 'The day that dog's pulse spikes from hard work, I'll buy a round for everyone in the pub.' I had to cover Spider's ears so he didn't take offence. He's a sensitive wee soul."

I snorted and nudged Spider with my foot. He gave a rumbling growl followed by a loud expulsion of intestinal gas, and I turned to Gil, rolling my eyes. "Oh yeah. He's sensitive all right. My first mistake was not giving him to Zach to train."

Gil raised a questioning brow. "The neighbour's son?"

"Yeah, he's great with dogs. He helped me train most of the others and frequently gets called out to help the search-and-rescue teams around these parts."

"Impressive." Gil swapped his feet around. "But all joking aside, I don't think Spider's true calling was ever in these mountains."

"Oh really?" I arched a sceptical brow at my dog.

"No. But I think he'd be an excellent service dog."

I studied Spider, thinking how he'd latched on to Gil so quickly and hardly left his side, especially during Gil's nightmares and panic attacks. The idea wasn't crazy. "You might be on to something there." I dug my thumbs into Gil's sole, and he groaned in approval, heavy on the groaning part which only had my groin tightening in response.

"Damn, that's good." Another groan.

"Will you quit those noises?" I hissed and squirmed to get more comfortable.

Gil eyed me, licked his lips, and groaned again.

I dug my thumbs in . . . hard, and Gil jumped.

"Ow."

I smirked. "Serves you right. But you might be on to something with Spider. I've noticed that he watches you a lot. And when he isn't watching, he's asleep at your feet or somewhere close by where he can keep an eye on you."

Gil lowered a hand to scratch Spider's head and smiled when the huntaway angled it away to get his chin scratched instead. "When I have a nightmare, like tonight, he's already at my side when I wake. He knows almost before I do. He's pretty great." He lifted his head and steadied his gaze on mine, his words careful and deliberate. "You *both* are."

And fuck me. My heart faltered at the heat banked in those dark eyes, silver-edged by moonlight. But rather than one of us breaking the moment, as usually happened, neither of us moved.

Then Gil licked his lips, his smile turning all kinds of wicked, and my mouth ran to dust, my heart hammering in my throat. Fuck, he was potent.

He slid his feet to the floor and reached out a hand to tunnel his fingers through my hair, his words soft and so fucking sexy. "I meant what I said today."

I frowned because he'd said a lot of things, but before I could ask him to clarify, his gaze swept my face and he took a deep breath, adding, "God, you really are beautiful. So . . . lovely."

I opened my mouth, then snapped it shut again because, what the hell did you say to that?

Gil frowned. "Has no one ever told you that?"

I felt very young and very awkward, my cheeks blazing in the darkness. "No." I huffed in embarrassment. "Hot, sometimes? Maybe sexy? Not that I believe half of what anyone says when they're trying to fuck you. God, how do you do this to me?"

"What?" His eyes danced as his fingers kept playing with my hair.

"This!" I groused. "Tie me in freaking knots with just a couple of words?"

He gave another of those soft smiles. "Luck, I guess. But just so you know, you're those things too, Holden. But you're also very, very lovely." His thumb traced my lips, sending a shiver down my spine.

"Not helping," I muttered, but smiled anyway. Then I asked what I'd been wanting to. "You said you meant what you said?"

He nodded. "About kissing you in the woolshed."

Oh.

He cupped my cheek, and the world stood still. "That it opened my eyes. And that it was the first time I'd felt anything in a long time.

I thought it was just the fact of kissing someone, *anyone*. Of having that kind of intimacy after so long. I thought it was about loneliness and feeling lost and maybe even distraction, or I wanted to put it down to that." The intensity of his gaze hit me in the chest. "And I'm sure that was part of it, but it was also . . . *mostly* . . . about *you*, Holden. Just . . . you. And it's taken me a bit of time to come to terms with the unexpected shock of that."

Oh boy. I swallowed hard. "And . . . have you?" I rasped, pressing my cheek into his palm. "Come to terms with it?"

Gil smiled and slid closer, our eyes locked, his body flushing hot next to mine. He leaned in, his mouth hovering just a breath away from mine. Our lips brushed, once, twice, little more than a rush of air, and then he ran his nose up the side of my face, drawing a deep breath from my jaw to my temple, and I was two seconds away from coming in my sweats.

"God, you smell so fucking good. Straight from bed." The timbre of his words reverberated in my balls, my cock stiffening at the sudden flood of sensations, and yet he'd barely even touched me.

I wasn't at all sure anything I'd done before had prepared me for Gil Everton.

"You are so damn delicious." His lips ghosted over mine once again, and a rush of goosebumps cascaded down my spine. My eyes fluttered closed as the tip of his tongue coasted along the crease, teasing, tasting. I groaned and chanced my hands around his waist. Hot, hot skin shivered at my touch and a groan rose from somewhere in Gil's chest.

"Yesssss," he breathed the word against my cheek, giving me courage to venture further.

God, is this really happening?

"I want to kiss you." He nipped at my lower lip, tugging it back before releasing it with a puff of air. "Tell me I can kiss you." Another brush of his lips, a fly-by, no pressure, just the hint of warm supple flesh against mine that left a bone-deep hunger for more.

And holy hell. If that was how it felt just to be touched by the man, I wasn't sure I was going to survive the full enchilada.

I pulled back just enough to cradle his face, the moonlight gilding those long black lashes as I made my answer as clear as I could. "Stop asking and just do it. You can do anything you want with me, Gil. *Anything*. I'm dying here."

His mouth turned up in a slow, sexy smile and pushed through my hold to nip the end of my nose. "That's a lot of latitude you're giving me, sweetheart."

Sweetheart? Fuck yeah. I never even blinked. "It is. *Anything* you want, *however* you want to do it. I've wanted you from the minute I laid eyes on you, and I'm up for it all. But this is your show, baby." I hesitated before returning a sly smile of my own. "Unless, of course, you'd rather it was mine?"

He gave a soft chuckle and ran a finger down my nose to my lips before pushing it inside my mouth. I circled my tongue around the nail and his pupils bled black in the grey light.

Then he put his lips next to my ear. "I told you if you were a good boy, I might let you drive home." He pulled away and winked, his finger moving slowly in and out of my mouth. "But right now, I don't want you to be a good boy. Right now, you're mine, Holden, and I'm driving. I feel like I've been waiting for this forever."

Gil leaned back to watch his finger thrusting in and out of my mouth, his breathing matching every slide, a dark stain creeping up his neck. I was way too close to losing that last bit of control and embarrassing myself, when his finger slipped free and his gaze rose back to meet mine, like nothing else existed in the world except that singular moment and that one conversation.

With our bodies flush, my heart thrummed against his, my skin too tight on my bones. Gil's frown lines deepened in the moonlight, a complex mix of emotions trading places on his face, difficult questions brimming in those beautiful eyes.

I said nothing. They were questions only Gil could answer.

And in the next few seconds, he did.

CHAPTER FOURTEEN

Gil

I cupped Holden's cheek and ran my thumb over that beauty spot I'd obsessed about for weeks. I thought about how he'd made me feel seen as more than just a grieving parent. I thought about his kindness and his easy-going nature and his sexy fucking attitude. I thought about all of that, and then . . . I kissed him . . . properly . . . like I'd been wanting to do since forever.

Like there was ever going to be any other outcome between us.

Like I hadn't known it would come to this.

Like I hadn't asked the question a million times. Why here? Why him?

Like I hadn't thought about what it would be like to have him. What he would taste like. What he would feel like in my arms, or me in his.

The sweet slide of his body over mine.

The spark of something far more dangerous in my heart.

His lips parted and he sighed into the kiss, his arms sliding around my waist, gathering me close. I scrambled into his lap and straddled his thighs, cradling his face to keep him just where I wanted him . . . and the world fell away.

"Oh god," he murmured into my open mouth, clutching me even closer. "I call an amnesty on swearing right fucking now."

I grinned against his lips. "Agreed. Now get back here."

But he hesitated, his eyes flashing with something I wasn't prepared to put a name to. "I just want you to know that I didn't dare think that we would . . . I never dreamed—"

"Hush." I sealed his mouth with mine. *I know. I feel it too.* But the words remained unspoken as he groaned and opened for me, his tongue sliding into my mouth to set my body alight one touch-starved cell at a time. *His* mouth on mine. *His* hands around my waist. *His* fingers slipping under my singlet to leave scorch marks on my skin.

I shoved my tongue down his throat, grunting in appreciation as his hips thrust up in response, and those clever fingers dipped under the waistband of my sweats. I knelt to give him better access and he brushed my hole, eliciting a filthy moan from my lips.

"Oh, shit. Yessss." It had been so fucking long. "Again," I demanded, pushing my arse out to make my point, but instead of diving in he pulled back.

"No. Not here." He glanced over my shoulder to where Emily's cottage stood, and I gave a small gasp of realisation and immediately wriggled off his lap.

"Come on." He grabbed my hand and tugged me toward the front door. "I don't want to rush this. I've been waiting too damn long."

Jesus. Heat pulsed low in my groin as my cock very definitely liked the sound of that. I raced to keep up, but at the door to his bedroom, reality hit and I hesitated, pulling him around to face me. "Just to be clear—" I swallowed hard. "—I'm not exactly sure how much I'm ready for. And I might not know where that line is until it happens."

Holden cradled my face and kissed me. "In which case, you're in charge, baby. But I have one rule."

I cocked my head. "This should be interesting."

He grinned. "At no point will either of us make any mention of who this bedroom used to belong to, or you'll likely witness the fastest deflation in the history of humanity, understood?"

I snorted. "Deal."

"Excellent." Holden stood back and held his hand out for me to take.

I stared at the awful wallpaper. At his dirty clothes strewn on the floor. At his . . . bed. I sucked in a deep breath and took his hand.

He pulled me close. "Thank you."

I smiled. "I wouldn't count your chickens yet. This is a work in progress."

He gave a solemn nod. "Understood."

I brushed my lips over his. "I tested negative after Luke left, and I . . . well, I haven't been with anyone since." And in case he missed the point, I added a reminder. "In over a year."

He simply smiled. "Lucky me. And *I* just happened to have been tested last week. Also negative."

I almost laughed. "Last week, huh? How very timely." I ran my thumb over his lips and he blushed furiously.

"Shut up. I was . . . hopeful, what can I say?"

I grinned and gave him a shove. "Get in that bed, Mister."

He stripped in two seconds flat and turned on the bedside lamp. Then he took a swan dive onto the mattress, where he immediately rolled to his back and crossed his hands behind his head, his hard cock swinging free.

Hard . . . for me.

And oh fuck. Saliva pooled in my mouth.

I closed the door on a very unimpressed Spider and then hesitated again as the enormity of what I was about to do hit me. I'd always enjoyed sex, always been confident in bed, but I hadn't been with a man other than Luke since we'd first met, and no one *at all* in the previous twelve months. I took a very deep, very shaky breath and rested my forehead against the door.

Do I really want this?

Yes. The answer came swift and sure, and with it, my nerves settled.

"Hey." Holden's soft voice broke through the crumbling wall in my brain as gentle hands slid around my waist and lips pressed to the back of my neck. "We don't have to do *anything* if you're not ready."

His words were all I needed, and I turned in his arms and kissed him hard, the rough skim of his scruff along my jaw a special kind of heaven. I tried to snapshot each and every second of the watershed of sensations tripping through my body to replay at a later date. "No, we definitely do have to do this," I murmured into his open mouth. "Because I want this, Holden. And I want it with *you.*"

I kissed along his jaw and down his neck, sucking at the base before kissing back up the other side. He groaned and his cock throbbed against my stomach, his lips finding my neck as I reached down and gently cupped his heavy balls.

He let me push him back toward the bed but didn't sit. Instead, he put his palms against my chest. "Shhh. Slowly, baby." He kissed me again and began to undress me, first my T-shirt, then my sweats, his fingers trailing over my bare skin and setting it on fire.

"So fucking beautiful." He kissed my shoulder, my chest, my nipples—giving each one a lick and a gentle suckle that rocketed my cock to attention. "I've waited so long for this." He knelt and kissed my belly, skirting my dick to kiss my thigh, his hands sliding down my back and over my arse, sending every neuron in my body sparking as he kissed down to my knee and then back up again.

He stood and took both my hands. "Come here." He sat on the bed and I pushed him flat. He scooted up the bed, moonlight striping his body as I straddled his thighs. He pulled me down on top, his mouth finding mine, his hands roaming freely over my body. "Jesus, you are so sexy," he rasped, his lips moving to my throat.

"You're pretty spectacular yourself." I pushed to a sit and grinned down at him. "And it's my turn now."

He chuckled and lay flat, spreading his arms wide. "Go for it."

Oh boy. I felt like a kid in a candy shop as my fingers trailed over his chest and down his soft belly, his skin pebbling at my touch. He was gorgeous, every centimetre of him. All those hard curves and sharp angles sliding under my hands. My fantasy of two weeks suddenly come to life and all fucking mine.

Almost ten years my junior, Holden wasn't muscle-bound or sleek or gym perfect, but instead he was lean in places and soft in others, with hard edges and gentle curves, and dotted with all the tiny scars that marked a life lived and worked on a farm. I took the time to kiss each one. Kissed the palms of his calloused hands that made my skin tingle. Kissed the dark suntan lines that marked his neck and arms. Kissed that glorious scruff, long and rough and not a waxed centimetre in sight. I crawled down his body and ran my tongue over his nipple, the grassy-earth scent of lanolin that clung to his skin making my lips hum.

He jerked, then groaned with pleasure, and so I did the same to the other, drawing it into my mouth to play with the hard nub.

"Oh Christ, that's good." His head pressed back into the pillow, flicking from side to side as I played a little more. Then suddenly he was done, and hands hauled me up his body to straddle him again. "Too damn close," he gasped, cupping my arse, the hard length of his dick clear and present under my balls as I pressed down.

Holden groaned in approval and shoved two fingers into my mouth. I sucked on them for a few seconds, watching his pupils blow wide. Then his fingers were gone, and as I leaned forward to kiss him, he hoisted up my right thigh and his slick digits rode my taint to glide over my hole.

"Oh, fuck yeah," Holden growled, wriggling his shoulder lower to get the angle he needed to slip a fingertip inside, just enough to get me all hot and bothered while he tongue-fucked my mouth, dirty and deep.

It was so damn sexy. The filthier the better had always been my motto, and Holden seemed well on board with that. And while he attacked me at both ends, I rocked my hips over his hard cock, providing some much-needed friction, our pre-come mingling to ease the slide.

"Is this okay?" he grunted between kisses.

I snorted and nipped at his lip. "Fucking outstanding."

"Excellent." He kept kissing and kept teasing my hole—dipping and retreating and edging me closer until I wanted to scream at him to just get the fuck on with it.

Then his fingers disappeared, and I blinked, disoriented for a second.

"Stay there," he ordered—like I was going anywhere—as he reached into his bedside drawer to pull out some lube.

I took the tube from his hand and squeezed a generous amount into his palm, slicking his fingers one at a time, drawing it out, watching his gaze intensify in the moonlight.

When I was done, he wiggled them in my face. "You want these inside you?"

I took his hand and brought his fingers to my lips for a kiss. "Three." I counted them off. "Deep as you can go. I like to ride that edge."

He flashed a sexy fucking smile and reached his hand through my open legs to find my hole. Then, with his eyes locked on mine, he slid a finger inside.

One knuckle, then two, and my head fell back as the first finger slid fully home and my arse ached for more. I bucked under the intrusion, our cocks sliding against each other to ratchet up the pleasure. Then a second fingertip slid alongside, and the stretch burned.

"Oh Jesus, fuck," I groaned filthily, falling forward on my elbows either side of his face, opening myself further as I breathed through the sting. It had been a long fucking time since I'd had that, but it didn't take long until the craving came again.

More. Always more.

"Three. Now." I huffed the order and swore I heard him chuckle.

"Open your eyes," he barked back, gruff and demanding, and I did as he said to find that wicked smile aimed my way. "That's better. Now, did I hear you say you wanted three?" He arched a brow.

"Yes, arsehole," I growled. "Three."

He grinned and squeezed in the tip of a third finger, his eyes scanning my face, watching, checking. He must've been happy with what he saw because he slid a little deeper and twisted them a fraction, and I'm pretty sure I keened. He groaned and kissed my face. "You are so fucking sexy. Does that feel good, baby?"

I grunted something—I wasn't sure what since I could barely form words let alone string any together, blissfully riding that fine line between pain and pleasure, my absolute favourite journey. The surge and crest as one fell into the other. The blur. The light and the dark. I held on to that knife-edge as my body adjusted and the sting edged over into deep fucking need.

I lowered my mouth to his and fucked my tongue deep inside before muttering into his mouth, "It feels so fucking good like you wouldn't believe."

He grinned and pumped his fingers in and out. "And how about this?"

"Mm-hmmm. Oh yeah, just like that," I gasped, pushing myself onto my hands and shuttling my hips to send his fingers deeper, our cocks rubbing and thumping against each other in some kind of erotic dance.

"Jesus, look at you," he murmured with wonder in his voice.

"Likewise." I rode my flat palm up his stomach to his mouth and slipped my fingers inside. He suckled on them and nipped at the tips. I slid them back to his groin to wrap around that thick cock and tugged it firmly. It jumped in my hand.

"Oh fuck." He gazed up at me, breathing ragged, his cock thrusting in and out of my fist, his words broken, his rhythm in my arse faltering but still lighting a fire at the base of my spine.

"You want to come like this?" he gasped, and I nodded. "Fucking hell, Gil. This is insane. Do you need me to—"

"No . . . almost . . . there."

"Oh god." His head fell back and he drove up with his hips.

Our coordination was falling apart—me pumping his cock, him finger-fucking my arse, my hips shuttling, his uncontrolled thrusts into my fist, and all while trying to breathe. Something had to give. I chose breathing, holding mine as I pumped Holden's cock faster, feeling his fingers tunnel up my arse, the squeeze on my prostate, the scent of him washing over my face, his grunts, my soft cries, faster and faster until—

"F-fuuuuck!" I threw my head back as waves of pleasure coursed through my body like they were cleaning house, flinging doors wide and rattling the chandeliers as my cock erupted, spilling creamy ribbons all over Holden's abs.

"Oh shit." He stared, his fingers sliding free as he continued to thrust into my hand. "Jesus, that's sexy."

I smeared it over his belly with my free hand, then wriggled to the side so I could take him in my mouth. He held himself steady, running the wet angry head around my lips before feeding it deep into my mouth. It had been so damn long, I almost wept from the pleasure, and then the taste of him exploded over my tongue and I did, tears running down my cheeks.

I glanced up and our eyes met, his expression soft and full of a million questions we'd been avoiding. He ran his thumb over my damp cheeks, and my lips spread tight around his cock. Then he cupped my chin. "I like this look on you."

I almost choked and he laughed, the fucker, and so I shut him up by taking him to the back of my throat and swallowing around him.

"Christ!" He fisted the sheet and thrust up into my mouth. "Shit, sorry." He looked horrified but I shook my head, pulling him closer and swallowing again.

He took the hint and gave another thrust. Then another—a little harder. And on the third he gave a strangled cry, wrapped his hands around my head, and poured himself down my throat. I swallowed as best as I could, and Holden dragged me up and licked and kissed every spilled drop until I was clean. Then he held me against his chest, and as we lay gasping for breath, his hands softly stroked up and down my spine like he was soothing some skittish kitten.

My breath caught at his tender concern. "I'm okay," I reassured him. "Look, Mum, no hands." I held one up for him to see, still and steady.

He smiled and lifted it to his lips, kissing the palm. "So, you're not spinning out about what just happened?"

I rolled off him and up onto one elbow. "So far so good. How about you?"

"Me?" He looked confused.

"Yes, you." I snuggled into his side.

Holden slid an arm around my shoulders and tucked me close. He pressed his lips to my hair, and when he finally spoke, his words were quiet and considered. "Hmmm. I think how *I* feel, apart from blissfully fucked out, thank you very much—" He kissed me again. "—will be very much determined by your answer to this question. What do you want to do now?"

And there it was.

The question I had no answer for.

"I don't know." It was honest and all I had. "What do *you* want? And be honest." I wasn't sure I even wanted to know his answer.

His eyes met mine. "That's hardly fair, because I don't want to scare you off, but I also don't want to lie either. You and me, just now, that was . . . well, shit, Gil, it was fucking amazing. I don't know *what* I'd imagined or fantasised, but that blew it out of the water. But to be honest, we could've just lain here and made out, and I'd have still thought it was magic. I just wanted to be with you, Gil, anyway you'd let me. And that's a first for me. I do sex. I don't do *relationship* stuff, which is what this feels like it's heading toward because I want more of you, a lot more, and not just sex. And I don't know how to feel about that. Confused, I suppose. Scared. Excited. But mostly terrified because it seems impossible and because I know it's not what you were looking for."

Oh fuck. I buried my nose in his chest, avoiding his eyes, mostly because I wanted all of that too. But that way lay certain heartbreak for one or both of us. "Holden, I—"

"Hear me out." He turned on his side and tipped my chin up, forcing me to look at him. "I like you, Gil. *A lot*. Would I like to try a relationship of *some* sort with you? Yes. Absolutely. No questions asked. It makes no fucking sense since we couldn't live more different lives, but you asked for honesty, so there it is."

"Holden—"

"*However*, I get where you're coming from. You're only here for three months, you're going through a lot, and if you want to forget this ever happened, then that's what we'll do. I won't fucking like it, because I really believe there's something here worth pursuing—" He flicked a finger between us. "But I won't mess with your plans. Just say the word. Okay, your turn."

His coffee eyes drilled into mine, stirring something almost forgotten in my heart. Something that felt a lot like hope and possibility.

Are you happy, Daddy?

I turned onto my stomach and propped myself up on both elbows. "Okay. Here goes. I like you, Holden, Lord knows more than I should. But my life is a mess and it's only just starting to turn around. Not to mention yours is complicated and stressful as well, with people who depend on you to be at the top of your game. We're both in the middle of big changes."

"I know, I know," he said dejectedly. "And I guarantee the next words out of your mouth are that these feelings are probably nothing more than a—distraction."

"Actually, no, smarty pants." I tapped my finger on his chest. "One thing I'm very sure of is that you are *not* simply a distraction for me. Far from it. I've shut down a ton of distractions over the last year, but when it comes to you, nothing works, and I don't know what to do with that. I can't offer you *anything*. I have no idea where I'm going or what anything between us could even look like."

"Then stop trying to picture it or put a label on it. Even I know that relationships don't work like that." He pulled me back down onto his chest and drew the sheet up, his thumb tracing circles over the small of my back. "Why do we need all the answers before we even start?"

Because I live my whole life like that. Because I'm so fucking terrified of this feeling, of you, of us, that I can taste my own failure as if we're already breaking up.

"If you want to stop, we stop," Holden continued, oblivious to the hurricane his words were fuelling in my heart. "It's as simple as that. But I'm not asking for promises, Gil. I'm not asking to make big plans with you. I'm not asking for you to consider anything beyond the time you're here if you're not ready. I'm happy to take what you can give for as long as you're here and just see what happens."

Just see what happens. It sounds so reasonable, so damn easy.

I twirled my fingers in the dark curls on his chest as a war of emotions raged in my heart. I could end the craziness right then. I could focus on what I was supposed to be there for. I could avoid more hurt, more loss, more . . . feeling.

Are you happy, Daddy?

I sighed and lifted my eyes to meet Holden's once again. "But, you see, the problem with stopping—" I kissed him softly, my lips lingering, my fearful, wishful pulse kicking up at the mere thought of what I was about to do. "—is that I think I might very well want all of those things that we would so carefully avoid talking about."

His eyes widened and then a smile lit up his face. "Is that right? So, um, what do you suggest we do?"

One foot over the cliff and I was still alive. "That we *don't* talk about them."

The flash of disappointment in Holden's eyes was there and gone in an instant.

I stroked his face. "Not *yet*. But I don't want to stop either." I put a finger to his opening lips. "I think we should do exactly what you said. See how it goes . . . day by day. I like it here, Holden. I'm feeling more . . . solid. And I don't want to have to leave just because things get awkward."

Holden's answering smile split his face. He rolled me onto my back and then piled on top of me, pinning me to the mattress and kissing me thoroughly. "You're not going anywhere." He pressed kisses up my neck until his eyelashes tangled with mine. "We'll take it day by day. And if it stops working for you, I promise to step away and let it go, no pressure. Okay?"

I side-eyed him. "This is probably the worst idea ever, you realise that?"

His lips twitched and he kissed me again. "The absolute worst. And yet somehow I'm okay with that."

I held his gaze a moment longer. "Okay. Day by day. But what do we tell the others? It's been hard enough trying to hide my interest in you before tonight." Holden looked far too pleased about that, so I pinched his butt.

"Ow!"

"That's for being smug."

"And irresistible." He grabbed my wrist before I pinched him again. "But as for the others, they already suspect something's going on, but I don't see why we should make it easy for them."

I groaned.

"But I think I should mention it to Mum. If anything was to happen while she was away, I—"

"I agree. Besides, she's already given me the 'don't hurt him' talk." I made air quotes.

Holden's eyes bugged. "She . . . what? Oh, Jesus no, I don't want to know. I swear that woman is clairvoyant. But how about I just make it sound . . . casual?"

Casual? I wasn't sure what I thought about that. "You mean sell it as a friends-with-benefits kind of—"

"No!" he snapped, his cheeks pinking. "Sorry. It's just—well, she knows I've done that before, and I don't want to put what we have in the same box."

What we have. I liked the sound of that far too much. I also wondered whether that past situation had involved our friendly veterinarian but decided it was none of my business. "So, that's *not* what we're doing then?"

Holden scooted onto his side and my hands slid around his neck as he kissed me. "No, Gil." His soft gaze hovered on mine. "That's *not* what we're doing and you know it. We're giving things a test run to see if we want to fork out on the complications of an actual purchase."

I couldn't help but laugh. "And here I thought you weren't the romantic type."

"Shut up." His smile slipped away. "If I told you what I actually thought, about how you make me feel, you'd run away so fast I wouldn't see you for dust. And you'd be right to do so. I'm hardly a proven commodity in the relationship stakes."

I traced my fingers over his lips. "You're not a commodity *at all*. You're someone very special, Holden Miller, and I'd be honoured to do a test run with you."

He pulled me into a long, slow kiss that curled my toes and sent warning bells jangling in my heart. It would be so easy to fall for him. Too easy. In fact, I was pretty sure I was halfway there already.

But I was also in too deep to turn away.

And I sure as hell *didn't* want to.

We took the making out into Holden's oversized shower where things escalated to lazy blowjobs, followed by idle conversation as we sat on the floor and let the water cascade over our tired bodies.

Holden washed me from head to toe, learning my body, setting his mouth on every inch, asking me about scars I carried. Appendectomy at ten. Sutures in my brow and a broken nose after a fall from a mate's horse at thirteen. The pucker where the drainage tube had entered my punctured lung after the accident. The screws and plates in my lower leg.

And I did the same for him, washing him down and cataloguing all his physical history—shearing nicks, cattle kicks, abrasions from sliding down scree, a quad accident, hammer injuries. The list went on and on. The man needed wrapping in cotton wool and locking away for his own protection.

When we were done, Holden led me by the hand back to his bed. We let a pissy Spider into the room to sleep on the floor, and knowing we were going to feel like shit in the morning, Holden fired Tom a text to say he wouldn't be there for mat time, and we reset our alarms for seven to claw back an hour or so. No one got going much before then, and the station would survive.

Holden then rolled me to face the window and crawled in behind, his hot body curling tight around mine, the big spoon to my little. He threw a leg over the top of mine, his arm firm around my waist like I might just disappear if he didn't lock me down.

It was so sweet all I could do was smile and snuggle in, revelling in the warmth of another body at my back—of *Holden* at my back. I stared through the wide crack in the curtains, through the moonlight spilling over the bed, and out toward the silver-dusted lake. And with Holden's soft snores at my back, I thought of Callie and Tuck, my work, and the accident. I even thought of Luke. None of them seemed to carry the sting they had just a few weeks before. Not gone, just not as loud, muffled by a towering cage of mountains, a rolling sea of tussock, and the softness of the arms that held me.

I didn't know where the hell Holden and I thought we were heading. Different parts of the country. Different ways of life. Commitments on both sides. His station. My practice. But I'd bought the ticket and I was going along for the ride, so help me.

Was it a bad decision? Maybe. But at least it was a decision. I was done with standing still. Standing still was going to bury me, slowly, one grey day at a time.

And I was done being scared to live again.

CHAPTER FIFTEEN

Holden

I woke with Gil still in my arms and a soaring lightness in my chest. He snuffled more than snored. It was pretty fucking adorable. Twenty minutes until the alarm went off, but I'd been awake almost an hour, watching him and reliving the night before. His body tangled with mine, our quiet conversations, and thanking fuck I'd had the courage to ignore my fears and join him on the deck when I had.

From the floor beside the bed, Spider scratched at his collar, then settled back to sleep. *His* snoring had been a lot less adorable. I didn't usually let him sleep in my room, but I was reluctant to break the special bond he and Gil seemed to have formed.

I lifted a lock of blond hair from Gil's lashes and set it back on his head. Then I ran my fingertips over the faint lines that gathered on his brow. I had so many questions—about him, about Callie, about his marriage, his work, his family, his life before he came to the station.

A test run? I swallowed a laugh. Who the hell was I kidding? I was hook, line, and sinker before we'd even fucked. Just the idea of calling it friends with benefits had been like a visceral punch to my chest.

Why?

Because I *knew* the difference.

And I suddenly understood something else as well. I understood that Zach had felt what I was feeling when I'd turned him down. Maybe even more, considering how long we'd been together and how well he knew me. I wasn't sure I could've made it any easier on him, but I did finally understand.

What if Gil had turned me down?

Gil's eyelids fluttered open and he blinked into the weak grey light seeping through the curtain. He rubbed his eyes, rolled to his back, and stared at me for a moment, confusion sliding into a slow smile that spread like sunshine over his face. "Hey, you."

"Hey, yourself." I pulled the sheet over his shoulders and tucked it in. "I have to say I like you in my bed."

His eyes sparkled. "It definitely has its advantages. What time is it?"

"Almost seven." I pulled him in for a kiss and he smiled against my lips, his hand finding my half-hard cock for an enquiring couple of tugs. "Mmm. I could get used to this."

I groaned and jutted my hips forward. "I kind of hoped you'd say that." Then I stole another kiss, and he wriggled in close until our bodies lay flush, our cocks nestled together, all friendly-like. "I thought one less pair of sheets to wash on a regular basis might be a selling point?"

He blinked up at me. "You mean sleep together in here?"

I shrugged and thrust into his hand. "Or in *your* room. And I was kind of hoping we might do more than *just* sleep."

"Is that right?" He gave me a sultry smile and reached for the lube, adding a dollop to his palm before taking both our cocks in hand.

The sensual slide of my dick alongside his sent a wave of delicious heat up my spine. "Of course, I'll pretty much agree to anything

—oh fucking hell—" I let loose a filthy groan. "—with my cock in your hand. Just saying."

"Good to know." He pressed up against me, his hand working hard, his breath coming in jerky gasps.

"Oh . . . Jesus." I grunted and buried my face against his neck.

"How about you stop talking and let me work here? Oh—" He gasped as I wrapped my hand around his and added to the pressure, my thumb gliding over his slit.

"Oh fuck! There . . . that . . ." He grunted, shifting his hips. "No . . . more . . . yes, there!"

It was quick and dirty and over way too fast, and our bodies fell apart, sated and slick with come, leaving us laughing and wiping ourselves down with the sheet.

"We're gonna be late." Gil scooted to the edge of the mattress and pointed to the damp sheet. "And you do realise that if we sleep together every night, it'll be *more* washing, not less." He began pulling on his sweats and I grabbed him around the waist and hauled him back into bed, both of us laughing.

"And your point . . . ?" I buried my face in his neck and blew a raspberry.

He snorted and pushed me aside. "Idiot. Come on, we have to get up. *This* is why it's not a good idea to sleep together."

"Bossy fucker," I grumbled.

"You love it."

I did. "Just five more minutes."

"No. Now get up. And that goes on the tally by the way. Amnesty over. And can I just say you don't have a chance in hell in winning?" He kissed me soundly, then shoved me off the mattress and I hit the floor with a grunt, sending Spider leaping out of the way with a surprised bark.

"You have zero respect for the fact I run this station," I groused.

"Aw, poor baby." Gil offered his hand to help me up and I jerked him down on top of me. He landed with a squeal, followed by a loud shout of protest. I wrestled him into submission, pinning his hands above his head, and kissed him thoroughly.

He stilled and deepened the kiss, and I sank to the floor alongside him. His tongue slid into my mouth with a needy moan, his legs circling my waist and bringing our dicks back into a close encounter. "Mmm," he hummed happily. "Maybe just five more min—"

"Of course, it's all right." My mother's cheery voice shattered the still of the morning, far too fucking close for comfort as footsteps crossed the deck toward the front door and Gil's horrified gaze met mine.

Oh, fucking fuck.

Gil deserved a gold medal for the speed with which he catapulted off the floor to check the bedroom door was securely snipped just seconds before the front door squeaked on its hinges.

Meanwhile, my mother's bright tone continued, "I'm pretty hungry, I have to say."

Harry said something I didn't quite catch before adding, "I don't want to interrupt—"

"It's fine," my mother insisted, and I kicked myself again for keeping the man at arm's length for so long.

"This is not how I want her to find out," Gil hissed into my ear, casting a scandalised look at my naked body.

Oops.

I retaliated by pointing to the crusty stains on his own sweats. "Likewise."

He glanced down and swore.

I leapt to my feet and rummaged in the wardrobe for some fresh clothes. "I'll stall them in the kitchen while you whip to your bedroom, baby."

He raised a brow and whisper-shouted, "Baby? Are we really going there in the light of day?"

I hesitated, heat racing into my cheeks. "Um, maybe? I don't know. Just between us?"

He studied me for a moment, then shook his head and planted a quick kiss on my lips. "Yeah, go on, just between us. Thirty-nine years old and the first time I've ever been called baby."

Oh. My stomach dropped and I reached for his hand. "Well, I've never said it to anyone either, so if you're not comfortable—"

He put a finger to my lips. "No, it's—" He smiled. "—nice. Now get your butt in that kitchen before they come looking for one of us."

"On it." I dressed at lightning speed—a shower could wait. "So, does the age difference make this a cradle-snatching thing—" I shoved my phone in my pocket. "—or a daddy thi—"

A pillow hit me on the head.

"I'll take that as a maybe." I ducked another pillow and scrambled out the door, pulling it shut behind me.

I've got this.

I found Harry and my mother talking quietly alongside the espresso machine as it came up to pressure. At fifty-five, Harry was a nice-looking man with gentle brown eyes and a warm smile. He worked with his receding hairline by buzzing the rest almost to the skin—a surprisingly successful look on him. Relaxed faded jeans covered a slight softening of his belly, and a short-sleeved white button-up highlighted solid forearms dusted with dark hair. One arm was slung loosely around my mother's waist and the intimate look they shared made my heart stutter.

My mother turned as I closed the door to the hall and Harry's arm instantly fell away. "Oh, there you are." She shot me a wry smile. "Office day, is it?" There was an amused glint in her eye, which never boded well. "And Gil doesn't appear to have started breakfast?"

"Morning to you too, Mum. And that's a lot of questions for this hour of the day. Harry, nice to see you." I walked over to shake his hand and then waved him to a seat. "Joining us for breakfast?"

Harry glanced at my mother, then nodded and took a seat.

"Thank you. I know you like to get started early, so I wouldn't want to hold you up."

"Clearly not *that* early." My mother chuckled.

I squinted at her and slid into a chair opposite Harry. "Yes, well, we were up late planning for muster and catching up on a few things, so I decided we deserved a lie in." It was worth a shot. "I think I heard Gil's shower as I came up the hall, so I'm sure he won't be long."

I'm pretty sure my mother snorted, although I couldn't be sure since she was standing with her back to me, but her shoulders were definitely shaking. For sanity's sake, I chose to ignore her and spoke to Harry instead. "And I'm really glad you came, Harry. I'm sorry I didn't make it clear much earlier that you're welcome to join us anytime."

"No need to apologise," Harry said, looking a little surprised. "I completely understand." He shot a look to my mother. "It's been the two of you for a long time. And you've had a lot going on."

I appreciated his words, but I'd still been an arse. "Maybe so, but I'm happy for the two of you. I really am." I glanced to where my mother stood wearing a pleased smile.

"Thank you, Holden." Her eyes shone like glass and the next second she was at my side, planting a kiss on my cheek. "You're a good son." A smile danced on her lips. "And a godawful liar."

Harry raised his hands and shot me a rueful look. "I apologise for your mother in advance."

My gaze narrowed on my mother. "Mum?"

Her mouth turned up in a wicked smile. "Gil *never* showers before you, Holden. I've been in here often enough to know. He always lets you get ready first. And even if he did, he's nothing if not organised. And yet the coffee maker is stone cold, nothing is prepped, and you've never been able to whisper to save yourself."

Oh fuck. I gulped.

"Not that I needed any of that, because if you really wanted to keep things under the radar, you shouldn't have made out on the deck on a still night. The house isn't *that* far away."

Oh. My. God. I nosedived into a mortifying rabbit hole.

"But don't worry—" She made no attempt to hide her glee. "We simply closed our window, didn't we, Harry?"

Harry rolled his eyes. "*I* closed the window. And then I whipped your mother back to bed lickety-split."

"Thank you." It came out as more of a squeak than anything.

Harry smiled affectionately at my mother. "She's happy for you, if that helps?"

Not really. "Please don't push this, Mum," I warned. "I don't want you—"

"Don't push what?" Gil strolled into the kitchen looking freshly showered and delicious, with damp hair and bare feet and smelling of everything I'd ever wanted.

And every filthy thought that hit my brain in that singular moment must've flashed in neon colours on my face, judging by the shit-eating grin that appeared on my mother's face.

"Sorry I didn't get the espresso machine on earlier." Gil walked unseeing past the desperate look on my face and headed for the scullery. "I was up late watching a movie and slept in. My fault entirely. Just as well Holden's working in his office this morning."

I groaned and dropped my forehead to the table . . . twice. Gil reappeared from the scullery, took one look at my woeful expression and the wicked grin on my mother's face, and the loaf of bread he was carrying dropped onto the island with a thud.

"They know, don't they?" He kept his eyes on me and I nodded. He blanched and immediately turned to Emily. "I swear when we talked before, nothing had happ—"

"Stop." She put her hand up. "It's none of my business, Gil."

"Oh really?" I said drily. "Could've fooled me. And this is not up for public consumption, understand?"

My mother frowned. "Of course not. What do you take me for?"

"Not even with the team."

She held up her hands. "They won't hear anything from us. But they're not stupid, Holden. They already suspect something between—"

"I don't care." It came out sharper than I'd intended, the sting hitting home in my mother's eyes. I was fucking up. "I'm sorry, Mum. But it's more for Gil. I've already told the team that I don't want Gil used as fodder for gossip."

Gil's eyebrows gathered in confusion because oh . . . right . . . I might've omitted telling him about that particular conversation.

"Besides, this is kind of brand new." I shot him an apologetic look. "And we'd appreciate some discretion."

"Hey." Gil walked over and squatted beside my chair, placing his hand on my thigh. "It's okay. You were going to tell Emily anyway, right? Before she left?" His hazel eyes held mine, and for a second, I lost myself in memories of our night together.

Without thinking, I leaned in and pressed my lips to his. His eyes flew wide for a split second, then he relaxed and kissed me back.

"Well, that's that then." My mother began pulling bowls from the cupboard. "My lips are sealed. Harry, you can be my sous chef. What does everyone feel like for breakfast? Pancakes? Eggs? Gil, you take a seat with Holden. This morning is my treat."

"But—" Gil flustered and stood to join my mother in the kitchen, but I grabbed his hand.

"Sit," I ordered.

He sat.

I found his hand under the table and laced our fingers together. He turned and I winked. "But you can kiss me again."

His eyes crinkled at the corners and his mouth covered mine in a soft kiss with just a hint of tongue.

"We've got this, right?" I ran my nose alongside his.

He hesitated just long enough to let me know he was as unsure about that as I was.

But he nodded anyway.

Two ostriches and a mountain of sand.

CHAPTER SIXTEEN

Holden

I jogged down the driveway toward the back door of the homestead, all the while trying to ignore the uptick in my heart just at the thought of seeing Gil. It had only been two weeks since that first night we slept in my bed, and I was hooked like a proverbial fish.

I'd never been one to finish work early—always the last to leave, needing to be shoehorned out of my truck. But things had certainly changed. I'd begun packing up first, grumbling if the others dallied, annoyed when they took the piss. None of it was helping my insistence that nothing was going on between Gil and me. Everyone rolled their eyes at my protests, except for Tom, who remained steadfastly silent on the subject. We weren't fooling anyone.

Case in point. Two thirty in the afternoon and I was heading for the mudroom, having left Alek and Charlie to return a hundred head of cattle back to the river flats and Sam to clean up on his own since Tom had gone into Oakwood. It was something I would *never* have done two weeks before.

And why?

All because when I'd sent Sam to the machinery shed for more tail paint, he'd heard Gil swearing black and blue in the kitchen and generally sounding upset. I hadn't gotten a thing done since, except screw up the colour code on a dozen head of cattle. Eventually Charlie whipped the can off me and told me to go play trains until I could get my head in the game.

And so there I was. Playing trains. Heading for the house because I was worried about Gil.

I barely recognised myself.

A month earlier and I'd scoffed at the very idea of a relationship with *anyone*. And yet suddenly that word wasn't scary anymore, just . . . frustrating. Because I wanted it badly. I wanted to make it official. And I wanted a whole lot more. A third of Gil's time on the station was behind us, and an odd sense of panic loomed in my chest. Like I was already running out of time.

If I'd had my way, Gil wouldn't have moved an inch from my bed. But it wasn't as easy as that. He'd insisted on sleeping in his own bed at least a few times since that first night together. And there'd been other times when he'd gone to sleep with me, but then left in the middle of night and I'd woken to find his side of the bed stone cold. *His side? Jesus, that happened fast.* All of those nights had been after days when things emotionally hadn't gone so well for him for one reason or another. The closer my mother's departure loomed, the more he stressed. He was a hardcore perfectionist. No real surprise there.

He didn't want me to witness the nightmares, that much was clear, but he wasn't as good at hiding them from me as he thought. I'd heard him up and about in the kitchen on those nights. He'd stopped heading to the deck where I might hear him, and I knew that was about me too. He was playing that part of himself close to his chest.

Well, fuck that and the horse it rode in on. I was planning on calling bullshit on it all very soon. I wanted as much of Gil as I could get, and that included all the not so pretty stuff. I might not have understood his PTSD anywhere near as well as he did, but since he wasn't keen on talking about it, I hadn't been above a bit of googling, and I'd learned some stuff.

Like there was no guarantee he'd ever be totally free of the nightmares and panic attacks regardless of how much work he did on them, but there was a good chance they'd lessen in frequency. I'd learned he might always need medication of some kind, or he might not, there was no simple answer. But the key to it all was ongoing work with his therapist and accepting support.

The first was in hand—Gil kept his appointments religiously. The second needed a little work. From what Gil *had* said, he wasn't really talking with anyone much beyond Leonard, not even Tuck, and he was protecting himself with me. If he let me into that side of himself, it was going to be harder for him to walk away.

And I got it, I really did. Because I felt exactly the same.

But I had news for him. I *wanted* it to be hard for him to walk away, just like I knew it was going to wreck me if things stayed as good as they were and he still left. But I also didn't want to push too hard.

I figured it would be like trying to force a bunch of merinos off the hill by running your dogs straight at them in full bark. They'd only start panicking, schooling like fish, and looking to make their escape. The best shepherds hardly even used their dogs. They worked with the natural temperament of their stock, using existing paths and opportunities to encourage the animals to go the direction they wanted, making them think it was their idea all along.

And since I ranked myself a pretty good shepherd, I figured I had experience to draw on. I just never imagined I'd be using it to muster myself up a boyfriend. Go figure.

But aside from that one hiccup, things between Gil and me were pretty . . . fucking fantastic. The sex rocked my eyeballs in their sockets. I wasn't sure if Gil was making up for lost time, but I wasn't complaining either. We hadn't taken things to full penetration, but I could tell it was coming.

Gil was as bossy as I was in bed, a fact which generally irritated me in a partner, but with Gil it was a huge turn-on. With him, I didn't give a shit who did what. I loved it all. And when he got that feisty look in his eye and refused to be ordered around, it lit a fire under my arse like you wouldn't believe. I couldn't get enough of him. My chafe marks had chafe marks and we'd already run out of lube once and had to raid the scullery until Gil got into town.

I loved the small reminders of his presence scattered through the house. His shoes in the mudroom. His recipe folder on the island. The lingering scent of his fresh cologne. And when I made my way to the kitchen each morning, regardless of the fact he might only have left my bed fifteen minutes before, that glimpse of his lean sexy frame was like crack to a craving so deep I wouldn't have thought it was possible. The ever-present flour that dusted his rumpled morning sweats, the cooking stains on his retro band T-shirts, or the porcupine tufts of cute as hell bed-tousled blond hair.

He'd ask about the team's plan for the day—whether we'd need lunch or snacks delivered. I'd ask what he was up to with my mother, how the winter bookings for the guest cottages were shaping up, whether the muster prep was on track, and did he need any help—for fuck's sake. He'd smile at every offer I made and politely turn it down, but I kept making them. Colour me ridiculous.

And all of that was bookended by the other end of the day when I'd arrive back to find Gil wandering the homestead gardens or checking the vegetables or talking to the chickens—looking lean and sexy and smelling of cinnamon or garlic or vanilla or curry or roast meat or lemon. It was a crapshoot which one. But I'd push him into whatever private space I could find and kiss him thoroughly until I guessed right what he'd been cooking. It usually took me a while since he was a way better liar than I was, but I couldn't possibly be wrong that many times in a row, so I figured he got a kick out of it as much as I did.

I loved him in my house, in my space, in my life.
I loved it all.
Loved?

Fuck me. I was also in desperate denial.

I wasn't even sure why we were trying to keep it quiet anymore, at least on the station. My feelings leaked through whenever Gil's name came up in conversation.

Off the station was a different story, especially when I talked with Zach. Every text exchange and phone call we shared were acid reminders of exactly how much had changed in the month since I'd last seen my friend. We'd yet to meet again in person, a state of affairs I'd initially been more than happy about, considering what Gil and I were doing, but time was running out and I knew I needed to have those awkward conversations with both of them soon.

When Zach asked how the *new guy* was settling in, I had to stop myself from gushing, and my prevarication said a lot about the guilt I carried. Not because I was taking another guy to my bed—Zach and I had never been exclusive in that way—but because I was hankering after something with Gil that I'd turned down flat with Zach. I wasn't sure I could explain it to myself let alone Zach, and I didn't want to hurt him further.

With all that churning through my head, I reached the back step only to be hit once again with the delicious aroma of baking. My mouth instantly pooled with saliva. It was one benefit of knocking off early.

I glanced up at the heavy grey clouds gathering over the western ranges and thought it was apt. A storm was about to break. Outside for sure, but maybe inside me as well. I leaned through the open doorway and raised my voice in an effort to be heard above the roar of the mixer. "Gil!"

No answer, just the relentless whirring of the beater.

I glanced at my dust-covered boots and winced. *Forgiveness, not permission, right?* I kicked the toes against the concrete step to loosen the worst of the grime and then tiptoed inside to find my mother's blonde bob just visible behind the hefty stand mixer.

Not Gil, then. I buried my disappointment because the sight still made me smile, and it was one I wouldn't see for the following six weeks.

A colourful bandana failed dismally to keep the sticky mixture from her hair. A chicken coop's worth of cracked eggs sat in a bowl at her elbow, a million squidgy brownies cooled on a set of racks in front, and an open tub of sugar the size of several heart attacks stood on a barstool at her side.

Brownies and meringues. My stomach growled. Miller Station's two favourite treats. I cast an eye around the kitchen to see if my guy was hiding somewhere, but there was no sign of the man I'd been hoping to catch a little time with.

"Hey, Mum."

She startled and her hand flew to her chest. "Dammit, Holden. Don't sneak up on me like that."

"I've been standing here for ages," I lied, and wandered across to peer into the bowl. "I was looking for Gil."

She shot me a warm smile and I realised how thankful I was that she knew. That *someone* knew. That I could relax in my own home. "He's in the same place as Spider." She added the last of the sugar from the cup in her hand and I watched as it dipped and folded into the pillowy sweetness. "In the vegetable garden. That dog's got a major crush on your boyfriend."

I hid my smile because Spider wasn't the only one.

My mother adjusted the mixer speed. "I thought you lot were finishing the cattle before that weather front hits later today. A month of grilling us like prime rib, and *now* it decides we need to be drowned in humidity before it rains like cats and dogs. If this is climate change, I'm over it. It better not delay my flight tomorrow."

"It'll have blown through by then." I snagged a still-warm brownie. "Your flight will be fine, the river will drop once more over the next week, and we'll get the muster done before the nasty stuff sets in—all as planned. And to answer your question, I left the others to finish the cattle so I could get to the wages. I need to confirm Gil's bank details." Not exactly a lie, kind of.

"A likely story," she scoffed, scooping another cup of sugar and trickling it into the mix. "But I'm glad you're here. Gil seemed a little off after I got back after lunch. Maybe he'll talk to you." She put the cup down and waited for me to meet her eye. "I like Gil, you know that. I just don't want things to slip around here in all your excitement over this new relationship. We can't afford to fall at the last fence with the buyer coming in a couple of weeks."

I blinked and took a second to tamp down my annoyance. "Do you really think I'd do that?"

She put the cup down and considered me for a moment. "No, I guess not. But I know Tom's worried."

I swallowed the irritation that surged again. "Then he needs to talk to *me*, Mum. He can't be spouting off about how I'm in charge one minute and need to step up, and then the next minute take his concerns to you behind my back. All it does is undermine me."

She hesitated, then she gave a sharp nod. "You're right. I guess we're all taking some time to adjust. I'll tell him next time."

I blinked. "You will? I'd, um, really appreciate that."

She smiled warmly. "I'm not a fool, Holden. I like Tom. He's family. But for better or worse, you're in charge now, and everyone needs to know that. Tom wouldn't have talked to Gran about Grandad behind his back, and he owes you the same courtesy. Which brings us back to Gil. You two aren't fooling anyone. I practically have to wipe both your chins every damn lunchtime. It's getting embarrassing."

I snorted because she was right.

"And get those boots off." She scowled at my feet.

"They're clean." I showed her the soles, which admittedly were less dust-free than I'd hoped.

She huffed. "Well, if you leave a trail of dirt through my house, you'll be cleaning it yourself."

"*Your* house?" I eyed her, half-amused, half making a point as I finger-scooped a mound of sugary deliciousness into my mouth. "Damn, that's good." It was almost worth the rap on my knuckles that followed. "Ow!"

She switched off the mixer and began scooping spoonfuls onto oven sheets lined with baking paper.

I reached for the beater and set about licking it clean. "So, you're happy leaving him in charge? You're not going to worry?"

"Not a bit. He'll be fine. We readied Folly Hut together two days ago. Then he did River Hut all on his own. I checked it early this morning and I couldn't have done it better." She slid three trays of meringues into the massive oven and then sat on the stool opposite mine. "What about you? Are you worried about the muster?"

Was I? I thought about that. "No. At least no more than last year. Just the usual logistical stuff and stressing about the weather. But as far as Gil's concerned, I've got no worries."

Her shrewd gaze pinned me to my seat. "So, what's eating you then?"

"Nothing in particular." I put down the sparkling clean beater and wiped my mouth. "I guess I'm still adjusting to Grandad and Gran not being here. To living in their house—" I looked around. "—with all their *stuff*. To being officially in charge, and Tom's part of that. And then there's the buyer's visit. Take your pick." I blew out a sigh. "We need that contract, Mum."

Her eyes softened. "You've done everything you can. The rest is out of your hands. But as far as the house is concerned—" A sly smile played on her lips. "—maybe you should check out your bedroom."

"My bedroom?" I narrowed my gaze. "And why would I want to do that?"

A grin split her face. "Just take a look. Groceries weren't the only thing Gil picked up in Oakwood yesterday. He's been a busy man this morning. And before you say anything, he checked with me first and the station is footing the bill. Go on."

With my interest piqued, I headed for my room only to come to an abrupt stop at the open door, my mouth hanging open in surprise. "What the hell?"

My mother appeared at my shoulder. "He worked at it all morning."

I stepped inside and a huge smile spread over my face. There wasn't a single rose in sight. Not a sugary painting on the wall. Not a cutesy knickknack to be seen. The wallpaper had been undercoated in white and gone was the fussy carved headboard. I recognised the two distressed leather armchairs from the guest cottages. They sat facing the lake atop a new soft grey rug. A simple table sat between them with a stack of my farming books to one side. And on the dressing table stood a line of test pots and a small paintbrush.

The room had been transformed. Gone were the ghosts of my grandparents, leaving a space that felt much more like me, like . . . us. I made my way to one of the chairs and ran a hand over its soft hide. I could picture myself sitting there to watch the sunrise behind the lake, maybe even with Gil if I was lucky. It was the first time I'd felt that maybe I could make a home for myself, after all.

I picked up the note that sat on top of the pile of books and read.

Thought you might like a temporary tweak to your room until it can be stripped and done properly. Decide on a colour and I'll paint while you're on muster. The furniture doesn't have to stay.

Gil

Warmth flooded my chest and my eyes unexpectedly brimmed.

"He wanted you to feel more at home in here." My mother's voice came from behind. "It can all be changed if you don't—"

"I love it," I said truthfully, spinning to face her. "So, this wasn't your idea?"

"No." She gave a soft smile. "It was all Gil's."

I swallowed the emotion welling in my throat. I'd let my doubts rule my feelings. Gil was as much in this as I was. He had as much to lose. He cared enough to do this for me, and that said a lot.

"Let him help you, Holden."

I turned back to my mother. "Help me?"

"While I'm away. You can't do everything on your own. No one can. Running this place is stressful, and Gil's a pretty good listener."

"We . . . talk," I said, my gaze landing on the stack of books. The one second from the top caught my eye, and I smiled. *Boss Versus Leader.* I almost laughed. Cheeky fucker.

"You're more like your grandfather than you know," she said softly, and it was all I could do not to flinch. "Running this place can be hell on a person, and you can't keep bottling things up like you've done all your life, like Grandad did, like so many farmers do. I want more than that for you. Talking about what's bugging you isn't weak, son. It's the exact opposite. I get that maybe I'm not the right person for you to talk to, and maybe not Tom either, but you need to have someone. Tell me you'll at least think about it. So I don't worry?" She batted maternal puppy dog eyes my way and I groaned.

"Oh, that was sneaky."

She grinned. "I'm your mother, what can I say?"

"Okay. I promise I'll talk to *someone* if things get tough."

"That's all I ask." She pulled me into a long hug, and for a second I considered spilling the whole sorry mess about my grandfather's calls and his increasingly vile diatribes that left me doubting my ability to run the place at all. But I'd been taking Gil's advice and limiting when I accepted Grandad's calls, along with the length of them, and it was helping. And since my mother was leaving the next day, I figured it could wait.

She let go and pushed me out of the room. "Now, go find Gil. And tell him I'll organise dinner. I thought it would be nice if we all ate together on my last night. Harry is driving me to the airport after breakfast."

"I'll tell him. And in case I hadn't mentioned it, these are awesome." I shoved another brownie in my mouth and ran for the back door, only just avoiding the spatula that hit the doorjamb as I passed.

CHAPTER SEVENTEEN

Holden

The term vegetable garden was a bit of a misnomer for something that was larger than most people's entire yard, including their house. The station didn't rely on its produce like it had sixty years before, but my mother and Gran had remained big fans. They'd set up a complicated watering system fed by the lake, but the growing season was drawing to a close and the garden was looking a little dry and worse for wear.

With the transformation of my bedroom still at the front of my mind, I rounded the stone pillar on the corner of the east deck and froze.

Holy Jesus. I'd found Gil.

The sexy man was clearing a large area of herbs and seeded spinach and looking like a sweaty, porno-worthy million dollars while doing it. With his Earbuds in place, he had no idea I was standing there, which gave me a moment to just enjoy the view.

He wore a wide-brimmed hat and a loose red Foo Fighters singlet that clung to his body and hid nothing of his hard sinewy shoulders.

Added to that, a pair of dirty jeans hung low enough on his slim hips to reveal a glimpse of his crease and merit an arrest warrant . . . or a solid fuck . . . It was a close call.

Because damn. The man was a walking wet dream, at least *my* wet dream.

Gil was nothing like the men I usually hooked up with who were either random tourists or farming and industry contacts. Gil was no tourist, and he wouldn't know a wether from a ram to save himself. But he took my breath away, regardless.

For a slender guy, he packed a ton of force into every slam of the shovel blade, and I wondered what the dry, thirsty earth had done to deserve it. When the creep factor finally kicked in—not as quickly as it should have—I wandered over, calling his name a couple of times to try and avoid startling him. But he never looked up, and when I tapped him on the shoulder, he jerked back with an audible gasp.

"Holden! Jesus—" He yanked out his earbuds and shoved them in the pocket of his jeans.

"I'm sorry." I raised my palms. "I tried to get your attention but . . ."

"No, it's fine." He jammed his shovel into a dry mound of soil and stood staring at the ground, his chest heaving.

Fuck. I ducked my head to catch his eye. "Hey, are you okay?"

He clearly wasn't, confirmed by the shaking hand he dragged down his face.

Way to go, idiot. Startling the guy with PTSD. I reached for his arm but he jerked away.

"I'm fine. I just . . . need a moment." He walked off a few metres and stood staring at the ground, his breathing shallow, his hands clenching and unclenching at his sides. Spider appeared from who the hell knew where and nudged Gil's thigh. Gil dropped a trembling hand to his head and scratched around his ears, his breath steadying.

Fucking wonder dog.

I watched as Gil dug in his back pocket and then snapped the lid on a small bottle to tip a pill into his palm.

I grabbed his water bottle from the ground and raced over. "Here."

His gaze jerked to the water, then up at me, those normally bright hazel eyes dulled to a muddy grey and edged with a shame that I hated on sight. "Thanks." He took the bottle and threw back the pill.

"If you need them, you need them," I said gently and tried for his arm again.

He didn't pull away. "I've been trying to cut down—"

"That's between you and Leonard," I said evenly. "I'm not your keeper, Gil. I don't need to know unless I do, right?"

His lips twitched and he shook his head. "Bossy fucker."

"Damn right. Now let's sit. And that one goes on the fridge, by the way."

He grunted and let me steer him to a bench parked under the misshapen old lemon tree that hadn't produced fruit in years but offered great shade. It was Mum and Gran's favourite place to sit with a wine in the evening and peruse their garden.

Gil's bare skin felt good under my hand, hot and slick with perspiration. He was too irresistible, and before we sat, I pulled him into my arms and kissed him.

He tensed for just a second, then relaxed and slid his hands around my neck, his mouth opening to deepen the kiss, allowing my tongue to sweep through. He tasted of salt and coffee and hard work and everything Gil, and my cock sprang to life of its own accord. But the tremble in Gil's hands was still fresh on my neck and I told myself to calm the fuck down.

"That was for my room," I said, stroking his damp cheek. "I can't believe you did that for me."

His eyes filled with pleasure. "So it was okay?"

"More than." I kissed him again. "I love it. But when it comes to choosing the final colour, I want us to do it together."

A crease formed between his brows, but neither of us stated the obvious implication of that.

"Now sit." I pushed Gil down onto the dusty bench and Spider dropped into the shade at his feet.

Gil sat staring at the ground. "I promise I don't usually—"

"How about we take a minute to breathe before all the self-recriminations start?" I elbowed him gently. "Then *I* can berate myself for startling you, and *you* can tell me how embarrassed you are about something that isn't your fault and that you can't control."

Gil's gaze rose to mine and something like gratitude flashed in his eyes. "Fine. Have it your way." He scooted down in his seat and leaned against me.

I took his trembling hand and we stared in comfortable silence across the vegetable garden and out to the lake like we'd be doing it for years. Two old men chewing over their day. And the idea wasn't . . . terrible.

After a few minutes, his shoulders relaxed and his breathing lost that worrying hitch. "That hasn't happened in the daytime for months," he said earnestly. "I promise I can still do my job."

I huffed dismissively, irked that he felt the need to justify himself. "Like I don't already know that, sweetheart? Just like I know you'd tell me if that ever changed." I studied his profile, the smooth line of his jaw, those long curling lashes, and that faint scar that ran across his eyebrow. He was beautiful at any distance, but close like this . . . "What happened today, Gil? Why are you assaulting our vegetable garden like it personally offended you?"

His lips twitched but he didn't answer.

I reached a finger to his jaw and turned his troubled eyes to mine. "Whether you tell me or not is up to you, but I'm in this all the way, Gil, the good, the bad and the ugly. And I like to think I could maybe do the listening thing too, that is, if you think that you can trust me." My calculating wiles weren't lost on Gil who promptly rolled his eyes.

"Sorry."

He snorted softly and studied me for a moment, like he was weighing his options. Then he pulled his phone from his pocket, scrolled for a bit, and handed it over. "I got this email from our lawyer just after lunch."

Our lawyer. I read the email twice. "Whoa." I winced and handed back his phone. "The other driver wants to meet with you?"

"With *both* of us." Gil ran his palms down his thighs, that edge of anxiety back in his voice. "I . . . I don't think I can do it."

I didn't blame him. "Have you talked with Luke?"

Gil sighed and looked away. "Not yet. I've been doing a good job of avoiding him since I arrived. I wanted some distance from it all. Tuck let him know what I was doing and why, but I haven't felt ready to talk." He flushed. "Pretty childish, right? But I did open the email he sent today after he'd received his copy from the lawyer. Here—" He handed back the phone and I read the email.

Luke sounded . . . desperate, for want of a better word. Like he'd been worried out of his mind about Gil. So much so that by the time I'd finished, my preconceptions of the guy were thoroughly shaken. He came across just as devastated as Gil was at the idea of meeting the driver responsible for Callie's death and more than a little concerned about Gil's reaction and his mental health in general. He sounded, not to put too fine a point on it, a pretty nice guy. *Dammit.*

And yes, I might've had a little bit invested in the man being an uncaring arsehole, so sue me.

"He sounds . . . worried," I offered cautiously.

"And with good reason," Gil said unhappily. "I haven't exactly been keeping him in the picture about me."

"But you two aren't together anymore," I pointed out. "You don't owe him regular updates, Gil."

He shrugged and added somewhat icily, "The divorce isn't final yet, so technically we *are* still married."

I said nothing, a knot forming in my stomach.

"I'm sorry." Gil reached for my hand. "You're right, of course. Luke and I *aren't* together, no matter what the paperwork says." His eyes searched mine. "And I don't want to be with him. That's finished. There's no going back."

I let out the breath I'd been holding and squeezed his hand. "That's good news for me." I chuckled joylessly and shook my head. "I wanted to hate him for what he did to you, but after reading that, I hate to say that I kind of don't. But I also don't like the idea that he knows you better than me. And yes, I'm behaving like a petulant child."

That made him smile. "Oh, I don't know. Possessive Holden is kind of hot." He kissed the small mole on my cheek, and I rolled my eyes. "Plus, we're still working on the getting to know each other part, right?"

I held his gaze. "I hope so."

He worried his lip at my non-committal answer, then dropped my hands and leaned back on the bench. "To be honest, I wanted to hate Luke too. And I *did*, for a long time, although maybe it was more disappointment than anything else. But now, I'm beginning to think he simply called time on something that had run its course long before. And he absolutely loved Callie as much as I did. He was a great dad. And maybe I'm more forgiving than I was because it's all brought me to you." He shot me a look. "So maybe he did me a favour in the long run."

Keep thinking that. "How's the breathing?"

He filled his lungs. "Much better."

"Hands?"

He held them out. "Could be worse."

"Good. Do you trust me?"

His gaze narrowed and that small scar disappeared into a tiny fold in his brow. "Yes." He blinked like the answer surprised him.

"Excellent." I patted his leg. "Wait here."

"Why?"

I silenced him with a look and he raised his hands. "Okay, this is me waiting."

"Mmm." I eyeballed him. "See that you do."

He smirked at my tone and I knew I'd pay for it later. I couldn't wait. I left him chuckling and headed for the kitchen.

Two minutes later I was back.

"What's that for?" Gil eyed the small knapsack I carried with suspicion.

"You'll have to wait and see." I held out the sweater I'd grabbed for him from the mudroom and then pulled him to his feet. "Come on, Mister Fancy Psychologist, the farmer is now in charge, and I say we could both do with a break." I started walking and he goosed my butt.

"Hey!"

"That's for being bossy." He sidled closer, his tone silky, "You want me to kiss it better?"

I so fucking did. But I gathered my dignity and side-eyed him instead. "I'll take a rain check, but it'll be more than a kiss if you know what's good for you."

"That can be arranged." He ran his mouth up my neck, sending a shiver all the way to my toes. Then he pulled away, his pupils the size of saucers, and Jesus, if I didn't want to strip us right there and then and have my way with him in the middle of the rampant zucchinis. And like he knew exactly what I was thinking, he ran the tip of his tongue along his lips and something combusted in my balls—

"No." I slapped a hand over his mouth. "Shepherd in charge, remember?"

"Are you sure about that?" He tickled my palm with the tip of his tongue and I yanked it away. "Then again, if you're talking ploughing or dipping or drenching or crutching—"

"Oh god, please stop." I grabbed his hand and tugged him after me. "Before I embarrass myself and scandalise my mother."

At the machinery shed, I handed him a helmet and he settled in behind me on our newest quad. "It gets steep in parts, so you better hold on."

"Aye-aye, captain." His arm snaked around my waist and he slid in close—his chest hot on my back, his breath loud in my ear . . . and yeah . . . I had to take a moment.

"Ready?"

He grunted what I took for a yes, tightened his grip, and we headed up the drive toward the woolshed, taking a right onto Dunwoody's beat before starting to climb. The destination I had in mind was about halfway up and off to the right of the main track. It was never meant for quads, and so when it got too steep, I parked the machine to the side and we continued on foot. Another fifteen lung-busting minutes—until the sweat ran from every pore on my body and my thighs burned like a motherfucker.

"Dammit, Holden." Gil paused, gasping at my back. "You could've warned me I'd need oxygen."

My laugh carried a distinct wheeze. "Would you have come?"

"Hell no." He sucked in another lungful of air and kept climbing. "Not in this humidity. I wish it would rain and just get it over with."

"Okay, timeout." I stopped and dropped my hands to my knees, taking a minute to catch my breath.

Gil followed suit, and while we were still bent over, we caught each other's eye and he chuckled. "You're insane, Miller."

"It's been said before." I lifted the hem of my T-shirt and wiped the sweat from my face, fully aware of Gil watching me. I lowered the shirt and shot him a wink. "We could always toss a coin . . . later."

He huffed out a laugh. "You wish. That gorgeous arse is mine, baby."

And it was, I realised with a jolt. Any way he wanted it.

Gil's mouth tipped up into a slow, sexy smile like he'd just read my mind.

"Don't look so smug." I flipped him off.

He laughed. "Don't mistake thrilled for smug. I'm already picturing how it's gonna go."

Oh god. "You have to quit saying that stuff." I adjusted myself and started walking again. "This way." I took a hard right off the track along one of the well-trodden sheep trails that crossed the face of the hillside. A few minutes on and we arrived at a large outcrop of boulders with the best view of the valley on the entire station.

"Welcome to the castle." I climbed up behind three of the largest boulders and then out onto the flat top of the slightly lower middle one, the other two acting as walls on either side.

"Sit." I scooted over and Gil squeezed alongside, the platform being just wide enough to fit two people snugly—a happy coincidence, nothing more.

"Oh. My. God. Wow." He looked out over the spectacular view of the valley. "This is amazing."

I handed him a water bottle from the knapsack, along with one of my mother's brownies.

His eyes crinkled in pleasure. "A picnic? You do realise this borders on romantic, don't you?"

"Hey," I protested. "I can do romantic." I omitted the part where I hadn't ever tried.

Gil snorted, seeing straight through me. "Exactly how many boyfriends did you say you've had?"

I elbowed him . . . hard. "None, and can I just say I regret having ever told you that embarrassing slice of my personal history? But it can't be that hard. Romance, I mean. Food, wine, candles, music . . . and a large, studded dildo."

He snorted and his lips met mine for the softest of kisses. "Aw, you say the sweetest things. Don't ever change." His face hovered close to mine, his eyes soft like he was seeing something he'd missed before. Then he sat back and raised the brownie in a toast. "Your mother's gonna nail your balls to the wall for nicking these."

I shrugged. "How do you know I nicked them?"

He arched a brow.

"Okay, I nicked them. But it'll be worth it."

"They're your balls." He took a swig of water, a large bite of the brownie, and groaned in pleasure.

"Actually, rumour has it that they're yours tonight." I took a bite of my own brownie as Gil choked on the remainder of his.

When he was done eating, Gil leaned back on his hands. "Damn, this is beautiful."

"So beautiful," I answered, and when he looked my way, we both knew I wasn't talking about the view.

His cheeks pinked and an almost-shy smile broke on his lips before he looked away again. "I think this is my new favourite place."

I dragged my gaze back to the view and tried to see the station through Gil's fresh eyes. It sat in a deep alpine valley—a kilometre at its widest point—as if carved with a giant's spoon into a steep-sided U. A mosaic of rock and scree and gravel moraines sliced through the faces, tumbling down toward tussock-clad terraces and billowing grasslands covered in hummocky dumps of rocks. And right at the bottom, a net of shimmering threads of water crisscrossed the valley floor toward lakes that glistened blue from glacial flour.

"I've walked up Dunwoody's beat a few times since I arrived." Gil's gaze swept the valley once again. "But I never thought to come this far."

"You can't see this spot from anywhere on the track." I filled my lungs with the moist air and let it out slowly. "I used to come up here as a kid. It was my own private castle, and this platform was the watchtower. It looks nothing more than a pile of rocks from the homestead, but because of the acoustics and depending on the wind, you can sometimes hear people talking in the backyard. Listen."

Gil did, and as the raucous cackle of the station hens climbed the valley walls, a slow smile spread over his face. "That's uncanny. And is that River Hut?" He indicated the sun glinting off a roof up on the top end of the valley.

"Yes." I pointed to the left of the structure. "And that's Folly Hut above the bush line. North Hut is around the furthermost bend where the Glendale River spills into the Havelock River, but we don't use that one so much."

Gil's eyes tracked where I was pointing. "It really helps to get my head around the geography. The station is so vast."

I slid an arm around his waist and pulled him close. "I can't remember the last time I did this," I admitted. "I love this land. It means everything to me. But I've been so caught up in worry about stock and contracts and feed costs, in the problems of the station, in my responsibilities, in Grandad, in everything that's happening, that I just forgot how plain beautiful it all is."

Gil turned and kissed my cheek. "It feeds your soul, baby."

I smiled and kissed his nose, losing myself in the calm of his gentle eyes. "My dad showed me this place." The words came from nowhere, but they didn't hurt as much as I'd expected. "I think that's why it became such a special place for me as a kid, especially after he left."

Gil regarded me with a tender expression. "You don't talk about him much."

"No." My gaze slid sideways to the valley. "And by not much, I take it you mean not at all."

His lips twitched. "Now that you mention it."

I took a deep breath and blew it out slowly. "I guess it still hurts."

His hand slid into mine. "Did you see much of him after he left?"

"Not as much as a lonely kid needed." I felt the truth crunch in my heart. "He came from farming, but not high country, and he and Grandad never saw eye to eye on the running of the station. I was eight when it all blew up. Mum and Dad's marriage was already dicey by then, and when Dad realised Grandad was never going to hand the reins over while he was still alive, he called time on everything, including us. He went north, got himself another family not long after, and now runs a huge dairy operation just out of Fielding."

"Wow." Gil's eyes widened. "That's a lot for a young kid to deal with. Did you ever go and stay with them?"

I shrugged, stamping down the pain that threatened to surface every time I thought of those years. "I visited a few times, and it was okay. But it was hard watching him so obviously happy with his new family and knowing he pretty much left me without a backward glance, so . . ."

Gil squeezed my hand.

"But it's not easy, this kind of life," I admitted. "It takes everything you give it and then sucks up the rest as well. The isolation, the unpredictability, the weather, the hard physical work; marriages, families, friends, they all get tested, and not everything survives."

Gil said nothing just squeezed my hand again, and I realised he probably understood those things better than most.

"Don't get me wrong," I finally said. "I like my dad. He's not a *bad* guy. He works hard and he's good with his family. He's just . . . oblivious, I guess. At least when it comes to me."

Gil pressed his lips to mine in the sweetest of kisses. "It still fucking hurts, right?"

"Yeah, it does." My eyes filled and he kissed each one in turn. "We should start heading back," I warned, noticing how the mushrooming clouds were thickening over the sawtooth ridges and starting to roll down into the valley. "We've got about forty-five minutes before it buckets down."

Gil flashed me a wry smile. "That's pretty impressive forecasting."

"Thirty years in these mountains teaches you a few things." I stood and dusted off my hands, then helped Gil up.

"Am I a coward if I don't agree to meet him?"

I chose my words carefully. "In my opinion, either decision is a brave one, and only you can decide what the best one is."

He frowned and looked away. "How very diplomatic of you." He jabbed at the rock with his boot.

"You know I'm right."

He shot me a quick smile that didn't reach his eyes. "It still doesn't help."

I wasn't going to be drawn. "What happened to him, anyway? The driver?"

Gil stretched and blew out a sigh. "He pleaded guilty to manslaughter and ended up in a Corrections Facility north of Wellington. Apparently, he had two children of his own, and a lot of people got up in court to say what a great father he'd been until he started using again after almost eight years clean. He lost his kids, his marriage, his freedom, and gained a lifetime of grief and guilt. I heard he could barely talk in court."

I tried to keep my elation in check. It was the first time Gil had ever talked about the driver of the other car in any depth. I risked pressing a little more. "The email mentioned he'd been through prison rehab?"

Gil rolled his eyes, looking unimpressed. "Apparently."

"You're not convinced?"

He chewed on his lower lip. "I don't know what to think. I can't decide if I feel hideously sorry for him or still totally fucking furious at what he did to Callie." He hesitated. "And what he put *me* through, as selfish as that sounds. And if that doesn't scream that I'm not ready to forgive and hold hands, then I don't know what does. *And* then, of course, I'm angry and disappointed with *myself* for thinking like that. I'm a psychologist. I'm *supposed* to know how to do this, how to learn to forgive for my own sake so I can move past it. It goes with the territory. And yes, I know I just swore." He massaged his temple. "But honestly, right now, I don't give a fuck. And that's twice. Shit." He snort-laughed. "Three times."

I squeezed his shoulder and kissed his hair. "Like I'm even counting. Did you come to any decisions while you were inflicting grievous bodily harm on the herb garden?"

He huffed out a laugh. "Only that I guess I need to suck up my pissy attitude and talk to Luke sooner rather than later. But I need to think about this first. Work out how I feel and what I want before Luke's feelings muddy the waters. And I want to get the muster and shearing out of the way so I have a clear mind. I emailed him and asked for two weeks to think about it."

I gave his waist a gentle squeeze. "Sounds like a start. You were both Callie's dads. He's gonna have the same decision to make for himself about the meeting."

Gil groaned. "God, I hadn't even thought about the fact one of us might want to go and the other not."

"It's possible," I agreed. "But that doesn't mean you have to meet this guy just because Luke might decide to. It's not your responsibility to ease this guy's conscience or offer him a listening ear, Gil. You don't have to be the professional in this. You get to be just you, a dad who's lost his daughter. Or aren't you psychologists allowed to be human like the rest of us?"

He snorted. "Fuck you."

I nuzzled his neck. "That's what I'm hoping."

A gust of wind funnelled between the rocks and fanned Gil's blond waves across his face. He pushed them aside and leaned back against the rock. "But if I don't go, I'll always wonder if I missed an opportunity."

I shrugged. "So, go see him. Or don't. Talk to Leonard and Luke and Tuck, and then make your own decision."

His smile made my heart trip. And then he kissed me, long and slow. "Ten years younger, and look who's the grown-up of the two of us."

I cupped his chin. "I just think that after everything you've been through, you have the right and the strength to do whatever you need to heal."

He studied me intently. "You barely know me, Holden."

I wasn't sure I agreed. "I know enough."

His brow knotted, but then he said in a softer tone, "Maybe you do at that." He pulled me close and kissed down my neck to the dip in my clavicle. My head fell back, and a hawk swooped under the swirling grey clouds above, there and gone in a second, riding the current as my heart thrummed against my ribs and Gil nipped his way back up my throat to press his lips to my ear. "You taste of hard work and chocolate, and you smell like wool."

I huffed. "Charming."

"Actually, it is." He ran his nose along my jaw, pressing clusters of butterfly kisses to the light stubble before continuing up the side of my face and into my hair. My eyelids fluttered closed, and he kissed each one. Then he leaned back and traced a finger down my forehead to my chin.

"I fantasised about what kissing you would feel like from the moment you slid out of that Hilux in Tekapo, looking every inch the sexy-as-hell young station owner. You even had the swagger down. I just never imagined I'd get the chance." He kissed the end of my nose, then pulled away and the world returned—a welcome breeze licking at my hot skin.

An engine roared somewhere in the valley and we both squinted at the cloud of dust moving at speed toward the homestead. It only took me a second. One glance at the ute and the motorbike lashed onto its bed and my mouth ran dry. *Zach.* "Shit."

Gil's gaze jerked to mine. "Who's that?"

"It's Zach."

"The neighbour's son? Paddy and Norma from Lane Station, right? Next valley over." The ute hit the cattlestop at speed, the clatter echoing through the valley and Gil huffed, "Well, he's sure in a hurry."

"And I bet I know why." *Dammit.* The last thing I needed was Zach and Gil in the same space. Fuck. My. Life. What would Gil think? I panicked. I should've told him. And Zach. What the hell was I thinking?

Gil's curious look went unanswered, and when a fat raindrop splatted on my cheek, I shouldered the knapsack and set off along the track at a fast walk. "Come on before we get drenched."

The sluggish raindrops intensified as I led the way across the steep face of the mountain with Gil following silently at my back. But when we got onto the quad bike, he grabbed my elbow and tugged me around to face him, his hair already dripping from the rain. "I'm not taking another step until you tell me what's going on." He cupped my jaw. "I know you too, Holden."

There was nothing but concern in his eyes and I was talking before I knew it. "I went to school with Zach. We've known each other forever. We're . . . mates." I aimed for casual, but heat crept up my throat.

"Uh-huh." Gil's tone and level gaze said I wasn't fooling anyone.

"But we also have . . . history. Friends-with-benefits . . . history. It's done, but—"

Gil's brows popped. "How recent?"

Oh God. "Can't we talk on the way?"

"No."

I sighed and slumped against the quad bike. "Zach's not out, and over the last few years we kind of . . . expanded on our friendship."

"Expanded, huh?" Gil's amusement was obvious, which gave me some relief. "So, you were fucking?"

I snorted. "We had a casual friends-with-benefits thing. It was safe for him and convenient for both of us."

"So, you were fucking."

I groaned. "Yes, but that's all it was . . . at least for me."

Gil huffed. "But not for Zach, I take it?"

I sighed and wiped the rain from his face with my hand. "No. Turns out Zach wanted more, and I'd missed it completely. It came to a head and I had to tell him I wasn't interested. We're still friends, but it hasn't been long, and he obviously doesn't know about you."

Gil rolled his eyes. "How long?"

I swallowed hard and screwed my eyes shut. "I ended it the morning I picked you up from the bus."

Gil's head fell back and he groaned. "Jesus Christ, Holden. And don't you dare count that, or any of the others." He studied me, hard, like he was trying to read me. "And you don't have any feelings for *him?*"

I returned his level stare with one of my own, willing him to believe me. "No, at least not in that way. I love him as a mate, but I've never felt for anyone what I do for you."

Gil kept staring, not taking his eyes off mine, looking for who the hell knew what? The truth, I supposed. Then his gaze flicked down to the homestead. "You said you knew why he was here?"

I sighed. "Zach's dad's a homophobic prick. The whole discussion about wanting more with me occurred that morning because Zach had been thinking of coming out to his parents and wanted to know where we stood if that happened. When I said I wasn't interested, I offered him a bed and a job if he decided to go through with it anyway. I'm guessing he did."

Gil shoved his fingers through his damp hair, his expression one of disbelief. "So let me get this right. A friend of yours, a *man* who's had his heart broken by you, and is likely still pining for what he can't have, and has no idea about us, is coming to stay and work on the station, and will have to watch you and I— Oh fucking hell." He groaned.

I grabbed his hand as thunder rumbled in the distance and the rain picked up. "I swear I was going to tell you about it this week. Did I screw up?"

Gil cupped my cheek and shook his head. "No. You did nothing wrong as such. It's just going to be awkward with a capital fucking *A*, right?"

He had no idea. "Maybe he won't notice—" The are-you-shitting-me look on Gil's face cut me short.

"Like we've been really successful at keeping things on the down-low so far, right?" He scoffed, his eyes dancing. "And exactly how do you think Zach is going to feel? I don't know what planet you're on, but everyone knows, Holden. *Everyone.* Which means Zach will hear the chatter. In fact, I was going to raise the idea of just making every-thing official tonight. Then at least I can kiss you anytime I want without worrying who might see."

I sighed because he was right. Everyone *did* know, which meant Zach would too within hours of his arrival. Then it struck me what Gil had just said and my stomach swooped. *Oh.* "Really? You'd be happy to make it official?" I stepped closer and ghosted my lips over his. "Because I'd like that a lot. Especially the part about you kissing me anytime you want."

He chuckled, gave me a way-too-small rain-damp peck on the lips and then shoved me away. "Yeah, you're far too fucking cute when you want to be. *That's* what you take out of all I said?" He slapped my butt. "Get on that quad, Mister. I'm too old for this shit. Whatever you need from me, you've got it. We'll keep us under wraps until you get a chance to talk with Zach, but you better be quick. Maybe not tonight if he's in a state. But tomorrow morning for sure. Yeah?"

I nodded. "I agree."

"Good, because we don't have the luxury of enough time together to waste any more of it," he finished.

A pointed reminder of something I was doing my best to ignore.

Gil cut another quick look toward the homestead and winced. "Oh god, he's not staying in the house, is he?"

"No. No." I leaned in to kiss the corner of his mouth. "I'll put him in my old cottage. Now come on. We're soaked already," I climbed onto the quad and Gil scrambled up behind, wrapping an arm around my waist.

"What the hell have you got me into?" His breath washed hot over the back of my neck.

I laid a hand over his arm on my stomach and steeled myself. "You don't want . . . to stop . . . us . . . do you?"

His hesitation wasn't exactly reassuring, but then he pulled me tight against him and nuzzled my neck. "Hell no, baby. We've barely gotten started."

CHAPTER EIGHTEEN

Gil

We made it as far as the bottom of Dunwoody's beat and the turnoff to the woolshed before the skies belched open and the rain bucketed down so hard, I could scarcely see the track over Holden's shoulder. Caught on the quad bike with zero cover, there was nothing to do but endure the solid drenching.

I'd been pretty buttoned-up in the adventure department, my adult life spent mostly between my comfortable office, the gym, or a walk on a nice day. And so, as we rounded the track for home, the childlike glee that unexpectedly bubbled up my throat and the race of adrenaline zinging through my blood kind of caught me by surprise.

I let go of Holden's waist, leaned back, and opened my arms to the deluge with a whoop of delight. I was sopping wet anyway, so what the hell did it matter? With my face laid open to the sting of the sheeting rain, the cool downpour ran over my parched skin and every cell burst alive in its wake.

"Whoooooooooooo-hooooooooooo." I heard a slightly hysterical laugh and realised it was me. Which only set me giggling.

Holden glanced over his shoulder, wearing a sopping, frowny face and demanded, "What the hell are you up to?"

I slapped him on the back. "Isn't this amazing? I am so fucking wet, Holden. I'm a mess. I'm such a fucking mess." I smacked a kiss onto his ear and then stuck my tongue out to catch the rain.

He turned to look at me again and immediately cracked up laughing.

"You know, I'd forgotten what this feels like," I shouted into the storm.

"What?" he yelled back over his shoulder.

"Happiness," I answered, my tears mingling with the rain to be washed off my face.

He laughed and punched the air, the two of us whooping like crazy people through the final three hundred metres to the shed. It lasted less than a minute but felt like hours—the force of the rain, the rare bubble of joy in my chest, the musical ring of Holden's laughter, his arse grinding back on my dick, his raw passion for his land, his home, his people . . . me.

The high country works its own kind of miracles.

Something ignited in my chest, something that felt a lot like hope. Endings and beginnings. The tail of one into the head of another.

We pulled into the shelter of the machinery shed, soaked to the skin and still laughing. I flung my arms around Holden's waist and planted wet kisses on the back of his neck, feeling truly alive for the first time in what felt like forever.

"Thank you. Thank you," I gasped, scrambling off the quad to stand in front of him. "That was . . . I don't know what that was. Except it was exactly what I needed."

Holden studied me with a soft longing. "You're welcome, baby." He ran the back of his fingers down both sides of my face, flicking the water to the ground. "God, look at you." He pushed back my sodden hair and cupped my chin in his palm. "You're so fucking gorgeous."

My heart swelled. "Likewise. A month ago, if you'd asked me if the last two weeks were possible, I'd have laughed at you."

"Same here." He drew me in for a hard kiss.

When he was done mauling me, I summoned my smuggest smile. "But I do believe that was another point against you, which, if I'm not mistaken, makes you a big fat loser."

He narrowed his gaze. "But *you* said *likewise,* which is the same as saying the actual word. And you said fucking mess and fucking wet—I've been had."

I snorted and gave him a light shove. "Expletives employed during psychological epiphanies can't be counted. You owe me pancakes, Mister Miller."

"Jesus Christ," Holden grumbled. "I never had a chance, did I?"

"I refuse to be drawn into your dodgy excuses," I said loftily.

Holden snorted and traced my lips with the tip of his finger, his eyes on mine, the sound of the battering rain on the iron roof matching the thunder in my chest. I was free-falling hard and I wasn't sure I could stop even if I wanted to.

"Holden? Is that you?" Emily appeared around the corner of the shed, holding a towel over her head to keep the rain off. She looked between us and her mouth tipped up in a smile. "Look at the state of you boys. You made a hell of a racket coming in."

Holden and I traded smiles. "I took Gil up to the castle," he answered, throwing me a towel from the stack I'd started keeping in the shed to stop the team wearing the worst of their grime into the kitchen every damn lunchtime.

Emily's eyes widened in surprise. "Did you, now?" Then she shook her head. "As much as I'd love to hear more, Zach's waiting on the deck, out front."

Holden sighed and dismounted the quad. "We saw him drive in."

She raised her brows. "I don't suppose he knows about . . . ?" She flicked her head my way.

Holden flushed. "Ah, no."

"Dear Lordy. I doubt that's going to go down well on top of everything else." She shook the water out of her towel. "Thank God I'm out of here tomorrow."

"So, he's told his dad?" Holden checked.

"Yes." Emily lifted the towel above her head. "But I only got the basics. He wants to talk to you. He won't even come inside."

"Shit." Then Holden caught my arched brow and groaned. "*That* one doesn't count. Besides, I already lost, according to you."

Emily glanced between us. "Don't tell me you boys are still running that bet?"

"Nope." I smiled smugly. "I just won."

She threw her hands in the air. "Sweet Jesus, I'm running a kindergarten. Gil, you're with me. We're gonna need coffee. Lots and lots of coffee."

We parted ways at the side of the house—Holden using the covered deck to get around to the front, while Emily and I took the mudroom route. I barely slowed to shuck off my wet clothes in favour of a pair of dry sweats and one of Holden's T-shirts before dashing into the kitchen. I wanted a good look at the man who'd caused all the kerfuffle, and yeah, okay, the man who'd shared Holden's bed as well. So, sue me. And if the only way I could do that was to spy on them through the window . . . it appeared I wasn't above that, either.

Did I feel pathetic and ridiculous? You betcha. Was it going to stop me? Not a chance.

But at least I wasn't the only one. Emily was already standing next to the window, a tea towel hanging limp in her hands, her right ear angled toward the open sash.

Her gaze shot to mine and a deep blush washed over her face. "Okay, so I'm nosey." She waved me over. "But I can hardly hear a thing above the rain anyway."

I looked over her shoulder and caught sight of a rather beautiful auburn-haired guy clinging far too closely to the man who'd come to mean a great deal to me. I immediately looked away, the uncomfortable clench in my belly feeling a lot like jealousy.

Emily shot me a sharp look. "Now don't you go thinking that's more than it is. Have some faith. I admit I once had hopes that those two might turn into a long-term thing, but Holden has been very clear that was never going to happen. You, on the other hand?" Her expression turned soft. "Well, let's just say I've never seen Holden like he is with you. He's never taken *anyone* to the castle, Gil. I doubt even Zach has been there unless it was as a kid. It was always Holden's thinking place. And that says a lot about what he feels for you."

I kissed her cheek, feeling all kinds of silly but more grateful for her words than I could say. "Thank you." Then I stole another peek through the glass. I couldn't help it.

The two men were sitting on the sofa. Zach had a tight grip on Holden's hand while Holden's arm lay across Zach's shoulders, and Spider bounced around them, clearly delighted to see the new arrival. The two men were relaxed with each other in a way that spoke of their long intimate history, and as I watched, Zach let go of Holden's hand and slid his arm around Holden's waist, exactly where mine had been not long before.

"Don't torture yourself." Emily tugged me over to a seat at the island. "You can trust my boy."

Funnily enough, I realised I already knew that.

"I've known Zach all his life," Emily explained, pushing a fresh coffee my way. "His dad is as redneck as they come and ignorant as hell. This has been brewing for a long time. Having said that, Zach's older brother Julian is cut from a much better cloth. He might be able to talk some sense into his father, we can only hope."

It was a timely reminder of how lucky I'd been with my own parents and the pain Zach had to be going through. I could do better than a little petty jealousy. "What about Zach's mother?"

Muted voices leaked from the deck into the kitchen and Emily glanced to the window. "She won't be happy, but Norma has never stood up to Paddy. Whether this will change anything, only time will tell. Either way, Zach will have a place here as long as he needs it." She eyeballed me then. "And that means you boys are going to have to find a way to make things work." Her eyes turned glassy.

"He'll be looked after." I took her hand. "I'll make sure of it."

She sucked in a shaky breath. "He's a good lad, Gil. He doesn't deserve this."

She was right about that. "No one does."

She squeezed my hand. "Do you still believe you're in the right place?"

I didn't need to think, and my answer was quick and certain. "Yes. I do."

That brought about a smile and Emily patted my hand and let go. "Then look after each other and let this place do what it's going to do."

"Emily." My tone carried a soft warning. "I'm leaving in two months. That hasn't changed." I didn't see how it could.

All she did was shrug, and for the next five minutes we drank our coffee in silence as the torrential rain beat a thundering tattoo on the roof of the homestead.

"Mum. Gil."

I spun in my seat to find Holden sporting dry clothes and leading a very pale Zach into the kitchen with Spider at their heels. Zach's auburn hair fell in damp waves around his face, his pretty eyes red-rimmed and haunted, his expression almost blank. He looked . . . devastated.

"Zach's going to be staying with us for a while," Holden announced, his tone thick with emotion.

Emily sprang to her feet and immediately enfolded Zach in her arms while I studied a weary-looking Holden. His dark brown eyes glistened, a matching redness to the rims that told the rest of the story. He caught my gaze and held it, and for a few seconds neither of us moved. I wanted nothing more than to pull him into my arms, but I stayed where I was. Holden's expression told me he understood but that he'd wanted it too.

What a mess.

After a long minute of silence, broken only by a few telltale hitched breaths from Zach, Emily finally released the man from her arms and waved in my direction. "Zach, this is our new domestic manager, Gil."

"*Temporary* domestic manager," I corrected, not missing the less-than-impressed look Holden sent me in response. "Nice to meet you, Zach." I crossed the room to shake hands.

"Same." Zach managed a half-smile that gave a glimpse of the handsome man in happier circumstances. He was heavier muscled than Holden, a few centimetres taller, and everything about him screamed fresh-faced country living. With all that cascading auburn hair, an intriguing splash of freckles across his nose, full lips, and bright green eyes, he really was a stunner.

"I hear you've settled in well," he said, looking me over, a tiny frown forming between his eyebrows.

"So far, so good." I shot Holden a curious look.

He shuffled on his feet. "I was just telling Zach how you're giving Mum a run for her money in the kitchen and how lucky we are to have you."

"Oh." My face grew warm at his praise and I flustered. "I ah . . . well, I wouldn't know about that."

Zach's gaze bounced between the two of us and that tiny frown deepened.

Luckily Emily saved us. "You're welcome to stay as long as you want. You can have Tussock Cottage now that Holden's moved out. I'll drop in some clean linen and breakfast supplies. I'm sure you know your way around the place."

Zach's pale face turned a pretty pink and he shot a mortified look Holden's way before quickly answering, "Don't worry, Em. I can go into town tomorrow."

"Nonsense," Emily scoffed. "I'll let you and Holden talk and come find you later for a chat. Right now, I need to finish packing."

She shot me a look. "There's dinner in the oven if anyone's hungry. Holden, Gil, I'll see you in the morning before I leave."

"I'll get some food on the table." I jumped to my feet and headed into the kitchen. "Zach, how do you like your coffee?"

"Black, please."

I shot Holden a look. "If you'd rather go somewhere private, I can bring it to you."

Holden glanced at Zach, who looked wary to say the least. "It's up to you."

I added. "I'm gay, as well, if that helps."

Zach's eyes widened and he shot Holden a curious look. "You didn't mention that."

Holden shrugged but said nothing.

Zach's shoulders slumped. "You may as well hear it from me rather than second-hand." Then he turned to Holden. "And I'll talk to Tom tonight so he can spread the word before everyone sees me and flips."

Holden nodded approvingly. "What'll you do with the dogs you're training? We have spare kennels if you need to bring them here."

"Nah, I'll ring the owners tonight. It's a week or so early for most of them, but that won't matter. I'll give some reason that I'm working here now and they can pick their dogs up from the station. Dad will be nice as pie to the owners, you can be sure about that. Apart from that, I've got a search-and-rescue training weekend at the end of next month, but otherwise, I'm yours."

I didn't miss the way Zach held Holden's gaze at the end, but Holden merely nodded and asked, "What about your own dogs?"

Zach immediately faltered. "I, um," his voice broke. "I had to leave them. Dad bred both of them from his dogs, so technically they're his. I figured if I asked, he'd make a point of saying no just to hurt me and I wasn't going to give him the satisfaction. I'll talk to Julian later. See if he can do something for me."

It was impossible not to feel crushed for the guy, and I spent the next hour refilling coffee cups and dishing up plates of Emily's food. It wasn't exactly how any of us had planned Emily's last evening to go, but it was what it was. Zach and Holden talked, sometimes including me, sometimes not, but Zach was surprisingly open throughout.

I heard his heartbreaking account of coming out to his father; the man's brooding and disappointed silence; his mother's attempt to talk her husband around; his brother Julian and his father shouting at each other; and then the only words Paddy Lane uttered directly to Zach during the entire debacle—

"You're my son, but I won't have this station, or my reputation become fodder for the local gossips. What you do off this property is your own concern, but if you want to stay on the station, you won't ever bring that sort of behaviour, or any man onto my land, ever. And I won't be having this conversation again, do you understand?"

And so Zach had left.

"What's the bloody point in coming out and then have to keep living a lie with the people who are supposed to love me the most, just so they can feel okay?" He let out a heavy sigh. "Jules wanted me to stay and fight. Said Dad would back down eventually." Zach's angry eyes locked with Holden's and the subtext was easy to read if you knew their history. "But I'm tired, Holden. I want more than just someone turning a blind eye. I. Want. A. Life."

"And you deserve one." Holden's hand covered Zach's. They sat close together at the corner of the table, elbows and knees touching—not that I was looking.

My throat thickened at the genuine affection in Holden's tone, but then his eyes met mine, and just like that it was as if we were the only people in the room and I understood exactly what he wanted me to know. I was it for him. Simple as that.

Holden leaned back and very deliberately lifted his hand, sparking immediate disappointment on Zach's face. I genuinely felt for him. Zach clearly had deep feelings for Holden, which meant I was going to come as a very rude and unwelcome shock.

Watching their closeness and similarity, I couldn't help but feel they fit well together. Zach was someone who could stand alongside Holden as an equal on the station. Someone who'd match him stride for stride. They shared that same rugged country appeal and a passion for the merino. The same profound love of the high country. And a long history that spoke of deep friendship and mutual respect.

I offered none of that.

I hung the tea towel I'd been slowly balling in my hands and approached the table. "I'm gonna go watch some television and leave you two to talk."

Holden frowned and looked about to say something, but I cut him a quick look, which silenced him.

"Nice to meet you, Zach," I continued. "I'm really very sorry about your family. You didn't deserve that. If you need anything in town, just drop me off a list tomorrow and I'll add it to mine. Until you're set up, you're welcome to eat with us whenever you need. There's always spare."

Zach looked surprised but grateful, and he stood and shook my hand. "Thanks, Gil. I appreciate that."

"No problem." I swallowed around a growing lump of guilt in my throat and made it almost to the west wing before Holden called out.

"Gil, wait up."

I came to a stop but didn't turn around, too nervous about what he might have to say. Then his arms slid around my waist from behind and I melted against him. He kissed the nape of my neck and then dropped his chin over my shoulder, and we rocked in place for a moment, the reassuring rhythm of his heartbeat on my back like a metronome in my head, my own heart shifting to match its pace.

"Can I come say goodnight when we're done?" He whispered into the side of my neck, my cock stirring at the gentle movement of his lips against my skin.

I didn't answer immediately. Holden still hadn't set foot in my room; I'd never invited him. He was always so careful to give me *my* space while at the same time opening *his* entire life for me to walk through. The disparity wouldn't have escaped him but he'd never said a word. And I'd been a jerk. A pointless attempt to protect myself, but from what?

I turned in his arms and kissed him hard. "Bring your PJs."

His smile could have lit up the hallway and I castigated myself yet again for being a selfish jerk.

I patted his chest. "Go to your friend. He needs you. Come find me when you're done."

CHAPTER NINETEEN

Holden

IT WAS A COUPLE OF HOURS BEFORE I CLOSED THE FRONT DOOR on an exhausted but much more settled Zach and made my way to Gil's bedroom at the back of the house. My heart ached for my friend. No one should have to make the choice between living true to themselves and being accepted by their family. I was gutted for him. But I also couldn't be there for him in the way he'd seemed to be hoping for.

When Gil left us, Zach had peppered me with questions about him until I'd shut the conversation down. Then he'd made it clear, without directly saying as much, that he wouldn't say no to company overnight if I was in the mood. I'd slid my hand free of his more than once and cut our final hug at the front door short when it looked like he might try and kiss me. I hadn't missed the flash of hurt in his eyes, and I dreaded the conversation coming the next day.

Gil's bedroom door stood ajar, the warm glow from his bedside lamp striping the honey-coloured floor. I pushed the door open and a grin split my face. He was asleep with his reading glasses falling off his nose and a book in his hand. *Man and his Symbols* by Carl Jung.

Spider sprawled on the mat at the end of Gil's bed. He grumbled his complaint at being woken, then fell immediately back to sleep.

"Traitor," I whispered as I tiptoed past, although I was secretly pleased that he'd chosen to follow Gil in favour of staying with Zach and me. Zach had certainly been surprised, which led to another series of questions about Gil.

At the side of the bed, I eased Gil's glasses off his nose and slid the book from his hands, placing both on the bedside table. My gaze lingered on the book's cover and I wondered, not for the first time, how much Gil missed working with his clients. His skills were wasted at the station. Even if he stayed past the three months, how much longer would it be until he got bored, or came to his senses and headed back to his life and the people who needed him?

A framed photo sat under the lamp and I picked it up, the poignant image hitting me like a fist to the chest, taking my breath away. A happy, laughing Gil held an equally delighted little girl atop his shoulders, the two of them clearly hamming it up for whoever was taking the photo. Luke, I supposed with an unexpected sting to my heart.

Gil was clearly still very much in love when the photo had been taken, and my eyes filled at a version of Gil I knew so little about. He'd shared bits and pieces about how he and Luke had ended but kept the other side of their relationship close to his chest. But in the photo, it was evident in full living colour.

The man behind the camera had Gil's total heart, no question, and there was an open trust and unguardedness to Gil that I barely recognised. I'd only caught glimpses of that Gil, little snapshots, like breadcrumbs that kept me believing more was possible.

What the hell had I been thinking, hoping Gil might want me in that same way one day? Jesus, I didn't even have a clue what that kind of commitment meant. All I knew was the ache in my heart at the reminder of what Gil had and then lost, and that I was like a fucking emotional child compared to that. What could *I* offer *him*? What did he even think when he looked at me? Gil had been right that afternoon when he'd said, I barely knew him. Hell, we barely knew each other.

I ran my fingertip over his face in the photo. He deserved so much better than what life had dealt him. Maybe he and Luke *would* have made it if they'd stayed together. Maybe they would have recaptured that love so evident in the photo.

"Luke's adopted cousin offered to be our surrogate, and Luke donated the sperm."

I jerked around to find Gil watching me with soft eyes.

He scooted up and patted the mattress. I hesitated, then sat, and Gil took the photo from my hands.

He studied it, a small smile playing on his lips. "Callie was like bottled sunshine. A cliché, I know, but it was true, nonetheless. Not that she didn't have a mouth on her or enough sass to drive you up the wall. She was like Luke in that way. Those genes run strong in his family." He gave a warm-hearted chuckle that made me smile.

"She was a beautiful child," I murmured, not entirely sure what to say.

Gil's expression turned wistful and he gently touched Callie's face. "She was. I was the primary carer since Luke's job as a domestic pilot meant he travelled quite a bit. Callie might not have had any of my genes, but we could talk, and that was way more important to me."

"I can understand that."

He offered me a quick smile. "She was smart, people smart more than book smart. She had a sense for people's emotions if you know what I mean? If I was worried, she often picked it up before Luke did. That sensitivity wasn't always a good thing. She knew Luke and I weren't getting on that well, and I could tell it worried her. In those last few months, she'd ask me all the time if I was happy. I'd fudge and say who wouldn't be happy with a daughter like her, and she'd look . . . disappointed, like she expected more of me. Like she knew how bad things were between Luke and me."

Gil put the photo back on the table and then pulled me down beside him. I rolled to my side, bringing us face to face. He ran the back of his fingers down my cheek. "She would've loved it up on Dunwoody's today." He smiled as he talked. "I thought of her while we were sitting there. She was way more adventurous than me."

"I dunno about that." I grabbed his fingers and kissed them. "You're here, aren't you? Way out of your comfort zone."

He thought about that. "You know, you're right. Go me."

I snorted and snuggled into his side. "How did you and Luke meet?"

"At the party of a mutual friend in my first year of university," he answered with a kiss on my forehead. "Luke was doing his pilot training at the School of Aviation and we just clicked. Things got serious fast, and a few years later we were married."

"Tell me about him." I held my breath as his brow wrinkled. "I want to know about the man who loved you. Not just the man who left you."

Gil hesitated, a troubled look in his eyes. Then his frown smoothed and he breathed out a long sigh. "Luke is a great guy, all of our difficulties aside. He's kind and thoughtful, and I was head over heels for him, and him for me. He's an excellent pilot and he gave up his international commitments so he could be home more for Callie and me. It was a big deal at the time but he never hesitated. And for a long while we were ridiculously happy."

Gil tucked me tighter into his side and I listened with a brimming heart as he slowly opened up about his life before Callie's death. About their wedding, about holidays and parties, Christmases, and the day Callie was born. About Luke's family and more about Gil's. About his love for his work and why he stepped back. Everything I'd been wanting to know.

"Did you always know you wanted children?" I asked carefully.

He grinned. "Always. There was never any question, and so

when Nina offered to be our surrogate, we leapt at the opportunity. She was hit hard by Callie's death. Luke's whole family was. They did their best to support us, but when Luke and I separated, it felt like I lost them as well. They rallied around him, but I . . ."

"You had no one." I lifted my lips to his and kissed him softly.

"Not entirely." He stared down at me, his eyes full of memories I had no knowledge of. "I had, *have* Tuck, and some friends who stuck close, but I still felt a little cut loose, I suppose. Then again, I didn't exactly make it easy on myself either. Luke tried to keep in touch, but I pushed him away."

"How did it happen between the two of you? The actual breakup." I pressed a little.

Gil snorted. "Very orderly and very grown-up. Probably because we were both so numb, I think. I'd switched off to Luke months before. I couldn't deal with Callie's death *and* our crumbling marriage at the same time. We'd given up on couple's counselling, mostly because neither of us had the emotional energy and were barely even talking. We'd stopped trying. I'm a fucking psychologist, you'd think I'd know better than that, right?"

"Hey." I put my fingers over his lips. "Why should you be perfect when everyone else gets to fuck up?"

He smiled against my fingers and wiggled closer. "Excellent point. But while we're on the subject of fucking—" He walked a hand down my T-shirt to cup my soft dick. "—do you think we can stop talking now?" Gil kissed down my throat to the dip at the bottom and sucked hard.

"Mmm." I drew him up with both hands around his face and covered his mouth with mine. "But this is better."

He groaned in approval and pressed our bodies flush, his hardening cock sending jolts of pleasure through mine. I trailed my hand down his back and under the sheet to cup his arse. His very *bare* arse. "You're naked," I pointed out, since I was kind of brilliant like that.

"Don't sound so scandalised." He threw the sheet aside. "Now, get them off." He tugged at the hem of my T-shirt and I whipped it over my head before quickly adding my sweats and socks to the pile on the floor.

"Mmm. Much better." He pushed me flat, got up on his knees, and kissed his way down my body to my toes before finding his way back up and swallowing my cock in a clever move that caught me by surprise.

"Jesus Christ!" I bucked, my hands trying not to fist his hair as he worked my dick in long hard sucks, his hands cupping my balls, teasing, playing, tugging lightly on the folds of skin.

I gave up trying to watch, the back of my head pressed flat into the pillow, my eyelids fluttering closed as I gave myself over to the sensation of Gil's tongue swirling around my shaft, over the slit and down the other side, his teeth lightly grazing over the sensitive spots, his hand making up the difference at the base where his mouth couldn't reach. It was hard and delicious and right on the edge of uncomfortable, exactly how I liked it.

Then his finger brushed over my hole and I rocketed to attention, our conversation from earlier in the day suddenly front and foremost in my mind.

"I want you to fuck me," I said thickly, thrusting lightly into his mouth.

He popped off and kissed back up my body until his face hovered over mine, lips swollen and slick, eyes glazed. "You want me inside you, baby?" He finger-tapped my hole while tongue-fucking my mouth, dialling the sexy way the fuck up.

Christ, he was potent.

"Like yesterday," I managed between kisses. "Condom. Back pocket."

His mouth curved up in a sexy grin. "How presumptuous of you."

I nipped his nose with my teeth. "You can always say no."

He lunged for the condom in my sweats and then rummaged in the drawer for some lube before throwing both on the bed. "Tell me how you like it?" He squirted a mound of lube into his palm and I ran a couple of fingers through it. He smirked. "Going somewhere?"

"Fuck yes, I am. You don't get to have all the fun."

He laughed and turned slightly so his arse was right there for my viewing pleasure. Then he retook my dick in his mouth, his slick fingers running across my taint to my hole, gently pressing until a single tip sank in.

"Oh shit." I groaned with pleasure and ran my lubed fingers down over his arse and into his crease. When they hit pay dirt, Gil's rhythm stuttered for a few seconds before finding its feet again as I slowly pressed inside. He was so hot and so fucking tight, and I was reminded he hadn't been fucked in a long time. Not that it seemed to matter as he groaned and shoved his arse down on my finger, sucking it all the way in while doing the same with his finger up mine.

He curled and hit my prostate and stars exploded in my eyes. "Yesssss!" I crooked my finger to return the favour and Gil jerked off my cock, leaving it to slap against my belly.

"Right . . . there!" He shoved his arse back onto my finger, so I added a second, and then the tip of a third, knowing how much he loved the stretch and burn, and he began pumping himself, all the while continuing to finger-fuck me into oblivion. One finger became two, but thankfully he didn't try three. I wasn't that guy.

"Fuck!" He pulled free from my arse and whipped around to face me. "On your stomach. Now!"

I grinned and flipped over. Bossy Gil was back and I fucking loved it. The second I was on my belly, he moved between my legs, grabbed my hips, and lifted me up onto my knees. Then he knocked them apart until I was spread wide for his pleasure, his hands ghosting over my cheeks as he murmured something in a soft voice that I couldn't quite make out. He kissed each cheek, then opened me wide and buried his tongue in my arse.

Lights out.

"Sweet Jesus." I jammed my face in the pillow as Gil licked a swathe up my taint and dove deep into my slack hole. I was almost at the edge on the first pass but I wasn't about to throw in the towel. This wasn't ending before I had Gil's dick where his tongue was, no fucking way.

"I'm too close!" I slammed my hand on the mattress to get his attention and he immediately slid to the side.

"Back or front, Baby?"

I answered by rolling to my back and holding my knees high.

"Atta boy." Gil stroked my hip and moved between my legs.

I grabbed his wrist. "But I want to finish on you."

His smile grew wicked. "Anything you want." He suited up and slicked, then pushed my knees a little higher. "Such a gorgeous arse." He trailed his fingers down my aching cock and over my tight balls to my hole where he slipped two inside for a few blissful strokes.

I'm pretty sure I whined, because he chuckled and then lined himself up, the head of his dick nudging tantalisingly at the entrance without pushing inside.

"Do I have to do everything myself?" I reached between my legs and slid a finger past his dick and into my hole.

"Oh no you don't," Gil growled and batted my hand aside, pressing forward so the head of his cock just breached the ring of muscle.

I gasped. "Oh fuuuuuuck." My head slammed back into the pillow.

He paused, and when I opened my eyes to see why, he was watching me closely. "Okay?"

I nodded, panting, struggling to find my words. Then Spider groaned from somewhere in the room and I summoned enough brain cells to shout, "On your mat."

"Is that a euphemism for fuck me?" Gil leaned down to kiss my chin, just as Spider gave another groan and hit the floor. "Because you never know with you farmer types." Gil kissed my nipples one at a time. "I've always wondered if . . . 'get in behind' . . . might have another meaning?"

I snorted. "Are you done talking? Cos I need to be fucked, and if you don't have the time—argh!" My arse burned in protest as Gil pressed inside in one long, slow slide, centimetre by centimetre, until he was fully seated, the painful restraint clear on his face.

"Oh god," he huffed. "You're so damn tight. Fuck me. And also . . . your call—" He winced. "—but anytime soon would be just grand."

I held up a finger as I panted through the burn, and when it eased to an aching need, I slid my hand around his neck and pulled him down for a kiss, the taste of him mixed with the musk of my body triggering a sigh of pleasure. I opened my eyes to find him looking at me.

"Ready?"

I grinned. "Bring it on."

It wasn't going to be pretty or take long. I was so fucking close I could've gone off like one of those puffball mushrooms. But Gil didn't look any better, his slow thrusts quickly morphing into a punishing rhythm as he bore down on top of me, my desperate cock squeezed between our bellies.

Perspiration coursed down Gil's face, his pupils blown to smithereens. He picked the pace up again and a few strokes later he tensed and jerked, dropping his mouth to mine, the groan of his climax echoing between us as he rammed me up the bed with the force of his final thrusts before collapsing on top of me, a sweaty panting mess.

I shoved him onto his side and knelt at his shoulder, grabbing hold of my cock.

He looked up, licked his lips, and opened his mouth.

Looking as fucked out as he did and eyeing me like I was the most delicious thing he'd ever seen, it only took a few strokes until I came with a shout and spilled all around and inside that sweet mouth. He never even blinked, just yanked me forward with a hand around my thigh so he could lick the last drop from my slit.

I did the rest, leaning down to lick the spilled drops from his throat and chin before kissing him long and hard to share the taste.

He groaned and threw the used condom onto the pile of clothes before pulling me on top and wrapping his legs around my thighs to hold me in place. "You are one sexy motherfucker."

"Back atcha." We kissed, and it was hard and passionate and orgasm-fuelled, and I felt it to the tips of my toes. Then slowly it changed and gentled, Gil's soft hum of pleasure sending a wave of happiness through my body, his lips languid over mine, his kiss full of emotion and promise and all the things we weren't saying to each other. All those things I so desperately hoped he felt so that I wasn't alone in this.

And whether it was that, or the fact that Gil had finally opened up and invited me deeper into his world, or maybe just the realisation of what he was coming to mean to me, I didn't know, but the force of my feelings hit me with a jolt.

I was so very royally fucked over this man.

I rolled off and onto my side, and Gil followed, the two of us facing each other. He pushed my hair from my face and kissed me softly. "What am I going to do with you?"

Anything you want. But I said nothing, sensing more to come.

He looked down and drew a wide circle around my left nipple and my breath caught in my throat. "I . . . I don't know what to do with this." He laid his palm flat over my heart, and his eyes lifted to mine, an unfamiliar nervousness swimming in their depths. "With you. With us." He cupped my cheek. "It's so damn unexpected." He smiled a little sadly and my stomach clenched.

"Why do you need to decide now?" I took his hand and held it to my lips, pressing a kiss to the back as he watched. "One step at a time, right?"

He thought about that, chewing the inside of his cheek before sighing and leaning forward for a deeper kiss. "Okay. One step at a time."

And that's how we fell asleep, face to face, wrapped in each other's arms, our bodies and limbs entangled. Gil's eyes were the first to close, allowing me to study his face as he slept, cataloguing every line and angle and sweet curve, and sure of only one thing.

If I lost this man, it would rip me in two.

"Shhh, Gil. It's okay," I whispered, trying to keep my voice calm and low as Gil's damp hand shook so badly it almost jumped from my grasp. But he gave no indication he even knew I was there, his panicked eyes wide with horror, his legs thrashing under the sheets.

He'd woken with a shout about thirty seconds before, dragging both me and Spider instantly awake with him. It wasn't like I needed to ask what was happening. *This* was what he hadn't wanted me to see.

Spider whined softly at the side of the bed, his chin on the mattress as Gil grunted and moaned, his skin slick with perspiration, his aching voice thick with grief, his head sweeping from side to side. "Callie!" The strangled cry tore my heart in two.

"Gil, I'm here, baby. I'm here." I made no move to restrict his anguished flailing, just tried to keep hold of his hand and watch that he didn't hurt himself.

A few seconds later he startled and sat bolt upright in bed, gasping for air, his sightless eyes scanning the room. His hand jerked free of mine and he dragged it down his face, gulping and sobbing.

I whispered his name and he spun to face me, eyes wide, taking a few seconds to even register who I was. But when he did, his shoulders slumped and he fell trembling into my arms. "H-Holden." He sounded half-relieved half-mortified, his pulse leaping in his neck. "Please, I need . . ." He reached out a hand and I grabbed his bottle of pills from beside the bed, tipping one into his shaking hand.

Then I helped him with the glass of water and he guzzled it greedily before falling back on the bed with his eyes closed, the breeze from the cracked window licking at his hot skin. His hand patted the mattress until he found Spider's head and the dog licked his hand.

"Good boy," he rasped, and Spider visibly relaxed.

I made a mental note to buy some better treats for my dog and then wrapped my arms around Gil and tried to pull him close. He resisted and I instantly loosened my hold.

"I can just lie here," I offered, desperately hoping he'd let me stay.

He frowned and looked about to shake his head, then he sighed and burrowed into my arms instead.

I tried and failed to keep a grip on the emotion that welled in my chest as Gil finally gave in and let me stroke his back as his heaving lungs settled. The trembling took a little longer to calm, and I wanted to scream at the man responsible for all of the grief Gil had gone through.

But I didn't.

Instead, I kissed Gil's head and anywhere else I could reach, murmuring reassuring nothings against his damp skin, telling him I'd be there, that I wouldn't leave him alone. That I cared. That he meant the world to me. And in time the shaking stopped, his breathing evened, and he fell heavily into my arms.

And as he slept with his eyelashes laced over his cheek, his heart beating strong against my chest, and his arm still tight around my waist, I whispered, "I love you."

CHAPTER TWENTY

Gil

I BLINKED AWAKE TO MILKY LIGHT SPILLING IN FROM THE HALL and no one in my bed, the sheet beside me cold to the touch. I sighed and rolled to my back, the pounding behind my eyes a stern reminder of the night's events, my pills always leaving me hungover and drained of fight.

Wash. Rinse. Repeat. The nightmare was always the same. The aftermath too. But something had been different. I'd fallen back asleep in Holden's arms, a fucking miracle in itself. An attack generally ended any chance of further sleep. But not last night.

The memory of lying safe against Holden's warm body spurred a rush of gratitude through my chest, and as I turned to find my water, my gaze landed on Callie's photo.

"Sorry, little girl," I whispered. "Kind of forgot you were there last night."

She stared back at me, her expression frozen mid-laugh.

"He's kind of great though, right?" I pulled the frame closer. "But ten years younger? Who'd have guessed?" I traced her face with my finger. "What am I going to do?"

Silence filled the room and I kissed her tiny face. "Yeah, thanks for that. Good talk." I settled the frame back on the table just as Spider's nose appeared on the bed. "Hey, boy." I stroked his furrowed brow as the events of the previous day and night rolled through my head.

A lot had happened in twenty-four hours.

I reached for my phone and blinked. Six? *Shit.* I'd slept through my alarm and Harry was taking Emily to the airport after breakfast. I frowned at a couple of missed calls and texts from Tuck, but they'd have to wait. Then before I could jump out of bed, another came through.

Answer your damn phone.

It rang in my hand, and I sighed and pressed Accept. "I slept in, all right?"

There was a pause on the line. "You *don't* sleep in. You are irredeemably anally punctual, and you almost always set an alarm even on your days off."

"I'm well aware," I flustered. "I don't know what happened, unless Holden—" *Shit.* I snapped my mouth shut.

"Unless Holden what?" Tuck said, picking up my little slip straight away because, of course he did. I could even see the smile on his smug little face. "Unless he turned off your alarm? As in your *boss* being in your bedroom, perchance? The hottie who runs the station—your words, not mine. Or maybe even in your bed? And please, God, tell me it's the latter, because fuck knows you need a bit of fun in your life."

I screwed my eyes tight shut and counted to five then squeaked, "Maybe?"

"Yes!" Tuck's glee erupted down the line. "I knew it. How long?"

I groaned. "A couple of weeks."

The line went quiet. "You've been fucking your cute boss for two weeks and I'm only hearing about it now? I'm deeply wounded, Gil."

"It's not like that," I flustered because god knew the alternative was going to sound ridiculous. "I . . . I like him, Tuck. He's . . . well he's really fucking nice." There, I'd said it. "I know it's stupid and crazy and probably the biggest fucking mistake but—" I didn't finish, figuring I'd said enough.

Silence poured down the line and I steeled myself for the words of caution my confession deserved.

"It isn't crazy at all," Tuck blurted, catching me off guard. "I'm so damn happy for you, I think I'm about to have a heart attack."

"But it's probably going to end in disaster—"

"So what?" Tuck scoffed. "At least it means you're still alive in there somewhere, and if this guy's managed to help you find that part again, then shit, Gil, I'll be grateful to him for the rest of my life."

A chuckle bubbled out of me. "He makes me laugh, Tuck. He's ten years my junior and got enough of his own shit going on, but he makes me laugh. And I can talk to him. He knows . . . everything."

"Everything?" He didn't have to expand.

"*Everything*," I repeated. "I even had an attack last night and he was pretty awesome actually."

"Are they lessening any?"

"The frequency is more variable than it was. Last week I went four days without one, which was a first." I failed to mention the two I'd had in the previous twenty-four hours, but who was counting?

When Tuck spoke again, there was a hitch in his voice. "Gil, I . . ." He didn't finish and disbelief rattled through me.

"Tuck . . . are you . . . crying?"

"No." He sniffed thickly, underlying the lie. "Of course I'm bloody not."

Which made me smile.

"Do you know how long I've waited to hear something more than a flat nothing in your voice? I've been so fucking worried. And just to hear you say this guy makes you laugh . . . God, Gil, I think I can breathe again."

His words touched me deeply. "I'm sorry that I shut you out the last year. I'm sorry if I hurt you."

"'S okay. We all do grief differently, right? It was just damned hard watching it consume you, and not knowing what the hell to do about it. I'm a fucking psychologist. I should know this stuff, right?"

I huffed. "How do you think I feel?"

We fell into silence for a while before Tuck finally asked the sixty-four-thousand-dollar question. "So, what are you going to do about this guy? Is it . . . serious between you?"

I sighed. "I don't know. I don't even know what it is, what we think we're doing. And it's only been two weeks. How serious can it be?"

"You've been around each other for a month," he reminded me. "And living in the same house twenty-four seven. It's hardly your usual dating scenario."

"Yeah, well. That's my problem to figure out." I decided to change the subject. "I take it this phone call is because Luke told you about the lawyer's email?"

"You need to talk to him, Gil. This involves both of you."

"I know. And I will once I've had time to think. But not until the muster and shearers are done. I need my head in the game for the next two weeks. This is what Emily employed me for, Tuck, and I won't let her down. I won't let that bastard get inside my head again." The fact he'd already managed to do that, I kept to myself. "He can wait for his answer."

"I don't give a rat's arse about the other driver," Tuck said evenly. "I was thinking of Luke. He's in a right mess about all this, as well. And you are the only people who can really understand what the other is going through."

He had a point. "I know. But what I said to Luke still stands. Let me get through the next two weeks."

He grunted. "It's your call."

Spider's head turned to the sound of footsteps in the hallway. "I have to go, Tuck. Holden's coming."

Tuck snorted. "I doubt it's for the first time."

I laughed. "Shut up. I'll call you later in the week." I slid my phone to the bedside just as the door squeaked open and Holden's freshly showered and bright-eyed face peeked around the corner.

"Oh good, you're awake." He strolled into the room carrying a tray loaded with food and a huge mug of what I desperately hoped was coffee to clear the fog from my brain.

"You brought me breakfast?" I couldn't keep the smile from my face as I pushed myself up and wriggled a pillow behind my back.

He slid the tray onto my lap, and my mouth watered at the sight of a stack of pancakes loaded with lemon juice and sugar. "I'm just paying up for the lost bet."

I surveyed the offering. "It actually looks delicious."

He huffed indignantly. "Don't sound so surprised."

"But you shouldn't have let me sleep in."

"Why not?" He joined me, sitting cross-legged on the mattress. "There's plenty of time before they head off. Besides, we both had a big day *and* night."

Heat raced into my cheeks. "Yeah, I'm sorry about that."

"I'm not," he said simply, his earnest brown eyes landing on mine. "It was a privilege to be there for you in some small way." He ripped one of the pancakes in half, took a bite, and then winced and put it back on the plate. "Jesus, that's disgusting. What the hell's wrong with maple syrup?"

I grinned and forked a mound of lemony deliciousness into my mouth, the acid sweetness zinging across my tongue.

"But, as for the panic attacks—" He stilled my fork and caught my eye. "It takes a ton of courage to face those on a regular basis. I admire the hell out of you."

I opened my mouth to brush his flattery aside, but nothing came out, because I realised in that moment that he was right. It did take fucking courage. "Thank you."

"You're welcome."

I swallowed another forkful of pancake and licked my lips. "Damn, Holden. These are good. You've got hidden talents."

He leaned forward and brushed his mouth over mine, licking the sugar off my lips before sliding his tongue into my mouth. "You have no idea how many talents I'm hiding."

I dropped my fork on the plate with a clatter and slid my hands around his neck to deepen the kiss, taking my time, licking into his mouth to taste coffee and lemon and sugar, and just below all that, a cloying hit of maple syrup. I put everything I was beginning to feel into that kiss, everything I wasn't ready to say, and it felt like Holden did the same, the two of us breathless and flushed when we pulled apart.

"Thank you again for last night," I said, catching my breath. "For all of it. I've never gone back to sleep so quickly after an attack, and that's definitely down to you."

His eyes softened at the corners, pleasure spotting his cheeks, and he kissed me again. "Anytime. Now, I'm going to leave you to finish your breakfast before I'm tempted to crawl back into bed and have my wicked way with you. I just saw Harry's car arrive, and Mum is coming up to say goodbye in a few hours. You've got time. Take it." He kissed me again and then headed back up the hallway.

I smiled at the plate of pancakes and loaded my fork once again. But before I could get it to my mouth, Spider appeared, drooling at the plate of food like he hadn't been fed in weeks.

"All lies." I regarded the huntaway with a wry grin and his brows bunched adorably. "Oh, for fuck's sake." I dropped Holden's remaining half a pancake into the dog's open mouth and he grinned all the way to his mat.

CHAPTER TWENTY-ONE

Holden

I'D ALMOST GOT THE MESS IN THE KITCHEN CLEANED UP WHEN Gil appeared with his tray, looking tired but still gorgeous in an Alice in Chains T-shirt and a loose pair of jeans that hung on his hips. He wandered over to where I was standing at the sink and put the tray on the countertop before sliding his hands around my waist and pulling me tight against him.

"Debt. Paid. In. Full." He smacked a kiss to my lips between each word and my cock rallied a little against his groin. "Are you ready for your mum to head off?"

"Yeah. We're gonna be fine. Are you?"

Gil laughed. "Hell no. I'm quietly freaking out about the muster, but that won't change until it's done. I just want to do a good job for her."

"I have zero worries about that." I slid my hand down his back and under the waistband of his jeans to grab his arse. "And this little gem is mine next time." I brushed my lips over his and dipped my finger into his crease.

He shivered. "I can't wait."

I withdrew my hand and slapped his butt. "Now jump in that shower before my resistance wears thin and I'm forced to spread you naked over that kitchen island."

"Ohhhhh. Kinky." Gil ran his nose up the side of my face and palmed my half-hard dick through my sweats. "We've got six weeks alone in this house until your mother gets back. There're all sorts of places we can try out for si—"

"Do you mind if I borrow a few eggs—oh."

My head shot up at Zach's voice just as he came to an abrupt stop, his gaze fixed on Gil's hand around my dick.

Fuck.

We immediately sprang apart and I huffed, "Shit, Zach, you couldn't have knocked?"

"I did." He looked between us, shock and hurt obvious on his face. Then he focused on me, his head slowly shaking. "Jesus, Holden, you don't mess around, do you?"

"I think I'm gonna leave you two to talk." Gil squeezed my arm and headed for the hall, saying a curt good morning to Zach as he passed. For his part, Zach said nothing, his face a mask, but his eyes followed Gil all the way through the door.

Once Gil was gone, Zach kicked it shut and marched over. "So, you're fucking him?"

I reeled at the anger in his tone, my face flaming. "Keep your voice down."

"Why should I? He's your goddammed employee, Holden." Zach regarded me coldly, icy fire in his eyes. "What the hell are you thinking? Did the sheets even get cold on the bed after I left that day before you had him in it? How very convenient for you. You barely had to draw breath. And how old is he, anyway?"

What the fuck? "That's enough!" I shouted and Zach's eyes flew wide. He'd always been the fiery one, not me. "You don't get to talk about Gil like that *ever*. Do you understand?"

Zach gaped. "I don't get to talk about him like that?" He blinked in disbelief. "What the hell does that even mean? Are you going to kick me off the station or something?" He started to laugh, then stopped just as quickly when I didn't answer.

Because he was right. It was crystal clear in my mind. If I had to make a choice, it would be Zach leaving, not Gil, regardless of what my mother wanted.

"What the hell, Holden?" He stared at me, furiously shaking his head. "I'm your best friend. And I was a lot more than that for a long time. What's this guy to you?"

I couldn't answer, wouldn't, not in anger, and I watched as the meaning behind my silence slowly began to sink in.

"Oh, fuck no." Zach's anger turned quickly to incredulity and despair, his whole body closing in on itself. "I don't believe this. So that's what last night was about." Understanding dawned in his eyes. He lurched to the table and sank into a chair. "I thought when you wouldn't fuck me that you were just looking out for me, not wanting me to do something I might regret. But you . . . you're *with* him, aren't you?"

Goddammit. I walked to where he sat and put my hand on his shoulder. "Zach, I—"

"Don't!" He jerked free of my touch.

I sighed and took a chair two down from him. "I was going to talk to you today."

Zach stared at the table. "How fucking considerate of you."

"Hear me out."

He shot me a glare and then looked away, saying nothing.

"It didn't happen straight away," I tried to explain, watching his shoulders stiffen. "But yes, it did happen. I don't know what to tell you, Zach. I really like him. He's . . . important to me. And I'm sorry if that hurts you. But you're important to me too, as a *friend.*"

Zach rolled his eyes and grunted something undoubtedly sarcastic.

I chose to let it go, but he wasn't getting it all his own way. "But don't bullshit me about the employee thing, Zach. *You* are technically my employee now as well. Didn't appear to stop you last night."

He threw me an "are you fucking kidding me" look, which . . . fair enough.

I took a breath and dialled things back. "Look, I know the timing is shit for you and I'm sorry for that. And I still want you to stay here. Really, I do. You've always had a home here and that hasn't changed. But Gil's not going anywhere, Zach. I like him. A lot. And he's not just . . . convenient. Far from it. He's . . ." I trailed off, knowing the truth wasn't going to help.

When Zach finally lifted his head and his eyes met mine, I saw an ocean of hurt in their green depths. "And you think that makes it easier for me—" He shook his head, his mocking laugh riddled with a pain that I couldn't take from him. "—knowing he gets to have you the way I wanted after only a few weeks? When I didn't have a chance after the years we spent together. Do you know what it feels like to hear you say things about him that you couldn't say about me?"

I kept my mouth shut. There would be no winners in trying to argue or justify myself.

Zach also fell quiet. And then, in a voice barely above a whisper, he said, "I'll leave tomorrow."

My heart sank. "No, Zach, don't do that, please."

He threw his hands in the air. "Well, I can't stay here and watch the two of you—"

"Zach." We both spun to find Tom standing in the open mudroom doorway. "Come with me, lad."

Zach fired Tom a pissy look. "Stay out of this, Tom."

"No." Tom waved him over. "Come on. We could do with your help to move the steers. Are you just going to walk away after all Emily's done for you over the years? This is a mess, sure." He shot me a lengthy for-fuck's-sake look that sent my cheeks blazing once again. "But it's times like these that show what you're made of."

It was a good pitch and I could see Zach wavering. He thought the world of my mother and Tom. Zach arched a brow at the older man. "So, you knew about Holden and me?"

Tom's expression softened. "We all knew, lad. You two would make the worst spies."

I stifled a smile and even Zach snorted.

"Come on." Tom waved him over again. "You get a free pass to bitch about Holden all day as much as you want, and we'll even join in. Lord knows there's enough to complain about. But tomorrow it's done and buried, understand? We're a team here, Zach, and we'd love your help on that muster, but at the end of the week, if you still don't want to be here, then that'll be that."

The kitchen fell silent, but I saw the second Zach gave in. He sighed and shot me a glare. "Okay, I'll stay for the week and see how it goes. I'm not a quitter and *I* don't let people down." His icy look added the unspoken element, *as opposed to you.*

I blinked and kept my mouth shut.

He continued in an equally cool tone, "But I'm done talking about this, Holden, so don't bother trying to find me to smooth things over. I'll talk when I'm ready and not before."

I nodded, catching sight of my mother standing in the hallway and unobserved by the other two. Her serious expression told me she'd heard enough to put the pieces together.

"That's settled then." Tom moved aside for Zach to pass. "Go ahead, lad. You can grab breakfast at my cottage and I'll meet you there."

Zach nodded, cast a withering look in my direction, and then left.

"You all right?" Tom's hand found my shoulder.

"I'm fine. Thanks for that. I get that this is going to be awkward for everyone, but if we can get him through the next couple of days, then maybe he'll stay."

Tom gave a dry chuckle. "Well, he was hardly going to stay on your invite, was he? But love triangles don't exactly bode well for teamwork, so I can't guarantee this won't start a lot of idle chat that we could well do without."

I bristled at his words and shrugged his hand aside. "Zach and I were *never* boyfriends, Tom. I didn't even know he wanted more until it was too late. There wasn't and isn't *any* triangle, not that it's any of your business."

Tom's gaze narrowed and his expression said he wasn't convinced. "That may be so, and I didn't want to say anything before, but this thing between you and Gil—"

"Also isn't any of your business," I said flatly.

He drew a sharp breath. "Look, son, all I'm saying is that the station needs everyone's full attention, but especially yours. You can't afford to take your eye off the ball until that contract's signed, if it's even offered. And from what I understand of Gil's reasons for being here, this thing between you two is a distraction that neither of you need. You have to keep your eye on the prize, Holden. Get your priorities straight in your head."

Anger stirred in my belly, and for some reason I bridled at his use of the term *son*. Mostly he said it in fondness, but for the first time I felt like I'd been put in my place.

"I'm not your son, Tom, although God knows I love you like a father. What I *am* is responsible for this station. I'm the owner, and it absolutely *does* have my full attention." My tone brooked no argument. "And I've done nothing *but* think about it for three long years. We're more than ready for muster and belly crutching. The work is up to date as much as it ever is. The accounts are current, we're ready for a contract, and we have a plan that will see us safely into the next twenty years, at least if I have anything to do with it."

Tom's expression grew uncertain and he shifted uncomfortably on his feet. "I didn't mean to—"

"I know you don't, Tom, and I also know you have the station's best interests at heart. I wouldn't have gotten this far without you, but I'm not a child anymore, and I deserve and am quite capable of having a life and a relationship outside of this damn station without it falling around my ears. My grandfather did and his father before him. Or do you think I should spend all hours of the day grinding away on this land and the remaining few hours cooped up alone in this house, like you've done in your cottage for twenty years?"

Tom blanched but I wasn't done.

"In this last month with Gil, I've felt more alive and prouder of this station than I ever have. Gil's not a distraction, Tom. He makes me better at what I do. Maybe we're long-term, maybe we aren't, but he's reminded me why I love this place and why it's worth fighting for. And I've realised that time away from the demands of what we do here actually gives me the fuel I need to keep going."

Tom swallowed hard and his gaze skittered off my face. "I guess I can see how that might be."

I sighed and rested a hand on his shoulder and his solemn gaze returned to mine. "Just bring any concerns you might have about the station directly to me and not to Mum. You've been telling me for three years that this is *my* station and that I need to step up and own it. Well, this is me, stepping up, doing what you wanted me to. You've done an amazing job getting me here, but I need to stretch my wings a little, hopefully with you at my side, because there's no one I'd want there more."

Silence filled the kitchen as we stared at each other, Tom studying me like it was the first time we'd met, and maybe in some ways, it was.

He licked his lips and looked about to say something, then stopped and licked them again, and finally, he spoke. "You're right. I should've come to you directly. I guess you're not the only one who's struggled with all the changes over the last few years. But I never meant that you shouldn't have a life, Holden. God forbid that you follow *my* example. I just want you to succeed because you deserve to. You're a damn good farmer and I guess I didn't want anything to get in the way of that. Sometimes I forget how much of a burden loneliness adds to this life, and God knows farming is tough enough without that. I had no right saying what I did. I'm sorry. Whether it's with Gil or someone else, I just want to see you happy. I hope you believe that."

I blinked back the tears. "Jesus Christ, I'm gonna hug you even though I know you hate it." I wrapped my arms around Tom's big square shoulders and crushed him against me. He grunted something that sounded like "for fuck's sake" before fondly patting me on the back.

"Yeah, yeah, yeah," he grumbled, good-naturedly. "But can you please stop before I throw up in my mouth?"

I huffed in amusement and let him go. "I'm sorry for jumping down your throat. It's been a hell of a couple of days."

"Yeah, well, we're family, right?" He eyed me with affection. "And families bitch at each other. I only want the best for you, but I get that it's time to take a step back. But fair warning—" He nailed me with a pointed look. "—that means I'll be letting you work a lot more out for yourself in the future. I'll be here if you need me, but you've got the reins. I will, however, be sure to let you know if you're about to *really* fuck up."

I grinned. "I'm counting on it. And I meant what I said. I do love you like a father."

Tom's eyes glittered in the glow of the kitchen lights and colour washed over his cheeks. "Well—" He cleared his throat. "—how about that? Mind you, the bar wasn't exactly set high after the other guy, was it?"

I snorted and shook my head. The man was nothing if not blunt. "You've got me there."

We exchanged a look that said more than any words could, and then he left, and I collapsed into a chair.

Two seconds later Mum plopped herself down in the chair opposite and Gil appeared in the open doorway, concern written all over his face.

I rolled my eyes and slid down in the chair. "Is this an intervention? Cos I have to tell you, I don't have the energy for it."

Gil huffed and made a beeline for the table, pulling me out of the chair and into his arms. He cradled the back of my head against his shoulder and I almost lost it then and there. "I am so fucking proud of you." His breath washed warm against my ear. "That couldn't have been easy, baby, with either of them, but you nailed it."

"You heard?" I mumbled against his neck, wincing at the emotion in my voice as the adrenaline crashed.

"It was hard not to," my mother answered softly from the other side of the table.

I eyed her over Gil's shoulder. "Not if you're hiding in the hallway, it's not."

Her cheeks turned a pretty shade of pink, but she said nothing.

Gil chuckled and let me go. "I wasn't exactly being discreet either. Zach was pretty damn angry and I wanted to stay close, just in case." He hesitated before asking, "Did you mean all that about me?"

I managed a smile at the image of Gil riding in to champion me and kissed him softly. "Every word."

He grinned and sat me back down in my chair. "I think we could all do with some caffeine. How's your time, Emily?"

She glanced at the clock. "We don't have to leave for another hour. Harry has some calls to make for work before we go." She reached out her hand to cover mine. "You did good, Holden. It was time."

I couldn't stop the smile. Her words meant everything. But it dissolved the instant my phone went off with an all-too-familiar ring.

Gil reached it before me, glanced at the screen and then held it out for me to take. His expression was carefully schooled, but the gentle caution in his eyes told a different story. *How much longer?*

I curled his fingers over the phone and pushed it back toward him. "Put it on mute."

His broad smile said it all. He leaned in and kissed me. "It'll be okay."

From her seat at the table, my mother shot me a questioning look. "Was that your grandad, Holden?"

I returned to the table and took her hands in mine. "We need to talk, Mum."

CHAPTER TWENTY-TWO

Gil

It was the day before the start of muster and the homestead lunch table was full. That afternoon everyone would head out to River Hut in preparation for a four in the morning wake-up call. Two shepherds from stations bordering the other side of Lake Tekapo had arrived to help, bringing the number around the table to eight. One more than I'd expected catering-wise for the week ahead, but I had tons to spare.

And as if my nerves weren't jangling enough, the atmosphere at the kitchen table measured equal parts excitement, anticipation, and a solid chunk of moody awkwardness. The latter mostly down to the singular presence of Zach—the first time he'd joined the team in the kitchen since that first fateful morning a few days before. I'd almost fallen off my chair when he'd walked in, head down and silent, and very obviously avoiding any eye contact, particularly with me.

According to Holden, Zach hadn't been a problem workwise. Punctual for mat time every day, he listened and did his work without complaint. And he was cheerful enough with the rest of the team, even if he barely broke the polite barrier with Holden. The eye rolls were still front and centre, virtual if not physical. All understandable, but I knew it was killing Holden.

They'd been close mates and a lot more than that for a number of years. But there was little Holden could do to improve things between them until Zach was ready to talk, which he'd made perfectly clear he wasn't. On the plus side, he hadn't simply packed up and left, which I'd half been expecting. I secretly hoped that time together on the muster—notably without me—might help thaw things a little.

But if things were awkward between Holden and Zach, things between Zach and me reached a whole new level. He never met my eyes, *ever*, not unless I caught him off guard while he was watching me . . . or us . . . uncomfortable either way. If he passed the house and I was outside, he ignored me, and he barely said a word other than please and thank you. Even those instances were usually through gritted teeth, namely because other people were present and he didn't want to appear rude, such as the day I'd stocked his fridge and pantry on the station's tab.

So, sue me. I wasn't above making a point, or for that matter, a little bribery.

And Holden and I had been doing our best to be mindful of his feelings, such as avoiding any cutesy talk or PDA when Zach was around. But it was becoming a hard pill to swallow since our relationship was now out to everyone else, something that should've felt freeing. The news had been greeted with not much more than a nod or an eye roll.

But where we'd expected—and were half looking forward to, half dreading—becoming the butt of everyone's jokes and being thoroughly roasted for it, everyone was instead walking on eggshells and avoiding the whole subject. All because of Zach.

The awkwardness had changed the team's dynamics and I didn't know how much longer Holden would be able to simply ignore that. Not too long, I figured. Not with muster on the horizon. In the mountains, they only had each other to rely on. Discord and friction fucked everything up.

Holden had done nothing wrong and neither had I, but it was beginning to feel like we were hostage to someone else's emotions. And with Holden gone on muster the next week and the business of crutching after that, I'd be halfway through my time on the station by the time I had him back around.

Something had to give.

The big wins of the week? Emily's arrival in London with no hiccups, and her complete support of Holden's issue with his grandfather before she left.

They'd rung Holden's grandmother together that very morning, and although she'd been devastated, just as Holden had feared, she'd eventually rallied and thrown her support behind her grandson. His mother had then called the unit and instructed them not to allow his grandfather to make calls unless they were pre-arranged with Holden and monitored by the staff. It was a good compromise, and the difference in Holden was immediate, like a huge load had been lifted from his shoulders.

What had transpired for Holden that morning, the conversations with Zach, Tom, and his grandmother, his mother leaving, and maybe even what had happened between the two of us the day before, had changed Holden in some tangible way, like he suddenly grew into his skin. His confidence blossomed, and the sight of it filled my heart. It also made me realise how much of my first impression of Holden had been bluster, a front, because if I'd thought that version of capable, bossy Holden was a turn-on, the genuine article, self-assured, take-charge Holden almost made me come in my pants.

The buzz at the lunch table took a turn toward the hilarious as Charlie tried to drum up support for a pre-muster party that evening.

"Come on. It's tradition," she insisted.

"I've stocked beer in the river crate if it's needed," I offered, referring to the metal cage suspended in the freezing alpine stream that ran past the hut. "I can restock tomorrow. It's not a problem."

"See!" Charlie's gaze swept the group. "Gil's on my side."

"I didn't say—"

"Yes, you did." She grinned. "We all heard you."

I groaned and threw up my hands in defeat.

"I'm too old for all that nonsense," Tom griped. "I've got half a bloody mountain to climb tomorrow and I need a decent head on my shoulders to get me there in one piece."

"Pffft." Charlie scoffed. "You've topped Green Pools a million times. You could do it in your sleep."

"I'm in," Sam piped up cheerfully.

"Yeah, go on then." Jackson, one of the visiting shepherds, shot Charlie a grin.

"Me too," his mate Logan agreed.

"Zach?" Charlie prodded Zach's calf with her foot. "Come on. Don't leave me hanging. I'll need some decent competition for the shot challenge."

Zach gave a sly grin and his pointed gaze caught Holden's. "Sure. I'm in. Holden can hold his own in that department too. Right, Holden? Remember Oakwood last year?"

I almost groaned, knowing that look *and* comment had been solely for my benefit in that "I know him better than you, and while the cat's away" implication. Well, I wasn't biting. One thing I knew about Holden—the man was loyal to the core.

And true to form, Holden's cheeks pinked and he slid me an apologetic look before saying, "Count me out. Someone needs to be firing on all cylinders tomorrow. And there'll be no shot challenge. Save that for the end of the muster."

I shot him a grateful wink, then turned back to the table. "I'll drop extra cans when I do my final run up there tonight. And make sure you eat first." I eyeballed Sam. "I'm putting you in charge of that. There'll be steak, cheesy potatoes, and two salads ready to go, plus butterscotch pudding for dessert. I dropped the dog food there yesterday, along with all the sleeping gear and toiletries, and the first aid kit is up to date. Holden will take the satellite phones. Take the rest of what you need this afternoon. The barbecue is clean and the wood-fired range is ready to go. But you can top up the firewood yourselves if you're going to be sitting around the firepit chewing through everything I cut and stacked. I'll have Folly Hut prepped by the time you're ready to move."

Holden looked confused. "But you're joining us for dinner tonight, right?"

"I, um," I flustered, my gaze flicking uncertainly over the others before returning to him. "I wasn't sure if—"

"Of course he's staying," Tom interrupted with a sharp look to Zach who flushed and looked down at his empty plate. "Gil's part of this team. Some might say he's the most important part, considering he's cooking all our damn food. Besides, it's tradition. Holden's mum and gran always stayed for the first meal."

Holden shot Tom a grateful look and received a quick smile in return.

"Then I'd love to join you," I agreed happily.

"Right, that's settled then." Charlie dusted off her hands. "I'll pack extra snacks."

"Vodka."

We turned as one to look at Alek who'd sat and said virtually nothing the entire lunch, which wasn't unusual.

"You can't have party without vodka," he said simply.

"Oh, hell no." Tom vehemently waved his hands.

"Yes!" Charlie punched the air.

"*After* the muster," Holden reiterated. "I'm not throwing any shade on you, Alek, I can well imagine you can hold your vodka just fine, but a night on that stuff with this lot, and they'll be more useless than Spider tomorrow."

Charlie snorted. "He means *he'll* be useless. We all know what happens when Golden drinks vodka, right, guys?" Her words were greeted by a sea of chuckles and nods.

"Golden?" I directed the question to Charlie.

"Oh god, don't." Holden slapped a hand over Charlie's mouth.

She peeled it away to gleefully explain, "It was Holden's nickname in school. Golden Holden. Because the arsehole couldn't seem to do anything wrong. Teachers loved him. He aced all his classes. He was on the swim team *and* the debating team—"

"It was a small school, okay?" Holden protested.

"Aaaand if ever he broke the rules, somehow, someone else always ended up getting the blame," Charlie finished with a flourish of her hand.

Holden groaned and sank down in his seat with his hand over his face.

"Golden Holden, huh?" I spread Holden's fingers so I could see his eyes underneath. "We'll have to see about that."

Everybody laughed.

Everybody except Zach.

"That's it." Holden pushed his chair back and stood. "I've been embarrassed enough. Let's get this party on the road. Take this afternoon for a bit of time out and to finish getting ready, and let's aim to meet at River Hut by five. Zach and Sam, you're with Tom."

Zach barely acknowledged the instruction, and to stop from rolling my eyes, I began collecting plates and walking them to the dishwasher.

Once Holden was done and the others were busy gathering their things, he wandered over to where I was standing and slipped an arm around my waist. I froze, my gaze instantly sliding over his shoulder to where Zach sat, pretending he wasn't watching everything that was going on between us.

"Holden—"

"No." Holden brushed his nose over mine. "I am done with not touching you. You, mister, are going to be kissed. So shut up and pucker up."

Had I mentioned bossy?

I snorted and leaned in to meet him halfway. He kept within PG limits, but at the end of it, there was no mistaking I'd been thoroughly kissed. And when Holden finally stepped away, a hoot went up from the table.

"Jesus, about time." Charlie clapped her hands, her eyes dancing. "Okay, now that's over with, there's ten thousand or so merinos waiting for us in them thar hills, give or take a ewe."

Everyone laughed and there was a scraping of chairs and a general move toward the mudroom door.

"So." I threw the tea towel over my shoulder and slipped a finger in Holden's belt loop to tug him close. "Golden Holden, huh? The swim team *and* the debating team. That's one very talented mouth you have there."

Holden leaned in and ran his mouth up my neck to my ear, whispering, "Oh, baby, you have no idea." And then he kissed me until my toes curled and the tea towel fell forgotten to the floor.

An hour later, the Ranger was packed with the remaining hut supplies including additional beer, and while Holden made a last-minute run to the woolshed for another tarp, I carried a coffee to the front deck to enjoy it in the warm autumn sun.

Spider had already taken his spot in the Ranger's passenger seat, looking unsure if he should be happy or not about the fact we were clearly going somewhere. All the dogs had a sixth sense about muster, their enthusiastic barking and playful shenanigans evidence they'd picked up on the general excitement that pervaded the station.

Little did Spider know that he was only going along for the drive. Holden had been adamant about leaving him with me. We hadn't talked about me being on my own for the week, but the fact Holden cared enough to make sure I had Spider for the nights I might need him did squidgy things to my heart.

I sipped on my coffee and reminded myself I was a man going on forty, not a love-struck teenager.

Love?

My coffee cup stalled halfway to my mouth.

Holy shit. Is that what I'm feeling?

I lowered the cup to my thigh.

Am I falling in love with Holden?

Am I in love with him?

I let the idea sit in my heart for a moment and . . . it felt good. Really fucking good.

And also . . . wholly terrifying.

I swallowed around the lump of fear in my throat.

Not a panic attack, just good old-fashioned chicken-legged fear.

I wasn't there to fall in love, even though I'd known I was playing with fire from that very first kiss. Three months on the station was only ever meant to be an escape . . . a chance to think. Falling in love had never been in the plans.

But what if I am . . . in love?

Would that be so terrible?

I swallowed hard. Yes. No. Christ, I had no idea. I had a private practice in Wellington, an apartment I leased, our old house we hadn't yet sold, and friends—although there was no guarantee how many were left after I'd abandoned them. And Holden's whole world revolved around the station, hundreds of miles and a whole one-eighty mindset flip from my world, my life.

I couldn't offer Holden *anything*.

Could I?

Are you happy, Daddy?

Oh god, what the fuck did that matter?

It matters.

The sound of an unfamiliar vehicle sent me to my feet just as a dark blue Hilux with Lane Station written in red letters on the side rounded the bottom of the lawn. *Shit.* I glanced toward Tussock Cottage where Zach's ute was parked, but there was no sign of him.

The blue Hilux veered right toward the cottage, no doubt recognising the ute, and I swore again. Most every visitor to the station came to the house first, regardless of their reason for being there. It was an integral part of high-country etiquette, so the fact this driver hadn't didn't bode well for why he was there.

The two dogs kennelled on the bed of the Lane Station ute gave a whine as they caught sight of Spider, and he gave a hefty bark in return. I wandered down to the Ranger and gave his ears a stroke while keeping a calculating eye on the ute.

Spider whined and shoved his nose into my hand.

"Yeah, I know, boy. I have a bad feeling about this too." I leaned my back against the passenger door, making no effort to hide the fact I was keeping an eye on the new arrival as he parked under an old liquidambar blazing in autumn colour.

A short stocky man in his fifties slid from the driver's seat wearing jeans, a red checked shirt, and a baseball cap that matched the vehicle's logo. He strode purposefully onto the small porch and banged on Zach's door before stepping back. Well back. Like he-didn't-want-to-get-close-to-his-son back.

He also never even so much as looked my way, although he had to know I was there. Rude bastard.

A few seconds later the cottage door opened and Zach startled at the sight of the man who I was fairly sure was his father. He carried all the right arsehole vibes.

"Dad?" Zach threw a slightly panicked look toward the house but didn't seem to notice me standing by the ute. "What are you doing here?"

I pushed off the door and wandered closer, wanting to make it clear to both of them that Zach wasn't alone.

"If you're not going to work the station, then you can take your dogs with you. I'm not feeding them on my dime. Lazy bitches." His father strode back to the bed of the ute and threw open the cage door. A huntaway and a border collie immediately leapt to the ground and scrambled over to Zach, tails beating furiously from side to side.

Zach fell to his knees and hugged the animals who gave him a thorough licking in return. He was clearly delighted to see them, and my heart caught in my chest watching the happy reunion. Spider barrelled down to greet the newcomers, and it would've been funny if Zach's father didn't look two seconds away from giving the excited dog a piece of his mind for the exuberant welcome.

Well, fuck that. "I wouldn't if I were you," I called a loud warning, and Paddy Lane shot me a surprised look before reluctantly stepping back and allowing the three dogs to hare across the lawn toward the lake.

"This is between my son and me," Paddy retorted. "Nothing to do with you."

"Maybe not, but this is Miller land." I kept my distance but didn't back away, leaving about fifteen metres between us. "Everything that happens on this station is Miller business. Just remember that."

He grunted something I was probably better off not hearing and then grabbed a couple of suitcases from beside the cage and dropped them on the veranda, spewing clothes across the dusty planks. "You can have these as well. No one else is going to want them."

Oh yeah, this guy was a right prick.

"How did you know I was here?"

Paddy looked his son over and grunted. "Where the hell else would you go? You've been tight with the Miller kid most of your life. Too tight, I always told your mother. Turns out I was right. We should've put a stop to your friendship as soon as he showed his true colours." He studied Zach, and just for a second I thought I saw a flash of something that almost looked like regret, but then that steely reserve returned. "I didn't throw you out, so don't go telling people I did. Leaving was *your* choice. All I asked for was a bit of respect."

Zach threw up his hands. "And live a half-life because you don't want me to embarrass you? I'm good enough to work my butt off on the station even though it's never going to be mine, but I don't deserve a little basic respect in return? You think anyone on that station cares that I'm gay except for you and Marty? And Marty's fucking seventy, Dad."

"Your mother—"

"Has likely known for years," Zach talked over his father. "And we both know this isn't about her. It's about you. And all it does is make you look like the small, mean little man that you are."

"You don't get off talking to me like that." Paddy's eyes flashed with anger. "The only reason you're even welcome on this station is because he's just as bad as you are. Don't think people don't talk about Emily's son, because they do. Well, congratulations. Now they'll be talking about you as well."

Zach stared his father down. "I don't give a fuck what they say about me." But there was a waver to his voice and his eyes were suspiciously shiny.

And I was done with this arsehole. "That's enough!" I made my way over. "This conversation is over."

"Just who the hell *are* you?"

"Gil Everton."

"Well, mind your own goddamn business."

"This *is* my business, *Mister* Lane. And you need to listen up." I'd dealt with a lot of bullies just like Zach's father in my time, inside and outside my office, and he didn't scare me.

Paddy's eyes narrowed. "Don't you threaten me." He glanced at something over my shoulder and I caught the sound of running feet.

"I'm not threatening you—" I took a few steps forward. "I'm simply stating fact. I'm the domestic manager of this station, and after listening to your sad performance, I figure this is every bit the domestic scene I was employed to manage. And let me tell you something, you don't get to come onto Miller land and bad-mouth the owner or anyone else on this station, not on my watch. From what I know of your son, he's twice the man that you are, and the station is honoured to have him working here. You, however, need to leave, and quickly. Oh, and next time you think about paying a visit, call first, unless you wanna be turned away at the gate."

Paddy's eyes bulged and his face turned a deep shade of red like he was about to burst a blood vessel. "You have no authority—"

"He has *every* authority." Holden appeared at my side, more than a little short of breath.

I was grateful for the support, but I didn't want Paddy to think I needed it, and I let Holden know that with a single raised brow. He caught on straight away and took a small step to the side. A very small step.

I returned my attention to Paddy. "I've asked politely, and now I'm waiting for you to comply." I caught the tiniest of grins on Zach's face at hearing my words.

"What's going on?" Tom joined the growing crowd, his gaze bouncing between Paddy and me while Sam and Alek arrived right on his heels, all of them gasping for breath.

"Mr Lane here is about to leave," I told them, not taking my eyes off Paddy.

Zach's father looked me over, his lip curling. "You don't want to mess with me, whoever you are. Stations rely on each other up here."

"And yet I'm strangely comfortable with that," I replied evenly. "You're not our only neighbour, Mr Lane. And you're certainly not our most important one." I had zero idea about that, but Holden's soft snort gave me courage to continue. "And when it gets out how you've treated your son, you might be surprised who ends up being isolated and gossiped about."

His eyes widened. "You don't know anything."

I let a smile escape just to piss him off. "I *know* Emily has a lot of respect in the Mackenzie, just like her parents do, something I'm sure you already know. And when she hears about this, what exactly do you think she's going to be saying to your farming peers?"

Paddy's gaze narrowed and I continued. "Now I'm sure you don't want to be thrown off this station, Mister Lane, but if that's what it takes, we'll be more than happy to oblige."

Paddy flushed red and looked past me to the group. "Tom? Are you going to just stand by and let this noddy talk to me like that?"

"I'd do as he says, Paddy," Tom answered gravely. "You're on the wrong side of this, mate."

Paddy's angry gaze landed back on Holden, but I could tell he'd lost his puff. "You're done in the Mackenzie, Miller. No one's going to want to work here after this gets out."

Holden never even blinked. "Goodbye, Lane. Don't let the gate hit you on the way out." They traded stares for a moment and then Paddy huffed and made his way back to his ute.

"And remember to call next time," I added, then heard Holden's soft snort of laughter at my words.

Paddy grunted something I was thankful I didn't catch, gave us a withering glare, and then tore up the track, spitting dust and gravel all the way.

The minute he was out of sight, conversation erupted at my back and Holden was peppered with questions. I let him deal with the explanations, needing a minute to calm my racing heart and get my shaking hands back under control. But when I looked up, I found Zach watching me, his expression hard to read, no doubt less than impressed with my interference.

I let out a weighty sigh. I had zero energy for any more bullshit. But before I could turn for the house, Zach stepped off the porch and offered his hand.

"Thank you."

I stared at his hand for a moment, then grasped it firmly with mine. "You're very welcome. He was way out of line. And I meant what I said. You're a better man than him and we are honoured to have you here."

Zach glanced down to where my hand still trembled in his and gave a tight frown. I slipped free of his grasp and broke the silence with a nod to his dogs. "Take them with you on muster. I'll make sure there's enough food."

Zach smiled at the three dogs watching us from the lawn. "Thanks . . . again."

"No problem." I was halfway to the house when he called out.

"Gil, wait up." It was the first time he'd used my actual name since everything blew up.

It stopped me in my tracks. And when he caught up, I could see everyone, including Holden, watching with undisguised curiosity.

Well, join the club.

"I'm sorry about what happened," Zach said so softly I had to strain to catch the words but I wasn't sure what he meant.

"About?"

"About your kid," he added, a high flush on his cheeks. "And your . . . marriage."

My eyebrows peaked.

He shrugged. "People talk. He, um, sounds like a jerk, by the way."

I bit back a smile and simply waited as he took a deep breath.

"I, um, might've been a bit of a jerk myself this week."

I fought another smile. "Apologies aren't needed. You were hurting, Zach. I get that." I held his gaze. "It just happened. It took us both by surprise. As you might imagine."

Zach shot a quick glance over his shoulder to where Holden stood, with a frown on his face, about ten metres away. Zach lowered his voice, "Yeah well, forgive me if I let him suffer just a little bit longer."

I huffed out a laugh and clapped him lightly on the shoulder. "I think I'm beginning to like you."

Zach snorted but his small smile was genuine. "It might take me a minute, but I think I'll get there in return."

We shared a laugh while everyone else pretty much gaped. Then I headed up the lawn and straight past Holden, who looked from me to Zach and then ran to catch up.

"What did he say?" Holden hissed, speed walking beside me. "And also, can I just say that I am so freaking turned on right now after how you put that arsehole in his place? That was the hottest thing I've ever seen."

I threw a glance over my shoulder, but everyone was still huddled around Zach. "How much time do we have?"

He checked his phone. "Thirty minutes?"

I stopped and spun to face him. "I thought we weren't leaving until four?"

He shuffled on his feet, looking guilty as sin. "We, um, have to do something first."

"We?" I narrowed my gaze but then remembered the thirty minutes thing and fisted his shirt. "I reckon we can do it." I cocked my head and waited while the cogs in his brain worked that one through. I knew the moment they did, by the sly smile that stole over his face.

"A speed test, huh?" He stroked the dark stubble on his chin. "First to come gets to drive to River Hut." He waggled his eyebrows. "You may as well give up now."

"Is that right?" I ghosted my lips over his and watched his eyelids flutter closed. Then I shoved him back and lunged for the house.

"Hey!" He windmilled his arms for balance and then ran after me, whisper-shouting, "No solo priming allowed."

I laughed and took the stairs onto the veranda in one leap, almost arseing out sideways on the hall rug before recovering my balance and sprinting for my bedroom.

Twenty minutes later we both lay blissed out and covered in sweat after the most vigorous sixty-nine blowjobs I'd experienced in my entire life, but at least they kept us clean . . . relatively.

Holden wiped my crease with the sheet and I winced. "Ow! You just had to try and get that extra finger up there, didn't you?" I grumbled.

He chuckled. "You ordered me to."

I leaned over and kissed him. "And yet you still lost." I collapsed on his chest and he grunted with the impact.

"Debatable." He coughed, stroking my hair. "Watching you come is my favourite thing in the world. Figure I'm a winner right there."

I lifted my head to find him watching me with soft eyes. "You threw the challenge?"

He shrugged. "Worth every cent." He drew me up until our faces were just centimetres apart. "I'm so proud of what you did out there."

"Then my work here is done." I leaned in to kiss him, but he held me back, his brown eyes swirling black with an emotion that stopped me in my tracks.

"I love you, Gil."

Oh god. My heart thumped against my ribs and then pretty much gave out as Holden stumbled on.

"I know no-nothing about love." His words tripped over each other, gathering speed. "Hell, I know fuck all about relationships, period. And I get that this thing between us is supposed to have a time limit, and looks impossible on paper, and comes with a whole lot of problems—"

"Holden—"

"—including the fact that you have a life in Wellington and you're only just out of your marriage, but none of that changes how I feel." He drew a quick breath before ploughing on. "And what relationship doesn't have its problems, right? And I'm really sorry if this screws up why you came here, or what's happening between us—"

"Holden," I tried again but he was on a roll, and the desperate longing in his face broke over my heart in a wave of emotion.

"—but I'm also not going to pretend that I don't feel what I do—head-rushing, parachute-gone, ground-coming-up-fast-with-no-safety-net in love with you. It kind of hit me like a truck watching you put that bastard in his place this afternoon. You're it for me, Gil. Story done. And I apologise now for the total idiot I just made of myself and for likely scaring you the hell away." He stopped and drew a long breath as I gently stroked his face.

"Are you finished?"

He shrugged adorably. "I think so?" His gaze shifted over mine, nervous and hopeful and so fucking beautiful. "Kind of depends on your response."

"Jesus, Holden, the things you say." I ran my thumb over his lips, joy and panic warring in my heart.

Like he could read my mind, he quickly added, "If it's too much, if you're not ready, I totally get it." He rolled me onto my back and stared down at me. "I've never felt this before and it scares the shit out of me as well, but not as much as not telling you does. I'd rather tell you and lose you than have you leave without knowing the place you've carved out in my heart."

I said nothing for what felt like the longest time, simply stared up at the sweetest, most complex, most beautiful man who'd come to mean so much to me. But as time passed, Holden's hopeful eyes turned troubled and wary, and he began to pull away.

"No. Stay here with me." I cradled his face and kissed his uncertain lips until they fell soft under mine. Then I tucked him into the crook of my arm and pulled him tight against me. "I've spent eighteen months doing my damned best to forget I existed, to forget the life I had before, to avoid thinking about any life that didn't have Callie in it. And I've been grieving a relationship that I'd once believed was going to last a lifetime."

Holden lay unmoving in my arms, like he was awaiting a death sentence, my thumb bouncing on the pulse point pounding in his throat.

I continued softly. "When Callie died and Luke walked away, I thought I was done with relationships. I never wanted to hurt like that again. I felt such a goddammed failure in my own life, and I think I came here partly looking for some kind of redemption."

"Did you find it?" Holden's finger started a small circle on my chest, round and around.

I tipped his chin up to look at me. "I think I might be seeing the shape of it forming."

He swallowed hard. "Do I . . . have a place in that shape?"

Far more than you know. "I'd like you to. Because I—" I took a deep breath and swallowed hard, my hand sliding up the side of his face. "I love you too, baby. So damn much."

Holden shivered in my arms, his body relaxing, and a huge smile broke over his face. "Well, fuck, that's good news." He stretched up to press a kiss to my lips and I kissed him back with everything I had, our tongues tangling, his mouth urgent and demanding on mine, and for a few moments I simply let myself revel in the miracle of the joy that flooded my heart.

But as the kiss slowed and softened, I pulled away and took his hand.

His gaze narrowed and fear crept into his face. "Oh, fuck. There's a but, isn't there?"

I blinked hard and gave a small shrug. "I still don't see how things could work between us. And if I'm honest, I'm so fucking scared to be back in this place again. I want to trust it. I want to believe in it. But, Holden, I'm barely getting my feet under me after losing Callie. I don't know if I'm ready for this. I don't know if I'm ready for being in love. I don't know if I could handle any more loss. I—"

He stole the last of my words with a kiss. "Stop borrowing trouble. If it's all right with you, I'm gonna stick with the part where you said 'I love you too'."

I grinned against his lips. "That's very . . . selective of you."

"Damn right it is." I got up on an elbow and studied him from above. "But it's also the only thing that's certain in what you said. I love you and you love me. We'll work on the rest. Do you honestly have a better solution?"

I didn't, but I knew it wasn't as simple as Holden was making it sound either. Then again, I figured he knew that as well as I did.

He arched a wary brow at my silence. "And if you say we should end things now, I'm gonna throw you in that lake. And when you turn into a popsicle, I'm gonna stick you in my freezer and bring you out on special occasions for a good licking."

I snorted. "That actually doesn't sound too bad."

But he didn't smile. "You haven't answered the question."

My answer came quicker than I expected. "We keep loving each other. See where it goes and work on the rest. Good enough?"

His smile lit up the room. "It's a good start."

He leaned in to kiss me, but the loud whump-whump of a helicopter blade had me shoving him unceremoniously aside and dashing to the window. "What the hell? This guy looks like he's going to land on—"

"Our front lawn? Yes." Holden beamed and grabbed my hand. "Yes, he is. Better get some clothes on, sweetheart, or you're gonna scare the locals."

I spun to face him. "What the hell's going on?"

Holden threw me my clothes and talked as we dressed. "I booked Wild Run for our pre-muster flight." He shot me a wink. "I thought you might like to come along for the ride."

Holy shit. Was he kidding?

"I even packed afternoon tea. The pilot is going to drop us off at Green Pools, the tarns at the top of Little Peak. Or maybe you'd rather stay here?" He shot me an insolent grin.

"Are you fucking crazy?" I was dressed and out the door in three minutes flat.

CHAPTER TWENTY-THREE

Holden

I scraped my unshaved cheek up the side of Gil's face and he groaned, a shiver running through his whole body from top to toe.

"God, I love the feel of that." He shoved my head back and scratched his fingernails through my three-day-old beard. "Muster is now officially my favourite time of year. Just look at you. All rough and ready mountain man and smelling of—" He took a sniff. "—yummy muster stuff."

I snorted. "Yummy muster stuff? Are you on something? Cos I stink of poor hygiene, sweat, smoke, sheep manure, lanolin, and those damn dogs."

Gil's mouth curved up in a slow, sexy smile. "As I said, yummy." He eyed me up and down, a sly smile tugging at his lips. "So, do you look like this any other time of year?"

I grinned and nuzzled into his neck, making him wriggle. "It can be arranged."

"Really?" He looked ridiculously hopeful and I laughed.

"You're clearly losing your mind." I shuffled onto my back under the sleeping bag and stared up at the stars. "It's been known to happen during muster."

Gil bopped me on the end of my nose and I felt twelve years old. "I lost my mind and a whole lot more the first time I saw you, Holden Miller."

I turned at his soft words and found everything I needed to in those night-darkened eyes. Firelight flickered over his face, highlighting every dip and curve that I knew by heart. I reached out and brushed the hair from his forehead then pulled the sleeping bag over his goosebump-covered shoulders. Night temperatures had dropped like a stone in just a few days, and snow was on the way. We'd get the stock off the hill just in time.

A log sparked in the firepit of the campsite I'd hastily built about a hundred metres from River Hut. I grabbed the extra sleeping bag Gil had brought with him and opened it over top of mine. Then I put an arm around his shoulders and tucked him close against me. His hand snaked around my waist and he sighed contentedly, his hot breath washing over my nipple, exciting the briefest flicker of interest in my spent cock.

We'd eaten a meal with the others, finished a couple of beers, shared some laughs around a River Hut fire, told tales—AKA lies—from the day's mustering, and then Gil and I had left the others to spend the night on our own. I'd caught a wistful look from Zach as we'd said our goodbyes, but he'd lifted a hand and even managed a tight smile.

Things between Zach and me had improved since Gil had confronted Zach's father that day. They weren't back to normal by any means; it was still all kinds of awkward, but I had hope we would get there.

Zach smiled more, joined in conversation, and even talked with me about neutral stuff such as the station, muster, the buyer visit, and my mother's trip. It was better than nothing. Best of all, the team had stopped pussyfooting around him regarding Gil and me, which meant our bubble had been burst and we'd copped a lot more ribbing.

Zach didn't join in, but he didn't leave the immediate vicinity either. I considered that a win.

We had two nights left at River Hut before the team moved to Folly Hut for the second stage, and I'd asked Gil to stay. He'd been reluctant at first, no doubt worried about nightmares in the tiny two-roomed hut housing ten bunkbeds like sardines in a can. The air was ripe with smoke and perspiration. The snoring was a nightmare, the farting even worse.

Sleeping under the stars on a still, clear night was a no-brainer alternative and Gil had jumped at the opportunity. Besides, bunk beds didn't offer the opportunity to fuck like bunnies if we wanted to, which we did. It had been two lonely nights without Gil beside me and I was becoming a fucking sap.

And so, I'd built a little private escape just for the two of us, and the marvel on Gil's face when he saw it had been worth every minute of my time at the end of a long-arse day climbing mountains. And with the dogs sleeping close by in their barrel kennels, the soft night bleating and snuffling of a few thousand merinos at our back, and the river gurgling not fifty metres away, I figured it was as close to heaven as I could manage on short notice.

"Damn, it's beautiful out here." Gil studied the carpet of stars that hung above our heads. "You never see a night sky like this in the city."

"Or pretty much anywhere." I rested my head on his shoulder. "The whole Mackenzie Basin is part of a Dark Sky Reserve. It's pretty special."

He kissed my head. "Have you ever been to the observatory by Tekapo?"

"Years ago." I raised my head to look at him. "Would you like me to take you?"

"Very much."

I lifted up and nipped the angle of his jaw, then sucked on it, the sound of his filthy groan carrying across the river and startling a few merinos in the process. His hot hands travelled the length of my back, fingers dipping just for a second into my crease before re-emerging to settle around my cock for a light tug.

"There's nothing in the tank," I warned with a chuckle.

"Nor mine," he answered happily. "Just . . . appreciating."

"In that case, feel free to appreciate away. I was wondering if you might like to walk up with me a way tomorrow?"

Gil dropped my cock. "Really?" The delight in his eyes made me smile.

"It's the final sweep and we'll be collecting a few stragglers," I explained. "I'm taking the west side of the cutting just above halfway. Tom caught sight of a few girls hiding up by the tarn. Sam and Tom have got the east side. Alek took a nasty slide down the scree yesterday and ripped the skin off his knee, so he's restricted to holding fort at the bottom for when the mobs arrive. We'll be up at four and heading off at five. I brought a spare headlight and that pair of hiking boots you bought in Oakwood, plus a heavier jacket."

His eyes narrowed. "So that's where my boots went?"

I waggled my brows. "I should have you back at the hut by midafternoon. That way you can be back at the homestead before nightfall. It's a fair hike though. Think you're up for it?"

"Of course I am," he scoffed. "I'm fitter than I've ever been in my damn life just hiking between the house and the woolshed a million times a week. And I *was* kind of hoping to experience a bit more of the muster than just the huts."

"Great. And the forecast is good. You'll be able to see your breath in the morning—might even be a frost the way tonight is shaping up—but you'll soon warm up. But the weather can change on a dime, especially up there, and you never know what the day will bring. You'll have to pack your jacket and some spare clothing of mine, just in case."

"Yeah, I already got the message about the drop in temperature thanks to my old leg breaks. Before I came here, I always imagined you mustered on horseback. Never dreamed you walked the whole damn way."

I chuckled. "Some stations still use horses, but most of our land is at altitude and the slopes are way too steep. There's no alternative except to walk them, but I kind of like that we do. I feel part of the station's history, I guess. It's how it's always been done here. A shepherd, his stock, a walking staff made from an old branch, and a dog. You can't teach that stuff."

"And a helicopter and a satellite phone and a ute," Gil added with a cheeky smile.

"Fair point." I grinned. "Animal husbandry in a modern world does have its advantages. But this right here—" I swept my arm over our surroundings. "—these stars, the hut full of snoring shepherds, the dogs barking with excitement, the shouts of shepherds ringing out across the valleys and hiking impossibly steep mountains to bring down thousands of merinos? It doesn't get any better than that, Gil. It doesn't get any closer to the land and our history. And *this* is what people come from all over the world to experience. Not to watch a chopper bring the animals down. But the chance to walk a muster with us. We could sell this experience ten times over every year, but I'd hate it. One or two tourists tagging along is just fine. But I always hand them over to Tom to look after, because this is *my* time and I fucking love it. It's like an annual blood transfusion when I'm gasping for air." I finished abruptly, feeling heat race into my cheeks.

Gil wrapped his hands around my face and planted kisses all over it. "Don't you dare hide that blush. You're a romantic, Holden Miller. And I love that about you."

I wrapped my arms around his waist and he buried his face on my shoulder. "I love you too."

And that's how we fell asleep, sharing space with a few thousand merinos; the Milky Way a canopy over our heads; the dogs snoring in their kennels; the fire crackling at our feet; content in each other's arms.

The outside world with all its dream-sucking reality remained safely shut away.

Gil

We woke at four, in the dark, to the penetrating sound of Charlie calling us for breakfast. Somewhere in the night we'd both burrowed under the sleeping bags, and I poked my head out only to whip it back inside.

"Fuck, it's cold out there."

Holden laughed and pulled me close for a smooch. "Better toughen up, city boy. The merinos are a bit short-tempered this time of year when the feeds running short, and they can smell fear a mile off. You're gonna have to watch your back."

My eyes bugged. "You're fucking with me, right?"

Another laugh. "Aw, I'll protect you, baby. What kind of boyfriend would I be if I lost you to a rogue sheep?"

I narrowed my gaze at him. "That's not funny. Shut up before I take my Ranger and go home."

He nuzzled into my neck. "You're not going anywhere." He pulled back to look at me. "You're always safe with me."

And we both knew he was referring to more than just the day's work, so I answered simply, "I know I am." Then I poked him in the chest. "But if you tease me one more time, I'm outta here."

"Got it." He crossed his heart and grabbed the top of the sleeping bag. "Ready?"

"No."

"Too bad." He threw the sleeping bag off and we scrambled to our feet, and goddamn, it was cold.

"Jesus." My balls rocketed northward to land somewhere under my rib cage and my dick instantly shrivelled to the size of a bean, and that was being generous. The fire from the night before had been reduced to little more than a few glowing embers, so we dressed like maniacs, shivering under a clear night sky with a temperature around the freeze-your-fucking-butt-off level.

That finally done and about half a degree warmer, we packed up our bed and ran laughing through the frost-crunchy tussock toward the glorious aroma of bacon and eggs and coffee. We passed an amused Tom, who was on his way to feed the dogs, and burst through the hut door just as the food was being dished up. We ate to a barrage of ribbing about our excursion the night before, including comments about the merinos needing therapy based on all the noises that had come from our camp, and could I add earplugs to the hut supplies the following year. Holden took it all in stride, giving back as good as he got, while I blushed like an idiot and took over the cleaning-up duties.

Overnighting at the hut had impressed on me the very real importance of food on these trips. A mustering day regularly spanned twelve hours, many kilometres, and could include a couple of thousand feet of elevation. I'd made a ton of mental notes to discuss with Emily when she returned, like the feasibility of a wood-heated outside bath, and increasing the solar panels to extend the power options. Only later had I caught myself with the realisation that I likely wouldn't even be there the following year.

I also had a whole new respect for Emily and the—mostly—women who had gone before her. It was no easy job. I drove out to the hut each morning to drop off food, replenish stocks, change out any clothes that needed it, and check the firewood. Then I headed back to the station to check off all my regular duties, including cooking, baking, ordering supplies, clearing out the vegetable garden, chicken duty, accounts, cottage bookings, and all the other sundry tasks my job entailed before falling exhausted into bed at the end of the day. On the plus side, I'd only had one nightmare in the previous four days, so I counted that as a win.

With breakfast done, lunches, snacks, and extra clothing packed and grazes and nicks dressed, the team was almost ready to go. Under Holden's instruction, I slicked some Vaseline between my legs to help protect from possible chafing, layered up in a pair of borrowed skins, a mustering lammy—sleeveless raincoat—and a thick woollen Swanndri I'd borrowed from the mudroom collection. I also carried my own daypack with emergency supplies and had a headlight strapped over my woollen hat so I could see where to place my feet until dawn broke.

When I was done, Holden handed me a smooth wooden pole almost as tall as I was. It had clearly been hand-fashioned, judging by the tool marks, and had a hole bored through the top with a soft leather strap tied to form a loop.

"This was my very first mustering stick, or nibbie, as we call them," Holden said, his gaze fastened to the pole. "Grandad brought me a piece of manuka from a friend's farm and I had to work on it myself. I've made a couple more since, but I'd like you to have this one."

I swallowed around the lump in my throat as I ran my fingers over the smooth contours of the wood. Holden's name and Miller Station had been carved along the length. "Thank you," I somehow managed to choke out and then kissed him softly. And then again. "I love that this is yours. That you trust me with it."

"Well, it's *yours* now," he said with a serious face. "Regardless of what happens." His eyes held mine for a long second before sliding back to the stick. "These notches are all the musters it's been on with me. You'll need to start your own tally on the other side." He avoided my gaze and we both knew why. "It's a useful piece of kit for walking and balance, but it can also stop you sliding on loose scree. Or you can use it to tie up a dog, ford a stream, gain traction on an icy slope or take a kettle off the fire. And when you're going downhill it can take the braking strain off your knees. I want you to have it."

I had no words, and so I just pulled him into a hug and whispered, "I love you."

"I love you too. Be careful up there today. I won't always have my eyes on you."

"I will."

Holden kissed my cheek and then stepped out of my arms to join the others who were making no effort to hide their blatant rubbernecking. Blinking back tears, I caught Zach's eye and knew the significance of the gift wouldn't have been lost on him. But rather than look away, Zach surprised me with a quick smile, then turned back to the group to listen to Holden and I quickly joined them.

Everyone paid attention as Holden revisited the safety considerations, who was walking with whom, the condition of the dogs, a radio and sat phone check, meet-up times, and then he opened the meeting up for any concerns. That done, we were ready to go, excited dogs bounding at our heels, including Spider who I'd brought with me the previous afternoon and who'd spent the night kennelled with his mates.

Adrenaline fuelled my body as I took those first steps of the day, unable to believe that unadventurous me was actually going to scale a fucking mountain to bring down a mob of sheep. *How was this my life?*

Like he could read my mind, Holden cupped my neck and asked, "You ready for this?"

"Abso-fucking-lutely not," I answered seriously. "Lead on."

He laughed as he unrolled my woollen hat down over my ears. Then he kissed me. "You look hella cute like that."

I squinted into the bright light fixed to his forehead, pretty sure my ears had turned pink under the stitching. I swatted his hand. "I'm too old to look cute."

He cradled my face and kissed me more thoroughly this time, the fog of our breath mingling with the swirling mist that filled the cutting. "You will always look cute to me. And I have to say—" He tugged up the collar of my Swanndri. "—this is a very sexy look on you, *Doctor* Everton."

I almost flinched at the casual reminder of a past life I was pretending didn't exist. "Blue-balled and drowning in merino you mean?"

Holden laughed and kissed me again. "Exactly that."

"Jesus, didn't you get enough of each other last night?" Sam steamed past with Thor at his side. "See you at the split, as long as this crap burns off. We're lucky it wasn't a blue duck." As the junior member of the team, Sam had been up an hour before everyone else. His job was to stoke the fire and get the range ready to cook, but also to do a quick scout of the adjoining hills and check the mustered mob. That could mean clocking a couple of kilometres and a few climbs before he even had breakfast.

"It's called delegating," Holden had quipped.

"A blue duck?" I raised a brow while watching Sam disappear into the mist and wondering how the hell he still had that much energy.

"It means when it's too wet or foggy to muster," Holden explained. "But this mist is gonna burn off pretty quick. Shall we?" He swept an arm toward the track and I nodded, excitement fizzing in my veins.

And with that, we entered the scrubby bush bordering the stream, and it began. My first muster. And quite possibly my last, I mused grimly, then shoved the gloomy thought aside, determined to just enjoy myself.

Holden talked as he climbed. Good for him. He scaled rocks and boulders like a bloody mountain goat. Whereas I was left gasping after only the first half-dozen switchbacks up the rocky ravine, and that was with the immeasurable aid of the mustering stick. Thank Christ for the timely gift which not only helped keep my footing secure, but reminded me that Holden had only been a boy when he'd first scaled these mountains. I could surely manage the same as a grown man.

Yeah, right.

Twenty minutes in, and it was all I could do not to throw in the towel and head home, my legs protesting the effort like I hadn't walked a day in my life. But then Holden would say something funny, or I'd get a peek at the scenery between the thinning misty swathes when dawn finally broke, or I'd catch the sound of the dogs across the valley, and I pressed on.

I knew damn well Holden was taking it easy on me. This had to be a much slower pace than he was used to, but he never said a word.

Spider stayed close at my heels, weaving back and forth behind me like I was one of his merino stragglers. I was so happy I'd brought him. His excitement at being on the hill with the others was contagious.

Time seemed to pass quickly, and when we finally left the ravine and the last bit of bush cover and crested the first rocky ridge, I gasped at the sight of the early morning sun glistening on the frosty tussock down in the valley. With the fog almost gone, it was like a magic carpet rolled out before us, and goosebumps fluttered across my skin.

Holden's arms slid around my waist and his lips settled on my neck without a gasp in sight, which only made me want to slap him. "Not a bad outlook, huh?"

I spun and caged him in with my stick around his arse so I could kiss him soundly. "Not bad? Understatement of the year. I have no words. How would you even describe this to people who haven't been here? Thank you so much for bringing me."

His look gentled. "*You're* the best damn view up here."

My cheeks burned hot because what the hell did you say to something like that? And so, I said nothing, just kissed him again, and that seemed to be enough.

"I think I've just found another use for this nibbie." I waggled my brows and yanked him flush against me.

He laughed and rocked his hips into mine. "I'm pretty sure that's in no history book I've ever read. My grandfather would be appalled. I must raise it at the next meeting of the Station Owner Collective."

"You do that." I let him go, took one look at the path ahead, and gulped. "Well, shit—" I took in the exposed, steep, rocky landscape, with its scree slopes and bare faces and lung-busting topography, and experienced a brief moment of panic. "—that isn't intimidating at all."

He laughed and took my hand. "Come on. You'll be fine."

"Have you met my lungs lately?" I groaned and he tugged me the next few metres before the path got too narrow and I slotted in behind.

A flash of green and bright orange whipped over my shoulder, the backdraft whipping at my ears. The bird landed just to my right less that ten metres away. "Shit!" I nearly jumped out of my skin, and Spider gave a rumbling growl followed by a deep bark. "Is that a kea?"

Holden turned and huffed at the massive olive-green parrot with its intimidating hooked beak. The inquisitive bird was walking toward us with his head cocked to the side as if deciding whether or not we were edible or whether we might provide something that was.

"Yeah, bloody thing. Shoo!" Holden waved his hands and Spider gave another bark and a mock charge that pulled up short.

The bird barely batted an eye, hopping all of a metre away before turning back to regard us all with wary curiosity. It looked completely nonplussed.

I chuckled. "That clearly told him."

Holden grumbled. "They might be big and pretty and smart as a whip, but they're a pain in my fucking butt."

"Kind of like me?" I bit my lip and he chuckled.

"Only if you *also* like to kill the occasional sheep by digging a hole just above their kidney to get to all that precious fat and then just leave them to die. I lose a number of animals each year to the buggers."

"Oh!" I re-evaluated my opinion of the impressive bird. "Well, that's a hard no, then. I prefer my lamb roasted, thank you very much."

Holden snorted. "They're rated next to primates in intelligence."

"A good reason to get going." I pushed him ahead. "I don't like the way it's looking at me. Like I might go well with a side order of bacon."

Holden laughed and the kea followed us for a couple of minutes before deciding we were a waste of energy and flying back toward the valley.

When we got to a wider portion of the track, I manoeuvred alongside Holden. "When we eventually start coming down, what exactly will we be looking for?"

"Sheep," he deadpanned, and I gave him a none-too-gentle elbow dig to the ribs. "Okay, okay." He chuckled. "When we get to the highest point, we'll have something to eat and drink first. Then we'll start coming down and mobbing them up as we go. Merinos mostly scatter in twos and threes, but there'll be a few groups of twenty or so dotted around. It's funny, but they quite often move about in the same peer groups from year to year."

I chuckled. "Kind of like hanging out with friends for the summer."

He grinned. "Yeah, something like that. They're creatures of habit, and their whereabouts are predictable up to a point because there are always the individualists who go their own way. But the predictability is why musterers like to keep the same beats year after year."

"Because they know where the hiding places are," I interjected.

He grinned. "Exactly. Now, you're getting it. Come on. We need to keep moving."

I groaned as we started to climb again, Holden continuing to talk while I followed, gasping my way up rocky slopes, traversing paths along narrow ridges, manoeuvring around or through scree slides—the stick proving its worth yet again—and all with views for fucking miles.

"Our job today is to bring our mob down from up top to Charlie, who has the middle beat. She'll then add them to hers and take them down to the bottom beat, who will finish the job. Meanwhile, we sweep and gully-rake for any stragglers left behind."

"These sheep of yours must have a good head for heights," I grumbled, grabbing onto a ledge as my boot hit some loose rock and slid out from under me.

"Yeah." He grabbed my arm to steady me. "They're a tough breed and surprisingly agile. You'd be amazed at the nooks and crannies they can get themselves into and just how high they go."

"Do you miss many completely?"

He chuckled. "You'd be surprised. There are a lot of places to hide up here. A few wily animals have even managed to miss several musters and have massive fleeces when we finally catch up with them. But double-deckers who just miss a single muster or shear aren't that uncommon."

"One for the sheep," I mused.

I'd stripped the lammie way back in the ravine, along with my Swanndri, perspiration pouring down my face. Spider picked his way with a surefootedness I admired but I knew was still hard on his pads. I'd watched the team tend to all the dogs' feet the night before, checking for nicks and scratches and applying ointment where needed. He shot to attention when a green-and-grey skink whipped across a rock in front of his nose, but he was far too slow and the tiny creature was gone just as quickly.

"I'd have thought it would be too cold for them up here?"

"This altitude is okay. Higher up they struggle. We've even got weta that can survive the freezing conditions. They've got some sort of antifreeze in their blood."

"Oh." I shuddered at the thought of the spiky little creatures. "Wonderful."

Holden simply chuckled.

Around the next switchback, we stopped to look at a small marker cairn that Holden had built as a kid, and we'd just moved past when a flurry of barking floated on the air.

"What's that?" I spun to trace the source.

Holden put his hand on my shoulders and faced me downhill, a groan of relief escaping my mouth at the chance to catch my breath and pretend my thigh muscles weren't about to burst into flame.

He pressed his hot body close against my back and whispered, "Listen."

I did, quickly realising that the barking I'd heard wasn't just random. It continued bouncing off the steep mountain walls, different dogs answering from side to side, like a monastic choir singing across a nave. Then Holden said something to Spider and the huntaway joined in with a series of deep barks that echoed through the mountains and likely all the way down to the homestead.

A huge smile broke over my face as I patted the huntaway's head. "It's like his superpower."

Holden laughed and slipped an arm around my waist. "It's called a bark-up. The dogs are sounding off to show where each musterer is. We could just use our radios, but Tom likes it old school."

I laughed and spun in Holden's arms to give him a hard kiss.

He pulled away, chuckling. "Well, if that's all it takes, I'll tell Spider to sound off more often."

The barking quieted and I shoved Holden ahead. "Come on. I want to get to the top so we can eat before I die, and also, your arse looks great from back here. At this point, it's the only thing giving me life."

He laughed and continued heading up the track.

I looked past his shoulder and gasped. "Fuck. Me. Now I know you're not taking me up *that*, right?" I pointed to a makeshift set of steps cut into the rock face. One that Spider was casually loping up like they offered no more challenge than the veranda stairs back at the homestead.

"Where the merinos go, we follow." Holden pointed above the stairs to where a dozen or so cream shapes were moving across the almost vertical slope and more huddling on the crest.

"Oh. My. God." I stared. "That wasn't in the brochure."

He held out his hand. "Come on, Edmund Hillary, I said I'd keep you safe."

I looked at his hand and then took it. Because I trusted him. Completely. And the truth of that didn't surprise me as much as it should have.

An hour and a half later, we'd traversed the rocky face safely, scouted out a few more groups of merinos along the way, and arrived at the highest point of our climb, thank god.

I collapsed on the closest flat bit of ground I could find, tried to fill my lungs, which was harder than expected, and held up a hand. "In the spirit of high-country naming practices, you can call this spot Gil's Gagging Rock or Gil's Demise. Either work for me."

Holden laughed and shoved a water bottle into my hand. "How about Gil's Goal, cos you made it, baby. All the way."

Huh. I got up on my elbows and took a look around. "Fuck, I did, didn't I? How about that?" I cut a smug look Holden's way. "Told you I was fit."

He snorted and waved me over closer to the edge of the ridgeline. "Come here and take a look."

I struggled to my feet, my body protesting all the way, and then wandered over to join him. "That's the Havelock River," he explained, pulling me down between his legs. "The Glendale feeds into it almost straight below us. We're almost two and half thousand feet above sea level here."

"Holy shit." I gaped at a river many times the size of the Glendale, the intoxicating view stealing my breath, as did the stiff breeze, which had appeared from nowhere to drop the temperature like a stone and dry the sweat on my skin. Holden unpacked our morning tea/lunch and then donned his Swanndri before handing me mine.

I put it on and started eating in silence, my gaze fixed on the scenery and the way the mountain dropped away just a few metres past our feet. The view from the helicopter flight a few days before had been jaw-dropping enough—cruising over an ocean of jagged, snow-tipped mountains that unfurled like a spiky grey-and-white carpet all the way to the Tasman Sea glistening in the distance. But there was something different and infinitely more personal about having my feet on those actual mountains—sitting on one of those peaks, feeling the hard rock beneath me, breathing the thin air, and wincing as the icy breeze cut into my cheeks. My heart soared in a way I couldn't put into words.

I sat between Holden's legs and leaned back against his warm body, devouring my food, savouring the view, and debating the relative merit of a heart-lung transplant on my return to civilisation.

Spider snoozed at our side, a few dog biscuits nestled in his tummy to pep him up.

All too soon we were back on our feet and heading downhill, mobbing up the stock as we went and moving them down. It took me a while to develop an eye for spotting the blighters unless they were grouped in sufficient numbers, whereas Holden had a sixth sense and eagle eye from thirty years of mustering these hills.

But after a while I finally cottoned on where to look and what to look for, even though I still missed more than I found. Thank God for Holden. And slowly, slowly, we worked our way down, the sun throwing shadows across the valley floor at our feet and into the deep ravines that split the faces.

The stock ebbed and flowed as the growing mob moved ever downward on the track. The stock was mostly compliant with the game plan—only the occasional troublemaker or freethinker needing to be gathered back into the fold by one of us or Spider. The huntaway was mostly on point, although he was easily distracted, and I finally understood his powder-puff label. He tended to work when he wanted. Then again, didn't we all, and it was hard not to smile when Holden got frustrated with him.

The relative quiet with which it was all done came as a total surprise. Holden whistled and encouraged the stock to follow the natural course downhill, whereas I'd imagined him driving them down with a lot of noise and barking. The truth was, Spider rarely barked at all unless Holden asked him. He mostly brought up the rear, swinging from side to side to discourage backtracking and occasionally disappearing down banks or between rocks to flush out the reluctant stragglers.

"It's all much calmer than I expected," I marvelled.

Holden grinned. "Good. That means we're doing it right. Too fast, too impatient, too much barking and yelling, and the mob can panic. Then before you know it, you have a smother of sheep on your hands and suffocation is a real threat, no different from what happens at concerts when people rush the exits."

"Jesus." I shook my head. "There's so much more to it than I imagined." And with that, I spent the rest of the day paying much closer attention to what Holden was actually doing and I realised it was like an intricate well-practiced dance. Sheep, shepherd, dog, and staff, all moving around each other on the rocky faces.

When I could get enough oxygen circulating in my brain, I was going to write down every bit of the day so that I didn't forget a single thing. It was... beautiful, and wonderful, and I loved every second of it. I took so many photos that the battery on my phone died halfway down.

And when we paused to catch our breath just before we made our descent back into the scrubby ravine above River Hut, Holden wrapped me in his arms and told me he loved me. My eyes met the dark heat in his, and in that moment, I knew I wouldn't need words *or* photos.

I'd never forget that day or that look in his eyes for as long as I lived.

I lowered myself into the canvas chair with a single loud groan, reliving every gut-busting vertical step of the day. I hadn't attempted the return drive to the station around three as planned, mostly because when we got back to River Hut at two, I could barely walk... or sit... or breathe. Mostly that last one.

And so, I'd made an executive decision in favour of an early meal for everyone. That meant I could rest up for a bit, get some food in me, and still get back to the homestead before night hit. The river was still low and the track wouldn't be a problem.

I gingerly stretched my legs in front and glared at Holden, who was doing his best not to laugh. "Shut up. Or I'll skewer your balls, along with anyone else's who even looks like they might smile my way." I scanned the group of equally amused musterers who lay scattered over the grass outside the hut, along with socks, boots, dogs, the first aid kit, beer, snacks, and other sundry items. "Then I'll whip up some pastry just for the occasion. It'll be my personal take on shepherd's pie."

Zach snorted and headed into the hut to keep an eye on dinner, a job which I'd delegated, having officially tapped out. Not that the pre-prepared meal would take them any time—butter chicken and rice, my secret recipe flatbreads, corn on the cob, and meringues with cream for dessert. An odd mix, but that was muster for you.

Sam eyed me warily for a few seconds, then scrambled to his feet and made a quick exit stage right to organise feeding the dogs who trotted along after him. Tom, Charlie, Alek, Jackson, and Logan simply smiled and went to help Zach. Either way, they'd all left, which meant I could whine to my heart's content.

I wriggled on the chair to try and get comfortable before finally giving up. I needed food and a foot massage and quite possibly a cushion before I parked my butt in the Ranger for the trip back home. I turned at the sound of my name, followed by hoots of laughter coming from the kitchen and shouted, "You're all a pack of arseholes."

Which was greeted by more laughter.

"Oh god, everything hurts," I grumbled to Holden. So much for thinking I was fit. Every bone in my body ached, my lungs felt like a steamroller had barrelled through them, my old tib and fib breaks were sending shots of electricity up my calves, and the two grazes I'd copped after an unexpected detour down a scree slide burned like motherfuckers. The fact that Holden looked barely puffed and was striding around the hut like he could go another mountain or two only pissed me the fuck off more.

"Sit down before I throw something at you," I groused. "I have a need to see you in a lot of pain. But first, hand me your penknife and my stick. I'm gonna notch the shit out of that thing for today. I think I left my colon on that last scree slide. Grazed the fuck out of my arse."

Holden laughed and handed me the muster stick and his penknife. "Want me to kiss it better . . . or maybe more?"

I shot a sneaky look toward the hut and grumbled, "No. It pains me to say that as good as you are in bed, I doubt I could stay awake past the amuse-bouche."

"I'm not even gonna ask." Holden knelt at my feet and took over rubbing my aching leg. "And stop whining. I saw your face. You loved it up there today."

My heart immediately melted, and a smile wiped the scowling frown from my face without permission. "I did," I admitted, running my fingers through his sticky hair.

"And you were brilliant. You coped super well. I've been walking these mountains for years, baby."

"He's right." Charlie was setting the plates and cutlery on the table. "Major kudos to you. That was a tough day."

"You're just being nice." I waved her flattery aside. "You went up a second time to get that last one. How the hell did you do that?"

She thought about that then grinned. "You know, you're right. You're a pussy."

I flipped her off. "Just because you haven't got literal balls doesn't mean you're safe."

She laughed and disappeared back inside the hut.

"My feet are sooo sore." I sent Holden a pleading look and added puppy dog eyes for good measure.

"Oh, for fuck's sake. Come on." He lifted my foot onto his lap and started kneading the sole, and I swore I scared half the merinos awake with my delighted groan. Then he lifted the foot to his mouth and kissed the toe. "But seriously, you did an amazing job today. I'm super proud of you."

His praise sent bubbles of happiness through my heart.

"You really enjoyed it, huh?"

My grin split my face from ear to ear. Enjoy didn't even come close to it. I was still riding a high the likes of which I hadn't felt since Callie had been put in my arms for the first time. "Like you wouldn't believe."

He beamed with pleasure. "Okay. Favourite part?"

"The views. But there was so much more than that. The silence when you made me stand still and listen. And I didn't get what you meant about merinos swirling like schooled fish until I saw it. And then lunch on that outcrop of rock overlooking the Havelock River. I had no idea it was so vast. Callie would've loved it. Her favourite story as a little kid was about a young girl called Elizabeth and her adventures on a river raft in Africa."

He slowed his kneading and smiled softly. "I wish I'd met her."

My throat thickened knowing she'd have loved Holden too. She'd have loved the station. All of it. "Yeah, me too. I had the best time today, thank you."

"My pleasure." He stood and bent down to kiss me. "Will you be okay driving back? You could stay."

I shook my head. "Nah, I need a hot shower. And I'm better than I make out. Just don't tell them." I nodded toward the hut. "They're having too much fun at my expense."

Holden grinned and added another hefty log to the embers before taking a seat next to me. It was the first time I'd noticed any weariness in him. I threaded my fingers through his and pulled his hand onto my lap.

He squeezed my hand. "Are you ready for the shearing gang Monday?"

"As ready as I'll ever be," I reassured him as Sam walked a couple of beers our way.

"Only a zero alcohol for you." Sam slid the cool can into my free hand, then gave the other one to Holden.

I chugged back a welcome draft and sighed happily. "Their cook sent me an email to check I was still covering morning and afternoon tea so he could gauge his supplies. Half of the gang are travelling out daily and the rest are bringing their campervans, so I don't have any cottages to stock. I've got this, Holden. No need to worry."

He turned sideways for another kiss. "I'm not worried. You could do this with your eyes closed."

It was a fact which we both knew to be true, and which we were pretending wasn't important in the scheme of where we were headed as a couple. As much as I loved what I was doing, I knew that eventually it wouldn't be enough. We both knew that. And one thing was certain: Holden wasn't going anywhere. He belonged on the station. He'd curl up and die like a fish out of water if he left, starved of the very oxygen he needed to survive.

Leonard had told me not to jump the gun and simply assume things couldn't work between us. Was that the sensible approach? I wasn't sure. Ignoring the problem was working in the interim and I wasn't about to mess with a good thing, but as sure as winter was approaching over the horizon, a reckoning was coming for Holden and me as well.

"Will you two please stop mauling each other?" Charlie collapsed into a chair with a scowl on her face. "I swear this has been the longest muster ever. We all need a cigarette just being in the same vicinity."

Everyone laughed, and I glanced to where Zach was standing at the wood-burning oven watching the water come to a boil. He didn't smile but he didn't look away either. I'd take that.

Another light beer, a huge meal, and a lot of laughs and friendly bantering around the fire, and I was ready to head back to the station with just enough light left in the evening to ease the trip. Holden walked me to the Ranger, with Spider running ahead to take prime position in the passenger seat. Hidden from curious eyes, Holden pushed me up against the driver's door and ravished me. There was no other word to describe being kissed top to toe, groped, licked, grinded on, and generally hung out to dry, still gasping for more.

"I'm gonna be wearing those hickeys for days," I grumbled. "And they didn't even come with a happy ending attached."

He cupped my dick and squeezed. "I'm sure I can fix that."

I groaned and thrust into his hand. "Don't tease. It'd be just our luck for Tom to walk around the corner and catch us, or Zach. And he's only just starting to talk to us again."

"Mmm." Holden ran his nose up the side of my face, as he was wont to do as often as possible. "I'm game if you are." He pulled a piece of dry grass from my hair, and then another. Then he licked his finger and cleaned something from the side of my face.

"Oh god, that was sheep shit, wasn't it?" I grumbled, rubbing my cheek with my sleeve.

He brushed my arm aside and kept cleaning. "How about you just shut up for a minute and let someone look after you for a change?"

"By washing my face with your spit?" I arched a brow.

"Yes." He eyeballed me, deadly serious.

I deflated under his attention and pointed to my other cheek. "I think you missed a bit."

His mouth curved up in a slow smile and he leaned in and kissed my cheek, his hot breath sending shivers all the way to my toes. Then he stepped back and turned my face from side to side. "I think that got it all. But make sure you change out of those clothes when you get home."

I almost laughed. "You're very bossy for a sheep farmer."

He grinned. "You seem to handle it all right."

I huffed. "Because I ignore you."

His smile turned all kinds of dirty. "Not always."

I bit back a smile because he was so right about that. "Behave." I pushed him off and climbed into the cab, setting my muster stick carefully on the passenger seat. Then I wound the window down and fisted Holden's shirt to bring him in for a final kiss. "Thank you again. For today. For yesterday. For last night. For the muster stick. For all of it."

"Any time." His kiss was soft and full of the sweetness I'd come to love about him. "I love you, Gil. And I'd like to think we have a lot more of these days in our future."

God, this man. I let go of his shirt and patted his chest. "Day by day, right?"

He stared at me for a moment like he'd been hoping for more, then stepped away and slapped the roof. "Drive carefully, baby."

CHAPTER TWENTY-FOUR

Gil

A week and a bit later, the woolshed home paddocks and races were full of disgruntled merinos and the shearing gang had been in full swing for almost three days—which didn't necessarily mean a break for anyone else. Holden and his team used the time to work through a range of other health measurements and routine analyses on the mob who hadn't had eyes on them since they'd been let loose on the hill months before.

For my part, I delivered morning and afternoon tea to everyone, chatted with the sweepers or rousies above the racket of music and electric shears, got schooled by the classer as to the relative quality of the fleeces, swapped recipes with the gang's cook—a weathered seventy-year-old Samoan woman by the name of Elsie—and won the shearers over with my meringues and beef-bacon-and-cheese mini pies.

Other than that, the shearing gang was a well-oiled machine, and with the belly crutch being a quicker clean up than the spring full shear, they didn't need that much from me and they'd be on their way to the next station by the end of the day.

When I'd lingered long enough to tick the friendly social box in the shed, I wandered over to the pens and races to catch up with Holden. I was finding a rhythm that worked and fed my heart on many levels. What had started as a novel experience to blast the cobwebs from my life had suddenly turned into something quite different—a growing connection with the land and the people who worked it and the food that grew on it and which kept all the wheels spinning—a sense of being part of something much bigger than myself.

And then, of course, there was Holden.

I was standing on the bottom railing of the race, watching my guy draft a constant stream of merinos into three different pens. *My guy. A sheep farmer. Go fucking figure.* But it required some impressive decision-making and sleight of hand with the drafting gate, and I was growing dizzy just watching him work.

"You feeling all right about the buyer's visit this morning?" I asked cautiously, knowing full well he was nervous.

"It is what it is," he brazened and kept his eyes on the fluttering ribbon of sheep, his beauty spot lost in the tight lines at the corners of his eyes. "Too late now. Besides, we won't know anything for a month or so if that."

How he could talk and still separate the mob was beyond me.

"True enough." I was hoping for a little more, but Holden steadfastly avoided my gaze. "Right, well, I guess I'll see you after she's been. Don't forget, we've got the barbecue tonight."

Still no eye contact. "I remember."

I waited a few seconds longer, then left him to it, getting halfway back to the homestead before I was grabbed by the shoulder and spun around.

"I'm sorry." Holden pulled me into a hug and I grinned against his sweaty shirt. "I was an arsehole back there, and if you want an honest answer to your question, I'm shitting myself."

"I always want an honest answer." I slipped my hands under his shirt and around his waist, ignoring the curious stares from some of the shearing gang watching through the woolshed doors. "But I'm a big boy, Holden. My feelings aren't hurt. I'll be here when it's done. When you're ready to talk." I tucked a long brown wave behind his ear and dropped a kiss on his lips. "Get back to your work. You've got this."

"Thank you." He kissed me again and then headed back to the yards at a jog.

Back at the homestead, I kicked off my boots, put on another load of laundry, and then made my way into the kitchen. A bright red Toyota Land Cruiser with SX Merino stamped on the side passed the kitchen window, heading for the woolshed, and I took a deep breath and crossed everything I had.

Three hours later, another unfamiliar vehicle rounded the driveway at the bottom of the lawn and I frowned, hoping Paddy Lane hadn't decided to pay a return visit. But when the black four-door BMW pulled in next to the path, I knew it wasn't Zach's father. Hell, it wasn't likely to be anyone connected with the station, not driving that thing. I dried my hands before heading for the front door, wondering just how much time this was going to take out of my party preparations.

I opened the door just as the visitor reached the veranda, but when he lifted his gaze from the stairs and our eyes met, my knees almost buckled.

"Luke?" I stared at my ex-husband, shaking my head. "What the hell are you doing here?"

"Hello to you too." He smiled sheepishly, a look which I'd once, but no longer found cute. "Surprise?"

Surprise? Was he kidding? Still in shock, I clutched onto the door like a life raft and stared blankly at him.

The cute smile fell away and Luke sighed. "Okay, so maybe not so funny. I'm sorry. I didn't want to drop in on you like this, but you kind of left me no choice. You said two weeks and I gave you that, but you're not answering any of my texts or emails and we need to talk . . . about a *lot* of things."

Pretty sure I was still opening and closing my mouth in a very unattractive fashion, I snapped it shut instead. Better that than risk the stream of angry thoughts running through my head getting any airtime. Not yet, at least.

When I didn't answer, Luke gave another weighty sigh and leaned back against the veranda, giving me my first good look at him. A few centimetres taller than me, Luke was as handsome as ever, with short dirty-blond hair, the brightest blue eyes, and a crooked naughty smile that promised fun with a capital F. But there was something about the defensive way his arms folded across his chest, the unfamiliar thinness to his face, and the way his jeans hung loose on his hips that gave me pause.

He looked . . . exhausted.

In truth, he looked a lot like I'd felt for so long that I'd forgotten I could feel any other way. Maybe he'd been like that since Callie's death and I'd simply been too caught up in my own grief to pay attention. An unexpected niggle of guilt and a swell of compassion wormed their way under my skin.

"How did you know—" I groaned. "Tucker, right?" I'd told Tuck he could let Luke know what I was doing, I just hadn't expected him to give Luke the actual name of the place.

Luke's gaze skittered sideways. "Don't blame Tuck. He was adamant you didn't want to see me, but I managed to wheedle the name of the place out of him. I mean, Jesus, Gil, I didn't know what else to do. I've been so worried. And . . . I've missed you." He swallowed hard, his eyes turning glassy. "No one else quite gets what it's like, do they?"

He was right, of course, but I kept quiet. Waiting.

His shoulders slumped and he shook his head, looking the picture of misery. "I don't blame you for not wanting to see me. I fucked up, leaving like I did. I know that. But do you honestly think things would have worked out any different if I'd stayed? We were tearing each other apart, Gil."

I finally found some words. "I guess we'll never know, will we?"

He blinked at that, his eyes suspiciously shiny. Then he dropped into one of the deck chairs and stared out over the lake. "This is a beautiful spot," he said absently. "I can see why you like it here."

Tuck had obviously said more than just the name of the place. "It is." It was as much as he was going to get.

Luke glanced back at me and sighed. "I-I miss her so much, Gil. So—" His voice broke. "—so fucking much, I can scarcely stand it. I'm sorry I left. So sorry. But we weren't talking. We weren't doing anything except hurting each other and I felt like I was drowning. Maybe it was the coward's way out, but I didn't know what else to do. If I could redo things, I'd stay. I'd try harder. I wanted so badly to talk to you about Callie but—" He swallowed hard, his breathing shaky. "Dammit, I'm sorry." He dragged his hand down his face and my gaze locked on to the green silicon wristband inscribed with the word Poppa. Callie had made me buy it for him one Christmas and my heart broke at the sight.

"It wasn't your fault. I didn't let you," I blurted but stayed where I was, my hands shaking too much to let go of the door.

"We didn't let each other." Those sky-blue eyes held fast to mine, full of regret. "But you had so much more going on. The nightmares. The panic attacks. We'd already lost each other somewhere along the way, and I don't think we even noticed what was happening until it was too late. But we should have. *I* should have."

Luke looked as miserable as I'd felt in my worst days and a cold wall inside me finally gave way. I let the door go and shakily made my way to the other chair, my legs as weak as jelly. I almost fell into it and Luke had to grab the chair to steady it.

"Gil, are you okay?"

I spun at Zach's voice. He was standing on the lawn watching Luke and me with a frown on his face.

"Zach, this is Luke, my . . . ex-husband. Luke, this is Zach, one of the shepherds."

I saw the penny drop in Zach's eyes and a decidedly unimpressed expression drew over his face.

Luke stood and offered his hand, entirely unsuspecting. "Nice to meet you, Zach."

Zach regarded Luke's hand like he might a three-day-old fish and left it hanging long enough that Luke was forced to withdraw it, his cheeks pink with embarrassment.

I almost smiled.

Then Zach turned to me. "I'll be in my cottage if you need anything, okay?"

I nodded, scrambling for a foothold in this weird rabbit hole where Zach Lane was somehow protective of me.

Zach then considered Luke for a moment, his distaste obvious. "You've got some balls showing up here, that's for sure." And with that singularly epic summation, one that I heartily agreed with, Zach headed for his cottage.

Luke followed his departure with an amused shake of his head. "Do I have a handprint on my face, cos it sure feels like I've been slapped?"

I snorted. "What can I say? They're a protective bunch. And they know my story."

Luke flushed again. "I can tell. Well, I'm happy you've got people who have your back. I've been worried. And yes, feeling guilty, and deservedly so. *I* should've had your back then, and instead I let you down. Can I ask you something?"

I nodded, trying to get my head around this contrite version of Luke that was so at odds with the way I'd demonised him for the last year.

"If I *had* stayed, do you think we would've made it?"

And there it was. The question I'd been churning over and over in my mind for the last year and the source of most of my anger at the man sitting in front of me.

But finally, I had an answer. "No. I think we'd long passed that point."

Luke's eyes closed in time with a long shuddering sigh, and he nodded with relief. "Me too." He said it like he could breathe again after months underwater.

And since I knew that feeling better than most, I found myself taking his hand.

He jerked in surprise, his eyes springing open to meet mine.

Somehow I managed a smile. "I think it was exactly like you said. Callie had the best of us those last years, and when she was gone, the holes showed up straight away. I don't think we knew each other anymore, and we certainly didn't know how to help each other through what happened. But I had as much a part to play in that as you did."

"Maybe." Luke spoke so softly I had to lean in to catch it. "But I still shouldn't have left *when* I did." His hand squeezed mine. "It was fucked up and I'm sorry for that. If nothing else, we've always been friends, and I should've stayed for that. I should've stayed because I'm your friend."

Tears welled in my eyes because it was what I'd missed the most when Luke left. The romance had been gone for a long time, but Luke had been my friend before anything else. "I would've appreciated that, but I didn't exactly make it easy for you."

"No." He looked out over the lake. "You didn't. But we both said a lot of things we didn't mean."

"We did," I agreed, but I needed to say the words. "But you should've stayed. Not for forever. But you had a whole family, Luke. Callie's extended family to rally around you. I had nothing even close to that. If it wasn't for Tucker, I don't know if I would've made it through those first six months after you'd gone. I get all your reasons and I own my side of it, and no, we likely wouldn't have lasted, but it hurt, Luke. It hurt so fucking much and I didn't have anything left."

"I know. And I'm so sorry."

"We needed *each other*." I kept going, determined to get everything said. "We needed to fall back on that friendship you were talking about. I'm sorry for pushing you away and making that almost impossible. I blamed you for a long time. But lately, I've been thinking that maybe I would've done the same thing in your shoes. I didn't want to let you in back then. I didn't want you anywhere close to me. But I didn't want you to leave me either."

"I know." He wiped his damp eyes with the back of his hand and then he wiped mine. "But the others weren't you, Gil. They weren't Callie's other dad. I knew I'd made a mistake almost straight away, but then you wouldn't take any of my calls or agree to meet, or talk, and I didn't know how to get back."

We stared at each other for a moment, years of marriage and a dead ten-year-old daughter between us, and suddenly the blame game just didn't matter anymore.

"We both fucked up," I said bluntly, and Luke grunted.

"Yeah, we did." He held up our joined hands and a small frown creased his brow at the faint tremble in mine. "You still getting the nightmares?"

I warmed at the knowledge Tuck clearly hadn't mentioned those. "Yes. But less often. Being here helps." It was as much as I was going to say at that point.

Luke looked around. "It *is* pretty spectacular."

I followed his gaze, remembering the first time I'd laid eyes on the station. God, had it only been six weeks? Six weeks, and somehow, I'd found a home here. With the people, the mountains, and the warm welcome of my kitchen. The station had burrowed under my skin and taken a piece of my heart without me even realising, just like the man who'd stolen the rest of it.

"It's not only the scenery," I clarified. "There's something about the people here too." *About one in particular.*

Luke studied me for a long minute like he wanted to ask more but didn't, turning back to the lake instead. "Callie would have loved it here." His words echoed my own to Holden just days before, and the realisation jolted me. "That girl loved animals and the outdoors."

Luke chuckled. "Not exactly your comfort zone though, if I remember right? In fact, I was surprised when Tucker told me what you were doing."

I shrugged a little defensively. "I don't *hate* the outdoors. I think I just got lazy. I got too comfortable with my routines. Same thing, different day. But when we lost Callie and the shit hit the fan, none of that old stuff was helping and I figured I needed a shake-up."

Luke gave an amused huff. "Well, you certainly seemed to have achieved that. Domestic manager on a high-country sheep station. Could've knocked me over with a feather. Then again, you love cooking, so I totally get that part."

"Yeah, that was the clincher. The animal side is a work in progress."

Luke chuckled. "I bet. Remember that petting zoo we took Callie to? You made me go in the pens with her so you didn't have to get too close."

A smile came unbidden. "And then that bloody calf pissed all over my shoes anyway." We both laughed, and the clear sound of it stirred so many memories of better times that I didn't know where to look. But when the laughter died, a deep silence filled the space between us. I looked for the anger and the pain I'd carried for so long it was like a part of my being but was surprised to find them missing. Not gone but undemanding of attention.

"So, what are you going to do about the practice?"

The million-dollar question and one I wasn't about to discuss with Luke. "I don't know." Because it was true. Silence fell again and then I said something I never expected to. "I did love you, back then, before everything started to fall apart."

Luke stilled, like he was too frightened to move. Then he took a deep breath and faced me. "I loved you too, Gil. So very much. I think we just forgot to look after it."

He was right about that. But then I thought of something that Holden had said a few weeks back and hoped he wouldn't mind me sharing it.

"The owner of this station once told me that animal husbandry is about more than getting the genetic basics right. It's about the whole package, and that poor feed, stress from weather, inadequate shelter, and a whole list of other things can screw with your perfect little breeding foundation. His comments struck me at the time, and I realised they kind of applied to all kinds of husbandry, not just the animal kind. You and I coasted on the great start we had, but we forgot to keep checking in when things got stressful. We stopped carving out quality time. Stopped feeding our love. And stopped sheltering each other when things got tough."

Luke's eyes glistened. "He sounds like a wise man."

A warmth flooded my chest and I couldn't have held back the smile if I tried. But it was a smile that I was pretty sure told Luke everything he needed to know. "He is." My gaze remained steady on Luke's. "He's a lot of things, Luke, including only thirty. His name is Holden. And I'm in love with him."

Luke blinked, hard. Then he blinked again and shook his head. "Wow. That came out of nowhere."

I shrugged. "Tell me about it. I wasn't exactly looking."

Luke studied me for a long time and I let him, content to let him find the truth of what I'd said, and I didn't miss the flash of grief that caught in those blue eyes when he did. But then he surprised me with a smile. "That's good, Gil. You deserve to be loved better than I ever managed to do. I'm happy for you."

Heat washed over my face. "Thank you." I scrubbed at my traitorous eyes. "Jesus, look at me. This place is turning me into a sap. But I'm not sure anything can come of it. My life is in Wellington, and I've only known this guy six weeks, Luke. *Six weeks.*"

"So?"

I stared at him.

"I knew that you were the one for me in just a few days."

I huffed out a laugh. "Yeah, and look where that got us."

"Don't do that." His eyes flashed with hurt. "Don't dismiss what we had just because it didn't work out."

He was right. "I'm sorry. Self-protection, I guess. Anyway, I heard you were seeing someone."

He winced and threw me a sideways glance. "Not *seeing* someone, just—" He shrugged. "—trying to feel something, *anything*, I suppose. It finished a few weeks after it started."

"Oh." I wasn't sure what to say to that.

"And I'm not flying anymore. I packed in my job."

I jerked around to face him. "What? Since when?"

"A couple of months ago. They asked me if I wanted to return to the international roster, but when I thought about it, I realised I didn't want to do *any* of it. So I quit."

I was gobsmacked. Luke had always loved his job. And it suddenly hit me that all the time I'd been thinking he'd moved on, turns out he'd been no different to me. Completely lost.

I stumbled around a response. "So, what are you going to do?"

He cast me a wry smile. "What are *you* going to do?"

I slumped in my seat with a snort of laughter. "Touché." Then I thought of something. "Holden's a pilot too. They used to have a Cessna on the station."

Luke arched a brow. "Two pilots, huh? Must be something in that."

I snorted. "Shut up. I was just saying you have something in common. Have you flown at all since you resigned?"

He nodded. "Just local aero club stuff. I'm actually kind of enjoying it. I even got into a chopper a few months back for the first time in a while. I was a bit rusty to start with, but I've been clocking up the hours since. Finding the fun again, I guess."

"I'm happy for you. You deserve to enjoy what you do."

He held my gaze. "We all do."

I studied him in return and then ventured, "It's probably time we got things rolling with the lawyers, right?"

Luke gave a soft smile and visibly relaxed. "Yeah, probably. It was actually one of the things I wanted to talk with you about, along with selling the house and what you think about this damn meeting proposal with the other driver."

My heart clenched at the reminder, but the idea that Luke and I could maybe face at least that one thing together was a big weight off my shoulders. It felt like a bridge of some kind between us. Between our past and whatever lay ahead for us in the future.

I got to my feet and noticed Zach standing on his veranda, keeping an eye on us.

Luke followed my gaze and chuckled. "I don't think your minder likes me very much."

I couldn't help but laugh. "Don't be offended, he hated me on sight too."

Luke cast me a puzzled look. "Sounds like there's a story in there somewhere."

"You have no idea." I gave Zach a reassuring wave and pushed Luke toward the front door. "Come on. I'll make us a coffee."

CHAPTER TWENTY-FIVE

Holden

"You run a tight ship," the SX buyer commented as we bumped our way along the river track back toward the homestead.

I smiled at the compliment. Rosie, as she'd asked to be called, didn't appear to dish them out readily. I'd spent hours showing the no-nonsense woman around the woolshed, the stock, the station equipment, and machinery. I'd left her chatting with my team and let her inspect the wool of a dozen stock I'd drafted off and penned separate from the others. Rosie had been tight-lipped the whole way. But she'd also been well prepared, having clearly read all the notes I'd sent before the visit, and that in itself was reassuring.

The company was taking my application seriously.

When she was done with all the rest, I'd driven her Hilux up the river for a hike up Widow's Walk to Lightning Tarn and its spectacular view of the valley all the way back to the station. The cool change made the steep hike a little more pleasant, although Rosie seemed more than up to the challenge. But we were still sweating bullets by the time we got down, and when I opened the chilly bin

Gil had packed to find it loaded with water bottles and some freezer-cooled wheat bags, along with a snack, I could've kissed him.

Rosie continued to make some notes on that damned tablet of hers, but when I handed her a wheat bag, she put the tablet aside, undid the top three buttons on her shirt and shoved it down the front with not the slightest hesitation.

I bit back a smile and she shot me a look. "What? I'm pretty sure you're not interested."

I raised a brow. "And you know this how?"

She snorted. "The high country is a small niche industry, Holden, and there aren't too many secrets between you. Not much better than a bunch of gossiping teenagers, if you ask me."

Her candour had surprised me.

"I don't think I'll ever get used to this scenery," she said, peering over her steering wheel to the run of mountain peaks on both sides of the track. "You're lucky to live here."

I followed her gaze. "I'd be even luckier if you guys offer me a long-term contract."

She shot me a sideways look and I braced as the Toyota scrambled up yet another shingle bar to exit the riverbed for the last time on the run back to the homestead. "I called in to see Patrick Lane yesterday," she remarked casually, and my stomach lurched. "His contract with Southwarm is up in a year, and he wanted to talk."

I breathed out a sigh. "I guess that explains the gossip thing. I don't imagine he had any nice things to say about me."

She chuckled at that. "He's not a fan, no. Although I'm guessing that's not news to you."

"Hardly."

She nodded. "He's . . . old school."

I snorted. "How very polite of you."

She grinned. "I told him I wasn't interested in anything but the wool you produced."

I caught her eye. "Thank you for that."

She nodded. "You're welcome. But his flock *is* top-notch."

It was, dammit. Paddy might have been a bigoted arsehole, but he was a canny breeder.

"But yours is a big improvement on last year," she quickly added. "I'm sorry about your grandfather. We know you aren't to blame for what happened, but if we'd been Southwarm, we might've let you go as well."

I swallowed hard. "But we're turning that around. You saw that in the fleeces."

"I did. The work you're doing here is a credit to you, and it fits well with our company's profile."

"With a contract I could invest more into my improvement program," I wasn't shy in pointing out.

A smile tugged at her lips. "I'm well aware. And we'll be taking everything into account. That's all I can say right now, Holden. You know how it is."

We rounded the woolshed and Rosie steered the Land Cruiser right toward the homestead. She dropped me at the back of the house and I waved her off.

It was done. All we could do was wait.

I crossed the backyard and smiled at the ring of chairs laid out around the firepit stacked with wood and ready to go. We were having a staff barbecue to celebrate the end of muster, crutching, and the SX visit. It was all Gil's idea and it was a great one. We'd let the social side of things slide when Grandad had become unwell, and that needed to change. Those bonds were the glue that made the station successful—something drilled into me since the first time Grandad had carried me into the woolshed on his hip.

But as great as the barbecue idea was, as soon as it was socially polite, I intended to drag my sexy domestic manager to my bedroom and roast his arse six ways till Sunday for as long as we could both keep going. Then I was going to fall asleep with him in my arms and remind myself what a lucky bastard I was.

Gil was halfway through his stay and I didn't know what the fuck I was going to do if and when he left, which he would surely do if I couldn't come up with a way to keep him there. I loved what I did. It was who I was to the core. The high country was bred into my DNA. And yet somehow, in six weeks, I found myself unable to imagine living this life without him in it.

And I wasn't going to.

He just didn't know it yet.

But I also knew I couldn't push. Gil's head was a complicated place, with good cause. I had to give him his head and let him find his own way to the same conclusion. Open the gates. Encourage, don't demand. Bring up the rear. Have his back. Help him follow the path of least resistance.

Right to the station.

I was going to shepherd Gil into my life for good.

That was if he didn't bolt along the way.

Because there was always that.

I kicked my boots off at the back door and hung my jacket on the hook. "Honey, I'm home."

When there was no reply, I walked into the kitchen to find a flushed Gil scrambling to his feet from the table where another man sat with red-rimmed eyes and a coffee in his hand.

With an unspoken apology on his face, Gil took both my hands in his, and then to my surprise, he leaned in and pressed a soft kiss to my lips. Over Gil's shoulder, I watched as the other man blinked and looked away.

Cradling my face, Gil mouthed, *I love you.* Then he stepped to the side and took a deep breath.

"Holden, this is Luke."

Luke? My gaze jerked to the man who was busy getting to his feet and then back to Gil who simply raised his brows and gave a tiny shrug.

"He just arrived," he explained with apology in his eyes. "I didn't know."

"That's true," Luke said from where he stood by the table, but I didn't take my eyes off Gil.

"It's okay." Gil squeezed my hands again, but I wasn't at all sure it was. Why was Gil's ex-husband in my kitchen? Did Luke want Gil back? But then Gil had just kissed me, so that didn't make sense. What the hell was going on?

"Luke just came to *talk*." Gil emphasised the word and I relaxed a little. He tugged me toward the table. "I'd like you to stay, if you're okay with that?"

Was I? I took in the handsome man sitting at the end of the table, because of course he had to be bloody handsome, didn't he? The man who'd ripped Gil apart by leaving six months after the death of their daughter. The man Gil had once loved. No, I didn't want to sit and get to know him. I didn't want anything to do with him. And I especially didn't want him on my land, in my kitchen, and sitting at my table with *my* Gil.

I didn't want any of that.

I just wanted to hit the fucker.

Then I remembered once again how Gil had kissed me in front of Luke, and I sighed. Gil had been making a statement. To Luke *and* to me.

And okay, that felt a little better.

"Nice to meet you, Luke." I offered my hand because what the fuck else was I going to do?

He took it. "I've heard a lot about you, Holden. All of it good."

My gaze once more shot to Gil, who simply shrugged . . . again. *Goddammit.* We were going to need to work on our communication.

So, failing any other polite alternative, I pulled out a chair and sat. And while Gil poured fresh coffee and kept an eye on us from the kitchen island, Luke asked about the station and my family, and we chatted about flying and the weather, and it was . . . awkward, and yet somehow okay. Colour me fucking surprised.

But there was something else. Gil's kiss had felt like a statement of sorts. And the way Luke scrutinised every interaction between us with obvious curiosity made me sure Gil had told him exactly what we meant to each other. That shocked me to the core, in the best possible way, because it meant that Gil felt just as deeply as I did, a question I'd avoided, too scared of the answer. It might not guarantee a happy outcome, but it gave me hope.

Whatever had been said between them before I arrived, they both looked wrung out, and Gil had been shaken enough to need one of his pills—I could always tell. But clearly a détente had been reached, and for that I was grateful. They seemed reasonably comfortable with each other, and there was an affection between them I hadn't expected and wasn't sure I liked, but it was better than hostility. Gil would fill me in however he chose, but I couldn't say I wasn't relieved when Luke finally scraped back his chair and said he should be going.

"You could stay in one of the cottages," I found myself offering, clearly needing a brain transplant and only too late noticing Gil vehemently shaking his head in the background.

"No, but thank you," Luke quickly answered, shooting a sideways glance to Gil. "As I told Gil, I have a motel in Tekapo."

"When do you leave?" *So, sue me.*

Another sideways glance to Gil, but I found that one was harder to read, and for some reason that set my heart racing. "Tomorrow. I have a flight late afternoon from Christchurch." But he was still looking at Gil, who in return looked . . . resigned.

Oh Jesus.

Luke and I shook hands again, but this time Luke's gaze locked with mine. "Thank you." His eyes flicked to Gil, then back to me, and there was no mistaking what he was thanking me for.

"My pleasure." What else was I going to say? *Fucking twilight zone, here I come.*

By the time Gil got back from walking Luke to his car, I was beside myself to know what had been said between them, but before I got a single question out, Charlie, Tom, and Sam walked in the back door with beers in hand. Gil directed them to take the snacks outside and get the fire going and then dragged me into the pantry for a thorough kissing, which I supposed was meant to reassure me but instead set my radar pinging. I thought back to the look he'd shared with Luke about Luke's flight, and my heart cracked open.

He was leaving . . . with Luke. *What the actual fuck?* My heart thundered in my chest. I told myself I didn't know anything for sure and that if he meant to leave, then what the hell was the kiss for? I needed to calm the fuck down.

I pushed the panic aside, and when Gil stepped away, I held his oddly sad gaze. "Tonight, you'll talk to me. Promise?"

He nodded. "I promise."

"Good. Then let's get this party over with so I can hear what you have to say." It was time to focus on the celebration. The team had earned it. I'd find out about the other soon enough.

And for an hour or so, I could almost pretend I was having a good time. As expected, the food was amazing. Gil had truly outdone himself. There were lamb cutlets flamed on the barbecue, salsa verdé, Hasselback potatoes with melted cheese and a sour cream sauce, and a garden salad. And to finish, there was blueberry parfait made with my mother's frozen berries and enough alcohol consumed to loosen everyone's tongues in a way that most were going to regret the next day.

We finished up with tall stories and the annual autumn Miller Muster Awards. Gil got the prize for the Loudest Sex Noises, much to his horror, and I got the Most Whipped, much to mine. Spider got the Laziest Herding Dog award but quickly made up for it with the Loudest Bark in the sound-off competition.

Alek got the Most Likely to Die in the Wilderness prize, having picked up another set of abrasions after falling down a rocky incline on the last day. Sam received the Up-and-Coming Party Animal award for falling asleep twice around the firepit after only one beer. Zach got the award for Most Personal Growth, which made everyone laugh, including him, and Tom got the Most Likely to Summon Noise Control snoring prize.

Jackson and Logan who'd come for the celebration got the award for the Fastest Downhill Sprint when they stumbled across a huge wild boar and had to leg it. And Charlie, who'd been responsible for coming up with the prizes, awarded herself Best Musterer of the Season to a jeering crowd throwing balled-up paper napkins.

At just after eleven, while the others were distracted playing a raucous game of statues by firelight, I finally grabbed Gil's hand and hauled him inside. I led him to my bedroom and sat him on the chair, then knelt at his feet and took his hands in mine.

"You're going back with him, aren't you?"

Gil blinked but didn't look away. Then he freed his hand, cupped my cheek, and kissed me. "You think you're so smart, don't you?" He rubbed his nose against mine. "But you know very well that I'm not going back *with* Luke. Not in *that* way. I'm in love with *you*, Holden, and that's exactly what I told Luke. I'm not in love with Luke. And he's not in love with me."

"Then why?" I held my breath, and he stared at me with the softest eyes.

"Because I need to. I'm owed a few days off. The shearing gang have gone and there's plenty stocked in the fridge and freezers for everyone—"

"You know damn well I don't care about any of that." I cupped his face. "Talk to me, Gil."

He licked his lips and drew a deep breath. "You and I are very good at pretending things will just somehow miraculously work themselves out over the next six weeks, but they won't, baby. And we both know that I have some thinking to do."

"But you can think here," I complained, then mentally kicked myself. *Open the gates, don't crowd. Don't bark up his arse.* I sighed and rested my hand over his. "Sorry."

Those beautiful eyes searched my face, and it was all I could do not to threaten to tie him to the goddammed chair and lock the door.

"I'm tired of life just happening to me," he said gently, sounding impossibly tired. "Whatever these next steps are, they have to be deliberate on my part or nothing will work. And for that, I need to leave the station at least for a few days. I need some perspective and I have to examine the life I left behind in Wellington. As long as I'm here, in this place, with you, it's like we exist in some magical bubble. I have to find out if—"

"If we're real?"

"Oh god, no, baby." He kissed me long and slow. "You and I are absolutely real. But I need to know if I can make the rest of my life real, along *with you*." He gnawed on his lip, clearly trying to find the right words. "We can't pretend my old life doesn't exist." He threaded his fingers through my hair to cup the nape of my neck. "Luke appearing today is proof of that. And it made me realise there are things I need to do. People I need to see. Luke and I want to start the divorce process, which means going through our stuff and getting separation papers signed. We need to talk about Callie, and we need to talk to our lawyer about that damn meeting with the other driver. I have an apartment and house to check and people to check-in with. I've been a crap friend, and—"

"Shhh." I got up on my knees and silenced him with a kiss. "I know. I hate it, but I know you need to do all that. And I want you to do what you have to do so that you can be sure. But there's something you need to hear from me."

A small smile broke over his lips. "Then tell me."

I traced his smile with my fingertip and then added my lips for good measure. *Open the gates. Have his back.*

"I want you. I want us." I pressed our foreheads together. "I love you and I want you to come back and stay with me, running this place however you see your part in that happening. I know that last bit is a problem, but I'm going to trust that the fucking universe hasn't thrown you into my life just to yank you away."

He cradled my face and kissed me, his tongue sweeping through my mouth like he couldn't get enough. I hoped he always felt like that. I hoped when he left that he'd always want more. When he finally broke away, I dropped my forehead to his knees and he stroked my hair.

"I love you, Holden. But I lost love once before because I didn't pay attention. I won't do that with you. If things are going to work between us, I have to be clear about my life."

"That is disgustingly sensible," I grumbled, getting to my feet and pulling him into my arms. "So, can we just shut the fuck up now? Because I want to be inside you or you in me so fucking bad I can't stand it. At least that's one happy ending I can pretty well guarantee."

"Please." It was all he said.

I walked him to my bed and stripped him, taking my time, savouring every second, and running my lips over every patch of smooth skin revealed. I sucked on his nipples and kissed down his throat, his spine, licking the dimples at the small of his back and nipping at his groin, first one side then the other. And when he was finally naked, his cock hard and dripping, I threw a condom and lube on the bed and took my time spreading him over the mattress like honey, marvelling at the moonlight playing over his peaches-and-cream skin.

Then I lowered myself alongside his lean-muscled body and covered his mouth with mine, kissing him thoroughly, trying to imprint myself somewhere deep inside his heart. Letting him know just how much he meant to me and that I wanted him in every way one person could want another, desperately hoping he felt the same. That whatever he discovered away from the station without me, it would still bring him home. That he would find his way back to me for more than just another six damn weeks. That he'd come back to stay.

I kissed his lips, his shoulders, the nape of his neck. I trailed my fingers down his sternum and belly, down his happy trail all the way to his cock, which he thrust against me. He opened his legs and I dipped behind his balls, a slick fingertip running up his crease.

"Fuck me hard," he rasped, frotting desperately against my thigh. "I want to feel you with me when I leave."

And so I did, opening him slowly with my fingers and then my tongue. Watching him writhe and groan beneath me. Taking him almost over the edge before laying him flat and rocking slowly into him, centimetre by centimetre, his legs draped over my shoulders, his bright hazel eyes lit silver at the edges, our gazes fixed on one another for every excruciatingly delectable second.

And when he was desperate and ready, I thrust deep into his body—no finesse, no taking my time. I gave him what he wanted. Let him feel me finding a home in his body so he'd remember. He seemed to want that too, his fingers digging into my arse, forcing me harder, faster, until the perspiration ran down our faces and a wave of pleasure crashed through my body. I cried out and spilled deep inside him, our gazes locked, his cheeks wet with tears, our hearts teetering on the edge.

Then I pulled out and took him in my mouth, his fingers gripping my hair as he thrust deep, once, twice, and then came on a cry and a flood of come pouring down my throat as he whimpered somewhere above me.

I licked him clean, disposed of the condom, and crawled up his slick body to encase him in my arms.

We drew the covers up and talked in hushed tones while the laughter and voices outside slowly quieted to silence. Gil told me about his conversation with Luke, about how Zach had his back, a fact which left me gaping. And I told him about the buyer and my hopes for the contract and how I didn't want to be without him, and how much I'd miss him.

And as much as it hurt my heart, I told him I'd support him regardless of his decision. That if I could only have him for another six weeks, I wouldn't sulk and I wouldn't try to change his mind—likely both lies. I told him I'd make them the best six weeks of my life and I wouldn't regret a second.

He kissed me sweetly, tears in his eyes, and told me he loved me. Then he pushed our bodies flush, buried his face in my neck, and that's how we slept—our bodies fused, the soft shuffle of thousands of merinos paddocked close to the house creating a lullaby of sorts.

Every time I woke, I kissed him.

And when the milky grey light of the morning stole into the room and the nightmares had been kept at bay for another night, I tried to take it as an omen that Gil was where he was meant to be.

With me.

And when he packed his bag and I walked him to the Ranger, I didn't try and convince him again.

I kissed him long and hard, imbuing it with everything I felt, and he returned it.

Then he stroked my hair and pressed his lips to my ear. "I'm coming back, Holden, you know that."

"I know you are." I couldn't look at him. "But right this minute is the last time I get to have you without knowing what your decision is whether we'll have a future or not. Everything will change after that."

He said nothing, just kept stroking my hair because we both knew I was right.

And as he headed down the driveway toward Tekapo, I made my way to the sofa on the veranda, the place where we'd first made out. And with my damp cheeks hidden from view, I watched his cloud of dust disappear up the valley.

It was out of my hands. All I could do was pray that the universe would find a way to bring him back to stay.

One thing was certain—if it didn't, I was pretty sure my heart wasn't going to survive.

CHAPTER TWENTY-SIX

Gil

It was hard to deny the buzz I felt stepping out of the airport in Wellington. I'd always loved the city, the arts capital of New Zealand, the Melbourne or San Francisco of our tiny country.

When things had been better between Luke and me, and when Callie was still alive, we'd bought tickets to most shows that came to town, visited art galleries, dined out at least once a week, and scoured the city for the best coffee places. When my world had fallen apart, I'd taken solace in the hype the city manifested, feeding off its energy to survive, or maybe just using it to hide behind. It was my home, the place I felt most comfortable in the world.

Or at least it had been.

The people, the cars, the energy on the streets, I'd missed it, not to mention the anonymity it provided. Nobody bothered you. Nobody really even saw you. Nobody wanted to know what was going on in your life. A smile, an occasional nod of the head, and then the world got on with its business, leaving you to wallow in yours if that's what you wanted. And I had. For a long time.

As soon as I landed, I texted Holden to tell him I'd arrived safely. Then Luke and I shared a taxi from the airport into town and he dropped me off at my apartment before heading to his.

When Tuck knew I was heading back, he'd asked to meet me there, but I'd put him off. He'd want to know too much about where my head was and what I was planning, and without any answers for him or myself, I didn't want his opinion to influence me. I wanted to be much clearer before we spoke.

But standing outside my apartment door, I couldn't help but wonder if I'd made a mistake. I'd been gone less than two months and yet somehow it felt like years. I could barely punch in the code my hands were shaking so badly, but I balked at taking a pill unless I had to. I wasn't about to head down that slippery slope again.

The lock finally buzzed clear and I sucked in a deep breath wondering what the fuck was wrong with me.

This is my home.

Is it?

I shoved that troubling question aside and pushed the door open, feeling more fucking nervous than I'd done in weeks. I was being ridiculous.

There's no monster waiting in this closet.

Are you sure about that?

I wasn't. Because the last year in that apartment had been the worst year of my life. If my personal demons lived anywhere, they lived there.

I stepped inside, closed the door . . . and froze, broadsided by a wave of grief so powerful it stole my breath and sent my legs to jelly.

Oh god. I'd forgotten.

Forgotten how I'd left the place.

Forgotten that the night before I'd caught the plane to Christchurch, I'd gotten drunk, alone, and then pored through old photos of Callie and our little family. Photos that were still strewn over the coffee table along with a glass and an empty bottle of top-shelf tequila.

Only the best for Callie.

And hanging over the back of the couch, Callie's Cirque du Soleil souvenir sweatshirt Luke had bought for her at the show, and the stuffed rabbit I'd given her when she was five.

Oh god. Oh god. I stumbled to the couch and reached for the rabbit so I could drink in its scent for the first time in weeks. It had been Callie's sleep companion and bore the scars of her affection—chewed ears and a raggle-taggle grey plush coat. I grabbed the sweatshirt and added it to the rabbit, holding them both up to my face as I fell back onto the couch.

It was a step back in time.

And just like I'd done the last time I'd held them, I cried.

I cried for everything I'd lost. I cried for Callie and my marriage. For me. For the part of me that would never be the same. For the daughter I'd never see grow up, never watch date or have a career or a family of her own. My defences crumbled in a gut-wrenching tangle of grief and anger, and it was like I'd never been away. Like my time on the station had never happened.

Like it had all been a waste of fucking time.

A familiar jolt of fear balled in my chest and tightened its grip. *Jesus no, not this as well.* I scrambled for my carry-on and rummaged inside for the bottle of pills. But just as I closed my hand around it, my phone on the coffee table buzzed with a text, and the name that flashed on the screen almost stopped my heart.

Holden.

I tapped the screen and almost cried.

Glad you arrived safe. Miss you so fucking much. I hope you find what you need. I love you.

And then it hit me.

I wasn't the same at all.

Not even close.

And the last six weeks had been anything but a waste of time.

I slowed my next shuddering breath and took the bottle from my bag. But rather than open it, I sat it on the coffee table and closed my eyes.

Focused on breathing.

In and out.

In and out.

Focused on mountains and clear water and dogs sounding off in the hills.

On a warm kitchen.

And on a pair of black-brown eyes and messy dark hair.

On a love I'd never expected and had no idea what to do with.

And slowly, a wrinkle of space formed in that tight grip around my chest, and I could breathe again.

It wasn't an answer. It didn't solve any of the problems I faced. But it was a start.

I opened my eyes and just let myself *feel*, the same as I had all those mornings on Holden's deck with a jumble of stars over my head and the world still asleep.

And as I sat, the afternoon turned to evening and the evening to night, and eventually I dragged myself into the shower and then into my unmade bed and set the box of Callie's ashes beside me.

"Goodnight, baby girl." I imagined Callie's face, and Holden's arms around me, and for the first time since I left the station, I smiled.

But if I thought I was off the hook, the savage panic attack that woke me in the middle of the night brought me back to reality with a jolt. I should've expected it after the previous couple of days, but it still sucked, and I missed Holden's warm body at my side more than I could say.

I took my pill, changed the wet sheets, got myself a glass of water, and stared out the window at the sparkling tapestry of Wellington city lights reflected in the harbour. It might not have been as pretty as the station lake with the Milky Way above, but I got through it just fine, and a niggling part of me wondered if that wasn't in fact the better option. If maybe the station, and Holden, and the little niche I'd carved for myself there were doing nothing but shield me from a reality I had to face on my own. It wouldn't be good to become overly reliant on someone or some*where* else to make me feel better.

I managed another hour or so of sleep on the couch before daylight pricked at my eyelids. The first thing I did after I showered was clean the damn apartment. Then it was breakfast at my favourite local café, since there was nothing in the fridge, and the barista greeted me like a long-lost friend. I ordered my usual then took a seat and looked around the crowded space, my mind drifting—wondering what Holden had eaten that morning and whether he'd remembered to defrost the muffins for morning tea and feed the hens. I'd left a list a mile long that he'd taken one look at and laughed himself silly, reminding me that he'd lived on the station for thirty years before I'd arrived.

Thinking of him and Emily's kitchen made me smile, and my heart ached in ways I couldn't afford to face. Not yet. But when my breakfast arrived, as delicious as it was, I was taken back again to the station. The eggs from my hens tasted way better.

I mentally slapped myself and made the calls I needed to. Luke and I had a lawyer's appointment in the afternoon and were planning to talk after. But I was free until then, and I had some long overdue apologies to make.

To that end, I lunched with two of my friends, the aftermath of which left me relatively unscathed. I was suitably scolded and then loved on and sympathised with. They asked a little about the station and why I'd gone there, but even though it was clear they weren't at all sure what to make of it, they told me to go with my instincts, and I kicked myself for not trusting people to be in my life when I needed them.

On the downside, neither of them mentioned Callie either, except to say how much they'd been thinking about me and how glad they were that I was *coming out of it,* whatever the hell that meant.

Callie was clearly still a touchy subject, and my friends were very careful to skirt around it. I winced, understanding that *I* was the reason for that uncertainty, my previous reactions hadn't exactly encouraged enquiry. It didn't mean they'd deserved to be cut out of my life, and it didn't make them bad people.

I left the lunch feeling strangely numb and set off to meet my new lawyer since we'd agreed that Luke would keep our old one. But our old lawyer was still handling any legal proceedings around Callie's accident and so I headed there afterward to discuss meeting the convicted driver.

Luke and I had talked *a lot* over the two days, including during the long journey from Tekapo to Wellington. We'd talked about Callie and our marriage and also about the divorce. In the car, there'd been tears from both of us, and more anger from me. Rebuilding our friendship would take time. I could see forgiveness in the future, but I wasn't there yet. And I was pretty sure Luke felt the same about some of the things I'd done as well. But we'd been on the same page regarding the divorce, which was a huge relief. And by mutual agreement we'd decided *not* to talk about the meeting request from the other driver until we had more information from our lawyer.

Once we had it, we headed to a café to talk some more.

"I checked our old house this morning like we agreed," Luke began, taking a bite of the mini lemon meringue pie he'd ordered. "It's in great nick, which is good news. I warned the tenants we'd be putting it on the market, and they were disappointed but they understood. I'm happy to deal with the real estate agent and all that, if you'd rather keep out of it?"

"Thanks." I swirled my spoon through my coffee, more than happy not to set foot on the property again. We'd been very grown-up and sensible about the divorce settlement proposal, both of us having savings and good jobs to fall back on. It was only the small details that needed crossing off. "We've already taken what we want out of the place, so as far as I'm concerned, we can sell the rest and split the proceeds. That should finish the asset division."

Luke nodded. "Agreed."

We finished the rest of our coffees in a silence that grew more awkward by the minute, both of us avoiding what we'd really gone there to discuss.

"I don't think I can do it," I finally blurted, and Luke's gaze shot up to mine. "I can't see him, not yet. I'm barely getting my shit together, finally, and I won't risk screwing with that."

Luke's hand covered mine, his eyes soft with understanding, and I was more grateful for his unspoken support than I could say.

"I've thought a lot about this in the last few weeks," I tried to explain. "And about what Holden said to me—that I don't owe this guy a shoulder to cry on just to appease his guilt. That I was allowed to just be me, a grieving father. That I had the right to take as long as I needed. And that if I didn't *ever* want to see him, that would be okay too."

Luke breathed a huge sigh and fell back on his chair, freeing my hand. "Oh, thank Christ." He almost smiled. "Because I don't want to see him either. It's too soon, right?"

"Right." Relief flooded my body, bringing a lightness to my heart that I badly needed. "I just . . . I get all the reasons I should see him. Why it could be good for everyone, and maybe that's true. And I can see maybe agreeing in the future, but just not now. But I don't want that to affect *your* decision, so if you want to go by your—"

"Hell no," Luke huffed. "I was worried *you* would. That your psychologist brain would think it was the right thing to do. Thank Christ for Holden's common sense. Jesus, that is such a fucking relief. Let's ring the lawyer right now and say it's a no, at least for the moment."

I got out my phone and made the call, telling the lawyer to check back in a year. Then I hung up, and Luke and I smiled at each other.

"So, have you decided what you're going to do?" He raised his brows. "About the sexy sheep farmer?"

I shrugged and looked away. "Not really. And also, that's way too weird hearing you call him that."

Luke snorted. "You might be right about that. But at the risk of getting my head chewed off, and as a man who was once in love with you and knows you pretty well, will you hear me out?"

My stomach clenched, but I sighed and met his eyes again. "Go on then."

He took my hand and lowered his voice. "You're allowed to grab a chance at happiness again, Gil. We *both* are. We're allowed to start feeling better without it meaning we don't miss her just as much as we've always done." Tears welled in his eyes but he kept talking. "I feel guilty every fucking time I smile, like my life should be in pieces forever in some kind of homage to her."

Oh god. His words sliced into my heart with a truth that made me gasp. I blinked a tear free and it splashed on my arm. Another quickly joined it.

He pushed on, wiping at his own tears. "I know you think I'm moving on too fast, but I'm not even close. I don't know how many times I've heard you talk about this stuff over the years. Things like you have to feel the pain first in order to heal it. And I know that's true. But Jesus, aren't we allowed to find a little bit of happiness at the same time? Isn't that part of the healing process as well? To start to feel again? I know *I* want that. I want to live again even if I'm also not finished grieving Callie. In some ways, I haven't even started. Or does it have to be always painful for it to be valid? I don't believe that."

I stared at him, seeing more than a glimpse of the man who'd stolen my heart all those years ago. I huffed a mirthless laugh. "Maybe you should be doing my job?"

The lines around his eyes smoothed. "I learned from the best."

I gave a soft snort. "Maybe. But how does someone know what's hope and what's just hiding or running away?"

He smiled and shook his head. "Gil Everton, you've never run away from anything in your entire life. It's one of the most irritating things about you. In fact, before we lost Callie, I'd begun to wonder if anything could ever really rattle you."

I blinked in surprise. "That's not true."

Luke sighed and let go my hand. "It's absolutely true. You've always been the carer. Always the one in control. Always with an answer at the ready; so sensible, so logical, so insightful. It makes you a great therapist, and you were always encouraging me to get in touch with my feelings as well, as painful as that was." He shuddered and I smiled. "But when it came to *you*, you never let anyone see the whites of your eyes. Do you know how fucking inadequate that makes the rest of us feel?"

I shook my head slowly, shocked at his words, not because they weren't true, but because I'd never realised he'd seen me that clearly. "I'm so sorry."

He shrugged. "Don't be. It's in the past and I'm as much to blame as you, and I let you get away with it. The only reason I'm telling you now, is because when I saw you with Holden, how you were with him, how much he clearly knew about you, I could tell that you were letting him close in a way you'd never done with me. To be honest, it shocked me. All those years together and you'd never looked at me the way you were looking at him."

"That's not tr—"

"I'm not talking about love. I *know* you loved me. I'm talking about letting someone else have your back. Trusting your secrets and your doubts to another person. You were letting yourself lean on Holden, and he wasn't taking any of your bullshit, not like I did."

I opened my mouth to disagree, then shut it again. I thought about the night before and my fears that I was becoming overly reliant on Holden, on the station. Like I was torn between feeling better and wanting to feel worse again, because I knew that space so well, and that was easier than living again, than thinking about maybe even being happy again.

Are you happy, Daddy?

When Callie had asked me that question in the last conversation we ever had, the answer would've been no. I hadn't been happy. Not for years. Not in my private life. Not with my husband. Not even in my work, which I could admit had become stale. Not with anyone except Callie. I'd learned to live with that. To accept that maybe it wasn't in my stars to be happy that way. And worse still, that maybe I didn't need it.

I had lots of other things to be happy about, right? My business. My clients. My metropolitan lifestyle. They counted, didn't they?

Except that recently, I *had* been happy.

And I'd been happy without any of those other things that I *thought* mattered so much. I still missed Callie like my heart had been flayed open, but that pain hadn't been my whole life like it had before. I'd started to live again. And I'd loved again. And I'd found a home and a place where I could laugh again. And a man that I could laugh *with*.

"You're allowed to heal, Gil. And I'm so fucking sorry that I couldn't be the one to help with that. But maybe *he* can. *Holden*. If you let him. You can't always have all the answers and there are no guarantees. That's why it's called a leap of faith. That's what all love is."

His words rushed my heart and I pushed to my feet and kissed him soundly on the cheek. "Thank you."

He grinned. "You're welcome."

But I hadn't missed the flash of sadness in his eyes or the way he scrubbed at them when he thought I was gone.

The minute I hit the sidewalk, I called Tuck. "We need to talk."

CHAPTER TWENTY-SEVEN

Holden

I sat in the kitchen hunched over my untouched sandwich and staring at the email I'd received that morning. The offer of a five-year contract with SX Merino just days after the buyer's visit.

And the crowd went wild.

Or not.

I tried to summon some enthusiasm for the most important thing to have happened to the station in years. A guarantee for the future. A chance to invest in the land and see my improvement plans bear fruit.

I should've been elated.

I should've run to the woolshed with the printout waving in my hand to share the news.

I didn't.

I'd simply fired Tom a two-line text and told him to pass it on to the others.

What the hell was wrong with me?

Like it was rocket science.

One word.

Gil.

The man had been gone three days and I was a total fucking mess.

Not outwardly, of course. Outwardly, I'm sure I looked fine . . . maybe . . . possibly. I got shit done, I joked with the team, and I had the cleanest office desk I'd had in years.

But inwardly, not so much. Inwardly my heart ached, terrified the answer Gil might come back with—would *likely* come back with—wouldn't be the one I wanted to hear. Because I was damn sure it would make sense to him.

Gil fought every effort to take care of him, after all, even with small things like letting me dry his goddammed hair after a shower. And I knew he was struggling to accept he could have a good life here, a great one, even if it was different from the one he'd been living before. It was an honest to God crapshoot how it was all going to go down, but the longer he was away, the more pessimistic I became.

I took a lacklustre bite of my sandwich and pushed the plate away. Every minute in that kitchen, every piece of food I put in my mouth reminded me of Gil and of what I had to lose. I was about to tip the rest of the sandwich into the bin when voices floated through the open back door and five pairs of smelly socked feet traipsed into my kitchen.

"Is that what you call dinner?" Charlie nodded to the one and a half sad lumps of badly sawn bread and peanut butter left on my plate.

I narrowed my eyes. "So, what if it is?"

She glanced at the others as if making a point. "I think we should tell Gil, right guys?" She pulled out her phone and I dropped the plate and raced back to the table.

"No, don't do that," I pleaded. "I was just too tired to cook anything tonight."

She huffed out a disappointed sigh and pushed me into a chair.

"You won the fucking contract, Holden. We should *all* be celebrating. Have you even told him?"

"Who?" I asked quietly, avoiding her shrewd gaze and knowing full well who she meant. *Another thing I felt guilty about.*

Charlie, of course, saw straight through me and said nothing, amping up the pressure.

"No, I haven't, all right? Not yet, anyway."

"Oh boy." She stepped back and swept her arm from Tom to me. "I believe this one's yours."

Tom sighed and took the chair opposite, waiting in silence until I caved and finally met his gaze.

"Go on. Say what you need to." I heard the exhaustion in my own voice.

"All right, I will." He folded his arms. "First up, I'm so proud of you. And your grandad would be too. We needed this to future-proof the station, and you got us there. This success is all down to you. But Gil deserves to know, son."

The term 'son' almost made me smile, and I realised I'd missed it.

"Regardless of what happens, that man cares about you, maybe even loves you. But more importantly, he's a part of this team, so don't you dare let him find out from anyone but you."

"I know. I know," I whined like a child because they were right. "Okay, I'll tell him. But just a text. I promised myself I'd give him space." I pulled out my phone and Tom looked disapproving for a second, then gave a resigned sigh, and I fired off the requisite text, wishing with everything I had that I could just call and pull him through that phone back where he belonged.

Charlie patted me on the back. "See, doesn't that feel better? You should always listen to us. Next on the list, we need proper food sorted. Sam, hop to it. Gil mentioned there was chilli and cornbread in the freezer. Alek, grab a few beers from Holden's stash. It's his treat."

I groaned and rolled my eyes.

"Zach, you set the table. Lord knows you should know your way around this place after bumping uglies with this guy for all those years nobody bothered to tell us about."

My eyes bugged, and Zach flushed red to the roots of his hair as he grumbled, "Jesus Christ, Charlie."

"What, too soon?" She fired him an innocent look and then shot me a wink before making a beeline for the study desk. Charlie lived by the mantra that shit was better out in the open than hidden away, but I wasn't so sure about her instincts this time. Zach and I had been getting on better, but joking about our friends-with-benefits thing was kind of a stretch.

With that in mind, I cast a nervous look Zach's way, surprised to find a tiny smile aimed back at me.

"Ugly being the operative word," he deadpanned.

Once I recovered from the shock, I flipped him off and he returned it.

Fucked if I knew how Charlie managed it but she did, and her shit-eating smile said it all, and the chaos in the kitchen resumed.

I appreciated their concern, I really did, but I just didn't have the energy. "Can someone please tell me what the hell is going on?"

"It's called an intervention," Charlie and Sam said as one as they carried on doing whatever it was they were doing. Then Charlie added, "You've been moping around ever since Gil left, and the guy *is* coming back, right? Jesus, even Spider's been pining like someone stole his best bone."

I caught her eye and recognised the worry underlying her humour. They knew. Certainly, Tom did from what he'd said, but I was guessing they all did. Maybe not all the details, but they pried enough from me to fill in the gaps. Gil had gone back to Wellington to sort out some shit and make some decisions. It didn't take a genius to work out what or who those decisions involved. Not to mention they'd been badgering me ever since he left about whether I'd heard from him.

The answer was no, bar a couple of nothing texts. Gil wanted space to think, and that certainly didn't involve me clamouring for his attention every spare minute of the day, although I had to admit, just once would've been nice.

Needless to say, they hadn't been impressed.

"Besides," Charlie continued, "this is supposed to be a celebration for nailing the contract, and that stands regardless of whatever our esteemed domestic manager has planned for the future." She grabbed the laptop from the desk and carried it to the table. "If Gil decides not to stay, he's fucking crazy, and I'm gonna shut him in the race with the rams until he come to his senses."

I snorted. "Idiot."

"Although why he's hankering after your sorry arse in the first place is beyond me." She took a seat. "Guess there's no accounting for taste."

I met her laughing eyes and gave her a wink. "Can I get a rain check on the ram idea?"

She laughed and pushed the laptop my way, and to my surprise, my mother's face stared back at me.

"Hello, darling."

My heart stuttered in my chest and my throat thickened. "Mum?"

"Oh good, you remembered me. So, you haven't completely lost your mind then. Congratulations on the contract. I knew you could do it."

I frowned at the screen. "I'm sorry. I should've called you first."

"Yes, you should have, but that's by the by. Now where is Gil?"

I sighed, eyeing the team who were shuffling their feet and looking suddenly awkward. "By the look of these bozos, I'm pretty sure you know exactly where he is."

"They were just worried," my mother continued as everyone else took a chair. "I only need to know one thing. Tell me you didn't let him go without telling him how you feel."

I blinked. "I'm not sure that's anyone's business, not even yours, Mum."

She said nothing, just gave me a patient look until I finally blew a defeated sigh. "Okay, yes, I told him."

"Good." She beamed. "Because we all want him to stay, don't we?"

There was a chorus of meddling and sticky-nosed agreement, and really, what had I done in my life to deserve this?

My mother's expression softened. "Don't give up on him. I think he wants to stay; he just doesn't know how to give in to that feeling."

Not helping.

"Can I have my son on his own please?"

The kitchen emptied in seconds and my mother looked at me with all the tenderness I remembered from growing up after my father had left us.

"You two boys are as bad as each other," she huffed. "Before he came to us, Gil cut himself off from most of his support, thinking he had to do everything himself. And as for you, you are always so careful not to push, not to ask more of people than you think they can give. It's part of what makes you a good leader, son. But sometimes people need a little push in the right direction. And sometimes you have to pull out your big guns."

Set the huntaway loose.

"He knows I want him back here for good, Mum. He knows I want him to stay. But it has to be his choice."

She sighed and leaned back on the headboard of whatever bed and breakfast she was staying in. "As you well know, I used to think someone like Zach would be the ideal match for you. But then I saw you and Gil together and I knew I was wrong. You need someone who's your equal, but not in the same way. You don't need help to run the station, you need a different kind of strength. Someone who has your back but doesn't work side by side with you. You're too independent for that. You need someone who complements you. And Gil does that beautifully. I'm so proud of you. Of what you've achieved and the man you've grown to be. Don't lose Gil without a fight, sweetheart. He needs you as much as you need him, and maybe he needs to be told that."

We chatted for a while longer about what she'd been doing and how Harry had unexpectedly decided to join her for the last two weeks of her trip, something I was delighted about. And when we were finished, I thought about what she'd said. I ran her words through my mind as the warm humour of the team washed over me and buoyed my spirits.

I thought about the many times a merino went rogue on the hill and wouldn't take the open path no matter how obvious it was, determined to ignore the opportunity even though it meant almost certain hardship. It was a timely reminder that sometimes an open gate needed a following nudge as well.

When everyone was done eating and the kitchen was spotless and the team were heading out the door, Zach lingered behind. He rubbed the back of his neck, looking all kinds of sheepish. "Can I just say one thing?"

My stomach clenched a little, but I nodded. "Go ahead. You're my best mate, Zach. You know me better than almost anyone."

The frown on his forehead smoothed as he gave a small smile. "Yeah, well, I can't say I liked Gil much at the beginning, for obvious reasons. But Jesus, Holden, I've never seen anyone look at someone the way he looks at you. I still might hate it at times—" He shrugged apologetically. "—but I can't deny it. And neither should you. We've known each other our whole lives and we've been through a lot of crap together. I think maybe we'll find a way through this too. I hope it works out for you with Gil. I really do. He's a good man. That's all I wanted to say."

Zach turned to leave but I grabbed his arm. "Thank you. Thank you *so* much. You don't know how much that means to me."

His eyes glistened.

"Can we hug?"

He narrowed his gaze. "Bro-hug boundaries."

I laughed and pulled him in for a quick, back-slapping hug, then let him go. He immediately headed for the mudroom and didn't look back.

When he was gone, I stared at my phone on the table for all of two seconds before grabbing it.

Gil picked up on the third ring.

"Don't say anything. Just listen to me."

"And hello to you too," Gil answered, and I could tell he was smiling, the fucker.

Then I heard Oasis singing in the background and had a slight moment of panic wondering if he was in a club. "Ah, where are you?"

"I'm driving. Hang on, I'll put you on speakerphone."

"Oh, right." Way to feel ridiculous.

Oasis faded. "Okay, I'm listening."

I cleared my throat. "Good, because first up, I know you want to work things out on your own, but I don't really think that's fair since this decision involves me too. I think we should be talking about this *together* . . . just saying. And on that same note, I don't think it's fair that you come back with a decision already made and simply tell me that this is how it's going to be."

I could almost hear his frown crunch. "Okaaaay." He hesitated. "But can—"

"I haven't finished."

I swore he chuckled.

"Second, I want us to make a real go of this. I want us to try, not decide before we've even really started. You aren't going to get the answers you want at some kind of safe distance. Life's not like that, Gil. It's messy and difficult and you have to get your hands dirty. *You* taught me that. The path isn't always clear and sometimes one or other of us will need leading to it. We'll need a . . . a damn huntaway—"

"A what? Holden, have you been drinking?"

"Third, I know I'll fuck up and so will you, but it's a long way to run from here, so I think we'll be okay. We can catch the other person before they make it to the road—"

"Holden . . ." And now he really was laughing so I simply kept talking.

"Fourth, you're not very good at letting people take care of you. And that's a problem. And I understand that it's hard with you being some high-brow psychologist and all. But you can't do everything on your own, baby. I want to help you, just like you help me. I *can* do that for you, Gil. And I'm pretty damn good at it, actually. Just ask my sheep."

He choked on another laugh.

"And last, I get that your skills are wasted here. I get that you have a whole life and a practice, business thing to consider. But right now, I don't care about those. I just want *you. Here,* with me. So do what you have to do, but you come back here, and I'll be waiting to talk. Not just listen. But don't come back and just say no without talking about options. I'm not losing you that easily. Give me a chance, please. This life suits you, baby. You might not be able to see it yet, but I do. You belong here. You belong with *me*. And I refuse to leave you on the hill."

I stopped, breathless, my heart racing in my chest. *Jesus, what have I done?* The deafening silence on the other end of the phone only added to the panic growing in my heart. Had I made a huge mistake?

Then I picked up the sound of Gil's breathing—short, sharp gulps thick with emotion. That was good, right? Wasn't it?

Headlights tracked across the back kitchen wall and a rapidly moving vehicle rounded the corner of the drive. Spider leapt from his mat under the table and ran barking to the front door. I was about to follow when my phone crackled to life in my hand and I lifted it to my ear.

"Get the fuck out here, Holden Miller." Gil's voice boomed down the line. "Your boyfriend's back, and I believe somewhere in the wonderful, fucking amazing speech of yours, you mentioned something about wanting to look after me. Well, here's your chance. I've just taken a goddammed leap of faith that scares the shit out of me.

I've got my whole life packed up in this ute and I could do with a little looking after right about now, if that's okay with you?"

I watched out the window as Gil's all-too-familiar Ranger came to a sliding stop with its front tyres skidding on the lawn. The driver's door flew open and I ditched my phone and raced up the hall. I made it out the front door just as Gil reached the bottom of the steps. I flew into his arms and wrapped my legs around his waist. He lost his balance and we toppled sideways onto the lawn with Spider making a beeline for Gil's face to welcome him home.

"For fuck's sake." Gil ducked his head to avoid Spider's rough tongue. "Get out of here, you crazy animal."

"Spider, away," I ordered, and he immediately backed off and lay down, although still whining with excitement. I straddled Gil's hips, pinning him on top of the dew-damp grass. He was so goddammed beautiful I thought I might cry.

"You got the contract, then." His smile broadened into a huge grin. "I'm so fucking proud of you, sweetheart. You deserve it all. Are you happy? All those plans you have. Now you can make them a reality."

Sweetheart. The word sounded so fucking good after too long without it. "I'm still getting used to the idea," I admitted, running my hands over every part of him I could reach. "It's been three long years and I thought it meant everything to me—" I hesitated, hearing the catch in my voice, and needing to take a second. "—but that was before you."

His expression turned impossibly tender, and I ran the back of my fingers down his cheek.

He was so beautiful.

"So, am I happy?" I bent down and brushed my lips over his. "Not yet. Not until I know if you meant what you said on the phone. Are you really staying?"

He cradled my face and beamed up at me. "Yes. If you'll have me."

Then a thought occurred to me, and I side-eyed him. "Just to be clear, define stay."

He chuckled. "Oh, ye of little faith. There's no catch. We've put our old house on the market and I've relinquished my lease on the apartment. I talked to Tuck and we agreed that he could buy me out of the business in six months if that's still what I want. I've put most of my stuff in storage other than a few things I'm having shipped down, so I guess that means you're stuck with me. Is that a good enough definition for you?"

Was he crazy? "But . . . what decided you?"

He traced his thumb over my lips. "You did. You and a few home truths from Luke. Kind of similar to what you just said to me on the phone."

I arched a brow, but he shook his head and said, "It can wait. Can we go inside now?"

"Not yet." I slid to the grass and stretched out next to him. "Keep talking."

He rolled so we were facing each other and traced a finger down my cheek. "Oh yeah, I've missed bossy Holden." Gil's gaze travelled over my face like he was drinking me in, and I knew exactly how he felt.

"And he's missed you too." My hand slid around his waist, needing to touch him, to reassure myself he was truly there. "Now talk."

He snorted and kissed me softly. "In the end it was easy. When I finally got my head out of my arse, I realised I'd spent every second of my time in Wellington thinking about *you*. I'd been comparing everything up there with my life down *here*, and none of it came even close to matching up. There *is* no comparison. My friends there will always be in my life no matter where I am. My future work might take some rethinking but I'm ready to sell the practice. It's time for something different. Basically, from the minute I left I wanted to come back."

"Thank God." Relief coursed through me. "I'm so fucking happy to hear that."

"There's more." Gil smiled and cradled my face. "Because being here has changed me. You, your love, and this place have all changed me. And not because the isolation here somehow shelters me from the reality of the outside world, but because it strangely does the exact opposite. I've faced things here that I've avoided for a long time. You can't hide from yourself or your feelings out here. The mountains, the quiet, the isolation, they strip you raw. When I'm here, I feel *everything*—the good and all the fucking bad as well. And yet somehow, it's all okay. I can throw anything at these mountains and they hold on to it until I'm ready to deal. And when I am—" He stroked my face. "—then I have you to talk to. Your quiet presence. Your acceptance. Your patience."

I held his gaze, blinking back the emotion rising in my throat. "I love that you feel that, but I know this is no magic bullet. Not this place. And not me. Just keep talking to me. I'll always listen."

He sighed. "Yeah, there's no hiding that I'm still a mess. Slightly less of one than when I arrived, but I'm still no walk in the park. I can't offer you any guarantees, baby. And I can't make any promises about future families or marriage or any of that. To be honest, I don't know if I can do all that again. I'm still working day by day here."

I took his hands. "Me too. And none of those are deal breakers for me either, just so you know. So, we keep talking, right?"

He nodded. "We keep talking."

"And your work?" I pressed.

His eyes lit up again. "Ah, well that's one of the best ideas that came out of the trip and from talking with you and Emily over the last couple of months. I chatted with Tucker and I have some thoughts. It would take a lot more research and planning, but how would you feel about me using one of the cottages for client stays? Like a retreat of sorts. Maybe even for stressed farmers. Somewhere people can come for intensive work on themselves for a few days or weeks, guided by sessions with me and surrounded by this amazing environment. The farmers could even help out if they wanted. It would be private and in their comfort zone. And I could also offer my services locally, either based on the station or an office in Oakwood a couple of days a week. That would let me carry on here."

"Or we could hire someone else to do the domestic manager job if you got too busy." I took a deep, shuddering breath for the first time in days. His words were everything I needed to hear. Everything I'd hoped for.

Gil's eyes danced. "Can I just say, I particularly like the *we* part of that sentence? But we're going to need to talk with your mum and gran about me staying on and exactly how that's going to work with the station."

"Of course." I took a second to let it all sink in. "So, we're really going to do this then? You and me. That's what you really want. I mean, we're kind of leaping in the deep end here. We didn't even date, not really."

"Yes, we're really going to do this." He eyed me coyly. "And I'm down with a little dating on the side. Or I could live in one of the cottages for a bit—"

"Fuck that." I shut him down. "The cottage bit, not the dating bit. You're not sleeping anywhere except with me."

"Soooo fucking bossy." He brushed his lips again over mine, whisper soft and teasing.

"Damn right." I rubbed our noses together. "But I expect to be dated, Mister Everton. I've never been dated, so yes, I definitely want that. I can't go through life without ever being dated properly."

Gil lifted a brow. "That assumes I'm the last boyfriend you're gonna have."

I held his gaze. "It better, at least if I have anything to do with it."

His cocky expression morphed into a wide smile. "God, I love you."

"I love you too."

"Then come closer. I need to kiss you properly." He tugged me close and suddenly he was all I saw—those gorgeous hazel eyes, that choppy blond hair, his smooth skin smelling of the city and travel and a sweet hint of promise.

The evening fell quiet on our tangled bodies as Gil took my face in his hands and pressed his lips firmly to mine, drawing a wanton moan from deep inside my heart. Then his tongue slid alongside mine and I sank into the kiss, home at last.

"God, I've missed this," he murmured thickly into my open mouth. "I've missed *you*." He pulled off and pressed kisses to my face in between soft snorts of contentment, and I knew exactly how he felt. "But do you think we might get up off this damn lawn so you can ravish me in your bed instead? I'm still waiting for the taking-care part of your offer to kick in."

I laughed and scrambled to my feet, then helped him up. "I'll have you know I aced animal husbandry at university. The human version might need a little fine-tuning but I think you're safe in my experienced hands." I counted off on my fingers. "Food, water, shelter, managing stress, and a good . . . breeding program." I waggled my eyebrows suggestively.

He laughed. "There is soooo much of concern to unpack in that one statement that I'm not even going to try." He threw his arm around my waist and we headed for the steps with Spider at our heels.

I leaned into his side. "Hey, I'm a great shepherd. I've got this."

EPILOGUE

Six months later

Gil

I reached for Luke's hand and he glanced my way, a nervous smile brightening his face for just a few seconds before it was lost to the more serious tone that had become his norm for far too long. The past six months had seen a strange ebb and flow between us. Almost like we'd traded places. I'd found firmer ground to walk on with Holden at my side, the station as my home, a new business that was beginning to find its feet, and this odd new family we'd somehow created.

Whereas Luke seemed caught up in the past. He wasn't looking for a job, and had bailed from yet another short-term relationship with some totally unsuitable—in my view—guy who'd wanted everything Luke wasn't ready to give. Luke was drifting, a state I knew only too well. Grief was a bitch that way. You never quite knew when it was going to rise up and bite you in the butt. It was never done with you, and no matter how much work you did on yourself, it always had something to say.

Luke had even spent a week in one of the station cottages, fishing and hiking and generally trying to help around the station. The team had given him a wary welcome, one that soon warmed up when they saw he didn't mind getting his hands dirty. All except for Zach, who'd maintained a cool distance ever since that first visit of Luke's to the station.

And as for Holden and Luke? After an awkward couple of days circling each other like wary tomcats, they'd finally bonded over flying . . . and me, funnily enough. Luke was very vocal about how much happier I seemed, and he was also quick to put Holden at the centre of why that was. It was hard to stay pissy with a guy who sang your praises, and Holden was no exception. Holden had even arranged for Luke to pilot a chopper flight over the station and played navigator for the man. Colour me gobsmacked. My ex-husband and my new partner chumming it up while I watched and waited for Armageddon to start.

Newsflash: it didn't.

I caught Holden's eye and waved him over. He and Spider were standing on a stony embankment a few metres behind Luke and me. With him were the newly engaged Emily and Harry, with Spider at their side. The rest of the team stood a short distance away, including Alek, who'd just got back from his second trip to Wellington for more form-filling and questions regarding getting his brother into the country.

Holden looked uncertain, but when I repeated the wave, he immediately ditched his footwear and picked his way through the freezing, gurgling shallows to take a firm hold of my other hand. Spider followed, of course, and positioned himself firmly against my leg. He rarely left my side, his warm body a reassuring presence in my life.

"Are you sure?" Holden checked again.

I gave a firm nod. "Yes. I want you right here with me."

Luke leaned forward and shot Holden a look. "Yes, stay, please. We wouldn't be here if it weren't for you."

Take a right down the rabbit hole. *How the fuck was this my life?*

I blinked the tears from my eyes and stared out across the gurgling shallows, swirling pools, and swiftly running deeper channels of the broad Havelock River, its waters crisp and clear and cold enough to freeze your balls, at least judging by what it was doing to my sockless feet.

Luke and I had chosen the place together. It was just outside the station boundary, wild and free of ownership, but was in easy reach with a four-wheel drive.

Luke handed me the small box of Callie's ashes and I held it with trembling hands. I needed my pills less and less as the months had passed. The nightmares were still there, the panic attacks too, but both had become less frequent. But on my therapist's suggestion, I'd relented and taken a tablet on the drive out, precautionary as much as anything. I wanted nothing to interfere with what we were about to do.

It had taken me a long time to reach this point. Two years of staring at our daughter's ashes in this box, not ready to let go, not ready to say goodbye, not until three weeks earlier when Holden and I were having a candlelit date up at castle rock. I'd been sipping on a wine, watching a satellite pass across a night sky jammed with stars when suddenly I just knew. It was time to set us both free.

There'd been any number of places I could've chosen, but the Havelock River was the only one that felt right. The memory of sitting on that rocky outcrop during the autumn muster, Holden at my back, staring down at the twisted braids and feeling Callie so close, so *with* me. Knowing how much she'd have loved it there.

It simply made sense.

Thrown into the river, her ashes would carry all the way downstream to the ocean, not tied to any one place, free, just as her ten-year-old heart had been.

I'd spoken to Luke and offered him half of her ashes to find his own place, but he'd surprised the hell out of me by agreeing immediately with my choice.

And so there we were.

I opened the lid, removed the plastic bag, and held it out for Luke. He stared at the bag like it might bite him, then he took a deep breath and grabbed a small handful. I did the same and we waded a little further into the freezing river, my old leg injury shouting its protest as the icy water hit the scars. The first throw was the hardest, the letting go, the saying goodbye. Luke reaching for my hand, Callie's green silicon band hanging loose on his wrist. My fingers threading with his. The tears. The choked cries.

But we got through it, Holden's arm around my waist, his body a solid wall at my side.

The rest followed more easily, and a minute later all of Callie's ashes were gone, floating across the surface of the river, dipping and diving, rolling over swells and around boulders, mingling with glacial water many millennia in the making, down, down toward the ocean, carrying all the dreams of a beautiful but too-short life along the way.

Holden pulled me back against him, his face buried in my neck. "I'm so sorry. I'm so fucking sorry."

I wrapped my arms over top of his, choking sobs erupting from my throat and tears coursing down my cheeks. Spider shoved his wet nose into my crotch and whined until I patted his head. "It's okay, boy."

I briefly looked for Luke, but he was stumbling from the water into Emily's arms. I left him in good hands and returned to watching my daughter complete the circle back to her beloved nature.

I watched until every last piece of her was gone. Watched until my feet coloured blue in the clear water, all feeling gone. Watched until Holden took my hand and gently led me out, sat me on a rock, and dried my feet before putting my socks and shoes on one by one. Then he wrapped a blanket around my shoulders and fed me cocoa from the flask Emily had brought with her and some of the caramel slice from our baking that morning—Callie's favourite.

I was getting better at accepting being cared for. I was learning to let Holden step in when he saw me struggling. Learning that it wasn't weakness, and that sometimes he saw what I couldn't. And colour me shocked that he was right more often than not.

We were making it work better than I'd ever imagined. It wasn't always easy and I'd packed my bags once in those first couple of months. But Holden had been right about that too. It was a long way to run from the station, and I hadn't even made it to the cattlestop before kicking myself in the arse and heading back to find him waiting on the deck. He'd taken me to bed for a few rounds of epic make-up sex, followed by a lot of talking, something I'd been neglecting, and the reason for the argument in the first place.

I did the same for Holden because he'd had his own challenges. When we'd visited his grandparents, his gran had been lovely, but his grandad left Holden feeling bruised and unworthy and guilty as hell. I'd actually had to call time on the visit and get him out of there, and Holden had spent the drive home coming to terms with the fact that things might not change between them, and none of it would be their fault.

And Patrick Lane continued to be a thorn in Miller Station's side, badmouthing the station, Holden's stock, and our relationship as often as he could manage. Thankfully he mostly kept Zach's name out of it, but it still stung Holden, knowing we were fodder for local chatter, and a couple of his contractors had become inexplicably cool soon after the infamous throwing-Paddy-off-the-station incident leaked out. But a lot of the backlash had blown over once Emily returned and set about correcting the local gossip in her inimitable way.

"We're all going to head back," Emily informed us. "I'll take Luke and Spider with me. We'll see you two whenever you get there. Take your time."

I glanced over at Luke, who still looked pale but a lot more composed, and then turned to Holden. "Can you give me a minute?"

He squeezed my hand and I walked over. "How are you doing?"

Luke shrugged. "Strangely better than I expected. I thought I was ready, then I didn't, then I did again. Weird, huh?"

I rested a hand on his arm. "Who knows about this shit, right? I've stopped assuming anything. Sometimes the things we fear the most end up being the best things for us."

He huffed. "Yeah, maybe you're right. I guess I'll have to wait and see. Are you two staying for a bit?"

I glanced at Holden, who was watching from a discreet distance, and found a smile on my lips. "For a while." I pulled Luke into a hug, then watched as they left in a bumpy convoy back toward the homestead. We'd join them later for a celebration of Callie's life.

Holden appeared at my side with a couple of blankets slung over his shoulder. "So, it appears we're all alone."

I turned into his arms and waggled my brows. "You wanna make out?"

He looked surprised. "Do you feel like it?"

"Maybe?" I pulled him tight against me. "Must be the adrenaline. Or maybe I just want to feel something different. Feel you. Just . . . feel. Today felt really important. Like turning a page. For me. For us. And maybe for Luke as well. You know when you feel sunshine on your face for the first time after days of rain? It kind of feels like that."

"Mmm." He ran his nose through my hair. "Well, I just happen to have brought *two* blankets with me. Top and bottom. It would be a shame to waste the opportunity since our house *is* fairly crowded at the moment."

He wasn't wrong there. With tourists in three of the guest cottages, Luke was staying in my old room in the homestead, a state of affairs which only added another factor of weirdness into the mix, not to mention putting a bit of a wrinkle in our sex life.

Holden kissed me on the nose and took my hand. "But as much as I want to get down and dirty with you, I think we should start with cuddles."

I pushed out my lower lip but couldn't hold the pout because Holden was right. It had been a huge day and I was already feeling the perk in my dick beginning to fail. "Actually, cuddles sound pretty damn good."

Holden led me toward a flat portion of the riverbank, which was relatively free of stones and with a large hillock at its back to break the wind. "But just in case the urge takes us, I happen to have a handy-dandy travel pack." Without looking back, he whipped a sachet of lube from his shirt pocket and waved it in the air.

"Well, of course you do." I didn't even blink. We'd ditched the condoms months before and had stashes of lube hidden all over the station. You never knew when the urge might take you, and a bit of ribbing from the team who occasionally stumbled across one of our hiding places was a small price to pay.

Holden found us a spot with a good view of the river and spread one of the blankets on the ground. He found a comfy position on his side and then pulled me down in front so that I faced the river. Then he wrapped himself around me and threw a leg over top for good measure. I wasn't going anywhere.

We'd only been there a short while when a group of merinos wandered onto the hillock above, completely oblivious to our presence. Holden gathered me close and we listened to them snuffle and eat while the sun danced on the rippling surface of the water, shooting small rainbows over the rocks.

Callie would definitely approve.

Are you happy, Daddy?

I smiled against Holden's forearm, an unequivocal *yes* shouting silently from my heart.

I turned and pressed a kiss to his cheek. "I love you."

Holden's hand snaked under my shirt to rest on my belly and draw me even closer. "I love you too. We've got this."

The End.

Want to keep up with all my news and releases, sign up to my newsletter HERE.

**Don't miss the next book in the series.
Pre-order Zach and Luke's story now.**

THE MECHANICS OF LUST
Mackenzie Country 2

I broke the rules and fell in love with my best friend. Newsflash. He didn't feel the same. I had to stand by and watch him fall for someone else. Moving on hasn't been easy since we all live and work on the same high country sheep station, but I'm finally getting there.

I'm building a new life, a new set of dreams, planning a different future, just me and my dogs. The last thing I need is Luke Nichols, the sexy, enigmatic, ex-husband of my nemesis, filling my head with a laundry list of cravings. Talk about complicated.

Luke is only in Mackenzie Country for a few months and I'm not about to put my heart on the line again just for a little fun. But the more I'm around Luke, the harder it is to remember exactly why Luke and I are a bad idea, the *worst* idea.

Things between us are about to go nuclear.

Maybe I'm wrong.
Maybe we *can* keep it simple.
Maybe I can satisfy my cravings *and* hold on to my heart.
And maybe pigs can fly.

Note TW: Contains references to past loss of a child.

Follow me on Amazon HERE.
Follow me on BookBub HERE.
Follow me on Instagram HERE.
Follow me on TikTok HERE.
Join Hogan's Hangout HERE.

ALSO BY JAY HOGAN

SERIES

AUCKLAND MED SERIES
Book 1 First Impressions is free at most retailers.

SOUTHERN LIGHTS SERIES
Book 1 Powder and Pavlova is free at most retailers.

STYLE SERIES

PAINTED BAY SERIES
(Includes Off Balance RWNZ 2021 Romance Book of the Year Award)

MACKENZIE COUNTRY SERIES

STANDALONE BOOKS

FOXED

UNGUARDED
(Part of Sarina Bowen's Vino & Veritas Series)

DIGGING DEEP
(2020 Lambda Literary Finalist)

AUDIOBOOKS

The following are available in audiobook format from most audiobook retailers including:

Spotify, Audible, Apple Books, Barnes & Noble, Chirp.

Auckland Med Series

Painted Bay Series

Southern Lights Series

Foxed

Unguarded

ABOUT THE AUTHOR

Jay is a 2020 Lambda Literary Award Finalist and the winner of Romance Writers New Zealand 2021 Romance Book Of The Year Award for her book, Off Balance.

Jay is a New Zealand author writing MM romance and romantic suspense primarily set in New Zealand. She writes character driven romances with lots of humour, a good dose of reality and a splash of angst. Jay has travelled extensively, lived in many countries, and in a past life she was a critical care nurse and counsellor. She is owned by a huge Maine Coon cat and a gorgeous Cocker Spaniel.

Join Jay's reader's group Hogan's Hangout for updates, promotions, her current writing projects and special releases.

Sign up to her newsletter HERE.

Or visit her website HERE.